The Broken World

J D OSWALD

PENGUIN BOOKS

PENGUIN BOOKS

UK | USA | Canada | Ireland | Australia
India | New Zealand | South Africa

Penguin Books is part of the Penguin Random House group of companies
whose addresses can be found at global.penguinrandomhouse.com.

First published in Great Britain in Penguin Books 2015
Chapters 1–13 were first published as part of *The Golden Cage* in
electronic form in Penguin Books 2013

001

Set in 12.5/14.75 pt Garamond MT Std
Typeset by Jouve (UK), Milton Keynes
Printed in Great Britain by Clays Ltd, St Ives plc

A CIP catalogue record for this book is available from the British Library

ISBN: 978-1-405-91778-0

www.greenpenguin.co.uk

To mum. I wish you could be here
to see how it all worked out.

I

Grendor's great-grandson King Ballah I, while still waging the war that would forge the land we know as Llanwennog, needed to identify his messengers and spies to those nobles he most trusted. To this end he had six rings made, each bearing his personal seal. Any noble, on being shown this seal, was to render up whatever aid the wearer of it required.

Such is the strength of the magic woven around these rings that all attempts to copy them have ended in failure. Nor will the seal reveal itself should the ring be worn by an enemy of the Llanwennog throne. It is said that the wearers can communicate with each other over vast distances and that the rings will summon them back to Tynhelyg should the king's life ever be in peril. Few have ever seen these rings, and many think them no more than myth, but to be charged with wearing one is the highest possible honour.

The Taming of the Northlands – A History
of the Kings of Llanwennog

'Fetch his lordship. He's coming round.'

Errol heard the words as if he were dreaming them. He wasn't sure where he was, but it was warm and comfortable. It smelled clean, the air fresh with a hint of dry grass.

He had been sleeping, he was sure, but he couldn't remember going to bed. Rolling on to his side, he opened his eyes and was nearly sick as waves of pain rushed over him. He had just enough time to register the vaguest image of a person standing over him, then everything dimmed again.

'Be careful. You've had a nasty blow to the head.' Strong arms cradled his shoulders, pulling him forward. Then something cool, more soothing than a mother's lullaby, pressed against the back of his skull.

'Fetch those pillows over, Mentril. Let's make our guest comfortable.' Errol felt himself pulled upright, but he still didn't want to open his eyes. Finally he was let back down again, sinking into soft cushions. The coldness was pressed to his forehead now, a dampened cloth that felt wonderful. He tried to relax into it, letting the pain slip away as he settled. Only when he was sure it was safe did he try to look upon the scene.

His first thought was that his mother had found him. A pale woman stared down at him, her concerned face framed by straight dark hair flecked with lines of grey. But as he regained some degree of focus, he could see that it wasn't Hennas. This woman was far better dressed than he had ever seen his mother, with the exception perhaps of her wedding day. She wore a fine silk dress in rich brown colours with a white shawl hanging loosely around her shoulders. His mother had never possessed such finery.

Without moving his head it was hard to take in much more than that worried, smiling face, but Errol could see that he was in quite a large high-ceilinged room, lit by a pair of windows. Even moving his eyeballs made his head swim, so he could take in no more than that. Perhaps he would be better speaking.

'Where am I?' The words sounded wrong, faint and hoarse in his dry throat. The woman leaned closer to him, bringing a soft lavender smell with her.

'You shouldn't try to speak. Rest. Conserve your energy. You've been badly injured.'

She was speaking Llanwennog, and as if that one realization was the keystone of a dam inside his head, Errol was flooded with memories. More than anything else, he feared for his life. He had spoken in Saesneg, the language of the Twin Kingdoms, his voice probably too quiet to be understood, but what if he had been muttering while unconscious?

'Where am I?' he tried again, this time in the local tongue, forcing the words out louder even though it made his head ache.

'You're safe. You're in Castle Gremmil, on the edge of the northlands. My husband found you dumped in woodland beside the Tynhelyg road. I guess you must have been attacked by bandits and left for dead.'

Errol tried to piece together his last memories, finding only snippets of images. He needed time to sort through it all, but he knew he was in a spot. It didn't seem like these people realized where he was from; if they had, he would most likely have been in a dungeon. He needed to come up with a good story, and fast.

'I don't remember much. I was heading for the capital. Came down from the mountains. I've urgent news for King Ballah. Stopped off at some village for food; I think the circus was there. But after that it all goes a bit blank.'

'An emissary for the king, eh? Well, Poul said you were carrying the king's seal. Rest a while and I'm sure everything will come back to you. Do you remember your name?'

'My name? Why, yes. Sorry. It's Errol. Errol Balch.'

'Well, Errol. It's nice to meet you. I'm Isobel, Lady Gremmil. And this, if I'm not mistaken, is my husband.'

Errol looked up at a noise from the far end of the room and immediately wished he hadn't. His brain felt like it was too big for his skull and was trying to fit in by squeezing out his eyeballs. Sparks flashed across his vision, and when they cleared it was to see a short broad man peering at him myopically.

'So you're a Balch, are you? I thought you had the family look. Pleased to meet you. I'm Poul Gremmil.'

'It was you who found me?' Errol took the man's proffered hand, squeezing it rather limply in his own.

'Well, it was one of my dogs, to be honest. Thought he'd flushed out some game, but when we went in after it, there you were, dragged under a bush with not a stitch on. Thought you were dead, but I guess you Balches are made of sterner stuff.'

Errol found that moving his arms eased the pain a little. He reached up to touch the back of his head, feeling a crusty mess of blood and hair.

'I'm very grateful to you, and your dog. But tell me, have I been unconscious long?'

'A day, maybe. Have you any idea who might have done this? Only it's a bad show, bandits attacking travellers on the king's road in my bailiwick.'

'I'm not sure, truly. I had to change some gold in Cerdys and I'm fairly sure I was followed from there. But there

4

were a few rough types in the circus. Did you see it when you found me?'

'The circus? No. They'd shipped out south before I came through. Seemed in a bit of a hurry to get to the King's Festival, by all accounts. But Cerdys? What in Gwlad were you doing up there?'

'Came down from the mountains; I was up there on a mission for the king. It's all very secret, really. I need to get back on the road as soon as possible so I can deliver my report in person.'

'Well, of course. But I doubt you'd stay on a horse more than five minutes with your head the way it is right now. You must stop with us at least another day or two. Give your brain time to recover.'

'You're right, of course. Thank you, my lord.'

'None of this "my lord" nonsense. We don't stand on ceremony out here in the wilderness, and any man bearing the king's seal will find aid here. It's Poul, please.'

'The king's seal?' Errol was puzzled. Now that he thought about it, Lady Gremmil had mentioned something about that too, and they were being far more hospitable than he might have expected, even if his face did make them think he was of royal birth.

'Your ring. I guess whoever attacked you must have missed it. You were clutching it so tight in your fist.'

Errol looked over at Lady Gremmil, who had reached for something lying on a small table beside the bed. She handed him a plain ring, and as he saw it, he remembered picking it up from the floor of the cave. He twisted it around in his hand, feeling an unnatural warmth in the metal, and as he did so an inscription began to form, writing itself in soft gold letters. Old-fashioned Llanwennog, arcane and hard to focus on even had he not been recovering from a nasty blow to the head.

The Hand of the King shall be treated as if he be the King.

'It's a long time since I've seen one of those. King Ballah doesn't grant that kind of boon to just anyone.' Lord Gremmil paused a moment as if trying to find a way to phrase the question Errol knew he wanted to ask. 'I don't suppose you can tell me anything about this mission, can you?'

Errol didn't answer straight away. Partly because he needed time to pull together the strands of the lie that had sprung so easily to his lips, and partly because he didn't want to seem too eager to give up state secrets. He rolled the ring around his palm for a moment, then slid it on to the little finger of his left hand. It was a bit too big, but it stayed in place.

'I can't be specific, you understand. It concerns the war with the Twin Kingdoms. We had intelligence of a possible route through the northern Rim mountains. King Ballah asked me to investigate, but quietly so as not to spark any panic. I've been riding the old trapping routes all spring and summer.'

From the look on Lord Gremmil's face, Errol knew he had the man convinced already. Lady Gremmil reinforced the lie by shuddering visibly, holding her hand over her face.

'And did you find . . . ?'

'Let me just say that it would be unwise to send all your able-bodied men to the southern passes. I think only a madman would lead an army through the great forest of the Ffrydd and over a poorly mapped high mountain pass, but we all know that Inquisitor Melyn is insane. Queen Beulah even more so.'

'I hear what you're saying, Errol. And you're right. This is the most important information. Rest now. I'll have a servant bring food. Then we'll see about getting you some clothes and a horse. This is grave news indeed. You must get it to the king with all haste.'

Melyn settled down by his fire, calmed his breathing and prepared to enter the trance state that would let him travel through the aethereal. They had reached the northlands of Llanwennog, and his scouts had reported back with the locations of the nearest settlements. Now it was time to contact Beulah and let her know how their plan was progressing.

It was not a task he was looking forward to. Back in the comfort and security of Emmass Fawr, or even the Neuadd, he wouldn't have thought twice about it. He'd even slipped away from his body while riding his horse along the Calling Road before, borrowing some of its energy to boost his own. But here he was in enemy lands, and the distance to Castell Glas, where the queen should now be, was far greater than anything he had travelled before. Neither could he contact her directly; he had to rely upon Clun. The boy had a natural talent for the aethereal, it was true, but nothing compared to the ease with which Melyn could communicate with Beulah. She was so close to him; he had trained her, moulded her for so long, he knew he could always find her. Clun was a new entity for him; it would be far harder to track him down.

And then there was the forest. He would have to traverse it, find his way through all that magical turmoil without losing sight of his own true body. All along the way he had been marking points that he could use to navigate. He should be able to retrace the path they had taken since parting with the royal procession, but he was not convinced that anything in the forest stayed the same for very long, especially when viewed in the aethereal.

Still, it had to be done. Without communication between his small army and the larger forces massing on the border, the whole invasion plan would grind to a halt. And so he relaxed, focusing his eyes on the flickering flames to help steady his mind.

The hubbub of the camp drifted away, not fading to total silence but sounding as if it were a good distance off. Melyn stayed in his body for a while, memorizing how he felt, setting it in his mind until he was confident he could return. Then, with a last look around the camp, he rose out of himself and into the air.

'Your Grace, I hope I'm not intruding.'

Melyn turned his aethereal body and looked down to see Frecknock a few paces away from his unmoving physical self.

'What do you want?'

'To help, if I may. Am I right in thinking you are about to contact His Grace the Duke of Abervenn?'

Melyn felt a tinge of his old anger rising; this creature had grown increasingly familiar and impertinent over the weeks and months of their journey together. She should be put in her place, should really be executed, as the queen had ordered. But she had also been of great help, and he found himself far more tolerant of her than he would ever have thought possible.

'What if I am?' he asked.

'Well, sir. I could watch over your mortal body while you are gone from it and do everything in my power to protect you from harm, but if you would permit me to accompany you on your journey instead, I could show you a much quicker way to reach Master Clun.'

'Very well, show me.' Melyn was surprised at how readily he accepted the offer of help, though any companionship on his difficult journey would have been welcome. Frecknock too was obviously taken aback by his consent, as she took a moment to compose herself before spreading her aethereal wings and leaping into the air. They were too small to support her bulk, Melyn noted, at least in the slow almost lazy way she used them. But there was an elegance about her aethereal flight that contrasted sharply with her waddling walk.

He followed her up into the air, over the camp and back towards the long valley down which they had travelled. When they had gone perhaps a mile, she descended to the ground, beckoning for Melyn to do the same.

'We needed to get a bit of distance from the camp, Your Grace. There's too much interference in the Grym with so many warrior priests around.'

'Why should it matter? I wasn't proposing to use the Grym.'

'Ah, but the aethereal is as much a realm of the Grym as the physical world. If anything it is more closely linked to it, since here you can do so much more.'

'How so?'

'It's easier for me to show, Your Grace, than tell. Please take my hand.'

Melyn did as he was asked, once more feeling that touch that should have revolted him, should have made his skin crawl, and yet was instead oddly comforting. Frecknock squeezed his hand, and he could see that she had closed her eyes in concentration. Then the aethereal view of the valley began to dissolve. There was an instant when Melyn thought he could see the whole of Gwlad laid out beneath him, a moment of darkness so complete it sent a shudder down his spine, and then he was somewhere else.

It was a small arena, roofed over and with a dry dirt floor. A few people sat around the edges, their forms more or less distinguishable in the aethereal, but it was the two figures in the centre that caught Melyn's attention. The first was quite obviously Clun; his features were unmistakable, even if he seemed to have matured years, rather than the months they had been parted. The second figure was something altogether different.

Melyn didn't think he had ever seen a horse so proud and magnificent. Or so big. Like all simple creatures, its aethereal form was detailed and rich, as if it was aware of nothing but itself. It held its head high, neck arched, tail jutting out as a warning to anyone who might approach from behind. As he watched, it pranced around the arena in a wild manner, throwing its feet out and tossing its head from side to side, circling and circling the boy, eyeing him up for the kill. Clun however seemed unconcerned, almost ignoring the great beast, refusing to make eye contact, turning his back at times.

Melyn looked around and spotted the queen sitting in the gallery overlooking the action. She glowed as if someone had placed a candle inside her, and her aethereal form showed the slight swell of her belly. Without thinking, he moved across, settling himself down on the bench beside her.

'Beulah.' Melyn spoke softly, in the way he had always done when trying to attract her attention to the aethereal. It was as much a game as a method of teaching, though normally she was aware of his presence even before he spoke. This time it was as if he didn't exist. The queen ignored him, her eyes only on Clun, and he felt a strange jealousy at her obvious devotion to the boy.

'She can't sense you, Your Grace. The child growing inside her . . .' Frecknock stood a short distance away, trying to make herself look small.

'I know. She's pregnant and that stops her from being able to see the aethereal.' Melyn turned his attention back to Clun. 'We were always going to have to communicate through the boy, but it looks like he's distracted at the moment. I could always attract Beulah's attention, but Clun needs to be a bit more focused.'

'You're very close to Her Majesty, Your Grace.'

'Her father put her in my care when she was only eight years old.'

'That would likely explain it. But if you will allow me, Your Grace, I should be able to alert Master Clun to our presence.'

Melyn nodded his assent, aware that once more he was depending on the dragon. He would have to kill her sooner or later, he realized; her influence on him was growing too great. But for now her aid was the only thing keeping his mission on track. And she fascinated him.

Frecknock stepped down into the arena, her aethereal form floating a hand's width off the dirt floor. Melyn watched the horse kick and stamp as it rushed round in a great circle. Then, when it was about to pass the spot where Frecknock's form stood, she stepped into its path.

The effect was instant. The stallion reared up, almost falling over backwards as it recoiled. It backed off several slow paces, then stopped, staring at the dragon with wide eyes and flared nostrils. Clun watched the horse, an expression of concern spreading over his face, and then his gaze moved around the ring as if he were looking for something. He swept over Frecknock and Melyn, then did a double take, his eyes going out of focus for a moment before finally coming to rest on the inquisitor.

'Mistress Frecknock, Your Grace. I'm very glad to see you.' Clun bowed, then stepped away from himself, his aethereal form leaving behind an almost identical double as still as a statue.

'You've been practising, I see. Good.' Melyn floated his own form down to meet Clun. He was dimly aware of motion all around him: no doubt people in the arena reacting to the sudden stillness of the Duke of Abervenn. He trusted the queen would understand what was happening, but no doubt some fool would try to go to Clun's aid and distract the boy. Or get himself kicked to death by the horse.

'Now listen to me carefully. We don't have much time.'

There was no doubt about it, the horse was magnificent. He was also completely wild. Beulah still wasn't sure why she had bought him and doubted he would ever be broken. But he might be put to some of the more tractable mares, she supposed. Foals with a bit of Gomoran fire in them would make fine warhorses.

Still, Clun was determined to try, and he was going about the task in a most unusual manner. It had taken ten men with ropes and a great deal of swearing to bring the stallion from the stone stable he had been trying to destroy and down to this training arena. At least two of the stable hands had broken arms, and by the way a third was walking his ribs were badly cracked. Those brave enough to watch had climbed to the back of the raised seating around the arena. Only Beulah herself dared to lean over the railings; Captain Celtin sat nervously behind her.

Clun stood in the middle of the ring as if it were the most natural thing in the world to be that close to an animal that could run him down in an instant. The stallion's hooves were each the size of his head, and tore up great clumps of dirt as it pounded around. And yet the horse didn't attack him, just ran and ran. Round and round.

After about half an hour of this, the horse began to settle down, perhaps no longer afraid of the strange situation, but more likely just bored. Beulah wasn't sure such a creature knew what fear was. At this point Clun turned his back on the beast and Beulah felt a surge of trepidation. Surely that was to invite an attack. But the horse continued its pacing, snorting and shaking its great flowing mane. Then, finally, it stopped, breathed heavily a few times, and walked slowly towards the centre.

Whether he sensed the approach or just heard a change in the beast's breathing, Beulah didn't know, but when the stallion was within ten paces of him, Clun turned and faced it, eyes with an expression of cold fury that reminded her of the battle he had fought with the dragon. The stallion kicked up instantly, but instead of attacking backed away, resuming its mad running around the arena. And all the while Clun kept his eyes on it, swivelling slowly on his heels to mark the endless circles.

Beulah watched, fascinated. She had never seen anything like it before. Breaking horses was a brutal business, she knew. This horse should have been haltered and hobbled, then made to accept a breaking saddle; then brave men would have attempted to ride it until it was beaten into submission. Until its spirit was broken. That was how it had always been done at Emmass Fawr and Candlehall. But experience said Gomoran stallions could never be broken that way. At least no one had ever succeeded. What Clun was doing was completely different, and apart from the fact that he was as yet unharmed, seemed to be completely ineffectual. Since he had never before owned a horse, let alone tried to break one, what surprised her most of all was that he should even be trying.

'By the Shepherd!' Beulah jumped and felt Celtin behind her tense as the stallion suddenly reared, almost falling over in its desperation to get away from something she couldn't see. Clun looked confused, as if this was not something he had expected. He searched around the ring, and then his eyes seemed to go out of focus. His hands dropped slackly to his side and his head drooped so much she thought he was going to collapse. But he stayed on his feet, looking for all the world like he dangled from an invisible rope with his boots just touching the ground.

Captain Celtin was the first to move, stepping reluctantly forward to jump down into the ring. Beulah stopped him, her touch making him flinch visibly.

'No, Captain. Wait a moment. I think I know what's happening.' She looked once more at Clun, then back at Celtin. 'Do you have any skill at the aethereal?'

'No, ma'am. I'm sorry.'

Beulah cursed her pregnancy once more. She tried to sink into the trance, tried to sense the presence she expected, but it was as if her head were wrapped in blankets. She looked around the arena, half expecting something to appear to her normal sight, but there was nothing to see apart from the curiously dangling Clun and the remarkable sight of a Gomoran stallion held motionless by fear.

'Be not alarmed, my lady. Inquisitor Melyn is here.' The words sounded distant, echoing from Clun's mouth without his lips moving. They were hard to hear above the muttering of the crowd.

Beulah shouted, 'Silence!' and a strange quiet fell upon the place. Even the stallion stopped its snorting.

'How is it you can speak, my love? Are you not in the aethereal?'

'I have news from His Grace the inquisitor, my lady.' Clun either hadn't heard the question or chose not to answer it. 'He has reached the northlands and will begin his planned actions in a few days' time.'

'Has he killed the dragons?' There was a prolonged pause after Beulah asked the question, minutes passing as if some long conversation were being held elsewhere.

Finally Clun spoke again. 'No. The wild creature

Caradoc escaped, as did Benfro. Frecknock is helping the inquisitor.'

'She's with him? Here, in the aethereal?'

'She is, my lady.'

For some unaccountable reason this made Beulah shudder. She hated not being able to see and move about the aethereal herself. It was a double torment to know that dragons might be spying on her, influencing her while she was so vulnerable. And why was Melyn allowing the dragon to accompany him? What could possibly have happened that could have made him trust her so? She longed to ask him more, but she was constrained both by the crowd of nobles who had come with her to the arena, and by the knowledge that anything she said would be heard by the dragon too.

'Tell Melyn that we will leave here tomorrow and sail directly for Abervenn. And tell him he would be wise to remember what we discussed before we parted. He knows what I mean.'

Clun fell silent once more, still dangling like a puppet in the exact centre of the ring. Again Beulah strained her senses to catch anything of the inquisitor or even the dragon. Was that why the stallion had reacted so fearfully? Was it an aethereal presence that it sensed, that had it almost cowering? Beulah had thought herself an adept, a master of the skill. But now she saw that for the lie it was. How little she knew about the worlds of magic.

'My lady, they are gone.' Clun's voice was back to normal now, and he pulled himself upright, turning to face her. 'The inquisitor said to tell you that he hasn't forgotten your words. He will carry out your orders when he feels the time is right.'

'Did he say why he had brought the dragon with him?'

'Mistress Frecknock has sworn a blood oath to protect the inquisitor. She wants to stay alive, and she knows the only way she can do that is by being useful. She is teaching Melyn and his men what magic she can to help them with their campaign, and she's doing everything she can to protect the inquisitor himself. I suspect she knows that if he dies, she will lose her head soon afterwards.'

If he dies. The enormity of what Melyn was doing hit home with those three short words. Beulah knew that the mission was a brave one, if not plain foolhardy. Five hundred warrior priests against an entire nation was not good odds. And the whole plan depended on them drawing the attention of a large proportion of Ballah's army. It would be a miracle if any of them survived.

'Do not fear, my lady. His Grace is very resourceful. He has his best warrior priests with him, and now he has new magic to help too. You'll see him again. I know it.'

Something about Clun's voice, his choice of words, made Beulah believe him. There was more to the Duke of Abervenn than the brave young man who had captured her heart. Beulah's gaze was so fixed on him that she completely forgot about the stallion on the other side of the ring. Only when he moved did she notice him, no longer afraid but striding into the centre. The horse was huge, his coat black and shiny with sweat. He had an aura of unstoppable power, of untapped menace and single-minded obstinacy. And before she could shout a warning, the stallion was upon Clun, who simply turned, calmly staring into those huge eyes, reaching up with his hand, letting the horse get his scent.

Slowly, calmly, the stallion lowered his head and allowed his ears to be scratched.

There was something wrong with his head. No matter how hard he tried to think, how much he shook the water out of his ears, still Benfro felt like he was muffled in thick, soft blankets. Neither was he quite sure where he was, though oddly that didn't seem to worry him much. Wherever it was, it was moving, lurching from side to side with a monotonous rhythm that swirled the fog around his brain and made it still harder to concentrate.

He tried to see what was going on, but wherever he was it was dark. A tiny sliver of light splayed in through a hole high above him, painting a fan-like pattern on a ceiling that appeared to be made of wood. But that couldn't be right. Hadn't he been sleeping in a cave? He'd lit a fire. No, he hadn't lit a fire, but there had been smoke. He was fairly sure of that. Or had he dreamed it? He remembered being tired, heavy, like he'd eaten too much. But he'd only had a couple of fish, and not that big. He remembered catching them in the river, filleting some to cook later when Errol got back.

Benfro started to piece things back together, bit by bit, memory by memory. It was slow work; he seemed only to be able to hold a few things in his mind at once. He had no idea how long it was since he had been in the cave, nor how long he had been in this moving wooden box.

This cage.

The idea came to him just as he started to notice the sensations from his arms and legs. It was as if he had forgotten what discomfort was and it had taken him that long to put a name to the feeling. Now that he had made the connection, he realized he had been uncomfortable ever since . . . when? He couldn't remember waking any more than he could remember going to sleep. But he must have done both at some point.

Benfro shifted his body, tried to sit up from the unusual lying position he found himself in. It was harder than it should have been. Not only was his sense of balance not working, but his arms and legs appeared to be tied together. He rocked back and forth, rolled over on to his front so that he could lever himself upright, but in the confines of the cage it was near impossible given the way he seemed to feel things only long moments after he had touched them. Finally he managed to reach some sort of tipping point, realizing as he did so that he had no way of staying upright. With a graceless certainty he toppled over, landing partially on something slightly softer than the wooden floor.

A voice muttered something harsh that he didn't understand.

'What? Is there someone there?' Benfro's words sounded oddly thick to him, slurred and heavy.

'I said watch where you're sitting. You're not the only one in here.'

'Sorry. I didn't know.' Benfro shuffled himself as best he could away from the voice, backing himself into a corner. Only then did it filter through his muddled thoughts that the words had been spoken in Draigiaith. Not only that, they were perfectly formed, the voice itself deep and old, slightly reminiscent of Sir Frynwy. Not the speech of men.

'I don't mean to be rude, but where are we? And who are you?'

'I am Magog, Son of the Summer Moon. But you can

call me Moonie.' Something shifted in the darkness, a looming presence dragging itself across the floor towards him. The light playing on the ceiling should have been enough for Benfro to see by, but the same cloud that fogged his thoughts robbed him of his keen eyesight. All he could make out was a glint, perhaps the reflection of an eye. Then he felt hot breath on his face, rancid with the taint of rotten meat. 'And you must be my brother Gog. I've been waiting for you. Where have you been all these years?'

'No, I'm Benfro. Sir Benfro.' The presence in front of him withdrew; there was a shuffling sound and something slumped against the far wall, upsetting the regular motion for a moment.

'A shame. And I was so sure. I was—' But whoever the creature was, Benfro didn't find out then. The cage stopped suddenly, throwing him forward so that he sprawled painfully on the floor. He heard the noise of bolts being drawn, a key turning in a lock, and then light flooded over him.

Benfro looked up to the far end, where the creature was slumped. It was almost impossible to make out the dragon who sat there, his colouring so perfectly matched the dark wood. He seemed thinner than Benfro, though otherwise much the same size. Except for his wings, which, while large for the dragons of the Ffrydd, were pathetic in comparison with Benfro's own. But what grabbed Benfro's attention most, what filled him with fear and pity and anger, was the expression on the dragon's face, the look in his eyes. He was frightened, broken and quite, quite mad.

Something hit Benfro square in the back. Whatever it

was that had been distancing his mind from his body dissolved in one instant of exquisite pain. He yelped, turning to see what had happened, and saw a man standing in the open doorway clasping a long whip in one hand. The man said something in a voice that sounded like it was used to being obeyed.

'I don't understand.' Benfro held up his hands. His wrists were cuffed in irons, a short length of chain looping between them.

'He says you're to behave yourself and stop spooking the horses. Otherwise he'll—' Benfro felt the tip of the whip fly past him across the cage and saw it strike the other dragon square in the face. Magog, as he called himself, shrieked, dropped to the floor and covered his head with his hands, speaking quick words in the same language as the man. He in turn hurled what sounded like abuse at the dragon, then turned to Benfro.

'So. Not speak Llanwennog, do you. Will learn. Not learn, not eat. Now be still.' And with that he slammed the door shut, plunging them once more into darkness. Moments later the regular rhythmic motion started again with a first sudden lurch that had Benfro sprawling on the floor again just as he was beginning to lever himself upright.

'Hee hee. You upset Tegwin. You don't want to be doing that. He can be nasty. And old Loghtan's worse still.'

Benfro started to struggle up again, then remembered the man's words and the pain of the whip. Perhaps when his head had cleared a bit more he'd teach this Tegwin a lesson, but for now it might be best to get rid of these chains. Taking a deep breath, he held his arms up in front of him and pulled them apart to stretch the links taut.

21

He thought of how they were an affront to his dignity, how they would be better off gone, and he tried to remember the feeling that had spread through his stomach before. Then he breathed out.

There was no flame.

Puzzled, Benfro took another deep breath and tried again. And still he failed to produce so much as a spark. It should have panicked him, should have angered him. Thinking about it, he realized that being in chains should have angered him too, and yet he had accepted it as merely a bit of an inconvenience. Something was deeply wrong with his mind, but he couldn't bring himself to care. Instead he settled himself back down on the floor, the weight of his body coming down hard on his arms. They would hurt later, when the circulation came back into them, but right now he was too tired, too confused to care. He closed his eyes, for all the difference it made in the darkness, and tried to sleep, but the other dragon kept muttering under his breath.

'Magog?' Benfro said, wondering how this pathetic creature had come by the name. The muttering stopped, so he assumed he was being listened to. 'What is this place? Where are we? And who's Loghtan?'

'Loghtan is the boss man. Oh yes. You think Tegwin's nasty with his little whip. Just wait till you meet Loghtan. Takes away your thoughts, he does. Takes away your mind.'

'But where are we? How did I get here?'

'We're in the circus, brave Sir Benfro. Oh yes. In the circus.'

2

Three parts of silver bane, one of root-wort berry. Twelve ground cloves from the islands north of Eirawen. Mix with honey from hives close to flax fields and strong Talarddeg ginger beer to mask the bitter taste. This potion will keep for upwards of six months, and must be administered with every meal. It will keep your dragon both docile and suggestible, the better to train it for the circus ring.

From the personal papers of
Circus Master Loghtan

Dafydd paced the rolling deck, listening to the constant chatter of gulls and the thrum of the wind through the rigging. He didn't understand why the ropes attached to the sails were called sheets, rather than the sails themselves, but during the course of his journey he had come to accept that there were many things about sailing he would never understand. For a start, why anyone would willingly choose it as a career.

Their passage through the Sea of Tegid had been calm enough, and they had even made it past the great looming cliffs of the Twin Spires of Idris without incident, but as they headed south into the Great Ocean the swell had risen and the wind strengthened. Dafydd had gone through seasickness: he was past huddling in a miserable heap beside the railing, clutching his aching stomach and waiting for the cold wind to blow the pain from his head. It had taken five miserable days, but he had finally found his sea legs during the storm that had sent them past the Caldy peninsula, beyond Bardsey Island and into the middle of the Felem archipelago. Now he felt fine, but he would never forget the torment he had endured.

It was made all the worse by the fact that Iolwen, who for months had been sick every morning and sometimes throughout the day, had taken to the rough waters with casual ease. Her mood had lightened, and she had become ever more beautiful in his eyes. She was radiant. Dafydd just wished that she would wear slightly less revealing clothes. Her pregnancy was well evident now, and it seemed somehow improper for a princess of the realm to parade her condition so openly among the common soldiers and seamen who shared their ship.

He found her, as usual, up at the front, sitting staring out over the huge carved figurehead. The late afternoon sun cast a golden glow around the edges of the myriad islets dotted about the sea here like so much chaff.

'Captain Azurea tells me he knows of a large island nearby where we can find fresh water and provisions. He plans to stop there for a few days to let the horses graze.' Dafydd settled himself down on to the scrubbed wooden deck beside his wife and understood something of her liking for the place. Ahead of the busy ship all you could see was the sea and the islands, all you could smell was the tang of saltwater and the hot sun-baked air.

'It's so peaceful. Sometimes I wish I could stay here for ever. Never go back.'

'Do you really?' Dafydd asked. 'It's nice, I'll grant you, and I'd far rather have peace than war any day. But I think I'd get bored very soon. And it's not always this tranquil either. Don't forget the storm that forced us here.'

He put his arm around Iolwen's shoulder and held her tight as the ship moved slowly through the narrow channels between the islets. They passed one rocky headland, a cliff of crumbling stone spearing out of the water several hundred paces high and streaked white with guano. Beyond it the sea was calm in the lee of a much larger island, the centre of which was dominated by a cone-shaped mountain wreathed in cloud. The ship turned towards the coastline directly beneath the summit, and as they neared the shore Dafydd made out a long stone jetty pushing into the bay. Behind it stood the crumbled remains of long-abandoned buildings shaded by tall palms and other exotic plants he didn't recognize.

'We'd best get out of the way of the sailors. They'll be wanting to drop anchor or whatever it is they do.' Dafydd stood and helped Iolwen to her feet as the ship turned towards the jetty. They picked their way back along the deck as all about them the bustle grew in intensity. Sailors scrambled up masts and began furling sails; a group of men prepared the longboats, breaking out heavy wooden oars; and all about them shouted orders were answered with curt grunts and the occasional oath.

It was much quieter in their cabin, and in the hour or so it took for the ship to finally come to a halt Iolwen busied herself selecting clothing more suitable for wearing on land. Dafydd watched her, wondering if he should tell her that the place was uninhabited. A knock on the door finally stirred him. He opened it to find Captain Pelod and Teryll waiting outside.

'We've docked, and the men are unloading the horses. Teryll and I'll see to the camp arrangements, but Usel wondered if you'd like a tour of the island. Seems it's got quite a history.'

Up on deck, Dafydd was surprised to see that the ship was moored alongside the jetty; he had expected it to anchor in the bay. But as he walked down the gangplank and stood on firm ground for the first time in far too many weeks, he could see that the stonework of the jetty, ancient though it was, still held firm. The crystal-clear water showed a pale sandy bottom many spans below the ship, shoals of fish darting about in the newly cast shadow.

Usel was already waiting for them at the landward end of the jetty. He had about him the air of an excited schoolboy, Dafydd thought. The man bristled with energy and was impatient to get going.

'There's something you really must see.' Usel didn't wait for them to reply but headed off along the beach towards the nearest of the derelict buildings. Iolwen strode off after him, speaking in Saesneg and just as full of excitement at being ashore. Dafydd shrugged at Pelod and Teryll, then jumped down on to the sand to follow.

It was a curious sensation to walk on ground that didn't move and pitch under his feet. Away from the open sea and its cooling breeze, the air was hot, the sunlight reflecting off the fine sand. Up from the beach the land levelled off into a wide plain before the sudden steep rise of the mountain. A fringe of trees marked the boundary between beach and plain, and beyond them lay a tangle of long grass and shrubs. Large lumps in the vegetation were the remains of yet more buildings, making up what must once have been a sizeable town.

'Who lived here, Usel?' Iolwen asked as they walked along a pathway through the brush which was obviously still well used.

'This is Merrambel, the most northerly outpost of the people of Eirawen.'

'What happened to them? Why did they abandon the place? Surely this must be a paradise to live in?'

'So you'd think. But Mount Merram's not as peaceful as it looks. The histories say it erupted violently over three thousand years ago. Many of the people perished, and those who survived were scattered throughout Gwlad. Most of them returned to Eirawen, but a few were blown north to the Twin Kingdoms. Some say that they were the first people to reach there and were the ancestors of Balwen's tribe.'

'Isn't that a bit far-fetched?' Dafydd asked.

'Not really, no. The cities of Eirawen are ancient compared to Candlehall and Abervenn. The people might be superstitious and backward now, but there was a time when they were as sophisticated as us, if not more so.' Usel led them down a steep slope into a river valley between the rows of broken buildings and the looming presence of the volcano. The vegetation on either side thickened, but the path was still clear, laid with flat stones butted perfectly together and formed into a series of long shallow steps. The shadows lengthened as they neared the bottom, though the sun still hovering on the western horizon shone up the valley past them. Usel was almost running now, so eager was he to get to whatever lay around the corner, and as Dafydd stepped past some overhanging fronds of vegetation, he understood some of the man's excitement.

The path down which they had walked opened into a wide clearing at the base of the valley. Immediately uphill the bulk of the mountain climbed away in a cliff. Vegetation covered it like the straggly hair of a drowned maid, but a great patch in the middle, perhaps a hundred paces wide and twice as high, had been cleared back to bare stone. And then it had been carved into the image of an immense dragon.

'Behold Earith the Wise. This is the god of the ancient peoples of Eirawen.' Usel's voice was full of fervour, almost devotion. But it wasn't this, nor the truly immense carving that made Dafydd gasp and Iolwen let out a tiny yelp of surprise. In the middle of the clearing, dwarfed by the statue, gazing up at its image and quite oblivious to the new arrivals, stood a real, live dragon.

The village was little more than a collection of rude wooden huts clustered around a well. A narrow track meandered away from it downhill towards the undulating plains of the northlands, ending at the scrubby village green grazed by a couple of thin goats and a few chickens, as if this was the furthest reach of King Ballah's long arm. Beyond the last ramshackle house was bandit country.

Melyn rode slowly through the houses, noting the signs of habitation, feeling out with his senses for the people who lived in this benighted place. They were small-minded, beaten down by the bleakness of their existence. Some time in the distant past a lucky soul had found some gold nearby. There had been a boom for a short while – Melyn had seen the ruins of a larger settlement on his way in, the scars in the landscape where men had toiled in search of wealth – but what had brought the people out here was long gone. The few poor souls still eking out an existence in this place were the losers, mindless optimists who used the vain hope of sudden riches to sustain themselves through a lifetime of miserable deprivation. He would, Melyn concluded, be doing them all a favour.

It took surprisingly long for anyone to appear. There were no dogs yapping at the heels of his horse, just goats shuffling up to see if he tasted better than the grass. He shooed them off, tying his horse to a rickety wooden rail by the well and drawing a bucketful of water for it to drink.

'Halloo. Is there anyone here?' Melyn's shout dissipated on the cold wind that never stopped whistling across the barren landscape. Shivering, he drew more power from the Grym, feeling its warmth in his bones. He was about to shout once more when he heard a scraping noise and turned to see an old man shuffle out of the newly opened door of the largest house in the village.

'Who're you?' The man's accent was harsh and unfriendly.

Melyn bowed his head slightly. 'I am Inquisitor Melyn of the Order of the High Ffrydd. Perhaps you have heard of me?' Melyn's Llanwennog was cultured in comparison.

'Don't know nuffin 'bout that. What you want? Taxes?

You can tell 'Is Majesty we bain't got no money fer ourselves. Let alone 'im.'

'I can assure you, I have no desire to take your money. Nor do I come here on behalf of King Ballah. I do, however, bring important news for everyone in this village. I take it you're in charge around here?'

'That I am.'

'Then I'd be grateful if you could call a village meeting. I don't want to have to say my piece more than once.' Melyn sent a compulsion with his voice, but it wasn't really necessary. The old man was going to complain about his back, his knees, the state of the roads, anything he could think of, but he was also intrigued to know what had brought this high-powered gentleman all the way out to his sorry village. He turned back to the open doorway and shouted to the darkness inside,

'Mabel. Send the lads out t' tell everyone I'm calling a moot. Don't argue, damn you. Jes do it.'

Melyn unstrapped a small travelling stool from his saddle, unfolded and set it on the ground beside the well. He saw two young boys dart from the back of the house, heading for the other huts. The message spread quickly, but even so it took several minutes before the first of the villagers began to assemble. Not once did the old man offer any kind of hospitality. Melyn found he didn't mind; anything offered would most likely have made him ill, and to refuse it would have been rude. Not that he particularly minded being rude to these peasants.

On his stool Melyn watched them assemble, feeling their excitement build as they saw him and exchanged whispered words with each other. The old man refused to say anything more than that this important man had a declaration that had to be made to the whole village. A few of the younger men tried to argue with the village elder, but he obviously still ruled the roost, and they backed down soon enough.

About fifty people had assembled by the time Melyn decided to speak. They ranged in age from a babe still suckling at its dirty-faced mother's breast to a bald-headed woman with a wall eye who must have been eighty if she was a day. They had a look about them, surly-faced and with eyebrows that met in the middle, which spoke of long years of inbreeding. For the first time, viewing the thin children and haggard women, Melyn began to wonder whether his plan was a good one. Nobody would ever miss these people. Nobody would notice them gone.

'Thank you all for gathering to hear me. Is anyone not here?'

There was a general shuffling, a refusal to make eye contact, some mumbling. Then the village elder admitted that there might be one or two men panning a stream a couple of miles out.

'To the west of here? A narrow gully with scrubby trees on the north bank?'

The old man nodded.

'That's all right. I've already spoken to them. We can proceed. Now, as I've already told your chief here, my name is Melyn. I am Inquisitor of the Order of the High Ffrydd. Does anyone here know what that means?'

No answer. He'd expected none, but it might have been more fun if at least one of them had known who he was.

'Never mind. I really only gathered you here to make my life easier. Captain, if you please.'

There was a shimmering in the Grym that Melyn felt through his bones, and a dozen warrior priests led by Captain Osgal appeared out of thin air. They had the villagers surrounded, and without a further word conjured up their blades of light.

'What's this? What're you—' The village elder was cut short by a ball of conjured flame thrown straight at him by Melyn. As it exploded in the old man's face, setting his clothes and hair alight, the women in the crowd screamed. Soon the men joined in as the silent warrior priests set about them with their blades.

It was over in less than a minute. Only the bleating of goats and the clucking of chickens broke the silence that descended on the village green. Melyn got up, folded his travelling stool and strapped it back on to his saddle.

'Pile them all up there.' He indicated a clear patch of grass and waited while the warrior priests did as they were ordered. Melyn was pleased to see that there was little blood; most of the sword cuts had been surgically precise. It made cleaning up easier.

'Stand back now.' He waited until the last body was in place and the warrior priests had retreated, then he reached out for the lines all around him. It was a difficult working, like conjuring a blade of light as big as a horse. And he had to deflect all that power away from himself or risk turning into a very brief and very bright star. It was magic he had performed before, magic he was confident he could perform now, but still he had to gauge the exact moment to release all that pent-up energy.

The fire started in the middle of the pile of bodies. No ordinary flame this, it consumed totally, eating away the substance as it absorbed the dead back into the Grym. A pyre would have left a pall of greasy black smoke hanging in the air like an epitaph, a heap of dirty grey ash to mix with the soil and flow down the slope with the next rains, but this fire took everything into itself, reaching out like a living thing. Melyn watched as his warrior priests retreated, feeling the magical flame grasping for them. He smiled to himself; he knew exactly how far it could go and stood just beyond its limit. The heat washed over his face, warmed his skin for a few brief moments and then began to fade away, pulling in on itself until there was nothing but a tiny glowing orb a few feet above the ground. Then, with a *pop* not audible to normal ears, that too disappeared, leaving behind nothing but a perfectly round patch of bare earth.

Errol spent a further three days in the company of Lord and Lady Gremmil, and every one of those days was torment. His head injury began to heal, the agony subsiding to a dull ache with time, but he still had to be careful about sudden movements. Every so often he would turn to answer a question, and the whole world would darken, his knees go weak. If he was lucky, he caught himself, but more than once he had ended up sprawled on the floor.

A physician had examined him that first day, not long after he had woken. A thin sombre man dressed in flowing black robes and carrying a heavy leather case which he never opened, he had prodded Errol, peered into his eyes, felt his pulse and temperature and declared him a lucky young man. Apparently the blow had bruised his brain, causing it to swell within his skull. Whoever had inflicted it had intended to kill. The physician offered to drill a hole and let some of the accumulated fluid out, but Errol declined. He had heard tales of trepanning from his mother and wanted nothing of it. Rest would be sufficient, as long as he could contain his eagerness to get away.

Lord and Lady Gremmil had a son, Evan, who was a little older than Errol but much the same size and build. Some months earlier he had ridden to Tynhelyg with a troop of men, the town's contribution to the war effort. Poul was obviously delighted that his boy was a captain, fully involved in the fight against the madmen from the south, but when Isobel brought Errol a selection of clothes far grander than anything he had ever owned before, he could see that she was worried about her only child. He felt terrible offering her sympathy and saying that he would look out for the young man when he returned to Tynhelyg. They were genuinely kind people, and he hated abusing their trust.

Gremmil was a grey town. On the edge of the north-lands, it had none of the gold to be found around Cerdys, but it had prospered well enough supplying food and equipment to the endless stream of prospectors who ventured north on the king's road. Errol didn't see much of it, keeping himself to the castle, but on the third day, when his balance was much better, Poul insisted on taking him down to the stables to pick out a horse.

'I couldn't possibly take a horse. I've no money to pay.' Errol looked at the line of stables, a long face peering from the open top of each double door. He knew nothing about horses except that one end bit and the other kicked.

'Nonsense, Errol. You're the king's man on the king's business. It's my duty to assist you in any way possible. And besides, you were attacked on my land. What kind of a lord would I be if I didn't compensate you for what happened?'

'Well, I suppose I could always send the animal back with your son when he next returns home.'

'I'll hear none of that. Come. I'll pick out a fine gelding and we can ride out a way so you can see if you think it suitable.'

That offer at least freed Errol from the dilemma of trying to choose a good mount. He had to hope that his meagre riding skills wouldn't show him up as the fraud he truly was. As it happened, the ride was not as traumatic as it could have been. Lord Gremmil was happy enough just to pass slowly through the streets of his town, exchanging pleasantries with the people and showing off some of its more substantial buildings.

'My father built up the town to what it is today. He saw the potential in supplying the miners, and the big cities for that matter. The land here's not as fertile as down in the south, but we produce perfect barley for malting. Something in the soil, I suspect. Most of it gets shipped down to Tynhelyg. Turned into beer and whisky.'

Errol nodded, unsure quite what to say as they rode out through the town gates and along the road for a while. He didn't really need to talk; Poul was happy to go on about his freeman farmers, his relationship with the grain merchants and his contributions to King Ballah's coffers. Finally they reached a group of large stone buildings arranged around a junction in the road. One of the structures was still being built, although it was nearing completion. An army of workers swarmed over it, putting the finishing touches to the roof, fitting freshly made shutters into the high windows. On seeing them approach, a tall man broke off from his work and hurried over.

'Your lordship, it's good to see you.'

'And you, Cerrin. How goes the work?'

'Very well, sir. We should be finished in a day or two. Well before the first harvest.'

'Splendid. Well, I'd better not keep you. I just thought I'd show our guest from the capital our new grain stores. Should quadruple our storage capacity, Errol.'

'Nothing like it in the whole of the northlands.' The tall man tugged his forelock, glanced at Errol and then ran off back to his work. A few of the other labourers had stopped briefly to look at the visitors, but they all turned back and resumed their tasks.

'Cerrin's father was the most skilled mason I've ever known.' Lord Gremmil walked his horse on past the unfinished building towards one of the completed three. 'It was his idea to build centralized storage for the barley. Before that it was kept on individual farms. The big merchants wouldn't come near us. It wasn't worth their while having to drag those huge carts around a dozen different farmsteads until they were full.'

Errol listened to his host drone on about farming practices and the importance of good logistics as he was shown the inside of one of the grain stores. Empty, it was a vast space, their footsteps echoing on the smooth stone floor. It had been built so that there were no pillars or buttresses inside, just smooth walls and wide doors at either end to make loading and unloading easy. As he listened to yet more of Lord Gremmil's enthusing, Errol realized that the noble was showing off his efficient demesne because he believed that Errol had the ear of the king and would put in a good word for him once he returned to Tynhelyg.

'So, Errol, do you like the horse?' Lord Gremmil swung up into his own saddle and they set off back to the town at a gentle trot.

'It's a fine beast, yes.'

'Then he's my gift to you. Along with the saddle and harness. No, don't argue. And we'll have to see about getting you some provisions for the journey. Oh, and here.' He put his hand in his saddlebag, pulling out something and throwing it to Errol, who caught it before he could see what it was. 'You'll probably need that too.'

Errol shook what he had caught and nearly dropped it in surprise. It was a leather bag that clinked with the unmistakable sound of coin, and judging by its weight there was enough to keep him going for months.

'Lord Gremmil, I can't—'

'Say nothing more of it. Let's return to the castle and make preparations. No doubt you'll want to leave in the morning. You'll dine with Isobel and me in the main hall tonight.' And, so saying, he kicked his horse into a canter and then a gallop. Errol stared at the bag of money, then at his fast-disappearing host and finally back the way they had come, the road to Tynhelyg. There was nothing to stop him heading off straight away; he had more already than he had arrived with, and every hour he spent here was an hour longer it would take him to track down the circus. And then what? Someone had overpowered Ben-fro, and they had not thought twice about leaving Errol for dead. What could he hope to do? Perhaps it was better to stay here, at least for another night. It was hard to maintain his deception, but he could always plead a headache and retire early, take a bit of time to try and work out what he was going to do.

Stowing his newly found wealth in his newly acquired saddlebag, Errol kicked his horse into a slow canter and followed the trail of dust back to the city. Poul was waiting for him at the gates, and they walked back through the busy streets at a more sedate pace before handing over the horses to a couple of stable hands. Isobel greeted them with a look of worried excitement on her face.

'Errol, it's good to see you up and about. I hope you're feeling better.'

'Much, thank you. But I'm a little tired. If you don't mind I'd like to have a rest before this evening.' Errol smiled and bowed. He could see that Lady Gremmil wanted to tell her husband something important, and he had no desire to intrude upon their business any more than he already had.

'Of course, of course.'

'Lord Gremmil, I am indebted to you. To you both.' Errol bowed once more, then turned away, heading for the stairs. But he couldn't help overhearing what Lady Gremmil had to say to her husband.

'A messenger arrived not ten minutes ago. The king has put out another call to arms, and he's sending one of the war council out into the country to see the job's done properly. Poul, he's coming here. He'll be here by nightfall.'

'Who's coming, Bella?'

'That horrid man, Duke Dondal.'

Errol almost fell down the stairs when he heard the name. He could feel panic rising in him. Dondal would recognize him in an instant. There was no way he could stay here any longer. Ignoring the ache in his head and the weariness in his arms and legs, he slipped past the stairs and out through a side door. The yard was a bustle of activity, but no one paid him any heed as he walked across the cobbles towards the stables. He was still wearing the riding cloak given to him by Lady Gremmil, and he pulled it around his shoulders, turning up the collar against the late afternoon breeze. The two horses were still tethered outside their stalls. A boy was taking the saddle off Lord Gremmil's animal. Errol hurried over, trying not to look anxious.

'Here, lad. Don't worry yourself with the other one. I think I'll take him out for another ride.'

'Not at all, sir. Less work for me.' The boy grinned and untied the horse. Errol pulled himself up into the saddle, grateful for Captain Osgal's rough tutoring in horsemanship.

With a nod of thanks to the stable boy, he kicked the horse lightly in the ribs and steered it out through the castle gates. Errol retraced his earlier journey down through the town, getting no more than a casual glance from the guards at the town gate, but as he rode away from the walls, heading out along the road through fields of swirling barley, he felt like his back was naked, just waiting for a killer blow. Any moment now, he thought, there'll be shouting and the sound of galloping hooves. A troop of men will run me down, take me back and throw me into a dungeon.

It took longer to reach the grain stores than before, and as he approached the huge stone buildings it occurred to Errol that they were too far from the castle to be easily defended. They had been built at the crossroads where they were most accessible to the local farmers; Lord Gremmil had no fear that they would ever be attacked, since they were deep in the heart of Llanwennog here. The town walls were a reminder of an earlier time, before the House of Ballah had united the country in peace.

So wrapped up was he in his musings that Errol didn't notice the shouting until he was almost upon it. Fortunately he was out of sight, hidden by the bulk of the nearest grain store, but he recognized one of the voices instantly.

'You're able-bodied men. Why are you here working on barns when the king needs every man for his army?'

'Your Grace, we're needed to bring in the harvest.'

'Harvest, pah. Women can cut barley as well as men. Are you cowards? Is that it?'

Errol slipped out of his saddle and let himself down to the ground behind one of the open grain store doors without a sound. Leaving his horse, he crept out of the shadow, hugging the wall of the building as he peered round the corner.

Duke Dondal sat on his horse, backed by at least two dozen men whom Errol recognized as from the palace guard. He was looking down his nose at the gathered workmen, who clustered behind the mason's son

Cerrin. It looked very much as if he had been volunteered spokesman.

'You'll all of you come with me now to the castle. If you're fit and strong enough to build follies for your lord and master, you're fit and strong enough to carry a pike to war.' Dondal's face was red with the temper Errol remembered all too well from his time as the duke's page.

'Sergeant, round up these men, and any more you find about the place. Bring them to the castle. Captain, you come with me. I need to have words with Lord Gremmil about holding back on his responsibilities to the king.'

Errol backed away quickly, only just making it into the shadow behind the grain store door as Dondal galloped up the road accompanied by half of the soldiers. He went to his horse, pulling it as much into cover as he could, and yet still felt desperately vulnerable as he waited for his inevitable discovery.

And waited.

Long minutes went past. Errol strained his ears to hear any noise that would indicate a search was under way. Or that the sergeant had decided it would be easier to wait until his captain and lord were both out of sight, then perhaps settle down for a quick smoke before taking the men he already had up to the castle and hang the bother of searching for any more. But he could hear nothing above the low swishing of the wind in the barley.

Finally he could bear it no longer; he had to see what was happening. He edged along the wall and peered round the corner. Seeing nothing, he moved on, still keeping his back to the stone, to look round the next corner, where the workmen had been standing before.

They were still there, sitting on the grass looking miserable. One soldier watched them from his horse, puffing contentedly on a short pipe, but the rest were nowhere to be seen. There were two other grain stores besides the unfinished one and the one Errol was hiding behind, but from where he stood he could see the doors to neither of them. It was as if the soldiers had vanished into thin air or been swallowed up by the still-green crops. But he knew they were somewhere, searching. He had to get back to his horse and hope they weren't being too thorough.

Errol felt the familiar but forgotten tingle as he began to turn, that sensation in the Grym. Too late he realized what it meant. A hand clasped his shoulder roughly, spinning him and making his head burst in waves of pain. He could hardly see, could do nothing about his knees as they folded beneath him, but he could hear the voice that spoke in rough city Llanwennog.

'Here, what's a lass like you doing here? Go on, get on home to yer mam. This 'ere's king's business.'

The hands that had spun him round now grabbed the front of Errol's too-long riding cloak and hauled him to his feet.

'Please, don't hurt me,' Errol begged, but then the soldier's words sank in. He'd called him a lass and said. 'Get on home to yer mam.' Could he possibly think that Errol was a girl? It was true his hair had grown long over the months since he had escaped from Candlehall, and his face had never been troubled by the need to shave. And his cloak was fine, its hems edged with embroidered silk in a flowery style that would suit a young merchant's daughter, especially given its length. Underneath it he was

42

wearing a man's clothes, but the soldier couldn't see them. No one at the castle had said anything; none had ever doubted his sex. Lord Gremmil had found him naked and beaten; the castle servants had washed him; the physician examined him.

'Go on. Get out of here. You've no hope moonin' after any o' these lads. They're King Ballah's men now.' The soldier shoved Errol away, back towards the grain store where his horse stood in the doorway.

'Sorry, sir. I'll be going right away, sir.' Errol tried to make his voice sound flighty, like the chambermaids who chattered in the corridors of Castle Gremmil. He took up his horse's reins and hauled himself into the saddle in what was probably a most unladylike manner. The soldier just laughed.

'Tryin' ter be one o' the boys, eh?' He slapped the horse on its rump, making it start. Errol reined it back, trotting out on to the road and heading back towards the town. Other soldiers appeared from behind the various grain stores, looking at him with puzzled expressions on their faces.

'Just a town girl wantin' ter play with the big boys,' the soldier shouted, which raised a laugh. Dropping his head as if in shame, Errol kicked his horse into a trot and then a canter. As soon as he was sure he could no longer be seen he turned into a field and rode far out into the barley, leaving the soldiers well out of sight as he made a long detour back to the king's road.

3

A dragon's word is her bond. And not just her own
promise but the promise of her tribe. An oath once
sworn cannot be undone save by release from he to
whom it is made. Or death, which ends all obliga-
tions.

Think hard before you swear such an oath, for it
will tie you with bonds of Grym, shackle you with
the force of Gwlad herself. To break it is to set yourself a hostage to cruellest fate.

Maddau the Wise, *An Etiquette*

There was something very liberating about having a simple task to do and knowing how to go about completing
it. Melyn found the cleansing of the northlands of Llanwennog a joy after the endless months of planning, the
long slog through the forest of the Ffrydd and the dash
through the Rim mountains. Now that he was actually in
his enemy's lair and laying down the foundations of his
great diversion, he was as close as he had ever come to
being happy. It helped that he was ridding Gwlad of the
godless Llanwennog; he could feel no sorrow in their
deaths, as he would feel no sorrow at the death of any
vermin. These people had long ago denied the word of
the Shepherd. Their fate was a just one.

So far they had only cleared villages and a few remote farmsteads. Out on the edges of settled country these people would not be missed for months, maybe longer, but it made no sense to leave too many enemies at his back. And so his scouts worked their way across the open plains, seeking out the next targets, while the bulk of the army remained out of sight. And hiding wasn't difficult: at first the terrain might look like one endless flat plain stretching to the horizon, but it was cut across with gullies, most dry at the height of summer, but some still filled with sluggish rivers.

They had camped on the edge of a large gully overnight, sheltering in some straggly woodland from the squalls of rain that swept in on sudden gusts of wind. Now Melyn was contemplating how best to attack Cerdys, the first sizeable town they had approached.

'There's no armed force stationed there?' Melyn interrogated a spy he had sent into the town, a short wiry fellow with enough of the look of the local people to go about unremarked. All the warrior priests were proficient in Frecknock's hiding spell now, so in theory any of them could go out and scout the area, but Melyn didn't believe in leaving anything to chance.

'There's a constable and two deputies, but they've no skill at magic as far as I can tell. They carry short swords, but since they spend most of their time in the tavern at the centre of town, I don't think they'll pose much of a threat.'

'Good. We'll surround the town and close in using all the roads. We don't leave until everyone is dead.'

The scout nodded, leaving to rejoin his troop. Captain

Osgal handed out orders to his sergeants, and the camp began to dissolve, bands of men heading off in different directions at timed intervals. Melyn left last, surrounded by a small band, Frecknock trailing just behind him.

They rode out of the woods and across the lush grass towards a point where the road could be seen winding its way across the plain. As soon as they were past the trees, the men began to shimmer and become indistinct as they wrapped the Grym around them like a cloak. Melyn let himself dip in and out of his trance state, seeing brief snippets of the aethereal. Here the men were clearer, some more sharply focused than they would normally appear. It was an interesting new insight into the two different forms of Gwlad's magic, for so long considered completely separate by the quaisters and librarians back at Emmass Fawr. The irony was not lost on Melyn that this knowledge had come from a dragon, one of the creatures the order had been created to destroy.

Just as he was dropping back into the real, something caught his eye, a glint in the aethereal. Melyn cursed silently, trying to calm his mind again and slip back into the trance. It came after a few moments, and he saw it again – a strange discolouration, almost like a bruise in the air, a few dozen paces off and not far from the road edge. For a moment he thought it might be a spy, one of Ballah's men with even more powerful concealment magic than his own, but it didn't move, just hung there. Noting its position, he rose back out of his trance and steered his horse over to the place. It was easy to find, a long dark patch of ash flattening the grass as if it had been dumped from a cart. The rain had washed it smooth, and in the

46

middle of the pile something glinted gold in the early-morning sun.

'Something happened here.' The thought was Melyn's but the words came from Frecknock, as ever following him like an obedient pet.

'Indeed, but what?'

Perhaps taking his question as permission to act, Frecknock stepped forward, stooped down and retrieved the shiny object. As her hand touched the ash, she shuddered visibly.

'What is it?' Melyn leaned forward in his saddle the better to see.

'A man died here, and then his body was consumed by the Fflam Gwir.' Frecknock stood once more, handing the object to Melyn. He turned it over in his hand, noting the pure gold and the worn stampings that marked it as a coin. It was no currency he knew, but he recognized it as something he had seen before. There had been a handful of them in the cave where Errol and the dragon Benfro had been hiding, left behind along with several other valuable trinkets.

'The boy was here, and the dragon too.' Melyn slipped the coin into a pocket in his travelling cloak, wondering who the man was and how he had died.

'Benfro did this.' Frecknock stood up, backing away from the pile of wet ash, and Melyn thought he saw her shudder again. 'Only a dragon could conjure this flame. But how? He has no herbs, no oils. He doesn't know the spells.'

'He doesn't need spells; he breathes fire.'

'He . . .' Frecknock lifted a hand to her mouth, her eyes wide. 'I can't believe . . . Not Benfro . . .'

'He breathes fire. Is that any more shocking than him growing wings and flying?'

'Your Grace, you have no idea.'

'Enlighten me then.'

'Breathing fire is something the old creatures did, before Great Rasalene showed us the way of the Grym. It's unnatural, bestial. No dragon would ever do it. The Fflam Gwir comes from Gwlad, not from us.'

'Well, this came from Benfro, which means he passed this way. And by the look of that ash, not long ago either. Another couple of heavy showers and there'll be nothing left to see.' Melyn looked up at the sky, dark with gathering rain clouds, then back at the patch of damp ash. There was something odd about it, and as he looked, it came to him. The grass was not burned. Fronds were poking up through the pile, paler green where they had been hidden from the sun for a while. He put his hand back in his pocket and drew out the coin. It was scuffed and worn, but a fire that could have rendered a man to ash would have surely melted it. Even the magical fire he had conjured to dispose of the dead Llanwennog villagers had burned with a terrible heat.

'How is it this coin survived intact? Why isn't the grass burned?'

'The Fflam Gwir burns only dead flesh and bone and scale. As we come from the Grym, so it takes us back when we are dead.' Frecknock sounded like she was reciting a passage from a litany.

'Then how do you account for Osgal's burns? How could Benfro produce this flame in the aethereal?'

'I truly do not know, Your Grace. He should not be

able to breathe fire at all. This is something I've never encountered before.'

Melyn could see Frecknock's fear as she spoke, and it made him feel better. She knew how precarious her position was; knew that she could be killed in an instant should she stop being useful. Admitting that there was something she didn't know meant that her end was a little bit closer.

'Well then, let us hurry into town before my warrior priests kill everyone. Perhaps one of the good citizens of Cerdys will be able to shed some light on the matter.'

Dafydd didn't know who was the more astonished, the dragon, Usel or himself. They all stood motionless, staring at each other for long moments. It seemed as if the chittering forest noise and babble of the stream had been cut off. It was Iolwen who finally broke the stillness.

'Um. Hello?' She spoke in Llanwennog, taking a single pace forward from their group and opening her arms wide in a gesture of peace. The dragon said something incomprehensible. Its voice was melodic, almost hypnotizing, and though he couldn't understand the words, Dafydd thought he would be happy to listen to it for ever. Then Usel spoke, and his words were a crude imitation of the dragon's, halting and uncertain but clearly the same language. Dafydd heard his own name, and Iolwen's, and assumed that they were being introduced to the beast.

She replied with a smile and a nod. He didn't know how, but he understood then the dragon was female. He had only ever seen one of her kind before, at a circus many years earlier. That creature had been male and nothing like as large or splendid as this one. Her scales glistened in the evening sunshine, reflecting a thousand different colours. Her tail coiled around her massive legs like some tame snake, its tip pointed and spiky. Long sharp talons sprang from her feet, and her fingers ended in lethal claw-like nails. Narrow fangs protruded past her lips, white as bone against the darkness of her face. She was fierce and yet also somehow unthreatening.

Dafydd listened as she spoke some more unintelligible words in that strange lilting accent. He felt at peace, relaxed and calm. The whole clearing was a safe place, a magic place.

'But this is wonderful.' Usel's words broke through Dafydd's reverie, bringing him back to the real world with a start. How long had he drifted? He had no idea. But somehow he had taken Iolwen's hand in his own.

'You can speak to her?' he asked.

'After a fashion. My Draigiaith is very poor, and she speaks a dialect I've never heard before. But I think I get the gist of her story. She's lost. One moment she was flying over the forests, searching the islands for more of her kin, the next she was in a land she didn't recognize. When she approached a town of men for help, they pursued her with weapons and magic, tried to kill her. She escaped and flew here, feeling the call of this place. But the carving puzzles her. She knows of no reason why anyone should have created it. No dragon has ever courted such veneration, she tells me. Her mistress would be appalled.'

'Her mistress? Who could command such a creature? Does this dragon have a name?' Dafydd's questions bubbled out of him as if he had no control over his actions.

'She is Merriel, daughter of Earith. At least I think

that's what she said. Not a dragon I've ever heard of, I have to admit. But as to her mistress, that's far more revealing. She is the dragon portrayed in this carving.' Usel pointed to the great rock face. 'Earith, favoured of the Shepherd. Gifted with the powers of healing. In human guise at least she is the founder of our order. Her existence as a dragon is . . . troubling to those who would see dragons as mere beasts.'

Dafydd began to ask how that could possibly be, but he was interrupted by shouts from behind and above. Whirling he saw Captain Pelod and his guards charging towards their little group, potent blades shining in the gloaming and eyes filled with bloodlust. On the ridge above them sailors appeared with crossbows, and before he could say anything the air was full of ill-aimed bolts.

'Hold!' Dafydd threw all of his will into the command, reaching out to everyone he could see. His voice echoed around the narrow valley end, bouncing off the rock wall and seeming to amplify with each repeat. A flock of brightly coloured birds clattered into the air from the nearby trees with squawks of alarm. The attack stopped as if it had run into an invisible wall. Pelod looked for a moment as if he had been slapped, and an unnatural quiet descended on the scene.

'What were you doing?' Dafydd asked as the guards extinguished their blades.

'We saw the beast attacking you.' Pelod's words were uncertain, as if he was no longer quite sure what he had seen.

'She was doing nothing of the sort. We're in no danger from this dragon.' Usel turned away and said something to the startled creature in its own language. Dafydd felt something brush his mind, like the touch of King Ballah, and then he understood her words.

'There is much to learn about this world into which I have stumbled. It is a place where men are cruel and wield the subtle arts with a brutality I've rarely seen. But you, Prince Dafydd, have shown me kindness. I shall not forget it.'

For a fleeting instant Dafydd felt something of the dragon's thoughts. She was old, far older than he could conceive. And she had seen much, felt joy and sadness through her long life. He caught glimpses of a world where dragons wheeled and turned in the sky, as numerous as crows, as elegant as eagles. Then that connection was broken, leaving him feeling flat. Merriel daughter of Earith bowed once to the small party, then stepped back and away from them. Dafydd knew what she was about to do and, still holding Iolwen's hand, he pulled his wife away.

'Come, Usel, you're in her way,' he said, and the medic looked startled as if he were a little boy caught dreaming during his lessons.

'What?'

'She needs room. Come.' Dafydd walked over to where Captain Pelod was standing at the head of his men. 'It's all right, Jarius. She means us no harm. Quite the opposite, indeed.'

Opening her wings wide to the last rays of the evening sun, the dragon took a couple of steps forward and sprang into the air. The wind washed over them as she passed, bringing with it the spiced scent of the nearby treetops. Once, twice, she wheeled around the valley, gaining height all the while. And then, with a haunting cry that filled Dafydd with melancholy, she sped off towards the horizon.

'Fly, beast. I know you can. Now fly.'

Benfro felt the sting of a whip across his back as he lumbered around a large oval ring formed by the parked circus wagons. He couldn't quite understand why he was running, why he didn't stop and turn on the hateful man standing on a wooden crate in the middle of the ring. Something wasn't right in his mind. He could think, and feel the rage building up in him, but he couldn't stop his body from doing what it was told.

'Up, I say. Up, beast.' The words were punctuated by nips from the sharp metal point worked into the end of the whip. Benfro knew it well. Every evening for over a week he had been forced to endure this humiliation. Hating himself and hating his captors even more, he opened his wings and leaped into the air.

It was difficult. The circus master's commands prevented him from going higher than the tops of the wagons, and the ring was too small for comfort. The ends of his wings were sore from repeatedly banging into things, and he had developed a sort of half-folded flight that made the muscles in his back scream in pain after just a few minutes.

'Now land.' Before he could even think about it, Benfro obeyed. It galled him that so commanded he seemed able to take off and land far better than he had ever managed in the months he had practised in Corwen's clearing.

'Good. That's better.' The circus master stepped down

off his box and walked over to where Benfro stood. Loghtan, he was called, and his son was Tegwin. Benfro wasn't sure who he hated the most. Tegwin was cruel because he liked it, and didn't confine his cruelty to the animals in the circus. Most of the people gave him a wide berth too, especially when he had been drinking. But Loghtan was cruel because that was the only way he seemed to know how to get what he wanted. Benfro didn't suppose the man had ever said please, or simply asked someone for a favour. It was his nature to demand, with a crack of the whip or a fist to the head to make sure his demand was met swiftly.

'You should have learned by now that I always get my way.' The circus master reached up and clipped a long rope to the chain halter fastened around Benfro's neck when he had first been captured. Loghtan wasn't a big man, not tall like Inquisitor Melyn's captain. He was short and wiry, with a dark face creased by an outdoor life. What little hair he had left curled tight around the edges of his scalp in shades of greasy grey, and spilled out of his overlarge ears. Benfro knew that he could reach out, pick him up and break his back in a single motion. He remembered the ease with which he had killed the man attacking Errol; they broke easily, these people. And he remembered too the fire he had breathed, reducing the dead body to nothing but fine ash. Well, a body didn't need to be dead first, did it? All he had to do was summon up the flame and breathe.

Instead he bowed his head, the easier for Loghtan to tether him like a dog. Though his every thought screamed 'Kill!', he could do nothing but collude in his own entrapment and humiliation.

Loghtan led him out of the ring through a gap in the wagons, and Benfro followed as docilely as any pack mule. He hunched himself down, his wings folded as tightly to his body as possible in shame as they went past the campfire. The circus performers were having their evening meal, and the smell of cooking meat made his stomach gurgle. Benfro had eaten nothing for days but the rancid scraps thrown into his cage each morning. He knew they were laden with whatever drug it was that Loghtan used to control him, and yet he couldn't stop himself from eating. One barked command from his new master was all it took.

The large wagon was parked at the edge of the camp, its sides down for a change, letting the warm plains air through the metal bars. It looked like one of the animal handlers had thrown a few buckets of water in, no doubt as a token gesture towards cleaning out the mess. The cage was large enough to house two dragons, but not so big that they could avoid fouling it. As he was led up the short ramp and waited for Loghtan to open the vast padlock, Benfro looked across to the nearest wagon, where the two lioncats sat, staring despondently at nothing in particular. They were so bowed down, so defeated as to be barely alive. He was beginning to know how they felt.

'In.' Loghtan's command was necessary; Benfro could do almost nothing without the circus master's express order. He bent low and squeezed through the small door. Inside the cage what little straw that hadn't been washed out was sodden and rank-smelling. The other dragon sat at the far end, staring at the sunset over the grassland. He didn't move as the door was slammed shut and locked again.

'Rest yourself. We'll have another practice in the morning before we leave. I want you to put on a good show for the king.' With a last flick of his whip across the bars, Loghtan strode off in search of some food.

There was nothing for Benfro, and despite the buckets that had been thrown through the bars, there was no water to drink either. He slumped down against the closed door, thirsty, hungry, but not tired. Most of his days were taken up with sitting in this dreadful cage, either cramped like now or more uncomfortably rocking back and forth as the circus rolled slowly south and east.

'Another day gone. Goodbye, sweet Arhelion.'

Benfro looked up from his musings. The old dragon spoke to the sunset as the last shimmer of red disappeared. He sounded so sad and lost that Benfro was left wondering how many times he had said the same thing.

'How long have you been in here?'

'Magog was always in here. Magog will always be in here. How long is how long?'

Benfro sighed. Getting sense out of the old dragon was like squeezing water out of a stone.

'But surely there must have been a time when you weren't caged like this?'

'This is Cenobus, Magog's home. Do not call it a cage.'

Benfro remembered the ruins deep in the heart of the great forest of the Ffrydd. It was difficult to decide which was worse: being stuck there under Magog's control or here under Loghtan's. At least he didn't dream here. There must have been something in the drugs he was given that made him sleep soundly. It would have been too much indeed to be caged during the day and forced to sort through the dwindling pile of dragon's jewels in Magog's repository through the night.

'Have you met many other dragons here?' Memories of his mother, of Sir Frynwy and the other villagers, of Corwen, reminded him of something he had forgotten under the influence of Loghtan's drugs. A shiver ran down his spine to the tip of his tail as his slow brain followed the logic of it.

'Magog has seen many dragons. They come to his court for his wisdom.'

'What about a dragon called Sir Trefaldwyn? Do you remember meeting him?'

The old dragon considered a moment, his rheumy eyes glinting in the failing evening light.

'No. I knew Palisander, of course. And Albarn the Bard, but no Sir Trefaldwyn. What manner of name is that for a dragon anyway?'

'How about Morgwm. Morgwm the Green?' Benfro studied the old dragon's face for the faintest flicker of recognition. But there was nothing. It was both frustrating and a relief; if this had been the sorry, mad wreck of his father, then what hope was there left?

'I knew a Morrin the Fool once. But he was no dragon. No, he was an ass, and a fine fellow to boot.'

'What happened to him?'

'Old Loghtan didn't like him, so he struck him down with an axe. Then they chopped him up and fed him to us. Very good he tasted too. You should be careful, young Gog. Loghtan doesn't like you much.'

'I don't think he much likes anyone.'

'Hee. Old Loghtan's a misery guts. That's for sure. But

you don't want to upset him. Oh no, sir. That would be bad.'

'Worse than this?'

'You think this is bad?' The old dragon laughed, a noise like pigs fighting in a sack. 'You don't know nothing, my boy. You don't know nothing.'

'What? We're locked up in this shit hole for days on end, drugged into submission, made to fly endlessly round and round, whipped . . . What could be worse than that?' Benfro's anger came out in his voice, but he was powerless to lash out, to kick and punch like he wanted to. His body was barely under his control. It took all of his strength just to find a slightly less uncomfortable place to sit.

'Old Loghtan's a magician, see.' The dragon went on as if Benfro had said nothing. 'He knows things. Oh yes, he does. He can do things to you. Bad things.'

'Like forcing you to parade in front of some king like a performing animal?'

'Oh no. Much worse, much worse. He can steal your memories from you.'

The sun was well below the horizon now, and the only light came from its reflection on the few high clouds sitting motionless in the evening sky. Benfro half-listened to the other dragon's words, responded because there was very little else he could do. His companion was completely mad, and he wondered how long it would take for him to get the same way.

'How can he steal your memories? Don't you mean he just makes you forget things?'

In the deepening gloom, Benfro saw the bulk of the

other dragon shift, shuffling in a stoop across the wagon to drop beside him. He was smaller than Benfro, withered with age and the treatment he had received at the hands of Loghtan and Tegwin. Benfro wondered how many decades he had been with the circus; how long it had taken for his spirit to be completely broken.

'See here, young Gog. See here.' The dragon turned his head away from Benfro, angling it as if he was trying to show something behind his ears. Benfro looked more closely at the leathery skin and fine scales. There was a rippled ridge of scar tissue running across the back of the dragon's head, perhaps a hand's width across.

'He takes away your memories.'

It wasn't hard to follow the route taken by the circus, but Errol found it impossible to catch up. Every time he stopped, the wagons had passed through some days earlier or camped for a night and then gone on without doing a show, much to the disappointment of the locals. It was the considered opinion of almost everyone he spoke to that the circus was heading as fast as possible for the capital, there to perform in front of the king.

'But they've left it very late.' The barmaid in this tavern was much like any number of barmaids he had seen in similar inns along the way. 'It's most unlike old Loghtan to be so late. Normally he'd have been through here a month ago, doing shows in every town until he reached the capital. Must have been something very special to keep him up in the northlands all that time.'

'I heard he'd captured a new dragon.' Errol watched the woman for any sign that she had heard this rumour from anyone else. It was too much of a coincidence for it to be anyone other than Loghtan's circus that had captured Benfro, but still he was plagued by the worry that he might be chasing the wrong quarry, and into the depths of the enemy's lair too.

'Well, I dare say that'd keep him back. But he's losing a lot of money not doing all these shows, and that's not like Loghtan.'

Errol chatted for a while longer, until his meal was ready, then retired to a table by the fire to eat. It had been a long day on the road, and he was anxious to get to bed. An early start in the morning and he might yet make up some time. His near miss with Dondal he could put down to bad luck, but the closer he came to Tynhelyg, the more chance there was of running into someone else who might recognize him. He wasn't quite sure what he'd do once he found the circus, but he wanted to get to it before it reached the capital.

He was finishing off his mug of ale when the rider entered the tavern. As the mud-splattered man approached the bar and ordered a drink, there was something about him that immediately put Errol on his guard. Perhaps it was his well-cut riding boots and functional but smart cloak. Maybe it was the way he held himself – with the air of one used to respect. Whatever it was, Errol knew the man was trouble. Making as little fuss as possible, he got up from his table and left the tavern. The rider had cast a casual glance over the room when he entered, but he paid no attention to Errol's departure, too busy taking deep swallows from his tankard of ale.

Light spilled from the kitchen door across the

courtyard. A second door, directly opposite it, led straight behind the bar. Errol stood outside listening intently, trying to make out the conversation between the barmaid and the rider over the general noise of the tavern.

'Oh, we get all sorts through here – merchants, nobles, soldiers on leave. Why I even had that Duke Dondal in here a few weeks ago. Mean old man waved his ring in front of me and expected to be fed for nothing.' The barmaid's words carried strongly. No doubt she had developed a good voice to cope with the more rowdy clientele. The rider, on the other hand, spoke softly, so that Errol had to strain to make out anything at all.

'Young man . . . through here . . . king's seal . . .' It was enough. It was to be expected, he supposed. Even if Duke Dondal hadn't known exactly who he was, Errol's hurried departure from Gremmil would have aroused his suspicions. No doubt Poul had recounted the whole tale, and Dondal would have surely put two and two together.

Errol went straight to the stables. He had no luggage other than his purse, no belongings other than his horse. The stable lad was nowhere to be seen, so he saddled up himself.

Out on the open road he felt a little safer. The rider may have been one of Dondal's soldiers, but he looked like a man who needed ale and rest. Errol doubted he would move beyond the tavern much before morning. Still, if there was one looking for him, there would surely be others. And soon the word would be out, his description in every tavern, with every noble between here and the capital.

Errol pressed on, riding slowly through the night. The

road was good and easy to make out in the dark, but every so often there were potholes waiting to catch out the unwary. It was bad enough being tipped off his horse, but if the poor creature injured itself he would be lost. Once he could no longer see the lights of the tavern and village behind him, he dismounted and led the horse instead.

It was a warm night, and the moonless sky was clear, the stars bright overhead. He knew he ought to stop somewhere, hobble the horse and try to get a few hours' sleep, but the thought of the rider kept him going. Only when the road dipped into another gully, lined on either side with scrubby trees, did Errol feel safe enough. He found a spot away from the road, tethered the horse to a tree and settled down against the trunk to sleep.

Dozing fitfully, he slipped in and out of dreams in which Isobel and Poul looked at him in dreadful disappointment. If he had told them the truth, they said, then they would have taken him in, protected him. Then he saw Melyn riding at the head of an army of warrior priests. Only they weren't warrior priests but dragons, and behind them the ground burned, black smoke boiling up into the sky. He tried to turn back to Lord and Lady Gremmil, but they weren't there any more. And this wasn't Castle Gremmil either. He knew where this was. It was Gog's palace.

Almost as if he flew, he sped along the corridors, looking for the long winding stone staircase that would take him up to the top of the highest tower. Errol knew he was dreaming, which added another layer of unreality to the dream. At any moment he might wake, might lose this opportunity, and knowing that made it all the harder to stay asleep.

He moved from the corridors to the tower room in a blink of an eye. Somehow that seemed more natural than anything he had experienced so far. The room was much as he remembered it from his previous visit, only this time he was seeing it from the air rather than the perspective of a young lad. His attention was firmly on the golden cage, still hanging from the rafters like some absurd aviary, and he soared up to it, past it, turning to see inside.

Martha lay huddled on a narrow mattress, asleep. She had rigged up a structure within the cage from bits of stick and blankets to give her some privacy, and to Errol it looked like she had stumbled into the nest of some vast bird. Her face was thin, her long hair ragged and matted. As he watched her, she shivered, drawing her knees up to her chest for warmth. He looked around the huge room, saw the fireplace empty and black, the desk strewn with papers blown about by gusts from the open window. How high up were they here? How cold would it get? Would she freeze to death here, abandoned? She mustn't sleep; he knew that much about the cold. You had to stay awake.

'Martha!' Errol tried to shout, but his voice sounded distant and muffled.

'Martha!' She rolled over, eyes still tightly closed, arms wrapped around her legs, head tucked in over her chest. Still his voice was too quiet, almost mumbled.

'Martha!' This time he shouted with all his might, and at the same instant he realized he had been bodiless, his muscles contracted, pitching him forward. For a moment too terribly short he saw Martha open her eyes, look up, see him. And then he was awake, back in the woods, gasping for air as his horse looked on placidly.

Errol tried to get back to sleep. He slumped back against the tree and closed his eyes tight, but his heart was racing, his mind fully awake. He gave up, full of anguish for Martha's plight, more determined than ever to find Benfro and the other dragon that might or might not be Sir Trefaldwyn.

The air glowed with pre-dawn light as he led his horse back to the road and mounted. Not a mile from his resting place he came upon a series of low buildings, labourers' cottages for a nearby farm. They were still shut up at this early hour, not even a dog or a goose running out to chase him as he rode slowly past. Some even had the look of being unoccupied, but at the last cottage a line of washing was strung between two gnarled apple trees. Shawls, blouses and skirts hung in a row, dry save for the lightest of morning dews. He was reminded of how his mother would sometimes leave clothes out when she knew there would be no rain in the night. 'It makes them softer,' she had always told him, though sometimes he wondered if it wasn't just that she had been too tired to bring it all in and fold it up.

It came to him in a flash, an idea so daring and yet so obvious he wondered why he hadn't thought of it before. A few dozen paces past the row of houses, where he was hidden from view by the trees that surrounded the small hamlet, he stopped and dismounted, then walked quietly back to the washing line. There was no fence separating the road from the garden, and it was a matter of seconds to help himself to what he needed: one skirt of heavy tweed, a pair of canvas trousers of the sort he had seen farm girls wearing, one white cotton blouse and a shawl.

Errol counted out coins from the bag Lord Gremmil had given him, more than enough to compensate for the purloined clothes, and placed them in the pocket of one of the remaining dresses, careful not to let them chink against each other.

By the time he made it back to his horse, the clothes rolled up under one arm, his heart was pounding. And yet he felt a thrill of excitement. He'd got away with it. Only once he had hauled himself back into the saddle and ridden away from the houses did Errol realize just how much he was shaking. What if he had been caught? How would he have even begun to explain to some burly farmer why he was stealing women's clothes?

He rode on, fretting that someone would come galloping up from behind. It could be the rider from the tavern, or the farmer, or Duke Dondal and the king's army. It could have been Inquisitor Melyn come to drag him back to Emmass Fawr. Shaking the fear from his head, Errol kicked his horse into a trot and scanned the horizon for the next copse.

After the incident at Lord Gremmil's grain stores when one of Dondal's soldiers had mistaken him for a girl, Errol had thought of taking a knife to his hair. Not having a knife, he had resorted to tying it in a long ponytail and tucking it down the back of his cloak. Dark as it was, it had gone unnoticed, or at least unremarked in all the places he had stopped since. Now he untied his hair and let it fall over his shoulders. He stripped off the clothes Lady Gremmil had given him, stowing them in his saddlebags along with the skirt, then pulled on the rest of the stolen garments. His cloak already looked like something a young woman might wear, but he brushed the worst of the road dirt off it before flinging it once more over his shoulders.

He would have liked a glass to check his appearance in, but as Errol rode into the next town he was confident the people glancing up at him would see not the fugitive boy wanted in two countries, but an apprentice healer heading to the city to buy exotic herbs for her mistress.

4

When all else fails, and your dragon becomes unruly even with the highest doses of calming potion, there is but one option left. Use camphor woodsmoke to render it insensible, then tie the beast firmly to the floor with its head laid straight. Behind the ears the skull is thinner than the rest and not protected by the hard scales that cover most of its body. With utmost care, it is possible to drill out a small section of bone, revealing the living brain beneath. And within the folds of this organ you will see the red jewels forming. Remove one, maybe two if they are large, being mindful not to injure the surrounding tissue. Replace the removed pan of bone, sealing it with the healing salve and Grendor's invocation. Be careful that your subject remains sedated for two or three days, for that is how long it takes a dragon's bones to knit.

This procedure should only be used as a last resort. Any surgery on a living brain is fraught with danger, and removing a dragon's jewels while it lives may result in the beast being rendered idiotic, if it survives the ordeal at all.

From the personal papers of
Circus Master Loghtan

The killing didn't bother him, but Melyn could never get used to the smell of burning flesh. It hung over the town long after the smoke had cleared, clogging the nostrils and clinging to clothes. Normally it wasn't a problem for him. The villages, with their tiny populations, succumbed to the Grym, the people burned away without smoke or ash. Larger towns he put to the flame, but always he had been able to ride away from the stench.

This place was different. There was little point clearing the northlands if no one knew. He needed word of his army to get out, to draw a large part of King Ballah's army away from the southern border. So at least some of the women and children would be allowed to flee. His warrior priests had met stiffer resistance here than anywhere else too. There had been Llanwennog regular soldiers billeted in the castle, some of King Ballah's personal guard among them. Melyn was glad he had encountered them in a town rather than open country. They had been mostly in their barracks and, far from the border, had not been primed for battle. He was lucky that none of them had been on gate duty either, since the town was well fortified. The alarm hadn't been raised until it was far too late. Even so, it had been their hardest test so far, and he had lost valuable warrior priests in the fight.

Now he sat in the main hall of the castle, trying not to taste the greasy smoke from the pyres. A frightened middle-aged lady stood by the window, staring out across a courtyard slick with blood, still piled with the bodies of the dead. She was pale-skinned for her race, probably a half-breed from one of the earlier vain attempts to bring the two nations closer together by arranged marriages between the noble houses.

'You need not fear for your life, Lady Gremmil. Nor for the safety of your serving girls. My men have orders not to harm them.'

'But they can do what they want to the men. To my husband. Will you leave any man alive?'

Melyn reappraised the woman. It wasn't fear that made her shake, but rage. 'This is war, my lady,' he said.

'War? Invasion more like. And just why do you need to wage this war anyway? What did we ever do to your precious Twin Kingdoms that you have to murder innocents?'

'There have been three separate assassination attempts on Queen Beulah since she ascended to the throne less than a year ago. All of them can be traced directly back to King Ballah. If your king wasn't so keen on toppling our rightful monarch and putting his puppet in her place, we wouldn't have to do everything in our power to stop him.'

Lady Gremmil turned away from him, not answering his accusation. He gazed at the back of her head as she stared out the window again. His captains would start reporting in soon. The town was taken; it was just a matter of mopping up.

A scuffle in the hall outside dragged both his and Lady Gremmil's attention to the door. It was kicked open, and Captain Osgal strode in, dragging another man by the scruff of his neck. He paid no heed to the lady, but hauled his captive up to the table where Melyn sat, then threw the man to the floor.

'I found him hiding in the stables. Thought you might want to talk to him before I cut off his head, sir.'

Melyn looked down at the cowering figure. He had grey hair and wore an expensive cloak. His fingers were covered in fine jewels, which flashed in the pale light from the window as he held his hands over his head.

'Well, this is a surprise. I didn't think to see you again so soon.'

The grey-haired man looked up at Melyn's voice. Duke Dondal had managed to avoid injury so far, which only confirmed the inquisitor's low opinion of him. Unlike Lord Gremmil, who had led his men against an army of shadows, trying to buy time for messengers to escape the city.

'Inquisitor Melyn? But how—' Dondal struggled to his feet, but Osgal floored him again with a well-placed boot.

'You stay on the floor in front of His Grace.'

'I had hoped we might run into each other eventually, Dondal. I'm anxious to hear how you managed to keep your head after plotting against your king. After introducing an assassin into his royal palace.'

'I had no choice, Melyn. The plot was uncovered before I even arrived in Tynhelyg. My only option was to persuade Ballah my plan had always been to hand the boy over to him.'

'How very convenient for you. And I suppose you gave Ballah all my gold as well. That might have convinced him of your loyalty. Not much consolation for poor old Errol though. Mind you, he fooled us all.'

'Errol? Errol who?'

Melyn looked up in surprise. He wanted Lady Gremmil

to witness all he did in the castle, so that she could report back to Ballah, but he hadn't anticipated any questions from her.

'He's of no concern to you. Just a spy.'

'Oh, so not the Errol Balch we found near death on the king's road then. Only he was a spy, of sorts.'

'Errol . . . Balch?' Melyn looked straight at Lady Gremmil, picking out images and memories from her mind. She was remembering a young man with long black hair and an earnest expression. She cared about his well-being for some unaccountable reason. So he had passed through Gremmil. Melyn wondered what had become of the dragon. 'He's calling himself Balch, is he? How amusing. I wonder if he knows. Tell me, when did you last see him?'

'It must have been a week ago. Just before Dondal arrived. He said he was carrying a message to the king about a possible invasion from the north. It would seem he was right about that.'

'The boy's still alive? I thought Queen Beulah had killed him,' said Dondal, first staring at Melyn, then at Lady Gremmil, then back at Melyn.

'So did she. But Errol's proved himself quite hard to kill on more than one occasion now. We can talk about him later. Right now I want to know how Ballah has deployed his armies in the south.'

'And why would I tell you that? Assuming, that is, I know anything about it.'

'Oh come now, Dondal. Why do you do anything? To save your scrawny neck. Osgal.' Melyn nodded at his captain and felt the telltale surge in the Grym as Osgal conjured his blade of fire. It cast an eerie white light over the room, harsher by far than the smoky daylight outside.

'Inquisitor, please. I can be of great use to you alive. Ballah would—'

'Ballah would sell your neck for a handful of beans, Dondal. Why do you suppose he's sent you upcountry when all the important things are happening in the south?' Melyn focused on the duke. He was easy to manipulate; his fear was real and intense. It was a shame he probably didn't know very much about the king's battle plans at all. Still, Melyn was determined to extract every last nugget. He built up an idea of what it might feel like for a blade of fire to burn its way through skin, cauterizing blood vessels as it bit its way down towards the spine, searing through bone.

'I only know what they discussed at the council of war before Ballah sent me here to recruit more men.' Dondal's words spilled out like water from a broken dam. 'Geraint was to take the main force to Wrthol to guard that pass. Tordu was in charge of the smaller garrison at Tynewydd. That should have been my command, but—'

'But Ballah couldn't trust you not to let me in without a fight. He's wise. That's why he's king and you're begging for your life. What of Dafydd? Is he in his father's army, or has Ballah put him in charge of the city defences?'

'I've not seen Dafydd for months. Nor his wife either. Ballah sent them to Talarddeg to get them out of the way. The boy kept coming up with wild schemes that would only end up getting him killed.'

'So who's guarding the city then?'

'Guarding it against what? Any attack would have to

get past Tordu or Geraint. And even then it would have to march for two weeks at least to reach Tynhelyg. Ballah would have plenty of time to prepare the city for a siege.'

'How many soldiers are garrisoned there now?'

'A thousand maybe. Plus two hundred of Ballah's palace guard.'

'So few?' Melyn probed Dondal's mind as he spoke the words, looking for the lie. But it wasn't there.

'Geraint wanted to leave five thousand men, but Ballah shouted him down. Said if he didn't want them they could go with Tordu's army. Then he sent most of his guard out with the army too.'

'And what of your own efforts? If the army that met us here is anything to go by, you've not been too successful in drumming up more men. When were you going to slink back to your master and admit your failure?'

'King Ballah wanted me back in time for the festival. And I've already sent three thousand men to the front, so I don't think he'll be too upset.'

'The King's Festival? I'd have thought with war looming that would have been cancelled. But no, I suppose that's not Ballah's style.'

Melyn settled back in his chair, digesting the information. If it was true that Tynhelyg was largely unguarded, neither Llanwennog army could ignore his threat. If there were just a way to isolate the king from his palace guard . . . They were the problem. A thousand men with iron swords were no match for even a hundred warrior priests, but two hundred well-trained magicians would ruin everything. Then again, if the king was outside the city, and with thousands of people gathered for the festivities . . . The

73

elements of a plan even more daring than his strike through the forest and into the northlands began to form in Melyn's mind.

'Lady Gremmil, I said you needn't fear for your life. I'm sorry, but I lied.' He concentrated on the Grym, summoning it to him, channelling it. Lady Gremmil turned at his words, but she scarcely had time to respond. With a mental flick he unleashed a surge of pure energy at her. She let out a tiny 'Oh' and crumpled to the ground, dead.

'You . . .' Dondal's eyes bulged in fear and anger. 'Did you have to do that?'

'Regrettable,' Melyn lied. He had rather enjoyed himself. 'But yes. I had hoped to draw the army from the passes by torching the northlands, but what more tempting a prize than Tynhelyg itself. Osgal.'

'Wait. Melyn. I can help you. I can—'

Contrary to the image the inquisitor had put in the duke's mind, this blade of fire cut without heat and didn't cauterize as it went. Dondal's blood sprayed wide over the wooden floorboards as his head clattered to the floor, separated from his neck by Osgal's swift stroke.

'Come on, you old nag. You can do better than that. Call yourself Magog? I've seen more convincing lizards.'

Benfro winced as each crack of the whip hit the old dragon's shoulders. He still couldn't call his companion in misery Magog, even though that was how he referred to himself. The mad old beast was running around the make-shift ring, his skinny wings held wide, flapping like a cockerel about to crow. Every so often he would leap up and glide a short distance before crashing back down to

74

the ground, stumbling, and running some more. Plainly it was no longer enough of a show for Loghtan.

'You can fly higher than that, you useless wyrm. Put some effort into it.' Loghtan let fly the whip again, and Benfro imagined himself getting up, ripping out the post to which he was chained, striding over to the circus master, taking him by the throat and squeezing until there was no life left in that hated body. But he stayed where he was, held still by the stupor of the drugs he was forced to eat.

'What is it now? Run, damn your hide. Ah, this is useless.' Benfro looked across to see the old dragon had stopped and was leaning against the nearest wagon, trying to catch his breath. Loghtan jumped down off his box and walked over to him.

'Right, you. Back to your cage. And don't think you're getting a feed tonight. You know the rules. If you don't work, you don't eat.'

But the dragon didn't move. Benfro could hardly believe it. Whenever Loghtan gave him an order, it was like his body was completely in the circus master's control, yet here was Magog – and suddenly he was Magog, Son of the Summer Moon – not so much defying the man as ignoring him completely.

Maybe he would reach out and pull off Loghtan's head. It would be easy, and then they would be free. But Loghtan's head stayed firmly on his shoulders. He dug one hand into the satchel he always wore over his shoulder when training the dragons, and pulled something out. There was a muffled *pop* and a cloud of smoke or dust enveloped the old dragon's head. Almost instantly he dropped to the ground in a heap, motionless. Loghtan looked at him for a moment, kicked him a couple of times, then walked to where Benfro was chained.

'Reckon two dragons might be more than any circus needs, if you understand me.' Loghtan selected a key from the heavy ring on his belt and opened the padlock securing Benfro to the post, handing him the heavy length of chain to carry. 'Now get over there and drag that useless bag of bones into the middle of the ring. Then wait here. I'm going to get Griselda to help me.'

Help you with what? Benfro thought, but he couldn't make the words come out. Instead his traitorous legs turned and carried him to where the old dragon lay. He could smell the dust in the air as he neared, an aroma that reminded him only of sleep. To his relief, Magog was still breathing. Benfro carefully moved Loghtan's box so he could place the dragon at the exact centre of the ring, then went back to the post where he had been chained, hating himself, Loghtan, the circus and the whole of Gwlad with every breath.

He didn't have to spend long cursing before Loghtan returned. Griselda hurried along behind him, and Tegwin brought up the rear, lugging a small wooden trunk. Benfro still didn't fully understand their language, but he could translate enough to get the gist of what they were saying. Their anxiety was obvious.

'It's too soon, surely. Once a year at most. Never twice.'

'Well, that's what the old man used to say. But he also said two dragons was bad luck. Maybe the youngster's sparked off something.'

They approached Magog, who was sprawled on the ground as if he had fallen from a great height. Loghtan kicked him a couple of times to make sure he was still asleep, then Tegwin put down the trunk and joined in.

'Give it a rest, boy. That's our meal ticket there.' Griselda put a hand on Tegwin's arm. He shrugged it off angrily but stopped kicking.

'What we need him for? I got you another one, didn't I?'

'Quiet, the both of you. This is delicate work.'

Benfro struggled to see what Loghtan was doing. The three clustered around the old dragon's head, bent down and talking in low voices. Then Loghtan opened the trunk and pulled something out. It looked like a hammer and chisel, though Benfro couldn't be sure.

He watched for an hour or more, unable to make out what was happening save that they were doing something violent to the old dragon's head. Then suddenly Griselda shouted, 'There it is! Be careful, Loghtan.' To which he merely grunted a wordless, angry retort. They all fell silent for a few moments, and then Benfro saw Loghtan hold up what looked like a pair of giant tongs. He dropped something into a cloth that Griselda held out ready. She wrapped it up and put it in her pocket, watched hungrily by Tegwin.

'Heal him up then, boy.' Loghtan dropped a number of metal implements into the trunk, closing the lid and standing up to stretch his back.

'Why do I have to do it?'

'Because I told you to.' Loghtan delivered a hard slap to the back of his son's head, then stooped and picked up the trunk.

Griselda stood, wiping her hands on her apron, leaving dark red stains. 'I'll give this a quick wash then bring it to your wagon, shall I?' she asked.

Loghtan nodded absent-mindedly, watching what his son was doing. Benfro thought he felt something rush past him, less solid than the wind but much more powerful. His senses were so dulled that it was impossible to be sure, but it seemed likely Tegwin was performing some kind of magic. Whatever it was didn't last long.

'That good enough for you?'

'It'll do, I suppose. We've got the other one, after all. This one can take some time to heal.' Loghtan handed the trunk to his son, who took it with a scowl and stalked out of the ring with it. Griselda followed him, and as she passed Benfro, he saw blood on her hands and face, so dark it was almost black.

'Pick him up. Carry him back to the wagon.' Once more the circus master's voice acted directly on Benfro's body, leaving his mind powerless to do anything but watch as he walked over to the unconscious form of the old dragon. The back of Magog's head and his shoulders were slick with blood. The scar line that ran between his ears was livid, like it had only just begun to heal. Benfro knelt down, trying to work out in his mind the best way to pick him up. His body carried on regardless, scooping the old dragon up and into his arms. He was lighter than Benfro had expected, but still heavy. Wings and tail trailed awkwardly as he carried him out of the ring, round the back of the wagons and away to the edge of the camp where their shared cage was parked. No sooner had he walked up the ramp and squeezed through the narrow opening than Loghtan shut the door behind them and locked it. The circus master walked away without another word.

Clumsily, Benfro laid the old dragon down on the thin straw that was all the bedding they had. Magog began to stir almost immediately, one hand going up to the back of his head even before he opened his eyes. When he did, he looked around the cage in startled glimpses, as if everything was new and alarming to him. Finally his eyes fixed on Benfro and stuck there.

'Who are you then? What are you doing in my palace?' The old dragon spoke in the language of the men, not Draigiaith as they had used whenever they were alone before.

'I'm Benfro, remember? What did they do to you?' Benfro used his own tongue and for a moment thought Magog didn't understand him.

'Benfro? Benfro? Never heard of him. Now if you were my brother Gog, that would be a different matter.'

Benfro slumped against the cage wall and tried not to stare at the old dragon as he prattled on, speaking as if he truly didn't recognize him. And then he remembered what the old dragon had said before, when he had shown him the scar on the back of his head. *He can take away your memories.* He saw in his mind's eye a pair of tongs dropping something small into a cloth in Griselda's outstretched hand. Something small and round and red. An unreckoned dragon's jewel, plucked from his living brain.

'Land ahoy!'

The cry came down from the masthead, where for days the sailors had been taking it in turns to scan the horizon for anything other than water. Dafydd instinctively looked out over the waves, though he knew it would be a while yet before he could see anything from the deck.

The ship was making good progress, with a strong wind at its back and all sails spread wide. Since leaving Merrambel they had followed the stars north and west across the southern sea towards the Bay of Kerdigen and Abervenn, but though weeks had passed until Dafydd was sure that they must be going the wrong way, still all there was to see was endless ocean and the odd lonely seabird.

Iolwen no longer sat at the prow watching the dolphins at play. Out here in the open sea it was too choppy, and with each passing hour she seemed to grow rounder still. She spent all day and all night in their cabin now. By Dafydd's rough calculations she was already overdue; their forced visit to the Felem archipelago had added over a month to their journey time. The sighting of land was the news he had been hoping for, dreading the thought of their child being born at sea.

Captain Azurea hauled himself up the ropes, surprisingly agile for a man of his size. Dafydd watched from the railings as he reached the top and scanned the horizon, arguing with the lookout then finally coming back down again. He bellowed something to the helmsman and the ship changed course a fraction. Only when the sails were trimmed to his satisfaction did the captain turn finally to the prince.

'We should be in Abervenn by nightfall, if this wind keeps up.'

'That's the best piece of news I've heard in weeks. Thank you, Captain.' Dafydd left him to begin readying his ship for port and went below to tell the men. The rest of the day was spent in frustrated waiting. The land grew slowly out of the horizon, first the mountain tops of the coastal range, then the tall cliffs, the Sutors, that formed the eastern side of the Bay of Kerdigen. The sea changed as they reached shallower waters, the long slow swell becoming choppier and bringing back a nagging nausea that reminded Dafydd of the long days at the beginning of their voyage. Locked away in her cabin, Iolwen stayed in her bed, too tired even to think about moving until they were in dock and motionless.

As the afternoon wore on to evening they began to see other ships. Merchantmen plied the coastal waters, and fishing boats ventured out much further than Dafydd thought wise, no doubt in search of the best catches. Leaning against the railings and watching it all slide past, he was joined for a while by Usel, who pointed out landmarks as they came into view.

'See there, that's the highest point on the East Sutors. Back when Abervenn was the capital of Hafod traitors were cast from there on to the rocks below. And over there – those flat-topped islands – they're the Thirteen Magicians. Legend has it King Brynceri raised them out of the sea so that he could fight a dragon marauding along the coast.'

'What happened to the dragon?'

'Oh, I suspect it was killed. Brynceri had a bit of a reputation for that. He founded the Order of the High Ffrydd to help him.'

'I know. I've made it my business to study my enemies. Is it true the inquisitor worships Brynceri's severed finger?'

Usel laughed. 'I'd love to see Melyn's face if you accused

him of idolatry. He keeps Brynceri's ring, which just happens still to be on the finger cut from the belly of the dragon Maddau. It's one of the order's most sacred relics, said to date back to Balwen himself. But he worships the Shepherd, like all the people of the Twin Kingdoms. Some say the Shepherd speaks to him when he prays, but I have my doubts about that.'

'You're not a religious man, I take it.'

'Oh, quite the contrary, Your Highness. I'm deeply religious. I am a coenobite of the Order of the Ram and I take my vows to the order very seriously. But I don't accept Melyn's view of the Shepherd as a warlike god visiting terrible vengeance on all who deny him. Rather I think he's a useful metaphor for the power that runs through the whole of Gwlad.'

'The Grym, you mean?'

'Of course, the Grym. But much more besides. Did you know that dragons believe in a being called the mother tree? She dwells in the forests of Gwlad and rules over us all with the dispassionate equality of nature.'

'I'd not heard that, no. But dragons are simple-minded creatures, aren't they? I mean, that one we met on the island. It was quite magnificent to look at, but all I did was order my men to stop attacking and suddenly it was pledging its life to me.'

'And why did you order your men to stop?'

'Well, it wasn't doing us any harm. The poor thing was confused, not a threat.'

'I only wish that more people felt the way you do, sir.' Usel turned and faced him with a look that Dafydd found oddly disquieting. It was an intense stare, those pale grey eyes boring into him, and for a moment he thought the medic was trying to read his mind. But there was nothing, not even the faint whisper he felt when King Ballah touched his thoughts.

'You truly love dragons, don't you?' Dafydd said. 'No, it's more than that, isn't it? You worship them.'

'Worship's too strong a word. The people of Eirawen worshipped a dragon who called himself Gog. Then there was a great calamity and Gog left them, though his spirit remained. Their scriptures tell of a time when Gog will come back and drive the unbelievers from Gwlad. Does that sound familiar to you?'

Dafydd considered. 'Change Gog for the Shepherd, and it's the same story. Melyn's justification for invading Llanwennog is that he's preparing Gwlad for the Shepherd's return. It's nonsense, of course. He just wants to rule the world.'

'Oh no. Don't ever think that the inquisitor is motivated by greed or a desire for power. Melyn's one of the few true believers. He knows he's right, which is precisely why he's so dangerous. He'll do anything his god tells him to. Or anything he thinks his god tells him to. Why do you think he hates dragons so much? When was the last time a dragon harmed anyone? But it's the sacred charter of his order to rid Gwlad of the beasts, so he hunts them down and slaughters them.'

'Well, when we've defeated Beulah and disbanded the Order of the High Ffrydd, if there are any dragons left they'll be welcome at my court. But we've got to win the war first. They'll have to look after themselves until then.' Dafydd looked over the water to the city of Abervenn spreading away up the hill from the approaching port. The setting sun highlighted the castle, perched on its rocky promontory above the harbour. It was a vast building, different architectural styles speaking eloquently of extensions added over many generations. He wondered what kind of welcome he would receive there, and for the first time since leaving Tynhelyg felt a frisson of fear.

'I hope the natives are friendly,' he said, but Usel didn't answer. When Dafydd looked at him, the medic was standing motionless, his arms holding the railing lightly, his eyes completely vacant as if in a trance. Dafydd followed the direction of that unfocused gaze and saw the tall masts of another ship in the harbour, larger even than the vessel in which they were sailing. A dark pennant flapped in the breeze from the top of its mizzen mast, but from this distance and angle he couldn't make it out.

'I think you had better go below, Your Highness.' Usel's voice was different, almost distant. Dafydd watched him closely until the medic's eyes focused again. He lurched slightly against the railing, muscles tightening in his arms and shoulders as he caught himself.

'I'm sorry, sir. I had to check something. I thought I felt a disturbance in the Grym, and I was right. There are warrior priests on board that ship, and look up at the castle – the flags flying.'

'You've got better eyesight than me.' Dafydd squinted at the castle.

'I didn't see them with my eyes, but that's not important. What matters is that you get out of sight before any loose-tongued fishermen see you. We can smuggle your party ashore after dark, but really I need to talk to Lady

Anwyn before we do anything. Damn, but this is inconvenient.'

'What is it? I don't understand. I thought we'd be welcomed openly here.'

'Normally you would, sir. But those warrior priests are not alone. They're here to guard the queen.'

The next few hours were nerve-racking. Dafydd sat on the edge of his cot in their cabin, staring at the darkness outside the porthole while Iolwen slept fitfully. Captain Pelod and his men had been forced to hide in the cargo hold with Teryll. Even Usel hid, his magic pulling him back into the shadows.

Finally, some time in the middle of the night, Dafydd heard a light knock at his cabin door. He rose and opened it, to find Anwyn standing there, Usel behind her.

'Your Highness.' Anwyn curtsied.

Dafydd gestured for them to come in. 'What's happening out there?'

'They arrived a week ago, far earlier than expected. Beulah's been parading her consort around ever since, trying to drum up support for the new Duke of Abervenn.'

'And is it working?'

'I don't think so. Oh, the people shout and cheer, but only because they know what will happen if they don't.'

'Anwyn? Is that you?' Iolwen's voice rose from the bed, and Dafydd turned to see her sitting up, clutching her swelling belly. Anwyn swept past him and went to her, kneeling on the floor.

'Your Highness, it's good to see you. Are you well?'

'As well as I could hope, given the circumstances. They say my sister's here. Are we safe?'

'As safe as anyone can be, but don't worry. Queen Beulah and her party will be riding out in a day or two. They're heading for Tochers to review the army. I think she means to lead her men into battle herself, by the way she talks. And in her condition too.'

'She's pregnant too?'

'Some months gone now, but not as far as you. By the Shepherd, Iolwen. Look at the size of you.'

Dafydd tuned out the pregnancy talk, turning instead to Usel. 'So we're going to be stuck on this boat until Beulah leaves?'

'No, sir. There's a wagon waiting to take you and the princess up to the castle. It's such a huge old place you can have a whole tower to yourself and no one will be the wiser. It'll be a lot more comfortable than staying here. Ships are fine at sea, but a harbour's not a place to linger long.'

'I'd noticed the stench. But what about my men? They can't very well ride through the town, can they?'

'No. Nor can we unload their horses without drawing too much attention. Captain Azurea will put to sea again tomorrow; he has cargo to deliver further along the coast. Captain Pelod and his men will disembark at a beach about half a day's ride from here. I'll go with them and guide them back to the city. There's plenty of ways into Abervenn by land.'

'Very well. When do we leave?' Dafydd glanced around at the cabin, suddenly keen to be gone from its confines.

It was Anwyn who answered: 'Now might be good. I think Princess Iolwen's about to give birth.'

The disparate territories and tribes that King Ballah I forged into the nation of Llanwennog were in ancient times a breeding ground for the many heresies that have deviated from the Shepherd's truth. Much of the warring between the tribes was directly at the behest of priests favouring one interpretation or another of the divine words. There were those who claimed the Shepherd had not left Gwlad at all, but merely taken himself into hiding; those who said he had been trapped in the stars by the Wolf and would only escape at the end of all time. Some mad sects claimed that the Shepherd was no more than a dragon in disguise, while others worshipped the Wolf in acts of great depravity. But perhaps the greatest heresy of all was that which triumphed and now flourishes under the present King Ballah. For it would deny the existence of Shepherd or Wolf, or indeed of any higher being, and put man himself at the pinnacle of everything.

The Taming of the Northlands – A History
of the Kings of Llanwennog

Melyn had taken to pacing the empty corridors of Gremmil Castle in the long hours he spent waiting for his scouts to report back. Dondal's information had opened up a tantalizing possibility, but it needed confirmation from a more trustworthy source. Failing that, he wanted supporting stories from as many separate people as possible, and he needed a timescale. If the King's Festival was in the next few days, then there was no way he was going to be able to get to Tynhelyg and put his men in place. But if it wasn't for three weeks, he had a chance.

The castle was eerily quiet without the bustle of servants. It was an old building, much extended and renovated, but like the town walls a relic of past times. Llanwennog had a long history of civil war before the House of Ballah had finally united it. Places like Gremmil had survived many a siege and launched many an attack.

Melyn was musing on how much easier it would have been to take the word of the Shepherd to the people if the nobles had still been at war with each other when he rounded a corner and found Frecknock standing in the corridor, staring at the wall.

'What are you doing here?' he asked, surprised more than angered. He no longer felt any need to keep her chained up. She immediately fell into her habitual crouch, dropping her eyes to the floor.

'Please forgive me, Your Grace. I was studying the carvings.'

Melyn looked at the wall, noticing for the first time an elaborate frieze running the length of the corridor. To his surprise he recognized the story it depicted, though many of the figures had been crudely defaced.

'Hah! This is the story of Balwen, when the Shepherd gave him the gift of magic so that he could look after the whole of Gwlad. I've not seen such a fine representation outside Emmass Fawr.'

'Is that what it is, Your Grace? I was wondering, what are those creatures in the middle panel? The ones that look like dragons.'

Melyn peered at the carving, then conjured up a ball of light to supplement the meagre illumination filtering through the grimy window on the far side of the corridor. Sure enough, in the fifth panel, where the Shepherd exhorted Balwen to look after all the creatures of Gwlad, there in the undergrowth were a pair of dragons.

'An interesting heresy. Andro would be fascinated. Maybe when this war is over I'll have this removed and taken back to the monastery for him to study.' He ran his free hand over the stone, walking down the corridor until he reached the end of the tale. 'But what is such a piece doing in a castle in godless Llanwennog? Unless . . .'

There was a door at the end of the corridor partly obscured by a pile of old furniture. Melyn shifted a few broken chairs until he could reach the latch, turned it and pushed. The door was either locked or set solid with years of neglect; either way it wouldn't move. Extinguishing his light, he slipped into his aethereal trance and checked the door for magical seals. The long-dead wood should have been a barrier even to his aethereal form, but it was strangely pliant, as if the room beyond were beckoning him. Sensing no danger, he stepped out of his physical body and floated slowly through.

To normal eyes it would have been too dark to see, but in the aethereal it was plain to Melyn that this was a long-disused chapel. There was an altar upon which still stood a small golden image of the crook, along with two fat candles, their wax pooled and solidified on the stone. The ceiling vaulted high above a space big enough for at least fifty people, and low benches were arranged so that the devout could sit while they listened to passages from the scriptures. There was even a heavy leather-bound book lying closed on a lectern to one side of the altar, and Melyn itched to hold it in his hands, to read the words within.

It was obvious that the chapel had not been used for worship for many decades, if not centuries. What surprised him was not so much that it was here; Llanwennogs had been drawn to the true word in the past, though converts were persecuted ruthlessly under the rule of the House of Ballah. What was so unusual about this chapel was that it had neither been desecrated nor pressed into use as something else – a storeroom or dungeon perhaps. It appeared to have been just forgotten, as if the faithful had said their prayers then left with every intention of returning the following Suldith. It had not been sullied; it was still sacred ground, and Melyn could feel the presence of his god all around him.

He floated his aethereal form towards the altar, kneeling in front of it even though he couldn't feel the stone against his knees. It was a strangely detached way to pray, and yet it felt like the right thing to do, as if the Shepherd had called him here. Melyn tried to close his eyes, as he would have done in any other chapel, but in the aethereal to close his eyes was to surrender himself back to his physical body. Too late he felt himself falling back, and with a snap he was standing on the wrong side of the door again.

'Ah, by the Wolf!' He thumped at the door, but it still wouldn't move.

'Can I help, Your Grace?' Melyn turned to see Frecknock standing several paces back down the corridor, waiting patiently as she always did. This was no place for a dragon, and the sight of her brought a flush of anger that he swiftly suppressed. But maybe there was something she could do for him.

'If you can move this junk and open the door, then you can be of service. If not, then get out of my way.'

'I can try.' Frecknock grabbed a heavy oak refectory table with one hand and pulled it back as if it weighed no more than the chairs Melyn had moved. The noise it made on the flagstone floor was enough to convince him that it was just as heavy as it looked.

The rest of the stored furniture dragged aside, the dragon put her shoulder to the door. At first it didn't move, but then with a sound of snapping metal the hinges collapsed and the whole thing fell in. Dust billowed up, shooting out of the open doorway like an explosion. Melyn covered his mouth, coughing through the fabric of his cloak, and stepped inside.

He was instantly aware of the Shepherd in the way his whole body felt younger, lighter. He stepped towards the altar, and a shadow fell across the shaft of light falling in through the wrecked door. Melyn turned to see Frecknock peering into the chapel.

'Get out! Get out! You must not sully this place with your presence!' He thrust the whole force of his will with the words, and the dragon sat back on her tail as if slapped. She backed quickly away, scolded, her hands held up in supplication. And then Melyn heard a voice that swamped his anger, rode over any feeling other than purest joy even as it chided him.

'Do not be so harsh on Frecknock, my servant. She has served you well so far.'

'But my lord, she is a dragon, a creature of the Wolf.'

'And as some of my creations have spurned me, might not his beasts turn from him? Did I not say you would find help in unexpected quarters as you pursued your quest?'

Melyn sank to his knees in the same spot where his aethereal form had settled just minutes earlier. He was humbled in the presence of his god, made to feel no better than the dribbling idiots who lived out their meaningless lives in the almshouses outside Emmass Fawr. His intellect was nothing, his skill at magic mere sleight of hand, his rise from abject poverty to the head of the most powerful order in the history of Gwlad a paltry achievement. He would have none of it without the Shepherd. And yet it troubled him that his god should be so capricious.

'My lord, your wisdom knows no bounds. Please forgive me if I don't fully understand.'

'You are my instrument, Melyn son of Arall. It is not necessary for the hammer to know why the carpenter wields it, only for it to strike the nail accurately and with as much force as possible.'

'Of course, lord.' Melyn bowed his head yet further in supplication and received a dizzying flood of youthful energy as a reward for his humility.

'You worry about the dragon's magic, I see. You fear that it is the Wolf's working and will corrupt your soul.

'Fret not, my servant. You will know the Wolf when you see him. The magic Frecknock and her kind wield is my magic. Stolen from me when Gwlad was young, it's true. But it is my magic nonetheless. Do you think I would have let you use it otherwise? Do I not watch over you at all times?'

'Lord, you are everywhere and in everything. I am honoured to be the instrument of your will. But I see the Wolf and his demons all around me, tempting me, trying to lead me astray. It has been too long since last I prayed to you. Please forgive me.'

'You have much on your mind, my faithful servant. Perhaps you would have been wise to consult me sooner. You think Duke Dondal lied to you. You do not believe that Tynhelyg could be so poorly defended, King Ballah so vulnerable. But it is true. I have made it so.'

Melyn's heart surged at the words echoing in his head. His greatest triumph was within his reach, and he could not fail.

'Ah, but you could all too easily fail, my faithful servant. King Ballah is a powerful sorcerer. He knows the evil magic of the Wolf, forged in his lair and alien to the power that runs through Gwlad. You will need all the help you can get just to reach Tynhelyg in time, and you will have to dig deep inside yourself to find the strength to defeat the Wolf's cub who lies there.'

'I am ready to take up that challenge, lord. It is what I've trained for all my life.'

'Yes, it is. And I have been preparing you all your life for this moment. You have Brynceri's ring with you. Take it. Place it on your own finger.'

'But, lord. The ring is sacred. I . . .'

'Are you forgetting to whom you speak, Melyn son of Arall? I forged that ring from my own breath. I gave it to Balwen so that he might protect Gwlad in my absence. It contains magic you cannot imagine. Wear it!'

Melyn felt the command as the merest hint of the agony that refusing would bring. He reached into his cloak and pulled out the slim wooden case, fumbling with the latch as he tried to open it. His hands shook as he removed the dry grey finger from its soft velvet nest. The ring hung loosely around it, the bright red polished ruby lit from within by a tiny spark that shimmered and flickered. It was the most sacred relic of the order. Only the inquisitor was allowed to handle it, and no one had worn it since Ruthin had cut it from the belly of the dead dragon Maddau. To do so had been unthinkable until now.

'Put it on, Melyn son of Arall, and feel the power of your god.' The Shepherd's voice was all around him, filling him with the certainty that what he did was right. Melyn slid the ring off the dead finger, scarcely noticing that he dropped it to the floor like a discarded chicken bone. He could feel the ring calling to him now; it was warm in his hand and almost leaped on to his outstretched finger.

It fitted perfectly, as if it had been made for him. Or he had been made for it. And as it snuggled down over his knuckle, the tiny flicker in the ruby blazed bright so that the whole chapel was painted rose. At the same time Melyn was suffused with a surge of such power and joy he felt he must surely die. The relief from aches and pains the Shepherd had given him before was as nothing compared to the strength and vitality that surged through him. It was as if he were twenty again, only better.

And then Gwlad opened up to him. His eyes were closed, but he could see the Grym linking everything. And on top of it he could see the aethereal. He could see the altar in front of him, but at the same time he could count the benches laid out behind him. He could even see Frecknock sitting in the corridor outside, waiting for him. But she was a different creature to the dull black shrunken figure he normally saw. Her aethereal image, with its elegant scales and large wings, fitted over her physical self so perfectly it was impossible to see where the real dragon ended and the imaginary one began. She shone with a white light, limning her outline like a halo and radiating a calm patience, a purposeful determination to do the best with whatever fate dealt her.

The flood of information was overwhelming: there was too much to process, too much power flowing through him. It was like conjuring a blade of fire and then losing control of it; he would surely burn up. But he knew how to control the Grym. Decades of mental discipline pushed their way to the fore, and Melyn slowly regained control of himself. He willed away the aethereal vision, then the softly glowing lines of the Grym, pushing everything back into the glowing red jewel burning in its band of silver and gold.

Sweat prickled on his forehead with the effort, but finally the inquisitor was confident enough to let out the breath he had been holding and relax his shoulders.

'I was right to choose you all those years ago, Melyn

son of Arall. Few would have the strength of will to come so close to me.'

'There's so much, lord. I can't begin to see it all.'

'It will get easier with time. Use the dragon's magic if it helps. She can show you how to reach Tynhelyg swiftly, and how to hide your men so that even the Wolf himself will not know they are there. Go now, Melyn, and be my hammer.'

There were times, Beulah thought, when having a husband was a distinct inconvenience. Now, for instance, when she was anxious to leave Abervenn and get on the road to Tochers, he was nowhere to be found. None of the servants had seen him in the main halls of the castle, and the two warrior priests on guard duty outside her chambers had no idea where he was either. Bored waiting for him to reappear, she had dismissed the guards, deciding to go and look for him herself.

Abervenn was an unnecessarily large castle, spread over the whole top of the hill, perched above the harbour city like some great carrion bird picking at a rotten carcass. It seemed to have been a madness running through the ducal family that made its sons want to build and build, and then build some more. The result was a mess of styles awkwardly meshed together, linked by a confusing warren of corridors. One moment she might be treading thick new carpet and walking past a gallery of fine portraits, then a turn and Beulah found herself in a servant wing.

She had looked already in the main hall, where the new Duke of Abervenn had met his vassals and taken their pledges of loyalty. A servant there had assured her that His Grace was not in the stables tending his horse, as he so often was since no one else could get anywhere near the beast. Neither was he in the exercise yard practising his swordsmanship. Frustrated but happier walking around than sitting with her increasingly large belly making her uncomfortable, Beulah headed for the West Tower, where Duke Angor's personal apartments had been and where his wife and daughter still lived.

Beulah had wanted to turn Dilyth and Anwyn out of the castle, stripped of their titles, and had been furious to find that they still had their old lodgings when she took up residence after the long voyage from Castell Glas. But Clun had persuaded her to let them stay, showing an understanding of diplomacy she would scarce have credited him with. Angor had been popular, but Dilyth was revered by the people, and her daughter too. Throwing them out of the castle would have been an open invitation for rebellion; instead of which Clun had charmed them, commiserated with them over the deaths of Angor and Merrl, and allowed them to retain much of their old life. He made a point of consulting them on matters concerning the running of the dukedom too, so it was possible he was even now paying them a visit.

But the audience chamber was empty, and the servants Beulah managed to find could not say where their new master was. So she climbed stairs and wandered corridors in solitude, staring at dark portraits, inspecting vast tapestries and occasionally gazing out of narrow windows. She had almost forgotten she was looking for her husband and was admiring a particularly fine pair of swords hanging over an unlit fireplace in an empty hall when a sudden noise startled her.

Beulah couldn't quite make out what it was. At first she thought someone was torturing a cat, but as that seemed unlikely she went to investigate and found herself in another of the plain servants' corridors. Then the noise came again, closer this time, and she knew what it was. A newborn infant screaming its first to the world.

Much to her surprise Beulah found herself drawn to the noise. Some hitherto unknown desire to give succour to a child in distress urged her forward where before she would have ordered a servant to eliminate the noise instantly. Her own unborn baby decided to give her a hearty kick at that same moment, and for a while she could do nothing but lean against the wall, her hand clutching her stomach as she waited for the nausea to pass. It was as she was standing there that a servant girl came out through a door a dozen paces down the corridor.

'What's going on in there? Whose child is that screaming?' Beulah moved towards the door, her head clearing with each stride. The girl saw her and nearly fainted. Then dropped to her knee in a deep curtsy.

'Your Majesty! Beg forgiveness. You startled me. I never expected. Is there something I can do for you?'

'There's no need to shout, girl. I'm not deaf.'

'Sorry, ma'am.'

'Never mind. I heard an infant crying.'

'Yes, ma'am. One of the chambermaids just this moment delivered a fine baby boy.'

'Show me.' Beulah still couldn't quite understand why she was interested. She had made it her business to avoid children ever since she had grown old enough to consider herself no longer one. Yet now she wanted to see, wanted to learn. Wanted to hold. The girl looked very alarmed.

'Lady Anwyn sent me for hot water, ma'am. And I'm sure you wouldn't really want to go in there. It was a hard labour, ma'am. Twenty-four hours since . . . Well . . .' She looked down at the floor, then at Beulah's own swelling stomach. 'You might not want to go in there.'

'Does Anwyn make a habit of attending when her servants give birth?'

'Why yes, ma'am. Or Lady Dilyth, but she's gone down to the harbour stores with His Grace the duke.'

Which explains why I couldn't find him, Beulah thought, and why the servants are all so fond of their former masters. Just then the baby let out another shriek.

'Away and fetch your hot water, girl. Don't keep a mother waiting.' Beulah dismissed the servant, who bobbed a curtsy and scurried off down the corridor. Then she took a deep breath and pushed open the door.

Dafydd had just handed his newborn son to Anwyn when the door to the tiny bedroom was pushed open and a strange woman came in. Before he was seen, he stepped back, drawing the darkness around him as Usel had taught him. He had never before used the magic alone, and though the woman didn't seem to register his presence, he still felt exposed.

It had been a difficult day and night since Iolwen's labour had begun. Smuggling her up to the castle had been easy enough, but then Lady Dilyth and Anwyn had taken over, shooing Teryll and him away. Their obvious

Llanwennog looks and the fact that neither of them knew Abervenn meant that they could do little more than hide in the suite of rooms that had been provided for them. Servants brought meals and hot water for baths, but all requests for news of his wife's progress had been met with protestations of ignorance. Dafydd had fretted and paced, stared out the window at the harbour and city below, tried to sleep and even sent Teryll off to seek information, though with his poor grasp of Saesneg the stable lad was less than successful. Finally, he had been about to force a servant at swordpoint to take him to Anwyn when the lady herself had appeared, looking tired but happy, and congratulated him on the birth of his son.

Now, scant minutes later, having only held the tiny infant for a few moments, and wanting nothing more than to comfort his wife, he was forced to hide by the un-announced entry of . . . ?

Dafydd looked closely at the woman who had entered. She was older than him, but not much. She held herself like someone used to being obeyed; perhaps he had noticed this about her instantly and that had made him hide rather than risk being seen by someone not sympa-thetic to his cause. She wore a simple dress, cut for ease of movement rather than high fashion but exquisitely made from the highest-quality material. Her hair was some-where between blonde and red, matching the spread of freckles that peppered the tops of her wide cheeks and bridged her small nose, but it was her eyes that surprised him. She had Iolwen's eyes. Then he noticed the bulge in her stomach and realization dawned.

'Your Majesty. This is most unexpected.' Anwyn

dropped to her knees, Dafydd's unnamed child still in her arms.

'I was looking for my husband.'

'His Grace the duke went down to the harbour with my mother, ma'am. She wanted to show him the excise warehouses in action, and a large merchant vessel arrived from Talarddeg this morning.'

'I heard a baby crying.' Beulah seemed almost distracted, Dafydd thought. As if she didn't really know why she was here. A sudden idea entered his mind. She was alone, unguarded. He could strike her down in an instant. The war would be over before it even began.

'One of my maidservants has just produced this fine baby boy.' Anwyn stood, blocking the path between him and the queen even as he began to summon his blade. It was as if she knew what he was thinking and had moved to stop him. And in that instant he realized he couldn't do it. However much he hated her, he couldn't strike down a pregnant woman; nor could he commit murder in front of his newborn child. In front of his wife.

Dafydd glanced at Iolwen, propped up in her bed, the covers drawn around her so that only her head was visible. She had suffered these past hours, and her face was pale, her hair matted with sweat. He had thought her asleep, but she was staring at the queen, her sister, with a look of alarm and disbelief. For the first time since entering the room, Beulah seemed to notice her too.

'Do I know you? Perhaps you have worked at Candlehall?'

Iolwen's reply was both weak and hoarse, her voice broken by exhaustion and hours of screaming. 'No, Your

Majesty. I've been in service to Lady Dilyth since I turned eight. My mam and da both worked here in the castle before me.'

'Worked? Where are they now?'

'Both dead, Your Majesty. Mam died when I was just little, and da didn't last long after she was gone.'

'How terrible.' Queen Beulah didn't sound as if she meant it. 'But you should know that the correct way to address a queen is to use "Your Majesty" only on first acquaintance. After that you may address me as "ma'am".'

'Yes, Your . . . Yes, ma'am.'

'What is your name, girl?'

'Iol— Iolo. Ma'am.'

'Isn't Iolo a boy's name?'

'It is indeed, ma'am. My da said he always wanted a boy.'

'As did mine, strangely enough.'

'Well, he's got one now, hasn't he.' Anwyn hefted the sleeping baby in her arms. 'Would you like to hold him, ma'am?'

Dafydd almost dropped his spell of concealment, such was his surprise. What was Anwyn doing, handing over his son to the enemy? Beulah herself looked momentarily perplexed too, as if she had not anticipated such intimacy. But before she could do much more than stare, Anwyn had handed the sleeping child over, showing the queen how to hold him.

'Oh, but he weighs nothing,' Beulah said. 'And he's so small. How can anything so helpless survive?'

'He will be well looked after here, ma'am,' Anwyn replied. 'The Dukes of Abervenn have always provided for the children of the castle, and many have gone on to serve them throughout their lives. He might grow to be a stable lad or a soldier. Or maybe learn his letters and become a clerk.'

'Or he may be chosen for the novitiate. He has an aura of power about him. But he is very dark. Who is his father?'

'A soldier, ma'am. Darrin's his name. He's gone to Tochers with the rest of the duke's men.' Iolwen was beginning to regain some of her composure, the initial shock of seeing her sister wearing off, Dafydd assumed. But as her strength returned, bringing colour to her cheeks, and the sweat dried from her face and hair, so she looked more and more like the princess he knew and loved, less and less like a serving girl married to a common peasant soldier. And even he could tell that her accent was different to the way the other servants spoke, closer to Anwyn's refined Saesneg. Fortunately none of the servants present had said a word, but it was only a matter of time before the queen began to suspect something.

'And does he have Llanwennog blood, this Darrin?'

'Many of the people of Abervenn have traces of foreign blood in them, ma'am,' Anwyn said. 'My own mother was born and raised in Talarddeg. Our trade with other lands is what has made this place so rich, and furnished your army with men and weapons.'

'I am aware of the role Abervenn has played in shaping the Twin Kingdoms, Anwyn.' Beulah's tone was sharp, but at that moment the baby gurgled and opened his eyes. The queen was distracted, her face softening as she looked down, and she held out a finger for the baby's tiny hands to grasp. Dafydd watched as the woman who had killed one sister and ordered the assassination of another cooed over the infant.

'He'll be of an age with my own child,' she said after a while. 'Perhaps he will be able to serve the heir to the Obsidian Throne. Who knows what fate has in store for any of us. Oh!'

Dafydd almost leaped forward. As it was, he was sure that for a moment his concealment collapsed. The baby let out a squeal not so much of alarm as of mischief, and Beulah pushed him away from her back into Anwyn's ready hands. Dafydd tried to work out what had happened, and then the spreading stain on the material of the queen's dress made everything clear.

'Your Majesty! Here, let me see to that.' Anwyn handed the infant to a maidservant, taking up a cloth and dabbing at the material of the queen's dress. Beulah stood helpless, a look somewhere between bemusement and rage on her face.

'Quick. We must get this into clean cold water as soon as possible or it will stain.' Anwyn hurried the unusually compliant queen out of the room just as the other maidservant returned with a bucket of hot water and towels. 'Ah, good. Gemma, please attend to mother and child. You know what to do.' And with that she was gone.

Dafydd stood motionless, still concealed, for a full minute, the room silent, all ears straining to hear what went on outside. Anwyn's effusive apologies and Beulah's occasional monosyllabic answers faded away and then disappeared entirely. Finally he could restrain himself no more. He banished the spell and stepped forward into the light with a great guffaw. Iolwen's face was creased in a tired smile too, and she took her errant son back from the maidservant gratefully.

'That was priceless. I would have given anything to see that, and I got it for free.' Dafydd chortled. 'Ah, my boy. This is a tale I will dine out on for years.'

'He's his father's son. To piss on the queen. But what shall we call him? He cannot be Divitie or Diseverin, no more than Ballah or Geraint.'

'True, true. But what about Iolo? That's as fine a name as any.'

Iolwen looked down into her son's eyes, then back to Dafydd, her brow wrinkled at his suggestion. Then, as if deciding she could think of no better, she smiled.

'Iolo it is then. Let us hope he lives long enough to be proud of it.'

6

Perhaps one of the wisest moves by King Geraint the Bald, son of King Ballah I, in the early years of Llanwennog was the creation of the King's Festival. A brave move too, for in its early years it resembled nothing so much as a re-enactment of the wars that had finally brought the nation together. You can still see the ancient divides to this day: Caenant folk will camp together and close to their northlands allies of old; Kais and Talarddeg keep themselves to themselves and far from the city walls; border mountain farmers and their neighbours from the central plains maintain a cordial but watchful distance. All, however, come to the capital every year, and nowadays the fights have developed into ritual games watched over by a benevolent king.

This yearly pilgrimage to Tynhelyg has become the glue that sticks together the nation once so fractured. And where once the representatives of the subdued tribes and regions came grudgingly to pay homage to their overlord, now folk come willingly, happily, to celebrate the richness and diversity of their proud kingdom.

The Taming of the Northlands – A History of the Kings of Llanwennog

As disguises went it was very effective, but Errol spent the whole of his journey to Tynhelyg wishing that there was some other way to keep from being discovered. The closer he came to the capital city, the more people he met on the road and in the towns and villages. Places to sleep were hard to find, and in some villages it was all he could manage to buy some bread and cheese. At least Lord Gremmil had furnished him with more than enough coin for his journey.

Errol fell in with some merchants and families who had already banded together. It made sense, since they were all heading the same way and travelling at much the same speed, and if Dondal's men were looking for anyone it was a lone young man, not a shy girl in a crowd. And yet he spent the first few days with the group in a state of nervous terror, waiting for someone to see through his disguise. With time, though, and as he got to know a bit about his companions, so he began to relax a little.

'You're always so quiet, Eleni. What's going on in that pretty little head of yours, I wonder.'

Errol took a moment to respond. He had chosen the name at random, not quite sure where he had heard it before. Perhaps one of the barmaids in one of the many taverns he had visited since losing Benfro. In fact he was wondering how the dragon was faring at the hands of the circus master; he couldn't help remembering the sorry state of the lioncats and the way everyone had been in fear of Loghtan. And what if Benfro couldn't keep back Magog? Would there be anything of his friend left to rescue? Or would he have to carry out Corwen's fatal wish?

'Oh, nothing. I was just thinking me there's not much other than grass around here. Where am I supposed to find me some healing herbs and suchlike?' He had taken to trying to make his speech sound more like the rough dialect of the northlands rather than the formal court tongue he had learned from Andro and perfected at Tynewydd.

'Dearie me, girl. Where'd you grow up? There's more than grass in the plains.' Mollum was a great bear of a woman, round and jolly with a forceful personality that made it easy to hide in her shadows. She was taking her family of young children to the city to stay with their grandparents, then she was going to head south to join her husband, stationed near Wrthol with the army. The King's Festival was a good way to distract the youngsters from the upheaval of the move. She had unofficially adopted Errol – or the apprentice herbwoman Eleni as he had to remind himself several times a day – the day after he joined the makeshift convoy. It had been easier to fall into her orbit than make a fuss about trying to stay private.

'It all seems so barren to me.' Errol repeated a sentiment he had expressed many times before. 'I'm used to trees and mountains. The sky's so big here.'

'Well, that'll change soon enough. We're almost at the city – not more than another day, I'd say. There's streets there where the houses meet at the top and cut out the sky altogether.'

Errol tried to look suitably awestruck at this description, though he knew already how narrow the streets of Tynhelyg were.

'And where will I find me my herbs there, if the sun never reaches the ground?' He rolled his eyes, flicking his long hair over his shoulder as he had observed some of the girls do.

'Ah me, Eleni. I don't think you'll have much trouble finding what you want in the city. Truth be told, a pretty little thing like you might find much more besides. Just don't sell yourself cheap, if you get my meaning.'

It was a favourite topic of Mollum's, and Errol was happy to let her do the talking as his horse kept time with her lumbering wagon. The afternoon wore on to evening in much the same way as many before, and when the setting sun made travel along the road dangerous, the caravan simply pulled off on to the grass and made camp.

There was much excitement around the fires that night as everyone reckoned they would reach the city by the next afternoon. Friendships had been forged over the long march south and east, and sitting out on the edge of the camp Errol could hear the beginnings of a great party. Tomorrow everyone would part, going to houses of relatives or the large encampment that sprang up on the eastern plains every King's Festival. Either way, the camaraderie of the journey would be over, so tonight was a chance to say farewell. The noise would only grow, and it was unlikely he would get any sleep.

The sky was clear, and a quarter-moon had risen, painting the rolling plains in eerie light, when Errol decided he might as well head off. He could get a good head start on the caravan and reach the city by mid-morning; he might even catch up with the circus before it found its spot and set up. Quietly he gathered his things and saddled his horse, making sure by touch that everything was properly attached. It was only as he was preparing to lead the gelding out on to the road that he sensed a presence behind him. Before he could turn, a fat fleshy hand clamped over his wrist.

'Be careful, Eleni. The roads are not to be travelled lightly, not alone and at night by a young woman. Nor even a young man.'

'I don't know what you mean, Mollum.' In his shock, Errol's voice was lower than the breathless high whisper he had adopted for his disguise, his Cerdys accent gone.

'It's your hands, boy. They give the game away. Don't worry, old Mollum won't tell on you. If I thought you meant ill I'd not have let you ride with us to start with. I dare say you've good reason for the disguise – maybe your father didn't want you to join the army. Reckon he's got more sense than you there, but you'll find out that lesson your own way.' She let go of his wrist, then ran her hand through his hair. 'Still, it'll be a shame when they take the shears to you.'

In the pale moonlight it was difficult to be sure, but Errol thought he could see tears in her eyes. 'You've been a good companion these last few days,' he said. 'I shan't forget you. I hope you have good luck in your travels.'

Before he could say anything more, Errol found himself swept up in a great hug, crushing the wind out of him. Just as he thought he would surely pass out from lack of air, he was released. Mollum took a step back, then thrust a small parcel into his hands.

'What's this?'

'A girl needs more than the one pair of breeks, and that

blouse won't wash clean any more. Go safely, Eleni.' And before he could protest, she turned away, waddling back into the darkness.

Errol led his horse on to the road, bewildered and relieved in equal measure. He walked away from the camp and its multiple noisy fireplace congregations, out into the moonlit night. Once he had crested a low hill and dropped down into the next shallow valley, he mounted and let his horse pick its slow way along the road, ever closer to Tynhelyg and the perils it contained.

'Is this it?'

'Is this what, Your Majesty?'

'The army of Abervenn? Is this the best you could muster?'

Beulah looked out over the men arrayed in something distantly related to lines across the large courtyard at the front of the castle. They were dressed in a hotchpotch of styles and colours, as if a dozen colour-blind seamstresses had been given a very rough sketch of what a soldier should wear. Some of the men had spears, some swords, but there seemed to have been no attempt to divide them according to their weaponry. And ranks had apparently been determined according to who had the shiniest and most ornate armour, no matter how archaic it looked. Cadoc was presumably general of this mob because he owned not only a shiny brass helm complete with red feathers, but also a complete set of armour for his horse. The poor animal snorted and puffed even standing still. Beulah was fairly certain it would be dead long before they reached Tochers.

'This is the last levy, Your Majesty.' Cadoc bowed in his saddle, and for a moment Beulah thought the weight of his ridiculous helm was going to tip him over on to the ground.

'The last?'

'We have already sent substantial forces to both Tochers and Dina, ma'am. These are the men who were left behind to bring in the harvest – a good one this year, as it happens. The grain stores are full to bursting.'

'I'm glad to hear it. We'll need all the food we can produce to feed the armies.'

'Indeed, ma'am. They're already consuming at a prodigious rate. Let us hope the campaign is short, or the city will surely starve.'

'I think that highly unlikely, General. Abervenn is rich enough and fertile enough to feed itself and my army for many years.' For a moment Beulah thought Cadoc was going to argue the point with her; certainly his thoughts betrayed a certain belligerence. But he managed to hold himself back, the discipline of his military training taking hold.

'Perhaps you'd like to inspect the men,' he said instead.

Beulah nodded, though she felt their time would be better spent in marching. Still they expected to be presented to their queen, and she owed at least that much to people who might soon die in her name. She nudged her horse towards the first rank of soldiers. They nervously watched her approach, a few retreating before being pushed back into line by those behind them. It was a rabble, a mixture of the old and the simple, which couldn't be trusted to hold against an attack. She hoped by the

Shepherd that the men already drafted were of a higher calibre.

'They're not the best of soldiers, are they, my lady?' Clun, ever the master of understatement, rode alongside the queen, his black stallion dwarfing her own fine mare. Perhaps it was the great beast making the men nervous, and with good reason – it had already broken one stable hand's arm and the leg of another.

'Are you sure that horse is safe, my love?' From where she was sitting, Beulah could look the beast straight in the eye.

'He's all right once you get to know him. He's just not—'

Whatever it was Clun was going to say, Beulah never learned. At that moment the horse reared up, its nostrils flared and eyes wide. For an instant she thought she was going to be crushed, but somehow the creature swivelled on its back legs, lashing out with its front at the conscripts. Panicked men tried to escape, pushing back into the ranks behind, tripping over each other and reducing the troops to a tangle of old armour and pikes, flailing limbs and shouts of alarm. There was a high-pitched shriek, almost girlish, cut suddenly short. And then the great horse settled back down again, Clun still perched in the saddle. The whole incident had taken no more than a half-dozen heartbeats.

'My lady, I'm sorry. I don't know what came over him.' Clun backed the horse away from the mess of soldiers as they scrambled to their feet. The chaos spread away like a fan from a single point, and there lay one unmoving man. Beulah looked down at him, well aware that he was dead.

No one could survive the hoof that had caved in the man's face. But it was not his injury that held her attention, rather what he still held clutched tight in his hand.

'What's that he's holding?' Beulah pointed, loath to dismount from her own horse. Her ever more obvious pregnancy made it hard to get comfortable, and once she was, she hated to move any more than necessary. General Cadoc seemed less than keen to dismount either, probably because he would need a winch to get him back into the saddle, so Clun slid athletically off his horse, patting the beast on its neck as if it had not just killed a man with a single kick. The stallion followed him like an obedient dog as he walked over and stooped to inspect the damage. After a few moments he stood once more, handing a slim wooden tube to Beulah.

'It had this inside.' Clun opened his other hand to reveal a short feathered dart, its head coated in some dark sticky mess.

'A blowpipe?' Beulah turned the weapon over in her hand a few times, then handed it back to Clun. 'Well, I don't suppose we need to guess who its intended target was. Captain Celtin?'

The captain rode forward. 'Your Majesty?'

'This man. I want his entire family rounded up and executed. Also all the men standing immediately around him in the line; they must have seen what he intended to do.'

'But Your Majesty!' General Cadoc nudged his horse into the space between Beulah and the soldiers still trying to scramble to their feet.

'This is an army, General. It needs discipline. As their commanding officer, the responsibility for that is yours.'

'But is it necessary to mete out such harsh punishment? The man is dead – can we not leave it at that?'

Beulah stared at the general, scarcely believing her ears. He was an old man and fat with it. His face was beaded with sweat, sweltering underneath his absurd armour. He was, she realized, all she despised about the nobility who hung about the royal court: a useless fop of a man who rode to war as if it were some great game. No doubt he would find himself a safe place to stay in Tochers, well away from the actual fighting, and there he would remain until it was time to lead his surviving forces back home. And it had been he who had suggested she inspect the men, he who had led her along the line to the assassin.

With far more effort than it should have taken, she conjured a short blade of light. A flick of the wrist and she whipped it through the air. There was a moment's pause, and then the general's head tipped forward under the weight of his absurd helmet, falling to the ground with a clatter. His body slid backwards off his horse, crashing into the still-floundering soldiers and sending a fresh wave of panic through the men as they were splattered with blood.

'Be still, all of you!' Beulah spoke the words quietly, but pushed the command out with her mind, her thoughts clearer than they had been in months. The result was instantaneous. The panic ended, and all eyes turned to her. She had their full attention.

'This is not some game, not some exercise in politics. I have no intention of going to the border and just rattling a sabre at Ballah and his armies. Four times now he has tried to have me killed, and four times he has failed. Know that if you plot against me or try to stop me, you will be crushed. But fight alongside me, take the war to the god-less Llanwennogs, and you will be well rewarded. We march now to the border. And from there to Tynhelyg itself. Follow me, men of Abervenn!'

A great shout went up from the soldiers as Beulah pushed out a feeling of excitement and adventure. The men's enthusiasm aroused, the army began its long slow march from the castle and out on to the road to Tochers. She let out a long sigh, releasing the tension she hadn't realized had built up in her. The blade she had conjured still burned bright, and for a moment she couldn't think how to douse it. Anger and shock had helped her conjure it; now she willed the power back into the lines. Sweat prickled her brow as it finally dissipated, and in her belly her unborn child gave an unwelcome kick.

Clun had remounted his horse and steered it alongside her once more. Her own mount was a fine specimen, taller than her beloved Pahthia by far, and yet it felt inadequate next to the stallion. She looked the beast in the eye again, feeling almost that it read her mind even as she tried to sense its own base thoughts. There was more intelligence there than she would have expected, and had not this horse saved her life?

'You've not named him yet, my love.' She reached out and patted the solid neck. As her fingers made contact a spark of the Grym passed between them, a last residue of her blade.

'He was your gift to me, my lady. I thought that honour should be yours.'

Beulah smiled. Clun's grasp of courtly manners and diplomacy was growing by the day.

'Very well then,' she said. 'Today he has proved himself my protector. And so I shall name him Godric in honour of that role and in memory of your father.'

Clun's face darkened, as it did whenever his family was mentioned. Then he reached forward, scratched between the horse's ears and slapped it on the neck.

'Godric. It's a good name.'

Black smoke rose into the morning sky, carrying a taint of destruction and death. Yet another town burned as Melyn led his army closer to Tynhelyg. They had sacked it, taking all they needed to replenish their supplies and replacing their wounded horses, leaving little behind for the women and children to live on. Winter would cull many more than had died under blades of light.

Progress was painfully slow. They could ride straight through the villages, confident they posed little threat, but the larger towns were another matter, especially old forti-fied settlements like Gremmil. These places had sent many men to the southern borders but retained some trained soldiers, and their lords were sufficiently well versed in warfare that to ignore them would invite prob-lems later on. Either they would band together and form a sizeable force to oppose him at Tynhelyg, or they would cut off his escape route, should he need one.

And so every one had to be sacked, which took time and occasionally cost men. Meanwhile the King's Festival was drawing ever closer, the capital reaching its point of maximum chaos and instability, and still Melyn was far from his goal.

'We need to move faster, and we need to move unseen,'

he said to Osgal as they cantered along the road. The army was not hiding itself now, though Melyn no longer wanted news of his approach to precede him. It was hard even for his most skilled warriors to remain invisible while moving at such speed, and the effort left them exhausted at the end of each long day.

'I've scouts out ahead, sir. We'll know about any towns or villages long before we're seen.'

'Yes, yes. But we still have to stop at each one in turn, and that's taking too long. At this rate, by the time we reach Tynhelyg the fair will be over and Ballah will be holed up in his palace again.'

'Your Grace, might I make a suggestion?'

Melyn looked down to where Frecknock ran alongside his horse. She moved with flowing grace, covering the ground easily and with no sign of exertion. She had changed a great deal from the pathetic creature he had spared back in the dragon village. Where she had been small and weedy, now she was lithe and well muscled from months of walking and running. Melyn shook his head, thinking he was seeing her with his aethereal vision, surprised to find himself admiring her beauty where before he would have felt only hatred. Without saying anything, he nodded for her to go on.

'There are spells which can shorten the distance, or spells that can make us travel at great speed, even though we barely walk. Either could get you where you want to be in time.'

'And you know how to perform this magic, I take it.'

'No, Your Grace. I don't think even Sir Frynwy knew how, and he was the most skilled mage I knew.'

Melyn's anger rose at the mention of the old dragon. 'Then what use is it telling me of such spells? Or are you so tired of your life you think to provoke me?'

'Nothing could be further from my mind, sir. I don't know how to do this magic, but I know of it. And you carry the secret of it with you.'

'I do?'

'The book, sir. The Llyfr Draconius. You'll find what you need in there, if you know how to look.'

'But I thought you said the book was dangerous.'

'Oh it is, Your Grace. Very much so. But together we might divine its secrets.'

'Together?' Melyn wondered at the temerity of the creature. She had to know he would not let her anywhere near the book; it contained secrets that might help her escape or inflict damage on him and his warrior priests. And yet his god had told him to use the dragon's magic if it helped. It was after all just the Shepherd's own magic stolen.

He had no time to think on it further, as a scout came galloping towards them with news of another town not far beyond the next rise. The routine was well established now, and the warrior priests soon resumed their magical camouflage. Melyn watched them with his newly sharpened aethereal vision as they surrounded the small town and set about ridding it of soldiers and all men of fighting age.

Even though it was little more than a large village, the sky had darkened towards evening by the time the grim work was done. The inquisitor was pleased to see there had been no losses on his side, not even a horse injured.

He wanted to press on, force the pace faster towards their goal, but he knew it would be unwise to push his men too hard. He ordered them to make camp outside the town, riding through to review the carnage. It didn't sicken him; these were people who had forsaken the Shepherd, after all. In better times he might have made the effort to convert them, but this was war. Any whose souls were pure would be welcomed into the safe pastures, and those who weren't could burn with the Wolf in his den. And yet he did not view the dead bodies piled high awaiting the pyre with the same satisfaction as once he had.

Perhaps he was tired of the road, or maybe he just wanted to get on to the prize. Whatever it was, Melyn left the smoking buildings and headed to the camp with a heavy heart. He needed something to get him past these endless delays. Finding two substantial towns within an hours' ride of each other was deeply frustrating, especially out here on the plains where there was nothing but endless farmland. It was almost as if the land was challenging him, setting deliberate obstacles to slow his new-found purpose.

His tent had been pitched and a fire started. Frecknock lay on the hard ground a few paces away from the circle of heat and warmth, as she always did. He remembered her earlier conversation and called her over to the fire.

'Is it really possible to shorten this journey? Can we get to Tynhelyg before Ballah hears of what we've been doing here in the north?'

'There is a tale told of ancient times in Marranem – what you would call Fo Afron now. The great eastern city of Voran was threatened by a volcano and the people were told to flee, but they were too slow, not wanting to leave their belongings behind. They would all have perished when the volcano erupted had Sir Flisk not been nearby. He took pity on the people, who had always treated him well, and cast a spell that made their every step like a hundred. So fast did they travel, it's said they crossed the Sea of Tegid without knowing they walked on water. When they finally stopped they found a fertile plain bounded by mountains to the west, the sea to the east, and decided to settle there. You know the city they founded as Talarddeg.'

There was something about Frecknock's voice, the way she told the simple tale, that Melyn found almost mesmerizing. With a start he realized that he had lost his concentration and snapped it back again.

'I'm not interested in your silly dragon stories; I want magic.'

'All our knowledge, all our magic is bound up in our stories, your grace. I do not know if the people of Voran really walked across the sea or founded Talarddeg, but Sir Flisk did a magical working that moved them rapidly away from danger. The magic exists; we just have to rediscover it.'

'And you want me to look in the book for it, even though it is dangerous.'

'I would watch over you, protect you from harm.' It sounded so trite Melyn almost laughed, but something stopped him. Frecknock was being completely honest with him; he could see it in her oddly alien thoughts. Ever since taking Brynceri's ring, the Grym had opened up to him. Quite apart from being able to see the aethereal without having to go into a trance, he could read the minds of his men with much greater clarity than ever before, conjure his blade of light almost without a thought. He was fitter than he had felt in months, as if the Shepherd were close to him at all times, blessing him as he had only done occasionally before.

Melyn got up from the fireside, went over to the saddlebags by his tent and pulled the heavy book from its leather case. As his ringed finger brushed the worn and cracked cover, he felt a surge of power that almost brought him to his knees. And suddenly she was at his side, her arms supporting him.

'Careful how you handle it, sir. No man has ever read the Llyfr Draconius before.'

Melyn sat back down by the fire, the book heavy in his hands. Uninvited, Frecknock settled herself down beside him, so close he could smell her over the smoke. It never occurred to him to chide her for such familiarity; it seemed the most natural thing in the world that she should be there with him.

The ring was warm on his finger, its ruby glowing in the fading evening light. He touched it to the leather cover once more, ready for the rush this time. The flames of his campfire were scarcely bright enough to read by, but it didn't matter. He could see everything in the aethereal. The book itself was strangely distorted, as if it were not one but endless volumes all occupying the same space. They whispered to him, promises of power beyond his wildest dreams, of knowledge long denied.

'Take my hand. Let me be your anchor.' Melyn looked up into Frecknock's face, saw into her mind, understood her concern. He reached out with his unadorned hand. Her touch was as warm as the flames in the fire, drawing them closer still so that he felt he could step inside her head should he wish. Certainly she was a curious creature, so desperate and downtrodden she allied herself with her persecutors. But the call of the book was greater still.

With a silent prayer to the Shepherd, Melyn opened the cover and gazed on the words within.

7

Dragons are by nature magical beings. They do not consciously manipulate the Grym like the great mages of history; nevertheless they are capable of simple acts of magic. Mostly these are reflex: the conjuring of a crude light or the casting of a thought. Some dragons are noted for their prowess in healing to the point where men even seek their advice. In truth, they are just natural channellers of the life force that is all around us. And the secret of their innate ability lies in their jewels.

A single dragon jewel can act as a lens for the Grym, focusing a wide area down to a narrow point, just as a reading glass might focus the heat of the sun to a tiny burning flame. A collection of jewels will amplify this effect many times, and the more jewels in the collection, the greater the distortion of the magical flow.

Father Charmoise, *Dragons' Tales*

'Fly faster. Now turn. That's it. Tighter!'

Benfro felt the snap of the whip in the air behind him, but he was too quick. Banking hard, he swooped around the end of the oval ring before clapping his wings together again and heading down the longer side. In the middle the object of his pent-up rage laughed.

'Brilliant. We'll make a show of you yet.' Loghtan coiled his whip and jumped down from his box as Benfro continued to fly in a long elliptical path, powerless to do anything else.

'You can stop now, dragon. Get some food and rest. We'll be performing for the king soon. I want you at your best for that.'

Benfro slowed and dropped, his feet hitting the ground with the lightest of touches. Had he not been so enraged by his treatment, he might have marvelled at how well he was landing now. But his mind was almost entirely eaten up with anger and with fighting the drugs that forced him to obey the circus master's every command. Turning towards the exit, he longed to crash his tail against one of the great central posts that held up the huge marquee, but the drugs wouldn't even allow him that much rebellion.

Outside it was organized chaos. Nobody paid him much attention as he slunk past smaller tents and piles of baggage towards the wagon he shared with old Magog. Benfro laughed bitterly. Magog. The only positive side to Loghtan's drugs was that he had felt nothing of the true Magog's presence in all the days and weeks he had been with the circus. Perhaps that was a side effect, or maybe the old mage was there but Benfro couldn't feel him. Without being able to see his aura, Benfro couldn't be sure if the rose cord still bound him to the tiny red jewel, or if the knot he had tied with his aura still held. His brain was too numb to concentrate on any of the subtle arts he had learned. All he could do was eat, sleep and train for his performance.

'You're back again early, Gog. And alone. Loghtan must

be pleased with you.' The old dragon was slumped against the end of the wagon cage looking as if he hadn't moved since Benfro had left him several hours earlier. Quite possibly he hadn't. Loghtan had left the door unlocked, confident that both dragons were under his control now.

Benfro still remembered the horrible surgery, the tiny jewel removed from Magog's living brain. He shuddered as he hauled himself into the wagon, reached for the half-rotten carcass of some unidentifiable animal that had been provided as food, and slumped down opposite his companion.

'I'm not Gog, you know. They call me that, but my real name's Benfro. Sir Benfro.' He had told the old dragon this at least twice every day since they had first met, but still he persisted in the Gog and Magog fantasy.

'You've always been a wily one, my brother. But I know you. Oh yes. Didn't Maddau always say we were the greatest of all mages. Why, we split Gwlad in two, you and I. Yes, we did.'

'Tell me about it.' Benfro wasn't sure why he asked. Maybe he just wanted to hear a voice that wasn't ordering him about. He eyed the rancid meat, knowing he had to eat but feeling queasy all the same. If he could just cook it a little, perhaps it wouldn't be so bad.

'Oh, but you must know the story. We fell out, you and I. Yes, we did. Couldn't agree which of us would have lovely Ammorgwm. Idiots, we both were. She wasn't interested in either of us. Ha ha. But we quarrelled. Oh how we quarrelled. Shook the ground with our tantrums, we did. Knocked down mountains and razed forests. The men weren't happy. Not happy at all, no. But they were so small back then it was easy to tread on them.'

Benfro was only half listening. He knew the story well enough, even if Sir Frynwy would have frowned at the unprofessional way this old mad dragon told it.

'Then she died. Sweet Ammorgwm. Was it you who killed her, or was it me? I don't know. Maybe it was both of us. Or maybe she did it to herself. Yes, that was it. She did it to herself. Not a dragon, really. No. Ammorgwm was a tree, so she was. Fancy that. You and me fighting over a tree. But then we never were all that bright. Strong, oh yes. Powerful in the subtle arts. But not bright.'

Benfro took a bit of meat, ripping it from the bone. It slid off with a sour taste, revealing maggots underneath. He spat it out at the same time as the old dragon's words penetrated his dull brain.

'A tree? How did you know that?' He remembered the mother tree appearing to him as a dragon of breathtaking beauty and infinite sadness. It felt so like a dream he couldn't be sure if she was real or not.

'She told me, so she did. And that's another joke on us, because she wasn't really dead after all. But we didn't care. No, no, no. We hated each other so much we couldn't be in the same world together. Couldn't breathe the same air. So we made a great spell, we did. The last thing we did together, even if we didn't tell each other what we were doing. We split Gwlad in two, made each bit half what it had been before. But you cheated, brother. Just like you always do. You left a window here, a window there, so you could spy on me and see what I was doing. So you could meddle in my Gwlad, but I couldn't meddle in yours.'

Benfro took another bite of the meat, finding a slightly better piece that he could chew this time. He was trying desperately to ignore the food and concentrate on what the old dragon was saying. But Loghtan had ordered him to get some food and rest, and that was what his body was trying to do. The taste of rancid flesh almost made him gag.

'You said Gog left windows. Where?'

'Forgotten, have you? Think your brother's good for nothing but remembering things so you don't have to?'

Benfro swallowed. The semi-chewed meat slid down his throat like phlegm and hit his stomach as if he had been punched. 'I'm sorry. I just thought you might like to tell me. Since you're obviously so much cleverer than I am.'

'Well, of course I am. I stayed here. It was you that had to go away. But you always liked your hall of candles, didn't you.'

Hall of candles. Candlehall. The Neuadd. Benfro went very cold. He had been there in his dreamwalking and seen something above that huge throne. A patch of different sky, like a window in the ceiling. How could he have forgotten that? How could he have not realized? And how could he ever hope to get there? It was half a world away, and the Neuadd was Melyn's place.

He let out a great roar, frustrated that he had come so far when his goal had been so near to home. Or at least he meant to roar, but instead, and much to his astonishment, a tongue of flame spat out of his mouth, engulfing the meat he held in his hands. The fire stuck to it, billowing around, sizzling the fat and charring the maggots. Where it touched his hand, it was warm rather than hot, and he could feel the weight of Loghtan's drugs seeping from his mind.

'Oh, how splendid! Do it again! Do it again!' The old dragon clapped his hands together, rocking backwards and forwards as the flames slowly guttered and dissolved, leaving a perfectly cooked apparently fresh haunch of beef. The smell of it filled the wagon, and all Benfro could think of was food. He sank his teeth into it, delighting in the taste and gulping down great chunks.

Only after he had finished almost half of it did he remember his companion. Benfro ripped off a great chunk and held it out. His head was clearer than it had been for days, and the old dragon's words came back to him with new meaning.

'You said a window here, a window there. Did Gog – I mean did I – have more than one portal between the two Gwlads?'

The old dragon took the meat, sniffed it, then started to suck at it as if his teeth were no longer up to the job of chewing. Maybe they weren't if all he had been eating for years was rotten flesh. He looked over at Benfro, the light in his eyes changing as if he too was thinking more clearly than he had done in an age. He opened his mouth to speak, but the voice came from behind.

'What's all this? Griselda giving you cooked meat? I'll have to have words with her about that.' Loghtan pushed his way through the door, whip in hand. Benfro thought for a happy instant that he could breathe flame again, turn this hated man into a charred mess. But despite his clear head he still didn't seem able to control his body.

'You, stay.' Loghtan pointed at Benfro. 'You, with me.' He pointed at the old dragon, who got slowly to his feet. Benfro raged in silence as his companion left the wagon. He had managed to clear the fog from his thoughts, but that only made the torment of his helplessness twice as bad.

'You're sure this is a good idea? You don't think I'd be better off lying low a bit longer?'

Dafydd paced back and forth across the carpet of the antechamber to the state room. Beyond the elegant wooden doors the collected nobility and worthies of Abervenn waited to meet him.

'There's nothing to worry about, Your Highness. News of Princess Iolwen's child has spread through the city already, and everyone is overjoyed. They want to see the boy, and they want to see his parents.' Usel walked across the room and made to open the doors.

'One moment, please, Usel.' Dafydd tried to compose himself. Standing beside him, their tiny baby in her arms, Iolwen looked more nervous even than he felt. He slipped his arm around hers.

'All right,' he said. Usel threw wide the doors, and Prince Dafydd and Princess Iolwen walked slowly through.

The state room was built on much the same scale as Abervenn castle itself – vast. The ceiling above them soared in intricately carved wooden arches. Tall windows bathed the room with light, and normally any sound would have echoed off the polished stone floor. But today there was a noisy silence hanging over everything, the sound of a thousand or more people holding their breath.

Dafydd didn't think he had ever seen so many people in one place before. After the confines of the boat and then the lonely suite of rooms at the back of the castle, to come forward now into this throng was more terrifying than going into battle. He felt Iolwen's arm tighten around his and knew that she felt the same.

They had emerged on to a dais raised above the heads of the assembled crowd. Two ornate chairs, not quite thrones, faced out across the hall, but Dafydd thought it wrong to sit straight away. These people wanted something from him. They needed something. He cleared his throat, suddenly dry.

'Fifteen years ago, King Divitie sent his youngest daughter to Tynhelyg as a hostage to peace between our two nations. She was only six years old at the time. I was not much older myself, and I remember thinking, what monster of a father could do that to his child?'

A low murmur ran through the crowd, though Dafydd could not tell whether it was of approval at his sentiment, or anger. He tried to scan the people's thoughts and emotions, as his grandfather had taught him. But it was one thing to do that when you were facing only one foe, quite another here.

'Over the years, Princess Iolwen came to accept her place at Tynhelyg. We tried to make her comfortable, but I know it wasn't easy for her, exiled through no fault of her own, forgotten by her father and his advisers. She grew up into a beautiful young woman. So beautiful, indeed, that I asked her to marry me. She agreed, and you have no idea how happy that made me. I was happier still when she told me she bore our child, but I could see the pain in her eyes when she thought her baby would most likely be born into exile, raised away from half of his family. So I brought her home.'

The murmuring was growing now, people exchanging comments with their neighbours, relaying his words to those at the back who might not have been able to hear. So far at least no one had thrown anything at him or shouted derogatory comments about his foreign appearance and the strange accent with which he spoke their language.

'It wasn't an easy journey; I'm sure you all know that the passes through the mountains are blocked. We travelled by boat, and were blown almost as far south as Eirawen before our captain could bring us safely here. And just in time too. For no sooner had my princess set foot on her native soil, than the baby started to come.'

The noise grew louder at this, as if the crowd had been waiting for confirmation of the news, and Dafydd had to raise his voice to be sure of being heard.

'Yes, it's true. Princess Iolwen gave birth to a son here in this very castle. He is the heir to both royal houses, and one day I hope he will unite both thrones and put an end to our futile warring. People of Abervenn, people of the Twin Kingdoms, may I present Prince Iolo.'

At first he thought he had gone too far. At the mention of thrones the urgent chattering had stopped, total silence once more returning to the hall. Iolwen had been standing slightly behind him, as if afraid to be seen by her people, but he pulled her forward, putting his arm protectively around her shoulder. Iolo slept on in her arms, a contented look on his face, oblivious to all. And then a shout went up from the back of the hall.

'Long live Princess Iolwen!'

It was followed by another, and another. Soon the whole hall seemed to be chanting her name. Then Dafydd heard the chant change.

'Long live Prince Dafydd. Long live Prince Iolo!'

He had not realized quite how tense he had been. The whole mad adventure had hinged on this moment, on being accepted by the people of a country with whom his family had been at war more often than not. But he didn't need Ballah's lessons in magic to know that these people were genuinely pleased to see him, ecstatic to see their princess returned and in raptures that her son should have waited until he reached Twin Kingdoms soil before being born.

The day passed in a whirl from then. All the noble houses of Abervenn presented themselves, pledging allegiance, men, arms, supplies – anything to help depose the hated Queen Beulah and her puppet duke. From what they promised, Dafydd got the impression they could not have sent any men at all to join the queen's army, and he said as much to Lord Ansey when they finally sat down to eat that evening.

'My son is captain of a troop of a hundred men,' Ansey said, his face grave. 'I had no option but to send them. The queen would have questioned my allegiance otherwise, and I would have ended up like poor old Angor. But my demesne can field an army twice that size still, and good fighting men too, not the old and infirm. Beulah's army is vast, but disorganized and ill disciplined. She has split it over two fronts, Dina and Tochers. Messengers take days to cover the ground between the two, and the generals have little idea of what is going on. If I send word to my son, he and his men will simply desert and come back here.'

'They would be better where they are right now,' Dafydd said. 'We have more than enough men to cause havoc with the queen's supply lines. And far better to have allies in the opposing army when we do meet them, as will surely happen.'

'I don't know. Most of the peasants have little appetite for war. Only the warrior priests keep them in line. An army that marches on fear is likely to fall apart under pressure.'

'Truly spoken, but we would have trouble enough from the warrior priests alone, if they decided to attack us. I don't relish going head to head with Inquisitor Melyn in a fight.'

'Me neither.' Lord Ansey shuddered as if the thought of the inquisitor was abhorrent to him.

'Which army is he with?' Dafydd asked.

'Who?'

'Melyn. Surely he must be overseeing the whole campaign.'

'I'm not sure. He wasn't with the queen when she came here, and he's not at Candlehall. He's probably riding back and forth between Tochers and Dina trying to impose some order on the chaos. That would be the sort of thing he'd do. Never trusts a lieutenant, does Melyn. Always has to do it himself.'

Dafydd tuned out Lord Ansey's moans about the inquisitor and his warrior priests, his mind skirting the edges of a new possibility.

'So neither the queen nor Melyn are at Candlehall.'

'What? No. It's a ghost city at the moment. All the nobles are either with the queen or at the front.'

'And what sort of military presence is there?'

'Very little, really. Mostly semi-retired soldiers. A few palace guards. Here! You're not thinking . . . ?'

'We don't need an army to disrupt supplies; everything comes from here anyway. If Abervenn decides not to send food up the Gwy, then it won't get to Dina. That's half of the army cut off at the knees. Meanwhile we can ship men up the Abheinn in barges. Candlehall might even surrender without a fight.'

Errol had never seen so many tents. They stretched for what looked like miles over the wide flat plain to the east of the city, right up to the distant blurred green edge of the forest. There were marquees large enough to hold whole villages and smaller tents for single families. Some travellers had no tents at all, taking their chances with the weather and simply laying their bedrolls around communal fires. He wondered how anybody could find where they had slept the night before.

At first the way had been clear and easy to move along, the camp neatly arranged in squares with wide avenues between them, but as he rode deeper into the site, so chaos took hold. People had arrived in groups and taken over as much space as they needed with scant regard for planning. There was obvious rivalry too – in the decorations, for space and for hawking pitches. Petty fights were breaking out all over the place, squads of soldiers constantly on the move, breaking heads and keeping order as best they could.

He thought he would have a hard time locating the circus, but Errol soon found there was little else being talked about – at least among the women washing clothes in the sluggish stream that wound its way through the camp.

'All the circuses set up under the town walls, lassie,' one florid lady told him as she slapped wet cloth against a shiny rock. 'But there's only one worth looking at. Old Loghtan's got hisself a new dragon, so they say. Even the king's gonna come see it when he opens the festival.'

'And when's that?' Errol saw the look of disbelief on the washerwoman's face, as if no one could be so stupid as not to know. It was a look he had grown accustomed to as he felt his way around Llanwennog society. 'It's just that I've been on the road so long, I've lost track of the days. You know how it is.'

The woman still looked doubtful, but she answered anyway. 'Day after tomorrow's when. But don't think you'll find any tickets for sale. Them had all gone before the wagon wheels stopped turning.'

Errol thanked her and led his horse away from the stream back towards the grey stone walls of the city. They loomed over the vast camp, growing ever higher as he came nearer. He had no great desire to enter; the city held too many memories of betrayal, torture, pain. And somewhere in there old King Ballah sat on his throne, casting his mind over the thoughts of his people, looking for enemies. Errol remembered the touch of that mind; he didn't want to feel it again.

Loghtan's circus was exactly where the washerwoman had said it would be. Quite the largest canvas marquee he had ever seen, of alternating red and white stripes, soared above the city wall at its highest. Smaller tents were arranged around it in groups, and as Errol approached he could see queues of people waiting to go inside.

'Roll up! Roll up! Come and see the bearded lady. Watch the snake man dance with his poisonous brothers and sisters. Marvel at the fish-boy, born with gills and forced to live underwater all his life.'

Errol felt himself compelled to go in. He almost forgot his horse, following obediently at his shoulder, and was pulling out his purse when he recognized the magic. It was a simple spell, crudely worked but effective if the length of the lines was anything to go by. He shook his head, dispelling the last of it, and walked on.

The nearer he got to the circus, the more certain he was that it was the one he had seen just before Benfro's capture. He thought he recognized some of the people, and the wagons seemed familiar, but it was impossible to be sure. The circus camp was pitched between the huge tent and the city wall, the wagons forming a tight wall, everything fenced off from view with wooden boards. These were brightly painted, bearing slogans, pictures of wild animals performing tricks and people in daft costumes. One particularly large picture caught his attention. It showed a huge dragon, its wings outstretched, soaring through the air. Another smaller dragon sat on the ground watching. The words, painted in letters as big as his head, read, THE GREAT MAGOG AND GOG. SEE THE FLYING DRAGONS OF LEGEND!

Errol stood back from the board. It was brighter than those around it, obviously newly done. And it was fixed to the side of a large wagon. There had been only one big wagon in the circus, the one Griselda had shown him, where the dragon was kept. The dragon. Just one. And now they had two. It had to be the right circus; it was too much of a coincidence.

There were a few people milling about, most of them heading towards the queues for the freak show. Hoping that no one was watching, Errol moved as close to the boards as possible.

'Benfro. Are you there?' He spoke as loudly as he dared, looking constantly back and forth to check he wasn't attracting too much attention. There was no answer.

'Benfro. Please. If you're in there, answer me. It's Errol. I've come to get you out.'

Still no answer. He tried to sense with his mind, feeling the different thoughts and emotions nearby. But there were so many people, and they were so excited, he could scarcely distinguish anything in the noise. The residual magic coming from nearby didn't help either.

'Well, you're a pretty thing, aren't you.'

Errol spun around at the voice, almost shrieking when he recognized the man who had spoken. It was the same man who had accosted them on the road weeks earlier, along with the gold trader Tibbits. The man who had escaped before Benfro could catch him.

'You wanting to see our dragons now, missy? Well, tickets are all sold out, but Tegwin here can get you inside. If you've something for him in return.'

Errol could smell the sour beer on his breath. Tegwin put one hand out, leaning against the boards and effectively blocking his escape.

'Pretty little thing like you's got plenty to trade. Come

all the way to the big city, ain't you. Well Tegwin'll show you around. Oh yes.' With his free hand he reached up to brush Errol's hair, then the side of his face.

Errol backed away, finding himself pinned against the boards as Tegwin reached down to clasp his waist. He felt strangely helpless, and then felt once more the touch of magic. It was far more subtle than the coercion spell that made otherwise sane people pay money to look at freaks. Errol could only assume that Tegwin didn't know what he was doing, what innate skill he possessed. No doubt many a maid had fallen for his inexplicable charm before, but Errol was no maid. He pushed Tegwin hard in the chest and at the same time pushed hard with his mind.

'Leave me alone, you disgusting man. Get out of my way.'

Tegwin staggered, tripped over his own feet and fell hard on to his backside. Errol ignored him. He knew that he had found the right place now, knew too how Benfro had been caught. It was all his fault, and he was just going to have to find a way to help him escape.

8

It is said that King Balwen fashioned himself an orb of clear glass and imbued it with such magic that, when correctly used, it would show the location of any other mage within a hundred leagues. Such a device might seem invaluable at a time when servants of the Wolf were striving to bring darkness to Gwlad, but the glass orb was rendered almost useless by the curious defect it had of identifying dragons as if they too were powerful mages. Since in those days dragons numbered far more than the few hundred surviving today, their presence in the orb obscured Balwen's true quarry. Some say the Wolf purposely gifted dragons with their innate magical ability so as to thwart Balwen in his task.

Historians and royal scholars alike have searched for this fabled orb, but if it ever truly existed it has long since been destroyed.

Barrod Sheepshead,
A History of the House of Balwen

The excitement of the show was contagious. Though he hated the circus, hated Loghtan and his whip, hated the drugs that forced him to do whatever the circus master told him, still Benfro found himself caught up in the frenzy. He had trained for this, however reluctantly, and he found himself anxious to do as good a job as possible. And he was nervous too, surrounded by men who had so far not tried to kill him and yet who might decide he was no longer worth having around if he should fail to perform as expected.

It was like a disturbed anthill, people running back and forth. Men wheeled heavy wooden apparatus in through the large opening at the back of the tent, herded animals dressed in elaborate costumes, shouted instructions to each other in hoarse barks. Soldiers in elegant uniforms assigned to protect the king loitered, got in the way and accosted the circus performers. Benfro and the old dragon had been forced to humiliate themselves in front of one captain, Loghtan making both of them grovel, bow, roll on to their backs and perform numerous other demeaning antics to prove that they were both under his total control.

'You're on next. Get over to the big top and wait for the master to call you.'

Benfro watched as Tegwin sorted through the large ring of keys until he found the right one, unlocking the wagon and throwing the door open. Unable to do anything but comply, he stepped out on to the grass, stretching his wings in the night air. The old dragon followed, moving stiffly, stooped by years in the cramped cage, and together they walked across to the marquee.

The tent was lit from within by hundreds of covered lamps, so that from outside it glowed like some monstrous striped grub oozing its way across the plain towards the city. Benfro stared up at the black shadows of the walls, feeling a terrible sense of dread sweat out of the stones.

Overhead low cloud reflected the endless fires and torches lining the rough avenues running through the mass of tents, as if the whole night burned. It was a terrible place, a terrible scene, like something from the mythology of men. The Wolf's lair.

Waiting by the open mouth of the entrance to the tent, Benfro looked into the circus ring and watched as Griselda performed her act with the lioncats. The creatures were thin and weak, but they too seemed fired up by the excitement of performing to such a large audience. The area around the ring was packed solid with people arranged on tiered seating that creaked and shook as they moved about. The tent had always been empty when he had practised before. Filled, it seemed a much smaller place; he wondered whether he could fly the circuit he had learned without his wing tips hitting some of the audience.

Part of him asked why he should care if a few men were killed or injured; his wings wouldn't be damaged. But Loghtan wouldn't allow him to harm anyone. And if he did, the soldiers who stood at strategic points about the ring would soon stop him. Benfro had watched them earlier, pushing their way through the circus, checking all the wagons and generally getting in the way. They were skilled in the brutal magic of men. Just as bad as Melyn and his warrior priests.

'You're on. Hurry!' Griselda's shout woke Benfro from his stupor. She dragged the two lioncats back towards their cage, their reluctance the first sign of anything resembling rebellion he had seen in the creatures. It was as if the ring was the only place they could be alive; everything else was just a living death. But he didn't have time to feel sorry for them. Loghtan's cry carrying over the noisy applause was the cue he had to obey.

'And now, ladies and gentlemen. From the depths of time, the most ancient of mythologies, I am proud, no honoured, to bring you the brothers Magog and Gog.'

The old dragon lumbered into the tent ahead of him. The applause petered out and excited murmuring took its place. Benfro counted twenty twin beats of his hearts, then followed into the warm muggy interior of the tent.

Silence.

All eyes were on him, and all voices stilled as he stepped from the shadows and into the ring. Even though the drugs Loghtan fed him had robbed him of much of his finer senses, still Benfro could feel the mixture of fear and awe he inspired in these people. Smiling inwardly, he looked around the ring for the royal box, where the king sat. He located the tiny grey-haired man and bowed deeply as he had been ordered. Then he stretched his wings as wide as he dared, took one step, two, three, and leaped into the air.

Some of the audience shrieked in fear, some clapped nervously, some scrambled out of their seats and tried to escape the battering they were convinced was to be their fate. But once he was aloft, Benfro found he had just enough space to fly the circuit he had practised. He could feel the closeness of the audience through his wing tips, but they never quite collided.

There was little to his act beyond flying around the ring while Loghtan told a very inaccurate version of the story of Gog and Magog. The old dragon ran along below him, leaping into the air and gliding short distances with his stubby wings, but Benfro knew no one was watching that sad display. All eyes were on him. He stared back, particularly at the king, whose presence made this such a special performance. Ballah was a small man, old and grey in a way that reminded Benfro of Father Gideon rather than Inquisitor Melyn. But the king exuded a raw cruel power, and he met Benfro's gaze with a fierceness that forced him to look away.

And then something else caught his eye, a sudden motion up in the shadows at the top of the tiers of seats. His circuit took him away from whatever it was for a while, and when he could look back again it had gone. But so too had the soldier who had been standing there. Puzzled, Benfro scanned the shadows, everywhere seeing dark shapes moving like thieves. Concentrating harder, trying to force his thoughts to clear, he almost flew into one of the great tree trunks that were the central supports of the tent. Making a quick correction, he swung tightly around the end of the tent, and as he did so his peripheral vision showed him what looked for all the world like Captain Osgal.

Astonished, Benfro almost fell to the ground. A great cry of alarm spread through the audience as he beat inelegantly at the air, trying to retain height without hitting anyone. He could feel the closeness of fleshy bodies, just inches from his wing tips as he struggled to remain aloft, then turned so that he was once more heading down the long side of the oval, past the elevated box where the king sat. And finally he was safe again, moving forward in controlled flight.

Benfro started on his next circuit of the tent, his wings beginning to ache. He desperately wanted to stretch them out and glide. But he was bound by Loghtan's drugs and could do nothing but fly and watch as one by one the king's guard disappeared into the shadows. Or to be more accurate, just disappeared. Even through his muddled senses Benfro could feel powerful magic going on, and dragon magic at that. But Loghtan, the king, the audience, even the old dragon leaping around beneath him seemed oblivious to it all.

And then the circus master was bringing his tale to an end, and Benfro almost missed his cue. He had to rear back, beating his wings hard against the air to slow so that he could land in the right place. Wind from his wings rocked the tent, swinging the lanterns so that the shadows danced and whirled. The audience was poised between alarm and exhilaration, and in that one instant before the applause began Benfro saw something that sent a chill through his hearts.

They stood silently like sentinels, invisible to all but him. Benfro realized now that he was seeing the Grym and the aethereal superimposed upon the mundane world, that state of perfect perception Sir Frynwy and Meirion-ydd had tried so hard to teach him. It was the key to understanding the subtle arts, the interplay between the forces of Gwlad and every living thing. He recognized the magic now too. It was the very first spell he had ever learned from Ynys Môn. The spell of concealment. Only this was far more powerful, far more pervasive than anything the old hunter had ever shown him. It was no surprise that the people filling the tent could not see what was hidden. What was truly astonishing was that it was men themselves who worked the magic.

Benfro swept his gaze across the whole of the tent,

turning slowly as if to accept the applause that he had hardly registered. With a feeling of utmost dread he realized that he was completely surrounded by silent, invisible warrior priests.

'Go on, get out of here. If you've not got a ticket, you're not getting in.'

Errol stared at the small crowd of people clustered at the gap in the temporary wall built around the circus. Palace guards flanked the entrance, and he knew they were posted all over the site, keeping unauthorized people away from the great tent and the king. He had watched Ballah arrive earlier, welcomed in by the circus master himself. Seeing the old man surrounded by his soldiers, Errol had felt a moment's terror. He had imagined the king singling him out from the crowd, capturing him, torturing him. But the moment had passed as swiftly as it had come upon him, and he understood it was all part of Ballah's magic, a projection broadcast to his subjects to keep them in awe of him. Now the king was inside, no doubt enjoying the show, and Errol was stuck outside, unable to find a way in.

Something brushed past him and he turned, hand instinctively going to the purse that hung at his belt under his cloak. The festival attracted every thief and pickpocket in all of Llanwennog, or so it seemed, and he had learned quickly to trust the instinct that told him someone nearby meant him ill. But this time there was no one close.

Errol stood in the shadows away from the flickering torches arranged along the roadside as it speared from the city gates. He had chosen the place as somewhere he might watch the entrance to the circus without being noticed, hoping that after a while the guards would lose interest, or perhaps that the crowd of hopefuls might disperse and he could try to charm his way in. After all, if Tegwin had fallen for his disguise, then maybe a palace guard would too.

Again he felt the sensation of someone brushing past him. Errol started and turned. Once more there was nothing. And yet he was sure someone had been there. It was a familiar feeling, the pull of the Grym when powerful magic was being performed, and it brought back memories of Emmass Fawr.

Thinking of the Grym was enough to bring it to his eyes. The lines defined the shape of the land, lighting it so that he felt he could walk confidently through the camp even if it were in total darkness. He felt the background murmur of their power, saw how the soldiers of the palace guard tapped them, constantly alert. And there was other magic around, indefinable against the noise of so much life, so many people gathered together in one small place. It chilled him; there was something wrong about it.

Errol drew further back into the shadows, trying to block out the noise and focus on something useful. He knew the immediate area was full of people, but it was a dragon he was looking for, and they cast a completely different sensation over the Grym. Tentatively, he reached out along the lines, looking for that telltale feeling, that sense of familiarity that he felt sure he would recognize from Benfro.

There was nothing.

He looked once more at the wooden boards painted with the images of two dragons. In the flickering torchlight they moved as if dancing. He knew that they must be

inside somewhere. Loghtan had talked up his show endlessly. Everyone wanted to see it. Even the king had come.
There were dragons; there had to be. So why couldn't he
sense them?

Closing his eyes, Errol tried to will away everything but
the Grym. He centred himself, as he had been taught by
the quaisters at Emmass Fawr and earlier still by Sir Radnor, then felt his way along the lines once more, searching
all the while for Benfro or any dragon at all.

It was a confusing mess of thoughts and images. He
pushed aside petty arguments over sleeping arrangements,
drunken anger boiling over to violence, the inconsolable
anguish of a child lost in a crowd, the eager anticipation
of an audience waiting for the main act to come on. And
then he felt something — the merest hint of dragon
thought, dragon empathy. It was something he had felt
before, and he reached for it instinctively.

There was that curious vision of an infant child
snuggling alongside a tiny dragon hatchling; of Father
Gideon, his face etched with worry and sorrow; of the
dead Princess Lleyn, her skin soft and pale, not tanned
and leathery. In the instant Errol recognized the touch of
Morgwm's jewel the world outside seemed to slip away.
The gentle breeze that had been rustling his long hair disappeared. The noise muted, softening as if he had stuck
his head in a box. The burned-grease smell of the torches
changed to a more delicate mixed scent of polished
woods, dusty linen and stale sweat. Opening his eyes, he
saw that he was no longer in the shadows outside the circus, but standing in a darkened room.

For a moment Errol was confused, but it didn't take

long for his mind to catch up. He had sensed Morgwm's jewel and in that instant stepped to the place where it lay. It didn't take a genius to work out that he must be in one of the wagons that the circus people used as homes, most probably Loghtan's own. Suppressing his excitement at having once more walked the lines, even if he was still unsure quite how it was that he did it, he set about searching the small wagon for his stolen bag.

Pale orange light filtered in through a pair of small grubby windows. Already accustomed to the dark, Errol could make out a narrow cot bed built into one wall, its sheets thrown back untidily, the pillow crumpled and stained. Directly in front of him a small table was strewn with bits of paper, plates of half-eaten food and two empty pewter goblets. Beyond it a large wooden cupboard with wide drawers at its base had been built into the end of the wagon. Errol opened the cupboard doors to release a stench of stale sweat that made him gag. Holding his breath, he went methodically through all of Loghtan's dirty clothes. There was nothing that hadn't been repaired many times before; even his boots were patched and re-patched. But neither was there anything resembling a large leather satchel of money with two dragon jewels wrapped in cloth at the bottom.

The drawers beneath were filled with all manner of junk, some of it probably quite valuable but so dirty as to be unrecognizable. There were broken bits of harness, goblets set with jewels that might have been valuable or might have been coloured glass, greasy rolls of parchment, their edges frayed and cracked with repeated mishandling. Errol pulled one out, squinting in the dim light as he tried to read the words scrawled upon it in looped handwriting. As far as he could tell, it was a spell of location, though from what he could read, he wasn't sure how it could possibly work. He put it back, rifling quietly through the rest of the contents of the drawers and turning up nothing.

Looking around the rest of the wagon, he couldn't see where anything might be hidden. It was a bare place, quite without ornamentation. Then his eyes fell once more on the bed. It was a raised wooden construction, about waist height off the floor, and the space underneath the mattress was blocked off by a plain wooden board. Errol felt around the edge of the bed, seeking a latch. He found a small hole just large enough to hook his fingers through and pulled up. Mattress, sheets, pillow and bed board lifted on well-oiled hinges to reveal a dark space beneath. There was even a hook and eye to stop it all from falling back down again.

At first Errol thought it was only more junk, a similar jumble to that in the drawers. But when he lifted out a dented metal jug its weight and lustre told him that it was gold. He put it back carefully, feeling in the darkness for something more familiar. Soon his hands grasped a thin cloth strap he was sure he knew. Gently he pulled out the bag that he had made back in Corwen's clearing. And by the weight of it nothing had been taken from inside.

And then the strap slipped in his hands, the bag crashing back into the junk with a noise that must have been heard on the other side of the city. Errol froze, his heart hammering away in his chest, his ears ringing with the noise as he listened for the sound of feet running to investigate. None came, and after a minute or two, still shaking but a little more composed, he reached back inside to pull out the bag again.

As he did so, he noticed a soft glow from something beneath it. Curious, he lifted out a small cloth drawstring pouch lit from within. Opening it revealed a perfectly round glass ball, like a child's marble. White fire burned inside it, although the ball gave off no heat. As his fingers touched its smooth surface, the light changed, swirling to form a picture. Errol stared into the orb and almost dropped it. Two tiny dragons sat in the middle of a packed-earth arena, surrounded by people. He looked over at the grimy window of the caravan and the great tent beyond. Was he seeing Benfro in there? And who was the other dragon?

A roar came from the tent, shocking Errol back to his senses. This was not a safe place to be. He dropped the orb back into its pouch and put it into his bag before lifting the whole thing out. Only then did he discover that the strap had been cut, so he had to reach underneath to take the weight.

Something brushed the side of his hand, and he felt a shock of familiar feeling run through him. It was like Benfro, like Morgwm, only different. Another dragon or something to do with one. Errol explored with his fingers, fetching out a small rectangular wooden box. It was no bigger than his hand but exuded a power that made it feel as heavy as a boulder. Putting it down on the table, he opened it to reveal a dozen small red jewels.

He snapped the box shut, remembering all too well the fleeting touch of Magog's unreckoned jewel. Bad enough that Benfro was shackled to one; how would he, Errol, survive under the onslaught of so many more? And yet there was something different about them. They should not have been here, should have been reckoned and laid to rest. He was filled with an urge to find the dead remains of whatever poor beast had yielded them up and . . . What?

Errol shook off the strange feeling and turned back to his bag. He dumped the whole thing on the table and opened it up, feeling around for its precious contents. Both jewels were still there, tightly wrapped in their cloths. He transferred them to the pockets in his cloak, along with the mysterious orb in its cloth pouch, and sorted through the gold coins, adding a few of the smaller ones to the money in the leather purse at his belt. He put the damaged bag back with the rest of the hoard and dropped the bed back into place.

It was as he was stepping over to the door that Errol heard the noise of keys being jangled on a chain, one slotting into the lock. He backed away, looking for somewhere to hide even as he knew it was too late, and saw the small wooden box still lying on the table. Before he could do anything, the door was open. A lantern held aloft cast yellow light over the interior of the wagon, and over the leering face of Tegwin, an odd smile on his lips.

'Thought I heard a little mouse in here, didn't I. Daddy got hisself a bit of slap and tickle fer afters, eh? Well, Tegwin don't mind sharing.' He threw the bunch of keys on to the table, hanging the lantern from a hook in the ceiling as he pulled shut the door with one hand, the other going to his belt.

Melyn watched the solid aethereal forms of his warrior priests move through the city like foraging ants. He sat in a comfortable chair in the distastefully opulent study of Master Cheldrum, the merchant who had for many years been his most reliable eyes and ears in Tynhelyg. He could see the ornately carved wooden panelling, the gilt-framed pictures of dour-looking men and women, the bow-legged table upon which sat a gold wine jug and several goblets worth more than a soldier might expect to earn in a life-time. And he could see further still, throughout the house, the street, the merchants' quarter of the city. He could even see Frecknock, though she was standing behind him. Her presence was reassuring now, an anchor from the pull of the book open in front of him.

It was without doubt a thing of great power. Perhaps equal to Brynceri's ring, the artefact that linked him directly to the Shepherd. Melyn knew he could spend several life-times studying the Llyfr Draconius and not even scrape the surface of what was contained within. Its magic had brought him and his army unseen across the central plains of Llanwennog to Tynhelyg in a day, a journey that should have taken a week at least, if not longer. It had shown him how to hide even more completely from sight, so that King Ballah's personal guards, trained as well as any war-rior priest, could not see him or his men even though they walked right past them. And now it allowed him to watch as his plan unfolded, delivering the city into his hands.

'I find it hard to believe that the city is so poorly guarded. I would never leave Queen Beulah with so few skilled warriors.'

'King Ballah feels no need of men to protect him,' Frecknock said. 'He's the most powerful magician in Llan-wennog; his ability to read the minds of those around him is legendary. And this far from the border he feels safe. They've all gone to the front.'

'Well, I don't intend to spurn the Shepherd's gift,' Melyn said. 'Come.' He shifted his focus, no longer needing to go into the trance that would let him slip into his aethereal form. He had been watching his men all the while, but now he concentrated on those surrounding the barracks. Inside its walls several hundred palace guards slept, ate, tended their horses or played cards. Mostly he could see them as indistinct forms, undisciplined flames of life, but one or two were more robust. These would be the skilled magicians and the few who might be able to see his hidden warrior priests. But they would need to go into a trance, and at their ease, in the barracks, they would have no reason to do that.

'Ah, here we go.' He moved forward, imagining himself flying over a long low dormitory building. Warrior priests entered at one end and made their slow way along the beds towards the other. One by one the flickering flames of life, sleeping soldiers, winked out, a silent stiletto to each heart.

Melyn pulled back, watching the whole barracks now, looking for signs that the alarm had been raised. They never came. His men were well trained and knew how to sow confusion in the enemy's minds. Soldiers wandered away from the mess hall and into unsheathed knives; they found themselves suddenly needing to go outside or wanting to be alone, and always there were warrior priests waiting. Aided by the book, the magic stolen from the Shepherd so many years before, they could hide the bodies from sight as well. At least until there was no one left to see them. It was all over in half an hour.

Melyn turned his all-seeing eyes to the palace and watched as a similar game was played out. Here there was a slightly different strategy. He had no desire to kill the servants, so their flames of life found themselves compelled to visit the festival outside the city walls, even though they should have been preparing meals, cleaning rooms or the hundred and one other things servants did. There were far fewer guards here, and they winked out of existence quickly. Satisfied that all was going to plan, the inquisitor pulled himself back to the mundane world, narrowing his vision to just what he could see with his eyes.

'It's time for me to go,' he said, closing the book and standing up. Behind him, Frecknock turned to follow him, but he shook his head. 'You must stay here.'

If she was disappointed, she didn't show it, merely nodding as she settled herself back down on to the floor by the window. She didn't really fit in the room, making it look tiny where in fact it was huge. At least it had large enough doors for her.

'As you order, Your Grace. But please go carefully.'

Melyn said nothing, unsure quite how he felt about her concern. She had proved her value to him many times over, and he had to admit she had saved his life more than once. His god had hinted that she might have spurned the way of the Wolf and accepted the Shepherd into her heart, but even so Melyn was reluctant to trust her. A lifetime of enmity was not so easily overturned. And dragons had two hearts anyway.

A squad of warrior priests waited in the hall outside the study. Melyn closed the door firmly behind him, beckoning them over.

'You two stay here and guard the house. If I've not sent for you by dawn, then you must assume we have failed. Take the book back to Andro at Emmass Fawr. And kill the dragon. The rest of you, with me.'

Outside the night was cool, stars pricking through gaps in the low cloud. They marched down the streets unhidden; there were few people out and about anyway and Melyn no longer cared that he might be seen. It wasn't far to the city wall, and the gates were thrown wide, unguarded as if Tyn-helyg had already fallen. Perhaps, he thought, it has.

Ballah was at the circus, that much Melyn already knew. As he approached it he could see a great crowd of people clustered around the entrance, no doubt trying to get in. He ignored them and the palace guard holding them back, walking instead alongside the wooden wall that sep-arated the circus from the rest of the vast tented city spread over the plain. Around the back there was a small entrance for the circus performers, and it too was guarded.

'You can't come in here, sir. Not unless you've got a pass.' One palace guard strode forward to meet him, the other staying back. Melyn noted their professionalism, for all the good it would do them.

'Do you know who I am?'

'I don't care if you're the king's cousin. If you've not got a pass, you're not getting in.'

'That's not what I meant,' Melyn said, then realized he was wasting time. 'Never mind.' He conjured his blade of light. The guard was dead in an instant, his head hit-ting the ground a split second before his crumpled body. His companion turned to run. Melyn reached into the man's mind, forcing him to stop. The guard was well schooled – he had mental blocks in place that would have turned back most – but he was not trained to face the Inquisitor of the Order of the High Ffrydd. He stopped in mid-stride, letting out an oddly strangled squeak, then folded up and hit the ground. Bending down, the inquisitor felt for a pulse, finding none. The power of the Shepherd flowed through him, Brynceri's ring glowing brilliant crimson in the dark night.

'Who's there? What's going on?' The voice came out of the darkness. A circus performer. Melyn didn't need light to see him. He reached out and turned off the man's mind with a single thought. There was the muffled sound of a body slumping to the ground, and he felt a surge of power once more, as if he had drunk the man's life force and found it more potent, more wonderful than any wine.

Behind him Melyn was aware that his warrior priests had stopped. He turned to them, feeling their fear. It was good.

'What are you staring at? We've work to do. Come.'

They rallied, stepped past the prone bodies and into the circus camp, but Melyn knew that they were afraid. Legend told of the old kings and first inquisitors who could kill a man just by looking at him, but no one had wielded that power in a thousand years. It filled him with an almost childish glee, both that he should be given such a wonderful gift and that his men should react to it so.

The great circus tent rocked slightly as he approached, as if something huge were trapped inside and trying to escape. Melyn heard the audience within give a great cry of alarm, then settle again. Somewhere in among the noise a lone voice was declaiming loudly, though he couldn't make out the words.

'Hide yourselves. Deal with the guards.'

He watched as his warrior priests shimmered out of sight, rushing to do his bidding. Alone, Melyn half listened to the story being told in the ring, a tale of warring dragons that sparked a memory in him, long suppressed. He must have heard the story before, he supposed, but it felt more personal than that. As if he had lived it, known the creatures well. Perhaps it was a side effect of the ring; it had been the Shepherd's gift, after all. It was imbued with unimaginable power and had been witness to great and terrible events stretching back millennia.

And then the voice stopped, the story ended. There was an instant of utter silence followed by tumultuous applause. Taking this as his cue, Melyn pushed aside the odd feeling of hiraeth. Now was not the time to be distracted by anything, let alone something as intangible as a longing for a past he couldn't even recall. He once more conjured up his blade of light, strode in through the wide opening under the tiered seating. Wood creaked and groaned as the appreciative audience stamped and cheered, their attention entirely focused on two dragons sitting in the centre of the great tent. Even with its back to him, Melyn recognized one as Benfro. With a surge of fury that turned his blade of fire crimson, he stepped forward into the ring.

9

Self-discipline is vital to winning a battle with a well-matched magical opponent. The key is never to let yourself be distracted; focus is imperative. But be aware that attack will come from many directions at once. You must not close your mind too hard, lest you fail to see your opponent's intentions in his thoughts. And yet you must shield yourself against his mental onslaught. Neither think that a powerful mage will seek to overwhelm you with sheer force when subtlety of touch will fell even the strongest tree. Be wary of the Grym but also open to it. Magic takes no sides, only does as it is bid. But most of all, when you lock wits with a magician, do not forget the physical. All the mental discipline in the world will not save you from a well-aimed arrow or hidden blade.

Inquisitor Melyn, *Lectures to Novitiates*

The applause was deafening, filling his head and blotting out all thought. Benfro felt his body bend into a bow, just like the one he could see his fellow performer making alongside him. He fought against it with all his will, and yet he could not control himself. Even though the ghostly images of a hundred or more warrior priests surrounded him, taunted him, mocked his weakness. They had killed his mother, and now this circus would kill him. Only where Morgwm had died in an instant, he would be slowly destroyed, his jewels ripped from his skull by the circus master. Better to go mad now than face that fate every day. And surely he was going mad. There were no warrior priests here. And that wasn't Inquisitor Melyn walking into the ring with his blade of light turned crimson like blood.

Before he knew what he was doing, Benfro was running. Pounding his way across the ring towards the hated figure. He vaguely registered the applause dying away, barely felt the power behind Loghtan's words as he waved his arms and spoke in an odd voice that sounded almost like Draigiaith. But mostly he saw Melyn, the hated enemy, alone and vulnerable. And that hatred, that anger, cut away whatever spells and drugs had bound him as if they were no more substantial than cobwebs. It boiled in his stomach too, filling him until he was ready to burst. With a roar that had been trying to escape since he had first been captured, Benfro belched out a huge flame.

Loghtan stood between him and the inquisitor. For a second the circus master looked astonished, and then he disappeared into the fire, screaming. Benfro paid him no more heed than to smile inwardly. He ran on towards Melyn, breathing in deeply, ready to burn the inquisitor to a crisp. The fire came easily, leaping away from him as if it had a life of its own. But Melyn simply waved his arm and the flame parted around him.

And then the fear hit.

Benfro reared back, a long-forgotten part of his mind

taking control of his body. This was far more terrifying than the fear that had swept over him when his mother had been murdered. Worse than anything Magog had ever thrown at him. Somewhere, deep down, he knew that the fear wasn't real. But that place was hiding from the voice that spoke in his mind.

'I knew I would find you soon enough, dragon. You're mine now. I will take you, crack your mind apart and find out what secrets it holds. And then you will cease to exist.'

It was Melyn's voice, but in his terror Benfro heard Magog's too, cackling triumphantly as it ate into him chunk by chunk. He scrambled to get away and crashed into something, tripping and falling to the dirt floor. Wide-eyed, he saw a pillar of flame running around the ring. It was Loghtan, burning up, screaming, scattering fire as he went.

There was uproar in the big tent as the fire spread far too quickly. It leaped up the great wooden poles and tore into the canvas. In no time at all huge chunks of burning cloth began to rain down on the hysterical audience. People were scrambling over one another to escape the flames that licked along the wooden seating.

'Hee hee. Gog's been a naughty dragon now. Old Loghtan didn't much like that, did he?'

Benfro shook his head, trying to push away the fear that still smothered him. The old dragon had appeared at his side, a wide grin on his wrinkled face and a light in his eyes far brighter than the flames surrounding them.

'You'd better come with Magog, hadn't you. Don't want to get all burned up in the fire.' He wrapped a bony arm around Benfro's shoulder and helped him up. Dazed,

Benfro was only too happy to be guided through the thickening black smoke towards where he hoped the exit was. He had lost track of Melyn, and the fear seemed less somehow, as if the inquisitor had been distracted from him. At least for now.

Benfro held his breath and together he and Magog pushed their way out into the dark circus camp beyond. Escapees from the audience were running back and forth, and some of the performers were trying to form a human chain to throw buckets of water at the conflagration – as if that would make a difference.

'Old Loghtan can't order Magog around any more. Oh no. Old Loghtan's gone to join the Wolf in his lair. See if he hasn't.' The dragon let go of Benfro's arm and danced a little jig. Then stopped all of a sudden. 'But where will Magog go now? Who has he got to go to?' His voice was suddenly sad and lost.

Benfro looked around. They were being completely ignored in the chaos; they could just walk out. But the question stood: where would they go?

'Come with me,' he said, heading towards the back of the camp, where the performers' wagons were drawn up.

'What? Where is Gog going?'

'I'm going to find your memories. Maybe then we can work out what to do.' He ran across the camp, pausing only to make sure the old dragon was following. With each step he could feel the stupor of the past weeks falling away, his anger growing all the while as he realized how helpless he had been, how badly treated. Loghtan's death was sweet, but there were others here who deserved the same.

The wagons were arranged in a rough circle around a central fire. Everything was deserted, all hands gone to try and save the big tent. Benfro went from wagon to wagon, throwing open doors and thrusting his head inside. He knew he would recognize the one he was looking for by its smell, but before he got to it, the door burst open on its own. An unwelcome and familiar figure backed out, struggling with something. Benfro didn't care what it was. He just shouted.

'Tegwin!'

As the circus master's son turned, Benfro backed up his cry with a roar of flame. And only then did he see what the man was struggling with. Dressed in women's clothes, a knife at his throat, was Errol.

Melyn ignored the flames as they surged up the poles and tore great holes in the canvas. Their heat was not intolerable, and he knew he was safest in the middle of the tent, rather than fighting to get out like the panicked audience. He pushed them from his mind too, along with his disappointment at seeing the dragon escape. He would catch that quarry soon enough; now there were more important matters to attend to.

'Are you afraid to face me, Ballah?' he shouted above the noise of chaos and fire. The old king sat still and calm as if he were on his throne rather than at the centre of an inferno. Without so much as a command from him, four of his guards leaped over the barrier that separated him from the ring. Their blades shimmered into existence as they spread out, trying to surround the inquisitor. Melyn chuckled and threw the full force of his mind at the nearest.

The soldier was prepared. His thoughts were tight, disciplined. He had no fear, no doubt. Melyn didn't care. He simply reached deeper in and turned his attacker's mind off. His blade flickered and disappeared as he toppled like a puppet abandoned in mid-play.

To their credit, the other three didn't flinch at the death of their comrade. Melyn almost regretted that he had to kill them; they would have made fine warrior priests if only they would accept the Shepherd into their hearts. But there was no time for mercy, and they fell before one of them could get within a dozen paces of him.

'You'll have to try harder than that, old man.' Melyn walked towards the still smiling king. The remaining two guards didn't leave his side, no doubt waiting for the inquisitor to clamber over the low wooden railing into the royal box. He would be momentarily vulnerable then, and that was when they would strike.

Except that he had no intention of getting that close. He reached out with his mind again, feeling the power of the Grym coursing through him, directed by Brynceri's ring. *His* ring. Gifted to him by the Shepherd himself, along with the secrets of the magic that the dragons had stolen. What harm could these second-rate magicians do him?

Melyn's arrogance was almost his undoing. He searched for the minds of the two guards, finding nothing there. And then he realized why Ballah had not moved, had not spoken. He was a projection cast while the inquisitor was occupied with the first four guards. The only four guards.

He whirled, blade of light at the ready, looking for the king. With a single thought the aethereal enhanced his vision and he saw him too close, lunging. Melyn stepped aside and felt the cloth of his cloak part as Ballah's blade appeared from nowhere and sliced at him.

'Not quick enough, old man.' Melyn twisted, bringing his blade down to slice into the king's back. It was a killing blow that would surely split the man in two, but it passed through without meeting any resistance. Melyn tipped forward, off balance. At that moment he sensed rather than saw the attack. He fell to the ground and rolled like he was twenty again, back on to his feet in a flash, blade held high to parry Ballah's blow.

It wasn't there. And the low chuckle he heard came from several paces away. Shaking his head, Melyn tried to calm himself. Distracted by the dragon, he had given Ballah the upper hand here; the king was just toying with him. Meddling with his mind. Well, two could play that game.

'Your soldiers are all dead, Ballah,' he said, erecting even stronger mental defences than normal. 'In here, in the barracks, in the palace. My men have taken your city and you didn't even know we were here.'

'Your arrogance is every bit as great as reported, Inquisitor. How long do you imagine you can hold this place when my army returns?'

'Long enough for Beulah to attack them from behind.' Melyn focused on Ballah's words, pushing the misdirection aside and turning to face the real king. For a moment Ballah was indistinct in the mundane, though he blazed bright and clear in the aethereal. Then he dropped all pretence of hiding, and Melyn felt a great rush in the Grym as the king drew its power into himself.

'She'll find only your blackened corpse.'

Before the words were even finished, Ballah had thrown a great ball of fire at him. Melyn lifted his ringed hand, forming the spell in his mind exactly as he had read it in the book. The fire hit an invisible shield two paces ahead of him, splaying out either side and bouncing back at the king. Ballah looked momentarily shocked, but rallied. Melyn felt the surge as the Grym was tapped for miles around; every living thing would have felt a sudden sickening weakness as its very life was leached. The king shuddered with the power of it all, and for a moment Melyn thought his work was done. Surely Ballah would simply explode, burn up like a novitiate conjuring his first blade of light before he was ready.

But incredibly the king held on to that force, concentrated it into a glowing orb about the size of his head, then sent it rocketing towards the inquisitor. Melyn didn't even bother forming the spell; he knew how it felt now. With a casual flick of his hand, he sent the ball spinning away. It missed the nearest tent pole but collided with the next, exploding with a deafening roar that sent splinters flying through the air. Melyn's shield protected him, but Ballah's face and hands were peppered with tiny cuts, making it look like he sweated blood.

Then Melyn saw the fear in the king's eyes and knew that he had won. He stepped forward, narrowing the gap between them, ignoring the screams as men and women were enveloped in burning canvas. He swung his blade of light, parrying Ballah's attacking thrust, countering it with one of his own.

'It's over, old man. I win.' Melyn feinted, parried, then

swung his blade with a flick of the wrist that brought it round in a neat arc, severing Ballah's arm at the wrist. The lifeless hand fell to the earth, and Melyn half-expected the king to explode as the concentrated Grym that had powered his blade flowed back into him. But even in his agony Ballah retained enough control to let it dissipate.

'You'll never live to see your precious Emmass Fawr again.' Ballah staggered as the shock began to take him. 'And Beulah will never rule over Llanwennog.'

'Empty words, old man,' Melyn said. And he drove his blade forward, burning a hole through Ballah's heart.

Errol had no time to react, even if he had been able to do anything. Tegwin had him in an arm lock, a thin dagger at his throat. One moment he was being pulled backwards out of the wagon, promises of sexual violence whispered in his ear, the next a voice mad with rage roared in the air. Then he was engulfed in flame.

It took a surprisingly long time to notice that he wasn't being burned. Far from harming him, the flames filled him with strength, caressing his bare skin like warm water, cleaning away the dirt of the road and the camp. He could feel the fire envelop his head, easing away the dull ache that had been with him ever since he had woken in Lord Gremmil's castle, the weariness of long days riding, walking, hiding, all gone in that warm, welcoming flame.

The knife at his throat dropped away; Tegwin's grasp relaxed, and only then did Errol hear a distant screaming, like a man being tortured. It reminded him of his stay in the palace dungeons. Then it had been him crying out as Ballah's guard smashed a hammer into his ankles, but now he was sure it was someone else in pain, and idly he wondered who it might be.

Slowly the flames faded, evaporating into the night. The last of them lingered around his feet and legs, filling them with a healing warmth as a foul stench of burned meat rose into the air. Something fell to the ground behind him with a noise like dried leaves trampled underfoot on a frosty morning. He turned to see a roughly man-shaped pile of ashes billow out on the dark ground.

'Gog breathes the Fflam Gwir. Hee hee. Old Tegwin's going to be sorry. Yes, he is.'

Errol's wits slowly returned to him. They brought a deep shudder with them, loosening his knees and tipping him forward. Strong arms caught him, arms that had held him tight as he flew over the Rim mountains and the plains of the northlands. He looked up into Benfro's concerned face.

'What are you doing here, Errol?'

'I came to find you. I've been following since they took you. I was going to try and break you out of here somehow, but ... What's going on?' Only then did Errol register the chaos, the flames leaping out of the big tent, the distant screams of fear and pain.

'Melyn's here.'

'Old Magog knew a Melyn once. Scrawny little kid, he was. Ran off to the castle, and no one ever saw him after that.'

Errol looked past Benfro and saw another, older dragon staring at him with a look of mild interest. 'Who are you?'

'I am Magog, Son of the Summer Moon,' the dragon said, his voice like a mummer rehearsing his lines. 'And this is my brother Gog. No doubt you've heard of us. We are the greatest dragons ever to rule the skies of Gwlad.'

'He was here before they captured me,' Benfro said by way of explanation. 'Loghtan did something to him, removed some of his jewels so he wouldn't remember who he was. He's been living his circus act for so long he truly believes he's Magog and I'm Gog.'

'Removed his jewels?' Errol wasn't quite sure he understood, but he remembered the small wooden box on the table in Loghtan's wagon. 'Hold on a minute.'

He sprang up the steps, his ankles feeling better than they had in months, and retrieved the box, handing it to Benfro. 'Can we put them back?'

'I don't know. Maybe Corwen could. The real Gog certainly would. If we just knew how to find him.'

'Well, we can't stay here. If Melyn's about, there'll be warrior priests everywhere. We've got to get away.' In all the excitement Errol had quite forgotten his unusual arrival in the middle of the circus camp, but now he thought about it, he didn't know which way was out. The big marquee had almost all burned away, but the blaze had spread to the smaller tents, if the flames and sparks leaping above the dark line of the wagons were anything to go by. Their dying light spread red over the nearby city walls. Opposite was the tented city, no doubt in uproar now, and beyond it the forest.

'We should head for the woods,' he said finally. 'We can hide there for now, try and work out what to do. It's not safe here.'

'Magog is not afraid of anything. Hee hee. Gog will keep him safe with his burning flame.'

Errol looked at the old dragon, then at Benfro and finally at the chaos of flames and screaming. A couple of circus performers ran past and he saw the major flaw in his plan.

'Can you fly still?' he asked.

Benfro nodded.

'And what about . . . Magog?'

'He glides a few feet off the ground and a few dozen paces at a time. Why?'

'There's a mile of tents and people between us and the woods. I don't know how they'll react to us just walking through.'

'I don't think we're going to be walking.' Benfro stepped away from the side of the wagon, his gaze shifting to the wagons on the far side of the campfire, now little more than glowing coals. Dark shadows moved in the gloom. Then a panicked-looking woman rushed out into the space. Errol recognized Griselda and was about to shout to her, but one of the shadows resolved itself into a warrior priest wielding a blade of light. Without a word he swung, cutting the old woman down with a single blow. She toppled forward into the fire sending sparks crackling up into the night. Momentarily distracted, Errol searched for the warrior priest, but he had gone, his blade faded into the shadows.

The shadows. They moved, spreading out. Four indistinct shapes defying the light that leaped up from dead Griselda's burning clothes.

'Oh my. That's not a good place to sleep now, is it, missy.' The old dragon's voice cut through the tense silence that had fallen on the scene. Errol couldn't see

Benfro anywhere. Then there was a high-pitched scream, a billow of flame as one of the shadows coalesced into the figure of a man writhing, alight. He crashed into a wagon, setting it ablaze.

The remaining three shadows resolved themselves into warrior priests, and as they did, Errol understood what they were doing. It was the same magic Benfro had used to hide himself, if far more subtle. But there was no time to reflect on that, as one of the men rushed straight towards him, blade of light held high.

'Melyn will reward me for your head, traitor!'

Errol stood his ground, unsure why he wasn't afraid. With a thought he brought the lines to his vision, seeing how the warrior priest tapped them for the power he wielded. And, overlaid, he could see the aethereal form of the man, so ill defined, his aura just barely containing that terrible force. It was simple to reach out with his own mind, divert a little more of the Grym and tweak that fragile hold. He had never done anything remotely like it before and yet it seemed so obvious.

The warrior priest didn't even have time to scream. He lit up like a beacon, then dissolved into the air. There wasn't even smoke, and as Errol watched, still seeing the lines and the aethereal superimposed upon the dark world of the mundane, he could see the man sucked apart as if he were no more solid than air, dissipating back into the Grym whence he had come. It wasn't until he heard another scream that he remembered there had been other attackers.

Instinct saved him. He ducked and felt the heat of a blade of light pass over his head right where his neck would have been. Looking up, fully expecting to see the blade coming back for the killing blow, Errol was instead confronted with the sight of booted feet, kicking wildly, at the same height as his head.

'You shouldn't be so rude to Gog's friend. Magog's not happy at all with you.' The old dragon had the warrior priest by the neck, two long talons curving under his chin as he held the man aloft. There was a fire in his eyes, as if he knew he should be angry but couldn't quite remember what anger was or how it worked. The warrior priest still had his blade of light, and flailed around with it, trying to cut the arm that held him tight.

'Now now. Don't be like that,' Magog said and squeezed. Errol saw the warrior priest's eyes bulge white in the darkness, his face darkening as veins stood out on his forehead. The blade shivered out of existence, a warm pulse of Grym flowing out along the lines, and then with a horrible wet crunching sound the man's neck snapped. The old dragon threw him to one side like a discarded bone. 'Not very well made, these men.'

The dragon stepped forward and Errol instinctively retreated, his back against the wood of Loghtan's wagon.

'Don't be afraid of old Magog, little man. You're Gog's friend and my friend too.' The old dragon looked suddenly confused. 'But . . . where is Gog?'

They both scanned the open space, lit clearly by the burning wagon on one side.

Benfro appeared from between two more wagons and hurried towards them. 'We've got to go. The last one got away. There'll be more of them soon. Melyn's seen me. He'll come for us.'

They hurried through the narrow alleys between the wagons, searching for a path that would take them to the edge of the circus camp without getting too close to the burning mess of the marquee. That was where all the noise came from – the panicked shouting, the screams of pain. Errol listened for any sound of pursuit, but there was so much din it was difficult to tell if any of it was directed their way. Still he knew they were being followed, and it was only a matter of time before more warrior priests appeared. Their last victory had been luck more than skill. Faced with a larger force they wouldn't survive.

Turning a corner, Errol was hit with a smell at once sickening and familiar. It was the taint of manure, a sickly heavy odour overlaid with acrid ammonia. He saw the animal wagons parked in a long line, their far sides forming the wall of the circus camp. A short distance off, the lion-cats gnawed at the iron bars of their cage, their eyes glinting in the reflected firelight. All the animals were terrified, trapped when their every instinct was to flee.

'Damn. I should have brought the keys.' Freeing the creatures would have added to the chaos and made their escape easier.

'These keys?'

Errol turned and saw the old dragon holding up a heavy bunch. 'How . . . ?'

'Old Loghtan won't be happy if he loses his keys, will he. Magog'll keep them safe for him for now.'

'Umm. Can I have them?' Without a word, Magog handed them over. It was almost as if he had to obey. Errol didn't want to think what terrible things had happened to him over the years to make him so compliant.

And mad. Instead he set about finding the right key for the nearest cage. It was slow work, there were so many. He was on about the fifth wrong one when massive gnarled hands reached over and took the ring from him, sorted one key from the bunch, inserted it in the lock and twisted. There was an oiled *clack* and the door swung open. Timid eyes peered at him from the darkness beyond.

'Magog knows all the animals, he does. Knows which key works for which.'

'Can you free them? Free them all?'

There was something about the word that brought a spark to the old dragon's eyes. He stiffened as if he had been stabbed with a sharp stick, then trotted off with surprising speed, sorting the right key for each wagon as he ran between them. Faster and faster he went, throwing doors wide, shouting encouraging words to the creatures, who poked their heads out of newly opened doors, until finally he reached the lioncats.

'Better put some distance between us and them,' Benfro said. He pushed between two wagons, leaning against the boarding until it splintered and cracked, forming a hole big enough for Errol to squeeze through. 'We'll come over the top.'

Errol stepped through, then watched as the planks were pulled back roughly into their original positions. He looked out over the tented city and saw a mass of people running here and there. Fires had broken out all over, and the air was filled with the stench of burning. Flaming rags of canvas danced about in the wind, carrying this way and that, falling to the ground and starting new fires. He doubted anyone would stop them passing through.

A blast of wind overhead was Benfro landing close by. A short while later the old dragon appeared on the roof of the nearest wagon. He spread his wings wide, nothing like as magnificent as Benfro's, and leaped into the air, gliding to the ground a few dozen paces away. Almost at the same moment a cry went up. Errol looked round and saw Captain Osgal running his way, two dozen or more warrior priests hard on his heels.

'Quick. To the forest.' Errol set off at a run, hampered by his disguise. It had not fooled the warrior priests for an instant. There was no need for it now, and he would gladly be rid of it. He stole a look back over his shoulder and gasped to see Osgal much closer and rapidly narrowing the gap. His face was a picture of pure rage, and his blade of light burned fiercest white.

There was no mercy in his eyes; he meant only to kill.

10

When girl-queen births in a servant's bed
And princeling tempted yet defies his king
The end times come, fear stalks the widening sky
A different sun will light the ancient hall.

The Prophecies of Mad Goronwy

'I only wish Iolwen could be here at my side.'

Prince Dafydd sat on his horse looking from the ridge across the valley of the River Abheinn towards the city of Candlehall. Behind him his impromptu army, the Abervenn Irregulars as they had taken to calling themselves, camped in readiness for the coming siege.

'She's safer back in Abervenn, believe me. And if Beulah and her army come anywhere near, Master Holgrum will have her and your son out to sea and safety before they're in any danger.' Usel nudged his own horse forward until it was alongside the prince's. He was never far away these days, Dafydd thought. Always popping up when he was least expected, always smoothing over the inevitable problems that a mad endeavour such as this campaign generated. It was just as well, really. Without the medic they wouldn't have even started out, and his knowledge of the Twin Kingdoms was vast: there wasn't a village or town they had passed through that he hadn't already visited and made friends with the nobility and common people alike. It had made their journey that much easier.

Now, however, with the capital in sight, there was little even Usel could do to avoid the inevitable. There were warrior priests stationed at Candlehall, many hundreds of them. And the two other orders, though less well suited to fighting, would likely side with Beulah against a foreign invader even if he commanded an army of locals.

'How do we get in without enormous bloodshed?' Dafydd asked, looking back to the high-walled city perched on its hillside and almost completely surrounded by the wide twisting Abheinn.

'It shouldn't be too hard to take,' Captain Pelod chipped in. 'We've control of the river, so they can't get supplies in. It's a busy city, filled with people not accustomed to hunger, and their queen's not around to encourage them. I'd guess it won't take more than a week to starve them out.'

'And meanwhile Beulah's force-marching her army back from Tochers. They could be here in a fortnight.' Dafydd strained his eyes, trying to make out what was happening at the city gates.

'We don't know that,' Pelod said. 'Chances are she doesn't know anything about us yet.'

'I'd rather not leave things to chance, Jarius. You know what a fickle mistress she can be.'

'I don't think you need concern yourself with a siege just yet, sir.' Usel kicked his horse into a walk that took it over the ridge and down the shallow hill towards the river.

'Where are you going, man? We don't want to give them any more warning than necessary.' Dafydd spurred forward to catch up with the medic, who had let his horse break into a trot. Behind him he was aware of Captain Pelod and the rest of his mounted troop of Llanwennog soldiers following. They soon caught up with Usel, but by then a similar party was riding out of the city to meet them. Dafydd's heart sank; he had hoped his advance had gone unreported, but in reality the city must have known of his approach for days.

Shadowed by the distant citadel on top of its hill, the parties stopped, leaving a space of some five hundred paces between them.

'Who are they – Melyn's men?' Dafydd asked Usel.

'No, indeed. Quite the opposite. I don't see any warrior priests there, which is most surprising. And that appears to be Seneschal Padraig at the front. I didn't think he even owned a horse, much less knew how to ride one.'

'Introduce me to them, will you? I'd like to parlay.'

'I think that's a very good idea.' Usel turned in his saddle. 'Captain, would you join us but stay a few paces back?'

They rode at a slow walk, seeing three riders break from the opposite group and trot towards them.

'The seneschal. I don't recognize the other man, probably a scribe. Oh, and my old friend Father Gideon. He must be representing Archimandrite Cassters. This does look promising.'

Dafydd kept his thoughts to himself, glancing nervously up at the citadel. It loomed over him, its shadow a portent of doom, and yet it was also a place of obvious power, calling to him in a way he had never felt before. As if he were meant to be here.

Twenty paces apart, the two groups stopped. Dafydd

was primed for a shouted exchange, but to his astonishment the grey-haired old man, Seneschal Padraig, climbed stiffly off his horse, handed its reins to the scribe and walked forward. Dafydd tensed, suspecting a trap, though he could sense no one within a couple of hundred paces but those he could see.

'Am I addressing His Royal Highness Prince Dafydd of the House of Ballah?' The seneschal spoke perfect Llanwennog without a trace of accent.

'You are,' Dafydd replied. The seneschal bowed deeply in response, taking rather long to rise again, as if his back were not used to such exercise.

'Then I bid you welcome to Candlehall, sir. We throw ourselves upon your mercy and hope you will not destroy our proud city.'

Dafydd stared at the man for some moments before realizing that his mouth was hanging open. He closed it, unsure what to say.

Usel stepped in for him. 'I am to understand, Your Grace, that Candlehall does not intend to put up a fight?'

'Quite so, Healer Usel. Our gates are open now, and they will stay open. The Order of the Candle has long argued for greater ties between the House of Ballah and the House of Balwen, and the Order of the Ram is well known for pursuing its own ends regardless of fealty.'

'But what of the High Ffrydd?' Dafydd asked. 'Are there not many hundreds of warrior priests guarding the citadel?'

'Most of them have been recalled to Emmass Fawr by Master Andro, at my request. Several hundred have gone to join the queen at Tochers. Those that remain are confined to barracks and will not be a problem. Not all of the Order of the High Ffrydd are as dedicated to Queen Beulah as Inquisitor Melyn, Your Highness. And no one has seen or heard from him in several months.'

Dafydd looked at the seneschal, trying to see into the old man's mind. It was like beating his arms against a stone wall. The other elderly man, Father Gideon, was just as inscrutable, though he had a warmth and friendliness about him that Dafydd couldn't explain but which soothed his nerves nonetheless. The scribe was terrified, dragged by the leader of his order into a situation that one such as he should never have to experience. But his thoughts were clear and easy to read: as far as he was aware, everything the seneschal had said was true. There was no great love in the city for Beulah, and the news of Princess Iolwen's return had cheered the people enormously. The scribe had even been present at meetings where Padraig and various other city luminaries had discussed how best to deal with Melyn's warrior priests and how to welcome Dafydd to Candlehall.

But it was all a bit too convenient, almost as if the seneschal had picked this young man particularly for his openness, then made sure he was fed all the information that Dafydd could possibly want to know.

'You'll forgive my suspicion, Seneschal,' Dafydd said after a period of silence had passed. 'But my grandfather long ago taught me that when something appears too good to be true, that's usually because it is.'

'King Ballah is a wise man, though I would not myself have provoked Queen Beulah in quite the way he has. But please, Prince Dafydd. There is no need to remain out here in the cold. You are welcome in Candlehall, your army too. I offer myself as hostage to the good behaviour of the citizens.' The seneschal bowed his head, and in that moment Dafydd saw the truth of his words, as if the old man had consciously lowered his mental defences.

'What do you think, Usel? Jarius? Should we ride up to the citadel?'

'Seneschal Padraig is nothing if not a man of his word. If he guarantees your safety here, then he truly believes you'll be safe,' Usel said.

Captain Pelod rode forward to join them. 'I would be delighted to take the city without bloodshed, but I'm still wary of a trap, sir. I'd feel very vulnerable going in there alone.'

'Then fetch your army, Captain,' Padraig said. 'As I said, they are welcome too.'

Pelod looked at him, and Dafydd nodded. 'Go,' he said and watched the captain gallop back to his troop. There was a brief discussion, then two riders headed back to the ridge, disappearing over it. Soon the first ranks of the Abervenn Irregulars appeared in their place and began their slow march down the slope on to the plain. Dafydd turned back to the seneschal.

'Very well then. Lead us to the citadel. I've always wanted to see the Neuadd.'

Padraig remounted, turned his horse and led the party back towards the city. The riders who had come out with him fell in beside Dafydd's men, keeping a careful distance.

The first point of ambush was the wide stone bridge over the river, and Dafydd tensed as they approached it.

Pelod ordered men to ride across and fan out on the other side. Others checked under the arches and shouted warnings to a few boatmen on barges, but there was no threat.

The city gates were thrown wide, and no soldiers stood on the battlements. There were, however, many hundreds of people waiting outside. For a moment all was silence save for the *clop* of hooves on hard stone, the chinking of harness buckles. And then a shout went up, followed by another. More voices joined in, adding to the noise until a great wave of sound echoed out from the city walls. Dafydd tensed himself for an attack, prepared to conjure his blade. His guard closed around him, brave Llanwennogs all, hopelessly outnumbered and yet ready to fight to the death to save him. But the people were not rushing forward to attack; they were parting, lining the route and cheering, throwing hats, confetti and anything else they could find into the air.

And Dafydd felt the combined thoughts of all those minds. These were common people, not soldiers or minions of the state. They were worn down by preparations for a war they didn't want and couldn't understand. They were disaffected with years of neglect by their old king and the callous contempt of their new queen. But above all they had hope that things were going to get better.

There was no way Seneschal Padraig could have engineered their enthusiasm; it was genuine and heartfelt. They wanted him to free them from tyranny.

'It's all right, Jarius.' Dafydd pushed his horse through the ring of riders, through the open city gates and into Candlehall. 'We're welcome here.'

More people lined the wide street all the way from the

gates, right up the hill to the citadel. Dafydd began to understand something of his grandfather's magic as he basked in the adulation of so many. It could be tapped – no, they gave willingly of their energy, and he gorged on it until he felt there was nothing he could not do. Should Inquisitor Melyn and a hundred warrior priests appear from nowhere to do battle he might have been tempted to take them on single-handed, such was the heady potency of his exaltation.

At the top of the hill the citadel walls too were unmanned, and the gates stood wide. The party rode into an open courtyard, and Dafydd got his first look at the mighty bulk of the Neuadd, rising above the palace buildings that surrounded it.

'We must dismount here, Your Highness,' Seneschal Padraig said, swinging creakily out of his saddle and letting himself slowly to the ground. Dafydd followed suit, feeling no danger in this place, the lair of his enemy, but only welcome, as if it had been waiting for him since the first stones were laid millennia earlier.

He followed the seneschal through a series of connected halls, ornately decorated but smaller than those in the palace at Tynhelyg. The place had much the same atmosphere as Ballah's castle – of great power barely contained. Then Padraig nodded to two pages waiting ahead of them. They pushed open a pair of huge wooden doors and the party walked through into a wide cloister, beyond which stood the great hall itself.

Dafydd was staggered by the size of the place. It rose far higher than the substantial buildings around it, as if generations of kings had not dared build anything that might look down on that one massive structure. Closer, he could see that it was built in a completely different style from the rest of the citadel, formed from what looked like one seamless piece of rock. He had a sudden image of an army of workers laboriously hacking the hall out of the top of the hill, not building it at all so much as sculpting it. There were intricate carvings all over the outer surfaces of the hall, but many of these had been defaced, as if someone had tried to erase the story they told. Dafydd knew his history, was aware of the Brumal Wars and the damage inflicted on the city by sieges and sackings, but this damage seemed somehow much older and on a much more fundamental level.

Everyone fell silent as they walked across the courtyard surrounding the Neuadd. It was difficult not to be awed by the place. Even Seneschal Padraig, who must have seen it every day, bowed his head as he hurried forward and pushed at the doors. They swung open as if they weighed nothing despite their great size, and Dafydd was almost knocked over by the wave of power that swept out.

He stepped in alone, going from sunlight to almost total darkness. Then his eyes adjusted, or the scene allowed him to see it; there was so much magic in this place it was difficult to tell which. He barely noticed the great windows that swept up from the floor to the arched ceiling high overhead, nor the polished floor, so shiny it could have been still water he walked on. All he could see, all his mind could focus on, was the enormous black throne.

Empty.

It could be his. It was his for the taking. And the people would not complain; they welcomed him here. Even the seneschal would swear allegiance to him. Queen Beulah had lost her throne and didn't even know it yet. He just had to climb on to that dais and settle himself into the place that was rightfully his. Dafydd stood motionless for some time, soaking up the power that hummed around him. It reminded him of the hours he had spent with his grandfather, learning the ways of the Grym. The old man would be proud of him now, he was certain of it.

But something wasn't right. This was too like the castle in Tynhelyg. When he turned to look back to the doorway, he could see the seneschal, Usel the medic, Captain Pelod and Teryll all staring at him, their expressions expectant.

Dafydd shook his head, casting aside the enchantment that had so nearly overcome him. 'This is not for me. It was never for me.' He walked away from the vast black chair, ignoring the pull that was like claws in his back, tearing his skin as it tried to wrench him into the seat of power. 'This is Iolwen's throne.'

Benfro thought he should take pleasure from the chaos spreading through the vast camp. As he sped towards the distant trees he could see people running in all directions, some shouting for lost companions, some bleeding from horrible wounds. There was fire everywhere, as if it were alive like the flames he breathed. It leaped from tent to tent, ripping through the dry fabric and setting alight trapped people. Their screams and the smell of burning flesh and hair filled his senses with a hollow feeling of triumph. These were men, his enemies, and they were dying. And he had killed some of them himself. He almost felt good about it. Almost, but not quite.

They were closing on the forest now and outpacing the pursuing warrior priests comfortably since Benfro had scooped Errol up into his arms. They would probably have been closer to their goal had the old dragon not kept stopping to point out things and exclaim in delight. No matter how much Benfro tried to explain the urgency of the situation, nothing seemed to penetrate that addled jewel-bereft brain.

Another scream went up nearby but different in tone to the general panic. Benfro looked back to see what was going on and saw Magog staring at a blazing tent, his head cocked to one side as if thinking. Then, before Benfro could do or say anything, he pushed his way in through the flames.

'What's he up to now?' Benfro put Errol down, searching the distance for their pursuers. It was difficult to see through the chaos; it was possible that they had lost the warrior priests, but he didn't want to count on it.

'I'm not sure. I think he's trying to help that woman.' Errol pointed to a figure standing by the blazing tent. Benfro trotted over just in time for the old dragon to come bursting out through the flames, shaking cinders out of his ears. He had his wings wrapped around him like a blanket, and once he was clear, he opened them, revealing a couple of terrified children in his arms. He bowed low and handed them to the woman, who stopped her screaming and stared.

'We've not got time for this, Magog. We have to reach the trees.' Benfro stumbled over the name – it meant too much to him of pain and suffering – but he could think of nothing else to call the dragon. 'Come. We need to run.'

'Can't leave the little ones to burn. Oh no. That would be too cruel.'

'Well, you've saved them now, so let's go.' Out of the corner of his eye Benfro saw something that sent a chill through him. Focusing on it he made out the dark shapes of hidden warrior priests. They moved slowly now, no more than jogging pace, and they were going methodically from tent to tent. As they passed each one, it burst into flames. Anyone close to them was cut down by brief flashes of conjured blade.

Then he heard a voice pierce the general noise: 'Dragon! To me, men.'

Benfro didn't need more warning. He grabbed his old companion by the arm, hauling him round. Ahead of them, Errol was running towards the trees.

'But what of the little ones? We can't leave them here.'

'We can't take them with us, either. They'll have to look after themselves.' Benfro snatched a quick look behind him, seeing the woman standing motionless, her two children clinging to her. They would be lucky to survive the next minute, let alone the night. He could do something about that – could fight the warrior priests even now rushing towards them – but he owed nothing to them. He had to leave them. Even so he felt a terrible weight of guilt on his shoulders as he did so.

Dragging the reluctant old dragon behind him, Benfro ran through the thinning lines of tents and on to a narrow strip of grass in front of the trees. He was just in time to see Errol stop at the forest edge and wave them on. Then the boy disappeared into the gloom. Not even bothering to look back, Benfro sprinted across the grass and fought his way through the thick-leaved shrubs that marked the border between grass and trees. He could hear the old dragon pushing through behind him.

'Dark in here, isn't it?' said Magog.

'And quiet too.' Benfro strained his ears, barely making out the sounds of mayhem out on the plain. A few dozen paces into the woods and it was almost silent, as if he had walked into another world. 'Errol? Are you there?'

There was a sudden noise, the cracking of a twig underfoot somewhere deeper in the trees, and at the same time Benfro also heard the crashing of many bodies coming through the shrubs and the harsh voice of Captain Osgal.

'Fan out, men. Find them before they get too deep.'

Benfro grabbed Magog by the arm again and headed in the direction of the broken twig. He moved silently – Ynys Môn would have been proud of him – but his companion trampled along with all the finesse of a stampeding ox. Pushing past low branches and watching out for roots that had no purpose other than to trip him, Benfro had to hope that he could maintain a decent speed, get enough of a lead on his pursuers. It was a forlorn hope; the warrior priests were dogged in their pursuit. Had they not chased him halfway across Gwlad already?

He reached the point in the dark woods where he was sure he had heard the twig snap, but there was no sign of Errol. It was too dark even for his keen vision, and the trunks of the great trees made it all but impossible to see far anyway.

'Have you seen Errol?' Benfro asked the old dragon, who stood motionless in the darkness, not even breathing hard.

'No. But we could ask this squirrel. Maybe he knows.'

It took a moment for the words to sink in. Benfro looked across, following the old dragon's gaze until he saw a familiar shape sitting on a low-hanging branch nearby.

'Malkin?'

'Benfro find friend. Benfro come quickly, before men arrive.' The squirrel jumped down from its perch, scampered over the ground and leaped into Benfro's arms, scrambling up over his shoulder and settling behind his neck. Benfro felt such a surge of happiness he almost fell over.

'Malkin! Where did you go? Where have you been?' Tears sprang from his eyes, and his voice rose an octave or two, breaking slightly.

'No talk now. Follow path now. Mother waits.' The squirrel slapped Benfro across the side of his head as if chastising him. Nothing could have made the dragon happier than to comply.

It was a surprisingly short distance, no more than a few hundred paces in all, and then they were stepping out of the tall trees into a vast clearing. The sky overhead was clear and sprinkled with stars so bright it could have been day. And there at the centre of the clearing, towering above everything else, the mother tree stood magnificent underneath a fat full moon. Benfro looked back and was sure he saw the trunks shifting together, blocking the way to anyone who might try to follow them.

The old dragon glanced around, sniffed the air like a dog, acting as if the sight of the mother tree was nothing new or special to him. Benfro looked for Errol, hoped he was somewhere ahead, safe already, but the clearing was empty. There was just him, Malkin on his shoulders, the other dragon at his side and the mother tree.

The boy was nowhere to be seen.

Errol held his breath, willed his heart to stop. Something cracked away to his left and he snapped his head round, straining to see in the blackness. He knew that Benfro and the other dragon were close; they had been just behind him when he had entered the forest. But Osgal and his men were nearby too, so he didn't dare shout or even whisper.

His back against the reassuring bulk of the tree, his cloak wrapped around him for protection and camouflage, Errol sank down until he was sitting on the ground with his knees tucked up to his chest. He tried to settle himself, to listen out for any movement near him. Perhaps if he just waited, the warrior priests would miss him and head deeper into the woods.

He almost believed himself. Almost, but not quite. He knew far too much about the Order of the High Ffrydd, too much about the warrior priests, too much about Inquisitor Melyn. They would never stop looking for him. Wherever he went, they would soon follow, bringing death and destruction with them.

A familiar feeling cut through Errol's musings: someone was close by. He had been motionless, but now he froze completely, not even breathing. He could sense another person, perhaps more than one, and then he began to hear noises. Hiding under his cloak had perhaps not been the wisest of moves. He could see nothing through the dark fabric pulled over his head, and yet neither could he move in case that was enough to reveal his hiding place. All he could do was hold his breath and try to gauge how many people there were from the noises they made and the indefinable sensation of their presence.

Moving his head just the tiniest of fractions, Errol opened his mind to the aethereal and, no longer blinded by his cloak, studied the scene. He had just enough time to make out the still figures of ten warrior priests standing directly in front of him. Unlike the usual indistinct flames of flickering Grym that people normally produced, their forms were oddly well defined, almost perfect images of the men. Then the nearest leaned forward, his arm sweeping down, and something hard connected with the side of Errol's head.

The world turned upside down in a flurry of noise and motion. And then nothing.

I I

All the dragons of the Ffrydd have sought out the mother tree, and she has blessed them with their choice. She is the beginning of us, and the end. Always we are welcome under her spreading branches, and her bounty is endless. But she is not like us: her ways are strange, and her aid is never quite what it seems. Accept her succour, for to refuse would be the action of a fool. But do not think her help comes without a price.

Sir Frynwy, *Tales of the Ffrydd*

At least the sickness had stopped; she had that much to be thankful for. Beulah was finding it increasingly uncomfortable to sit in a saddle, however. Not to mention the difficulty of getting on to a horse in the first place. She had known the child would grow large inside her, but nothing had prepared her for quite how large, and how inconvenient, the baby would become. If she didn't receive word from Melyn soon, she might have to leave the army and return to Candlehall before the campaign started. There was no way her heir was going to be born in a dingy little town like this.

Tochers was a mean-spirited place set at the southern end of the narrow Rhedeg pass. Even in times of peace between the two nations travellers had seldom followed this route to Llanwennog. It was easier to take a boat from Abervenn, sail around the Caldy peninsula and up the Sea of Tegid to Talarddeg; easier yet to go through the Wrthol pass and across the border country. The Rhedeg had no doubt been named ironically; there was no running through its twisting valleys and steep climbs. But it was still possible to march a hardy army through, especially towards the end of summer when even the most persistent snow had thawed and the dry season had shrunk the rivers until they were easy to ford. And so it was that Tochers existed, little more than a guard post on the back door into the Twin Kingdoms.

The army had camped on a ragged upland plain between the small grey town and the entrance to the pass. Since her arrival several days earlier Beulah had made it her business to ride along the neatly spaced lines of tents and through the training grounds. She knew the value of being seen by her soldiers, of mixing with the men who were going to fight and die for her cause. Had she not been heavily pregnant, she would have been tempted to pitch a tent in the middle of the camp and live there, but Clun had persuaded her to stay in the relative comfort of Castle Tochers instead.

Watching the ranks of soldiers practising their swordsmanship, Beulah couldn't help being impressed with just how far her rough peasant army had come. The quaisters and warrior priests Melyn had posted to the armies had worked hard to drum some discipline and skill into the conscripted labourers and journeymen.

'They're quite a sight, aren't they, my love?' she said as

Clun rode over on his huge black stallion. Soldiers melted out of his way, and she could feel their fear of the creature, though they tried their best to hide it. That too was a positive sign.

'They've trained well, my lady. It's true. But I don't know how much longer we can keep them here. Some of these men have been away from their homes for months.'

'Well, it won't be long now. We'll hear from Melyn soon. Then we can march.'

'You're very confident. What if the inquisitor's been captured? Or killed?'

Beulah stared at her consort. She brushed the edge of his thoughts, looking for signs of mutiny or fear, but as ever he was just stating what to him was obvious. It was, however unlikely, a possibility, and as such had to be considered.

'Melyn won't fail us – trust me on that. I'd know if anything had happened to him.'

'I believe he'll succeed,' Clun said. 'But every day I search the aethereal for a sign of him, and every day I find none. He should have contacted us by now, surely.'

Beulah didn't answer. Now that Clun had voiced the possibility of failure, it weighed heavily on her mind. Yet she was certain she would know if the inquisitor had come to any harm. They had a connection she couldn't fully explain. He had always been able to sense her feelings, even when she was miles away, and she in turn could read his mood though she was in Candlehall and he back at Emmass Fawr. But her pregnancy had severely hampered her ability to control the Grym and cut her off completely from the aethereal. What else might it have affected? The question went unanswered as she was distracted by a messenger who hailed her from a distance, bowing deeply.

'Your Majesty, Your Grace. General Cachog requests you return to the castle. We have news from Dina.'

'We'll come immediately. Assemble the troop captains in the castle yard.' Beulah kicked her horse into a trot, steering it towards the town as the messenger saluted. Clun's stallion outpaced her mare without difficulty, and she was tempted to push her mount harder, but a twinge in her belly, her child moving awkwardly, stopped her. Even a bouncing trot was supremely uncomfortable, so she slowed to a walk, breathing slowly and deeply to ease the pain. By the time she reached the castle courtyard, lowered herself out of the saddle and walked into the dimly lit main hall, the rest of the party was already assembled.

'Your Majesty.' General Cachog bowed his head and motioned for someone to come forward from the shadows. 'We've just received a bird from Dina.'

The man wore a heavy leather apron, and thick gauntlets hung from a hook on his wide belt. His face was a mess of new cuts and old scars, and as he bowed stiffly and handed her a small scroll, Beulah could see he was missing the ends of several fingers. Carrier hawks were notoriously vicious beasts; she hoped the bird in question was securely caged.

The message was short and simple, and it made Beulah's heart soar. She turned to Cachog. 'The bulk of Geraint's army has been seen marching from Wrthol and heading back towards Tynhelyg at great speed. General, do we have any news from our scouts?'

'The last report was the same as before. Tordu has his men camped around Tynewydd. Too many for us to storm the pass.'

'Well, that might be about to change. Send a bird back to Dina. Tell General Otheng to begin his attack immediately. By the Wolf, I thought it would be Tordu who'd break and run; you can defend Rhedeg with a much smaller force. What's Melyn done to get Geraint so worked up he'd risk losing Wrthol?'

'He's killed Ballah and taken Tynhelyg.'

Beulah whirled to see Clun standing as if he were held up by ropes. His hands hung limp at his sides, his shoulders slumped and his face was strangely blank. She felt a shiver run through her, as if someone were caressing her face, stroking her hair.

'Melyn?'

'He is here. In the aethereal.' Clun spoke in a higher voice than normal, the words without inflection. It was unnerving.

'How? No, never mind. What is the situation? What do you mean you've killed Ballah and taken Tynhelyg? You were meant to be sacking the northlands.'

There was a pause as if Beulah's words had to be relayed over a great distance. General Cachog stared nervously at Clun, while the bird handler had turned white, making his scars stand out on his face like a cruel game of noughts and crosses.

'The opportunity arose. It was worth the risk. He cannot stay long. The city is in turmoil and there is much work to do. Begin the attack. Relieve the siege.'

'What siege?'

But Clun didn't answer. He dropped to his knees as if his ropes had been cut and would surely have toppled forward to the floor had not General Cachog caught him. Beulah was at his side in an instant, cradling his head. His face was cold and clammy with sweat, his eyes tight shut, teeth clenched as if he fought some inner battle.

'Clun, my love. Are you all right?'

'Where am I? My lady . . . ?' Clun opened his eyes and stiffened as he came to his senses. Beulah pushed him down as he tried to get to his feet.

'Take your time, my love. You were speaking to Inquisitor Melyn. How did he appear to you? What did he say?'

Clun said nothing for a while, his eyes darting about the room as if he had never seen it before. Beulah watched the colour slowly come back into his face.

Finally he spoke. 'It was . . . I don't know. Strange. It wasn't like the aethereal. I wasn't in a trance, not properly. You were giving orders and then suddenly Melyn was standing there beside you. Only he looked different somehow. Like there was someone else there too.'

'Never mind that,' Beulah said. 'What did he say?'

'I . . . He said that he had taken Tynhelyg, that he had killed Ballah and captured the city. He knows that Geraint will force-march his army back to the capital as soon as he finds out his father is dead. They are preparing for a siege and expect our forces to relieve them. General Otheng knows already; there are warrior priests at Dina who are adept enough to glimpse the aethereal, and Melyn is so much stronger now. I don't know how. I wasn't looking for . . . He put me in the trance.'

With those last words Clun pushed himself upright,

running his hands over his face and rubbing at his eyes as if he had just woken from a long sleep.

'It wasn't a very nice feeling.'

'But it was definitely Melyn?' Beulah asked, although she knew the answer already. However faint it had been, she had felt his touch. And through her pregnancy too. Clun was right: something had happened to the inquisitor to make him much more powerful.

'It was him.'

'Then we had better get started. General.' Beulah stood and General Cachog helped Clun to his feet. The bird handler stepped forward, bowing nervously.

'Do you still want me to send a bird to Dina, Your Majesty?'

'No, that won't be necessary.' The man's relief was palpable. He bowed deeply and scurried away, no doubt to treat the wounds that had not yet formed into scars.

Out in the courtyard the warrior priest captains were assembled and waiting. Beulah stood on the steps outside the main castle door to address them. With a conscious effort she tapped into the lines, feeding her words directly to her audience to add emphasis to her voice. Only, as she was about to speak, she felt something very strange, as if a cloud of coldness had slipped over the sun even though it remained as bright as before. The warrior priests felt it too. She could sense their controlled alarm, their readiness to fight. And then, with a sickening feeling in her swollen abdomen, she remembered where she had first encountered that unpleasant distortion of the Grym – in a foothill village a thousand miles from here, swathed in fog and empty of people.

Looking up, she scanned the sky for anything moving. It was bright and blue, the sun high overhead and scarcely a cloud in sight. But there, to the south-west, was a tiny speck. Closer and closer it came, until it resolved itself into two birds flying side by side. Then large birds. Then too large for birds. She had never really believed that they were birds at all.

A pair of dragons flew lazily through the air, wingspans wider than anything she had seen before. Their scales glittered in the sunlight and their long tails whipped up and down with each great beat of their wings. Either they could not see the town and the army camped beneath its walls, or they chose not to. Their destination seemed to be the mountains.

Beulah felt a hum of power flow through the lines around her. She dragged her eyes from the dragons and saw Clun, his gaze locked skywards, his hand moving forward.

'No, my love. Do not draw their attention.' She spoke as loudly as she dared, hoping her voice would carry at least to the front row of warrior priests. 'No one is to conjure their blade unless I tell them to.'

The hum subsided as a hundred warrior priests relaxed. All eyes were fixed on the dragons. From so far she could not tell if either of them was Caradoc, and a chill ran through her at the thought there could be three such beasts loose in her realm. Where had they all suddenly come from?

The dragons climbed, dwindling back to bird-shaped specks as they rose over the mountain pass. In what seemed like an age but was no time at all they had disappeared against the grey rock and purple heather, heading towards Tynewydd and Llanwennog beyond. And still they all stared, tense, waiting for the creatures to come diving back, talons outstretched in attack.

The sound of galloping hooves on the stone road broke the spell. A lone rider hurtled through the castle gates and pulled his horse up. He dropped out of his saddle and shouted at the nearest soldier.

'Bring him forward,' Beulah commanded. The man was jostled across the yard and up the steps. He was filthy with dust, his hair matted as if he had ridden non-stop for days. When he saw the queen, he dropped to his knees and bowed his head.

'Your Majesty, I bring grave news. Candlehall is taken.'

The old dragon wandered about the clearing, peering at things. Occasionally he would bend down, scoop up a fallen branch or a flower, look at it closely and then put it back again. He seemed quite unperturbed by the abrupt change from deep forest night to the other-worldly light of this place. Benfro only wished he could be as relaxed.

'What happened to him, Malkin? What happened to Errol?' He paced back and forth at the edge of the clearing, trying to see through the thick shrubs that marked its edge. The squirrel still perched on his shoulder rocked back and forth with each change of direction, digging its claws into his neck.

'Malkin not know Errol. Malkin just look for dragons. Malkin find dragons.'

'Yes. Yes, you did. Thank you. But my friend is out there still, being hunted by men.'

'I am afraid that they have captured your friend,

Benfro. I'm sorry, but he was too far away, and there were too many for me to hide him from them all.'

Benfro swung round so fast that Malkin almost flew off his shoulder. Standing just a few paces away from him, the mother tree bowed her slender head in sorrow, and for a moment it felt like the clearing had been plunged into winter. Then she looked up again, and the night sky filled with light. It was hard to be worried in her presence. She filled him with a sense of peace and calm.

The other dragon seemed less impressed. He sauntered up to where she stood, sniffed loudly and offered her a flower he had just plucked. 'I am Magog, Son of the Summer Moon,' he said. 'And this is my brother Gog. We are the greatest dragons ever to have lived, you know.'

'I don't think so, Sir Tremadog. You are a better dragon by far than Magog ever was.'

'Sir Tremadog? Eh? Who's he then?' The dragon blustered, but Benfro could see a change in him, as if the name had woken some deep-buried memory. Memory. The old dragon's jewels. He looked down and saw, still clasped tightly in his hand, the small wooden box that Errol had given him. How had he managed to hold on to it all this time?

'They took his jewels out, one by one. Can you put them back?' He offered the box to the mother tree. She took it from him, opening it and picking out one of the tiny red jewels.

'I could, Benfro. And I can see that you have only the noblest of aims when you suggest it. But to do so would render him quite mad.'

'But he's mad already.' Benfro tried to speak softly,

though the other dragon was paying no attention to them any more, having wandered off to talk to some rabbits hopping around in the grass.

'He's confused, simple. He doesn't remember anything of his past. But he's not mad. If I were to put these back in his head, it would be filled with unconnected images, memories of great pain and torture, of loss and betrayal. They would plunge him into a madness such as you cannot imagine.'

'Is there anything you can do for him?'

'Of course, Benfro. I can keep him here, where he will come to no harm. In time he will get better, though he'll never be the proud dragon I remember. But come. You look starved, both of you. Let us eat, and you can tell me your tale.'

A table laden with food appeared in front of him, filling the air with a smell that made his mouth water and his stomach gurgle. Benfro couldn't remember when last he had eaten, and breathing fire had left him completely empty. But even as his legs propelled him towards the feast, he remembered the world outside this unreal bubble.

'I can't,' he said. 'I've got to try and find Errol. I have to help him.'

For a moment the whole scene shimmered, fading away. Ranks of tall trees overlaid the clearing like ghostly shadows, packed so tight together even the starlight couldn't penetrate. Benfro wondered if he had done something wrong. Had anyone ever refused the mother tree before? She looked at him with a glare that reminded him of his mother and then relented. The moment passed.

'You must eat, Benfro. You'll be no use to your friend

if you're weak with hunger. Now sit and tell me about this young man. I'm surprised that you would befriend one of his kind after what they've done to you.'

'He's different. He helped me fight off Magog when he didn't need to.' Benfro glanced nervously at the point in the air between his eyes, though he couldn't see his aura just then. He was tired, not thinking straight. He should have checked his mental defences as soon as he had thrown off Loghtan's control. But it was difficult to stay worried for any length of time here. Benfro could feel nothing of Magog's presence. Something kept it away for now, so he might as well make the most of it.

The mother tree took her seat at the head of the table, long white hair tumbling over her shoulders, slender, angular ears protruding through it on either side of her head. She took an apple in her long-fingered hand, caressing its shiny red skin but not eating. On the other side of the table Sir Tremadog had settled himself down and was tucking in noisily.

'I have to get rid of Magog,' Benfro said, 'and I need to find a way to Gog's world. Even if Gog's dead, there must be other dragon mages there who would know how to break the curse. Or how to find my way back to the place of the standing stone. Magog's bones lie there; with them I could reckon his jewel and be free of him.'

'Gog's world, eh?' Sir Tremadog said. 'I knew a dragon once who was trying to find a way there. Looked all over Gwlad for it, he did.'

'But you told me the window was at Candlehall,' Benfro said. 'I even saw it. Or at least I saw something.'

'Old Gog's forgotten again, hasn't he. I can't go

anywhere near the hall of candles. Makes me ill just to think of the place. But I can't let you have your world and not know what's going on. So I made me a window too, in a place where you won't know about it.'

It took Benfro a moment to work out what the dragon was saying. Benfro had never accepted the roles of Gog and Magog that Loghtan had given them. And until a few seconds ago he had forgotten the incident when Sir Tremadog had begun to tell him of the windows between the worlds.

'Where did you make this window?'

'Well I'm hardly going to tell you, brother mine. After what you did to me.'

'Perhaps then, good sir dragon, you would tell me?' The mother tree leaned forward, and in the same motion she changed, once more taking on that shape of perfect dragon beauty.

'Ammorgwm?' Sir Tremadog dropped the handful of food he had been transporting to his mouth. It landed on the table with a dull *plop* as he stared intently at the vision in front of him. 'You came back?'

'I want you to tell me about the window that you made between the two worlds. Where is it?'

'Close. Not far at all. But I can't tell. Not with Gog listening. He mustn't know about it. Oh no. That would spoil the surprise.'

'I'm not Gog.' Benfro dropped his head to the table. 'I'm not your brother. I'm Benfro, son of Morgwm the Green and Sir Trefaldwyn of the Great Span.'

'He will take time to adjust, time to reorder what memories he has.' Benfro felt a hand on his arm and looked up into the great black eyes of Ammorgwm, the mother tree. He was tired, the effort of their escape and the trauma of his captivity beginning to catch up with him. It would be so easy to surrender to those eyes, to let sleep take him over, but the last time he had done that, he had lost months. Errol could be dead in hours.

Shaking his head to try and clear it of sleep, he pushed thoughts of rest as far from his mind as possible.

'O Benfro, I should know better than to argue with a dragon whose mind is made up. Here, eat these. They will give you the strength you need.'

The mother tree waved her hand and a plate piled with strange fruit appeared in front of him. He hesitated, but she nodded her head. Mindful of his manners and conscious that he really did need to eat, Benfro took a piece and bit into it. His mouth was filled with a wonderful flavour. As he swallowed, he could feel his strength building in a way that only emphasized how weak and tired he had been. He took another piece. It was better than the first and it filled his stomach with a warm glow. The third was tastier still, and he started cramming the food into his mouth. Only after some minutes did he remember his manners, put down the last piece of fruit uneaten and push the plate away.

'Thank you,' he said, all too aware that the mother tree, still wearing the form of Ammorgwm the Fair, had watched him like an indulgent mother might watch a hatchling. 'I could eat more, but then I'd fall asleep. Already it's been too long; I must go back for Errol.'

'You won't find him in the forest. If he were here, I would be able to help him.' The mother tree stood and

Benfro automatically got up from his bench. 'They've taken him to the city, where my influence is diminished. But there are ways. Please, follow me.'

Benfro found himself beside the great tree that towered over the centre of the clearing. It had been distant while he had eaten, although he had hardly walked more than a half-dozen paces, yet now he could reach out and touch the rough bark. It split beneath his fingers, opening up into a dark cleft.

'You'll find what you seek inside.'

He looked back, seeing the table still laden with food. Sir Tremadog sat on the bench, his back to them, his arms working away as he fed himself.

'He'll be all right?' Benfro asked.

'You don't need to take responsibility for every dragon, Benfro. I will look after Sir Tremadog. He will be happy here. Now find your friend. There's much still you have to do.'

Benfro stepped into the cleft in the tree, feeling the grass give way to soft dirt beneath his feet. The opening became a narrow fissure dropping down into the earth. It smelt musty and dank, like forest loam disturbed, and behind that powerful musk there was a drier, dustier aroma reminiscent of Corwen's cave. Turning once more, he saw the entrance closing, the serene face of the mother tree watching him go.

'Thank you, again,' he said, but whether he spoke quickly enough, he didn't know. Noiselessly the bark sealed and he was plunged into darkness.

Something of the ease and comfort of the mother tree stayed with him for a while, and Benfro felt no fear as he descended. At first he went by touch, feeling the walls with his hands. But soon his eyes adjusted to the darkness and he could see the faintest of illumination far ahead, red like the glow of dying embers. The warmth of the clearing faded slowly away, the moisture of the forest drying out with each new step, and as he moved along the tunnel, so his feeling of security dissolved like autumn mist. Unease took its place, a familiar gnawing fear that almost had him turning back.

Then the rough earth of the tunnel wall abruptly changed. Now his talons traced their course over smooth stonework, his feet felt the cold of ancient flagstones. In the gloom ahead he could make out the arched ceiling of a small aperture leading through to another space still obscured from view. One step, two steps, three. Benfro kept going, though he knew already what sight was going to greet him.

Squat pillars held up a low ceiling, marching away from where he stood and on into the indistinct darkness. The air was cold, with a scent of winter trees stripped of leaves and life, and everywhere there was that dull glow of red, too familiar to be anything but uncomfortable.

Row upon row of small alcoves had been cut into the stone, and in each one sat a pile of unreckoned crimson jewels.

12

The child will come too early to its world
Its mother's love, its father's pride
Will leave its fate for beast and bird to decide.

The Prophecies of Mad Goronwy

The palace held far more secrets than he could have ever anticipated. There were moments when Melyn felt like he was a child once more, discovering all the wonders of the world for the first time. Each new find increased his respect for Ballah and at the same time filled him with a sense of unstoppable power. He had killed the king who ruled this domain, after all. And now all that Tynhelyg held was his to command. His to use.

Ballah's throne room was less ostentatious than the Neuadd, the great carved wooden chair a pale imitation of the splendour of the Obsidian Throne. Still he had felt a surge of power, of being connected directly to the Grym, when he sat upon it. Achieving the aethereal had been simplicity itself, and he found the whole of Gwlad laid out before him. It had been the work of moments to find Prince Geraint's army striking camp on the plains outside Wrthol. Melyn had spent some time watching the mounting chaos as the Llanwennog army prepared to march back to Tynhelyg. He was not worried; by the time they reached here he would either have the city under his complete control and prepared for a siege, or he would have fled back to the northlands and across the mountains. Either way, the proud Llanwennog kingdom would be in ruins, and the Wrthol pass wide open to Beulah's peasant army. The queen knew what was happening; relief would come sooner rather than later.

But there was no time for resting on his laurels. Swift though the fall of the city had been, persuading the people that they were better ruled by him and his warrior priests was not going to be easy, and there was so much here in this palace to discover, he really didn't want to have to give it all up. Neither did he want to march back through the forest. Even with the dragon to help, he would lose valuable men, and time.

The dragon.

Melyn cursed, looking out the windows to the pale glint of dawn over the palace gardens.

'Get over to the merchants' quarter. Bring the dragon Frecknock to me at once.' He watched the young warrior priest scurry out of the throne room on his errand and hoped it wasn't too late. He didn't know what had made him order Frecknock's execution. It seemed like a lifetime ago, not a few short hours. But everything had changed, and he wanted to show her just how much he had achieved.

'Your Grace?'

Melyn looked up to see a small group of his men standing nervously several paces from the throne as if he were a terrible king whose wrath was to be feared. It was good that they were afraid of him again; the months on the road had bred an unwelcome familiarity between the different ranks of his warrior priests.

'What?'

'We've brought you the king's . . . that is, Ballah's personal effects.' The leader of the group held up a bundle of rich velvet and cotton clothes, neatly folded. On top of them were a few items of jewellery and a small wooden box. This was a disappointment. Melyn would have liked a crown, even though he knew that Ballah had never worn one.

'Bring them to me,' he said, not rising from his seat. The bundle was placed at his feet. 'What of Ballah?'

'His head adorns the south gate, as per your instructions, sir. His body is on the pyre with the rest of the dead.'

'Good. Leave me. Get some rest.' Melyn dismissed the men, watching them troop out, seeing how tired some of them looked. True adepts would take the energy they needed from the Grym and had no need of sleep. Had he let his standards slip so far as to bring second-rate warrior priests with him on this mission?

Shaking the thought from his head, Melyn turned his attention to the pile of clothes and jewellery. It was much as he would have expected, except that Ballah had worn soft silk undergarments more suited to a woman than a great king. His clothes were in the main well made from the finest materials but not showy like some of the garments paraded about Candlehall. His jewellery was similarly understated, though some of the items hummed with power. He examined them carefully, looking for traps and finding several that would have certainly killed anyone trying to use them.

He was about to turn his attention to the small wooden box when a noise from the far side of the room distracted him. Looking up, Melyn saw Frecknock standing in the doorway flanked by the two warrior priests he had left as her guard. She bowed when she saw he had noticed her.

'Your Grace.'

'Ah, Frecknock. Come. Tell me what you think of these baubles.'

She walked briskly across the room, her talons digging into the thick carpet and pulling up small tufts with each step. Her two guards had to trot to keep up, and Melyn couldn't quite understand why he found this amusing. Nor why he was so pleased to see that she was alive. Still, there was something in the way she deferred to him completely, bowing deeply before accepting the collection of rings, amulets and other trinkets Ballah had worn about his person.

'Some of these have been imbued with great power,' she said, swiftly discarding those items that were simply ornamental. 'This one helps you to achieve the aethereal trance, but it's got a nasty curse on it. And this one . . .' She held up a plain silver ring. 'This one has a linking spell woven into it. I suspect there are several other such rings, maybe as many as six. They would make communicating over great distances much easier than using the aethereal, particularly if you wanted to talk to someone who didn't have the skill to see in that plane, or if you were not sure where they were.'

Melyn took the ring, rolling it around in his hand, feeling its warmth. 'But who has the others?' he asked. 'Where does Ballah have his most important spies?'

'I would advise caution if you are considering using the ring, sir. It's protected by some very subtle spells.'

'I know. Perhaps you might help me in undoing them. But first let's see what Ballah kept on his person but didn't wear.' Melyn picked up the small wooden box and ran his fingers over it. There was a familiar power about it, an echo of something he couldn't quite put his finger on. But whatever it was, he could sense no danger from it. Flipping up a tiny metal latch, he opened the box.

Inside, nestling in a shaped velvet liner, lay a simple silver ring set with a single dark crimson jewel, its face cut in an ancient style. Melyn looked from it to the ring on the index finger of his right hand, the ring given to King Balwen by the Shepherd and then to Brynceri by King Balwen. The two were identical.

'What trickery is this?' Melyn reached for Ballah's ring, then he thought better of it, handing the box to Frecknock. 'Here, what do you make of this?'

She took the box from him, her enormous hands dwarfing it and yet somehow holding it elegantly. She didn't take the ring out but ran her dark fingers over it with soft caresses, as if feeling for blemishes on the surface of a mirror. Finally she handed the box back to him.

'There are no curses on this, but it is a thing of great power. I cannot begin to understand how King Ballah came to have it, but it is something of your god, the Shepherd. It feels the same.'

Melyn looked at the ring again, debating with himself what it could mean. The dragons had stolen their book of magic from the Shepherd, so it was possible that Ballah's ancestors had stolen this ring. But why had he never heard of it before? Why had the Shepherd not told him of it? It was, he knew, unwise to question the ways of God, but he couldn't help being concerned.

'Should I touch it?' He spoke the question even though he had meant to keep it to himself.

'There is no ill intent in it, sir. But it is an artefact of great power. One without sufficient skill in the subtle arts might well be overwhelmed by it.'

Melyn looked at the dragon, seeing her eyes properly for the first time. They were not pure black orbs, but flecked with tiny speckles of gold, like a night sky spanned with stars. It was hard to read her intent, hard to understand the strange thought patterns of a dragon. And yet he couldn't help feeling that she was on his side in this. She wanted him to master the ring as he had mastered her.

At that moment Melyn knew that Frecknock was truly his creature to command. She could no more see him come to harm than she could throw herself from a cliff on to broken rocks. Her secrets, her knowledge of magic, were his for the asking. And this ring, this enigma, was just the beginning.

He was reaching for it, about to pluck it from its velvet cushion, when the double doors to the throne room burst open. Captain Osgal pushed his way through, dragging something behind him. His face was dark, his cheeks bloodied and torn as if he had been fighting some wild animal. As he came closer, Melyn could see his robes were ripped, hanging from his large frame in tatters.

'My men are still hunting the dragon,' Osgal said, hauling his cargo round and dumping it on the floor in front of the throne, 'but we caught this one.'

Melyn looked down at the unconscious form curled up like a hibernating caterpillar. For some unaccountable reason wearing women's clothes. Errol Ramsbottom. With Brynceri's ring helping him, the boy's secret would soon be his.

He ran down the corridor, no thought for the noise of his feet on the flagstones, which echoed through the emptiness. It was important he get wherever he was going as quickly as possible, though he wasn't sure whether it was fear that drove him on or desperation. In truth, he wasn't quite sure where he was at all; it seemed familiar, like something from a dream perhaps. But it was too real to be a dream. His breath was too short, the cold stone beneath his feet too hard, the oily smoke from the far-spaced torches too acrid as it burned his throat and eyes. He looked down at his hands, seeing them as if for the first time. The fingers seemed too slender, the skin paler than he remembered.

Stopping at the end of the corridor, he bent down, hands on knees, gulping down deep breaths as he tried to sort out the tumble of images and memories in his head. He knew this castle, knew the people who lived in the lower levels and the dragons who walked the upper halls. But there was something wrong about that too. Men hunted dragons, had all but wiped them out. It made no sense for them to be living together like this, even less for the dragons to be the masters.

The staircase rose from the other side of the hall formed by the intersection of two corridors. He knew that he had to climb all the way to the top. That was where the old dragon lived, and the dragon had told him to come as soon as he felt the slightest strange thing happening to him. Well, this must count as strange, otherwise why would he be running? And yet he couldn't actually remember the old dragon speaking to him.

The stairs were uncomfortably large for his short legs, and it wasn't long before they began to ache. Thin cold air rasped his throat as he climbed ever upward. All his focus was on the climb; there was nothing left to spare for thought. Only when he finally reached the top and stood in the freezing wind that blew across the great room from one open window to another did he realize that he couldn't remember his name.

Had he been in a dark wood? There was some memory of that and of fear, of hiding. Then pain. He tried to remember, but his mind was a blank.

'Hello?'

The voice sent shivers down his spine that had nothing to do with the icy breeze. That one word cut through him. He had been searching for something for a long time now, and that voice was surely it.

'Hello? Is there someone there? Is that you, Xando?'

Xando? He supposed that might be him. It seemed to fit, even though it wasn't quite right.

'I . . . Where are you?' He looked around the room, expecting to see the dragon, but something told him the open windows meant he was away. There was no telling how long he would be gone either.

'Up here, stupid. Where I've always been.'

He scanned the room, looking finally up into the rafters, where a cage of thick gold bars hung from a long chain. It swayed slightly, and a head poked out through the bars. The head belonged to a young woman, not much more than a girl really, her long black hair matted and unkempt. But the sight of her made his heart soar. He even knew her name.

'Martha.'

'Well done, Xando. That's only what, six months it's taken you to remember?'

He twisted through the clutter of giant tables and drawers, benches and strange apparatus that filled the room, finally stepping out into a clear area directly underneath the cage. A few logs had burned down to almost nothing in a huge open fireplace. What little heat they gave off was lost in the chill air that swirled from the open windows. There was a smell of fresh snow, and he remembered another castle, different, more terrifying.

'I don't suppose you could let me out of here?'

He looked up again, seeing the young woman peering down at him. She fixed him with a gaze that seemed to go straight to his soul.

'I don't know how.'

'No, you wouldn't. He'd hardly share that information with his servants. Same as he won't let me wander free when he's not here to keep an eye on me. Well, perhaps you could throw some logs on the fire; it's freezing in here.'

He went over to the fireplace, hauled some logs from where they were stacked and placed them on the charred remains. Flames licked up immediately, but it would take a lot more than that to heat up the room.

'Why don't you tap the Grym?'

The question came to his lips along with an understanding of what he had been doing but not how he had learned, who had taught him. Martha snapped her head around when she heard the words.

'This cage cuts me off from everything. And what would you know of the Grym anyway, Xando? I thought old Gog forbade our kind from knowing anything of the subtle arts.'

'I . . . I don't know. I just . . . knew.'

Martha leaned as far out of her cage as she could, straining her neck to get a better look at him. He was happy to stare back, drinking in her radiance. Even half-starved, caked in grime and unwashed, she was still the most beautiful thing he had ever seen. Her green eyes were like forest pools, deep and calm, and he remembered dragging her lifeless body from the water, a stern voice commanding him, telling him how to save her, the taste of her cold lips on his.

'Errol? Is that you?'

He opened his mouth to reply, but something that had been nagging him for as long as he could remember began to make itself known. His head was sore, as if he had been hit hard with something unyielding, and now the pain was growing impossible to ignore. His thoughts were cloudy, muddled. He remembered another girl – older, dressed in red. He had loved her, hadn't he? Or had he been a novitiate, sworn to uphold the charter and serve his inquisitor with unswerving loyalty?

'How is it that you're doing this?' Martha's voice was an anchor, but he was finding it increasingly difficult to concentrate on anything. Waves of tiredness and nausea pulled at him. Then rough invisible hands began to shake him.

'Where are you, Errol? Are you close?'

He tried to answer, but he seemed to have lost the ability to speak. And now his vision was fading too, blackening at the edges, so that all he could see was Martha's face staring at him. The edge of panic in her voice was a double blow: she was the one who always knew what was happening, was always in control. If she couldn't deal with this situation, then what chance did he have?

'Don't go. Please. Fight it.'

He tried, but he knew he was going to fail. With the last of his will he reached out, seeing someone else's hand respond to his command. Martha stretched her arm out of the cage towards him, but he knew as well as she did that the distance between them was too great.

'Errol.' Her voice flattened, the emotion draining from it as his vision darkened to almost nothing. Her face was just a memory as he felt a mixture of happiness that he had found her, that she was still alive, and deepest despair that he couldn't reach her.

'Errol. Wake up now.' The voice was different, male. It came with more shaking, sending pulses of red pain through his head. He gasped and tasted a different air, warmer, filled with the smell of unwashed men and polished wood.

'I know you're awake, Errol.' This time the voice spoke directly into his head. It was all over him, probing his thoughts, looking for memories that weren't there, digging out that last hopeless image.

'So you're still moping after that girl, eh? I should have known she was trouble the first time I saw her.'

He tensed against the invasion, trying to force whoever

it was raiding his thoughts out of his mind. But he knew it was hopeless. He was outclassed, captured, defeated. He had enjoyed the briefest of respites, but now he was finished. He just hoped the end would be relatively painless.

Errol opened his eyes, saw a distant ornate plaster ceiling softened by tears. Rough hands held him pinned to the floor, and then a hated face moved into his ill-focused vision.

'I'm so glad you could join us.' Melyn flexed his hands, and Errol saw a ring on one index finger. It glowed with a malevolent light mirrored within the inquisitor's eyes. 'It's time to find out what goes on inside that head of yours.'

For a moment Benfro thought the mother tree had played the cruellest of tricks on him. He was back in Magog's repository underneath the ruined castle of Cenobus. The alcoves, carved into the rock, covered every available surface, climbing the thick pillars and lining the walls. They contained the work of his dreamwalking – the returned jewels he had sorted through in the months of restless nights before he had swallowed his pride enough to accept Errol's help. He was reaching for the first set, about to begin the task of putting them all back in the great pile at the centre, when he finally saw the crucial difference.

These jewels were all red.

He snatched his hand back, the jewels untouched. Bad enough that Magog's had made Benfro's life a misery; there were tens of thousands here. He walked slowly along the aisles, hugging his wings close to his body, holding his tail straight and rigid, terrified lest he accidentally brush against some unreckoned memories.

There were no torches in the cavern, but the dark red glow from the jewels was more than enough to see by. Benfro felt the power of them filling the place, a heady thing yet tinged with bitterness like the screams of a host of tortured souls. It made him shiver to think about the terror those long-dead dragons must be enduring, locked away, slowly drained until nothing was left but the echo of a once-proud life.

After a while he began to make out something of a pattern. The aisles were arranged like the spokes of some giant wheel, and he was walking slowly towards its hub. They grew wider near the centre, and some of the piles of jewels were white here – reckoned. He wanted to go to them, take them out and pile them together, but he wasn't sure quite how he would deal with the sudden appearance of confused, alarmed and possibly quite mad memories. He also wasn't sure where to put them or indeed exactly where he was. The Llinellau ran through the room, merging at the centre, but rather than an open space, a massive black stone pillar rose to the dark ceiling.

He walked up to it and ran his hands over its glass-smooth surface, then remembered where he was, what he was doing. Instinctively he pulled back, but the pillar hadn't hurt him. It was powerful, and all over it, somehow underneath its glossy surface, were Draigiaith runes too indistinct to read.

Something pulled at Benfro's mind, and for a moment he thought that Magog was back to his old tricks. A quick look at his aura showed this wasn't so: if anything the rose cord was paler and more insubstantial than he had ever seen it. Perhaps the knot he had tied around it, still tight despite everything he had been through, was slowly choking the life out of the connection. Maybe if he could keep it up for a bit longer, Magog would be gone altogether.

As if hearing his thoughts, the cord started to glow, pulsing slowly and arcing away from him in a wide loop. He expected it to connect to the Llinellau nearby, but instead it swooped around the pillar, and as he concentrated on it, he felt it tug at him then pull hard.

Benfro stood his ground, fighting the power for as long as he could, but the pain built up swiftly. It was as if someone had put a hook in his brain and was trying to pull it out through a tiny hole in his forehead. He took one small step forward, and instantly the agony lessened. All too soon it came again though, and he had to take another pace, and another, following the cord as it pulled him around the pillar.

On the opposite side of the pillar a doorway had been cut into the stone, leading to a narrow stairway. It reminded him of Magog's retreat under Mount Arnahi, only these steps weren't worn smooth and slippery with damp. The cord tugged him with a doomed predictability; the strength of its force must surely mean that Magog's jewel was close by. Unable to resist, Benfro climbed, circling the pillar at least twice before stepping out into a small room. Low urgent voices filtered through an opening on the other side, and his nose caught a scent he both wanted to confront and run from. The pull of the cord stopped abruptly. He stood silently, holding his breath, wondering what to do.

There was an opening in the wall to his right. Daylight fell through it, and that was where the voices were coming from. Benfro edged his way over to it, meaning to listen, to come up with a plan. But at the last moment he tripped on a loose floorboard and stumbled into the space beyond – a great hall where Inquisitor Melyn stood over Errol, flanked by a dozen warrior priests.

And, most astonishing of all, Frecknock.

13

Sailors will often tell impossible tales, especially when they've a belly full of rum and an audience of gullible landlubbers to impress. Most have heard of the ship-eating kraal that rises from the depths of the Great Ocean, and many will know of the sea maidens who lure unsuspecting sailors to their deaths. But the greatest mystery of all concerns the lost civilization of Eirawen, and unlike many other sailors' tales this one is true.

Far to the south of the Twin Kingdoms, fully a month's sailing from Abervenn, lies the empty land of Eirawen, the home of wise Earith, if the histories are to be believed. Certainly a great people once lived here, for their cities are still there, a little ruined now and overgrown by jungle but magnificent all the same. Some say that they are our own ancestors and volcanic eruptions drove them north millennia past. And it is true that Eirawen has more than its share of those smoking, fiery mountains. But the cities are not damaged by soot or ash or lava, merely abandoned. As if the entire population decided one day to leave and never came back.

From the travel journals of
Usel of the Ram

Osgal dropped Errol to the ground, perhaps rather more roughly than was necessary.

Melyn gazed down at the unconscious form of the boy. He was thin, his skin almost pale enough to pass for a Twin Kingdoms native. His hair was as long as a girl's and matted with blood at the side of his head. He wore a woman's loose shift and travelling cloak, and would have easily passed for a maid. It was a good disguise: in a crowd he would have been invisible.

'We found him in the eastern forest, sir. Hiding at the base of a tree. There was no sign of either dragon close by, but I left a couple of troops to continue the search.' The bitterness in his voice was plain; he wanted to catch and kill Benfro. Perhaps understandably, given what the dragon had done to him.

'Patience, Osgal. The dragon will come to us. He'll want to help the boy. Only this time Errol will be under my complete control.'

Melyn rose from Ballah's throne, feeling a slight resistance, as if he didn't really want to disengage from the warm embrace of the Grym. He broke through it, reminding himself just how easy it would be to lose his mind to the chair. He still held the small wooden box with the dead king's ring in it in his hand. That was a mystery that would have to wait for now.

'Take this. Study it. Let me know what secrets it holds.' He thrust the box at Frecknock, who accepted it with a startled expression. Osgal scowled, his animosity towards the beast as fierce as ever. Well, he'd just have to get used to having her around.

Melyn stooped to look more closely at the boy. With

his smooth skin he looked almost younger than when he had entered the great monastery at Emmass Fawr. He'd be almost seventeen now, he supposed. Old enough to take on a man's responsibilities but still too young to shave.

'Clear the room, Osgal. I need to concentrate.' Melyn knelt beside Errol's unconscious form, noting for the first time how much he looked like his mother in the shape of his nose and the set of his eyes. Or maybe it was just the way the long hair framed his face, the way Lleyn's always had.

'Your Grace, you should have some men with you at all times. The city may not be totally safe yet.'

Melyn looked up at Osgal. There was a time when he would have reduced the man in rank and had him publicly flogged for questioning an order. But he was right. The palace was riddled with unmapped corridors populated by servants who might yet harbour some lethal loyalty to their dead king. And he needed to concentrate totally to get back into Errol's mind.

'The dragon will protect me with her life,' he said finally. 'You can remain with a few men. But I don't want to be disturbed. Understand?'

'Sir.' Osgal clattered his fist off his breast in salute, then turned away to give his orders. A half-dozen of the warrior priests who had entered with him formed a neat line behind Osgal a short distance from the throne. The rest left the room without a sound.

Turning his attention back to the boy, Melyn felt out along the lines nearby, drawing the power of the Grym into him and the ring on his finger. He reached forward, touched Errol's forehead and slowly closed his own eyes.

Unconscious subjects had no barriers to keep him out, but it was more difficult to make sense of the disjointed images, to weave them into a false memory. Melyn had hoped that his earlier work would help; he knew his way around Errol's thoughts. But what came to him was even more disjointed and disorientating than he had expected.

He saw a landscape of mountains and steep-sided valleys at once completely foreign and yet hauntingly familiar. High in a cloud-flecked sky dark shapes twisted and turned like carrion birds circling over a dying animal. But he knew they were not birds. He saw a castle, impossibly large, covering the whole of a mountain top, its tallest tower reaching for the sun. No such place existed in the whole of Gwlad, of that he was certain. And yet it stirred ancient memories deep inside him.

Picking his way through the images, sifting and searching, Melyn began to wonder whether this actually was Errol. For what seemed like an age he could find nothing of the boy who had caught his attention at a rustic wedding in the Ffrydd foothills. There was no imagery of Emmass Fawr, nothing of the time he had spent here in Tynhelyg, nor of the dragon Benfro or the great forest. There was just more of the castle: its interior, the faces of people linked to feelings of fear or hatred, an ancient but huge old dragon hunched over a writing desk in a vast and cluttered room, a cage with bars of gold hanging from the rafters and in it a girl.

Melyn smiled to himself, knowing he had found what he was looking for. Here was Errol, hiding deep in his make-believe world. With a bit of patience and skill he could rebuild the boy's memories, fix his loyalty to the order and then unravel his greatest secret.

He started with a simple idea, pride at being chosen for the novitiate. It was something Errol had always wanted, something he had worked hard to achieve. And he had succeeded where so many from his village had failed. Errol responded, the whirl of images beginning to include scenes, snippets and people Melyn recognized. Where he saw himself and the warrior priests he tried to spread a sense of calm and trust, but it was getting harder to maintain control as the boy slowly began to regain consciousness. He pushed a little harder, drawing more power through the ring. He could feel it warm on his finger, knew that it glowed even though his eyes were tight shut.

And then the boy started to slip away from him. It was like nothing he had ever encountered before. Errol's memories faded to darkness, leaving him with just the other images, of the castle and the girl. For an instant Melyn felt like his mind was being stretched over an incalculable distance, as if his soul were being sucked into the Grym. Instinct and training kicked in together, and he snapped his own mental shields up, pulled back out of Errol's mind with such force that he lurched backwards.

'Wake him,' he said. Osgal stepped forward, knelt and shook the boy hard.

Melyn watched for a moment, then slid back into Errol's thoughts. He saw the girl again, only this was a much earlier memory. They were both cold and wet, and he was kissing her. The intimacy repulsed him, but it also showed him he would never be able to overcome Errol by stealth. Theirs would have to be a battle of wits, but Melyn was confident he could crush the boy's spirit.

Osgal shook the boy once more, and Melyn sensed that he was about to wake. He leaned over just as Errol opened his eyes; it was important he was the first thing the boy saw and that he was overcome with a sense of helplessness and defeat. It was no use fighting any more, might as well surrender to the inevitable.

Just as he was starting on Errol, just as he was about to break him down and unravel his secrets, a noise distracted him. Melyn looked up and saw the dragon Benfro stumble out from behind the throne, trying to stay on his feet. Indoors he looked bigger than ever, his folded wings reaching up towards the ceiling. He must have been fully the size of Caradoc, and his eyes blazed with a cold fury.

'Kill him!' Melyn barked the order, but it wasn't necessary. All the warrior priests sprang forward, and the inquisitor felt the drain on the Grym as they conjured their blades of light. Only Frecknock stood like a statue, her mouth slightly agape.

Melyn pulled Errol to his feet. The boy's head lolled woozily as the inquisitor dragged him away from Benfro. And now Melyn felt something even more strange, a twisting in his mind that made his ears resonate. The ring on his finger burned so bright and hot that the pain made him yelp. He let go of Errol, watching as the boy slumped back down, his eyes barely open, but before he hit the floor, before he was even halfway there, he simply vanished. Melyn had barely enough time to register what had happened when someone screamed an alarm. He turned to where his warrior priests should have been surrounding the dragon and cutting it down, only to see a wall of flame rush towards him.

Benfro leaped forward, talons outstretched, wings unfurling as the inquisitor's warrior priests conjured their blades and ran to meet him. He had no time to think, no time to be afraid of them. He brought his wings together in front of him with such force that his claws cut grooves in the wooden floor as he was pushed backwards. A great wind sent the warrior priests sprawling. Ignoring them, he headed for the inquisitor, who held Errol in his arms and was trying to drag him away.

Then Errol disappeared, and without even thinking Benfro let out a great belch of flame. As it billowed towards the inquisitor he could hear Frecknock shriek and had a second to wonder what she was doing here, why she was still alive. But Melyn raised his hand in an almost contemptuous wave, and the flame washed out around him, dissipating into nothing.

'You'll have to do better than that, little dragon.' Melyn was unscathed. His eyes blazed red, and the room was suddenly filled with fear. 'I killed your mother, and I'll do the same to you.'

Melyn conjured a blade of fire, and only then did Benfro remember the warrior priests behind him. He whirled, lashing out with his tail as they struggled to their feet. Another burst of flame and several were howling in agony as their flesh melted away. Turning back, he ducked just in time to feel Melyn's blade swing through the air where his neck had been. But the inquisitor's stroke had brought him in close, and Benfro was ready. He lunged forward, talons outstretched, ripping them through cloth and flesh.

Melyn fell back, his face white with shock. Still he was quicker than Benfro had anticipated, swinging his blade back around in an ugly arc. Benfro knew even before it hit that he could do nothing about it. The blade swept through his wrist as if it wasn't there.

It was curiously painless. He watched astonished as his hand fell to the floor. There was no blood, and as he lifted his arm to look, his aura swam into vision. He could see how it flowed and bunched over the damage, as if trying to stop anything from leaking out.

'Kill him, you idiots!' The inquisitor's voice penetrated his shock. Benfro swung round again, belching out more flame at the warrior priests. They screamed like children as they burned.

'You can't beat them all, Benfro. You have to run.' Frecknock's voice was in his head. He looked to where she had been standing and found instead that she was kneeling beside the inquisitor, tending to his wounds. His rage at her doubled. How could she ally herself with the man who had slaughtered her entire family?

'I do what I must, Benfro. Now go before anyone sees I'm helping you.'

The doors burst open at the far end of the room. Warrior priests swarmed in like wasps. Too many of them for Benfro to take on, and his stomach was gurgling and empty now. He had to escape, but how? If he went back down to the cavern beneath the throne room, he would be trapped.

'Use the Llinellau, Benfro. I know you've done it before.' Frecknock's voice was calm, quite unlike the hectoring tone he remembered. It reminded him more of Corwen and the first time he had seen the Grym. Unbidden the Llinellau appeared in front of him, thick and powerful and converging on the throne. He gazed at the lines and at the aethereal overlaying everything else, and there, behind the throne, just like he had seen in Candlehall, was a small window. One strand of the Grym snaked its way through, one strand that didn't lead straight back to Magog's retreat at the top of Mount Arnahi.

'Benfro, you have to hurry.' Now Frecknock sounded more like her old self. He looked at her and then across just long enough to see that the warrior priests had reached the dais and were almost upon him. She was sheltering Melyn, who sat on the floor shaking, but she looked up and winked at him, just once.

'Go!'

Benfro turned his attention back to the Grym, feeling out along the line that must surely take him to Gog's world. But where on Gog's world? He didn't know any place to go. How could he walk the Llinellau to somewhere he had never seen? Then he remembered the strange dream he had shared with Errol, of flying over a huge castle, being attacked by other dragons. He had dropped Ynys Môn's jewels. Somewhere out there his friend and mentor was waiting for him.

Benfro pictured the scene: the old dragon sitting in front of a campfire on which their day's hunt cooked, sipping from a flask he would never share, telling tales of ancient times when dragons were proud masters of all they surveyed. He could feel Ynys Môn out there, just a step away.

But his hand, he couldn't leave that behind. He had to find a way to mend it. Turning and stooping in one swift motion, he snatched it up as the first warrior priest leaped towards him, face blistered and burned, blade long and silent and deadly. It was Captain Osgal, somehow still alive.

Benfro froze for an instant, watching the blade swing down in an arc that would cut his head in two. His severed hand slipped from his grasp and tumbled back to the floor. Too late to do anything with it now.

He closed his eyes and jumped.

The plain outside Tochers was a mess. The army had packed up, and the first companies of men were marching down the low valley on the road to Candlehall. Beulah watched them go, once more cursing her stupidity. Melyn had come up with his plan to cause a diversion in northern Llanwennog, to draw most of its army away from the passes. Of course Ballah would have thought to do the same thing.

What galled her most though was knowing that Abervenn had turned against her. Her own people had risen up in rebellion and accepted the leadership of a foreigner, a Llanwennog, Prince Dafydd. And perfect little Iolwen; she should have disposed of her little sister right after Lleyn. But then the shock of losing two daughters might have killed her father, and long years of regency would have lost her the Obsidian Throne just as certainly.

'Damn her. By the Wolf!'

'My love? Does something ail you?' Clun rushed to her side; he was never very far away these days.

'My sister. Iolwen. She was there in Abervenn Castle. Why didn't I see it? She gave birth to a son. I held him in my hands, my own nephew. And he pissed on me.' She dared Clun to laugh, to even smile. But he didn't. His face darkened instead, his brow furrowing in anger.

'Are you sure it was her? I thought you said she was a serving girl.'

'That's what Anwyn told me. But I thought she looked familiar. And why would both Anwyn and her mother look after a serving girl giving birth? Surely they'd have servants to do that.'

Beulah fumed. She had been tricked, and it was all the fault of her unborn child. Without its presence damping her magical skills she would have seen through the subterfuge in an instant.

As if sensing her rebuke, the baby kicked. Beulah tried not to wince, but Clun saw it nonetheless. He took her arm and led her to a nearby chair set on the ramparts of the town wall so that she could watch the army leave.

'You need to take it easy, my lady. The baby will be along soon.'

'Nonsense, Clun. It's not due for weeks, I'm sure.'

'Your Majesty. I have news from the pass.' Captain Celtin climbed the steps to the battlements and bowed, keeping a discreet distance until Beulah waved him forward. 'This just came by bird.' He handed over a small scroll of parchment.

Beulah broke the seal and unrolled it. The message was quite long and complicated, written in tiny letters that she had to squint to read. Yet as she worked her way down to the bottom, her heart lifted and she chuckled.

'Oh, but this is priceless!' She handed the scroll back to the captain, then stood up and grasped Clun in a warm embrace.

'To think that I once wanted all their kind killed. Well, I still do, but perhaps not today.'

'What are you talking about, my lady?'

'Dragons, my love. Or more specifically the two dragons that flew over here yesterday. Apparently they attacked Tordu's army and drove most of it away from Tynewydd. His men are scattered over the Caenant plain. The pass is unguarded.'

'But how—'

'There's no time, my love. We have to move swiftly before he can regroup.' Beulah turned her attention back to Celtin, who had finished reading the message and was grinning too. 'Celtin, I want you to summon the generals for me. We need to alter our plans.'

The captain saluted then ran down the steps on his errand. Beulah set off after him at a much slower pace, the bulge in her stomach making anything more than a sedate walk impossible. With Clun's help, she reached the street below as General Otheng and a number of other senior officers hurried to meet her.

'Is it true, Your Majesty? We have dragons working for us now?'

'I doubt they care who they attack, General. We must thank the Shepherd these two decided Llanwennogs taste better.' Beulah uttered the words without thinking, then remembered how Clun's father and stepmother had died. 'I'm sorry, my love. That was insensitive of me.'

Clun's face was unreadable, and he said nothing.

General Otheng broke the silence. 'How are we to play this to our advantage, ma'am? We still need the army to retake Candlehall.'

'The forces that were to defend this end of the pass will march to Tynewydd. If this intelligence is correct, we can take the town without major loss. And once we have it, our men will defend the other end of the pass for when we return.'

'A wise plan, ma'am. But don't forget the pass can be deadly in winter. Our forces could be left to fend for themselves for months.'

'Tynewydd will be stocked for Tordu's forces, and it has a deep well. You'll need to take warrior priests with you in case the dragons return. And you'll need to march soon and fast, before Tordu has a chance to regroup. I will lead the army back to Candlehall. We should have the city back in our hands by month's end.'

Beulah watched as everyone set about their tasks. Only Clun stayed with her, and together they walked back to the castle. They were hardly within its gates when the baby gave another great kick. Still a month to go, but it was as feisty as a ten-year-old. She clutched at her stomach, waiting for the waves of nausea to go away. Something convulsed inside her, as if she had been punched in the gut, and she let out an involuntary gasp. Strong arms caught her as her legs buckled, and only then did she feel the warm liquid trickling down her legs.

'What's happening, my love?' Beulah was only dimly aware of her surroundings as Clun picked her up and carried her through the castle hall.

'Be calm, my lady. Try to relax. I think your waters have

broken,' he said quietly, then yelled to a servant standing nearby. 'Fetch the medics. Now! Her Majesty has just gone into labour.'

The first thing he noticed was the grass pressing against his head and hands, wiry and dry like the end of summer. Then the smells came to him: dry earth, dust, something strangely spicy. Slowly sounds trickled into the chaos of his head: the chittering of a million million insects, the background hiss of the wind, the croak of a crow about its solitary business, something small rustling in a nearby bush.

Errol tried to sit up, but as soon as he tensed his muscles to lift his head, he was engulfed in pain. It felt like someone had shoved a knife through his temple and straight into his brain. Lights burst like explosions in his vision. Gasping, suddenly breathless, he slumped back down again, waiting for the pain to pass.

It seeped away slowly, leaving a dull ache as a reminder of what would happen should he try to move too quickly again. But he had to move before whatever was in the bushes came for him. He needed to find shelter, somewhere to rest safely while his head cleared. And he needed to find out where he was.

This time Errol pushed himself up slowly. His head throbbed, and his balance was completely off, but eventually he managed to lever himself into a sitting position. It took a moment for his vision to clear enough to see, but when he did, he was still confused. It was sort of the forest of his dreams, only different. This was the place where he had seen Martha walking. There was the path, hugging the shade beneath the canopy, meandering back and forth as if it didn't want to venture into the light. But the trees looked different, the grass dry and yellow. Turning slowly, he saw the clearing with its distinctive rocky outcrop, but it was not quite right. In his dream this place had been lush and green. Now it was as if no rain had fallen in centuries.

Errol sat in the long grass slowly taking it all in. It began to dawn on him that this was not a dream. It was too real. Unlike his previous visits, he could hear the wind, feel the wetness seeping through his clothing, smell the autumn scents. Perhaps if he waited long enough Martha would come along and he could stop her from walking out into the clearing, save her from being captured by the dragons. But that couldn't work. She had been captured, he knew. He had seen her trapped in a cage of gold at the top of the tallest tower in the vast castle. Or had that been a boy called Xando?

He shook his head tentatively, trying to make sense of the jumble of memories. The pain washed over him again in dizzying waves, if anything making it even harder to think. It was obvious he had taken a nasty blow, and the best thing he could do was to find somewhere safe to recover.

A sudden noise attracted his attention. He turned his head too quickly and almost fainted. Beyond the tree under which he sat a line of low shrubs and bushes climbed a nearby rise. One of them was moving independently of the others, as if it had its own wind to play with. Or was concealing something. He stared hard at it, waiting for his vision to clear again.

'Is there somebody there?' His voice sounded strange

to him, hoarse through his dry throat and deeper than the woman's voice he had been affecting for weeks. The bush rustled some more, and then a head poked out through the leaves.

For a moment he thought it was Martha. The girl looked at him with that same quizzical expression, head cocked slightly to one side. But where Martha's hair was dark and fell long and straight past her shoulders, this girl's was short, spiky and ginger. Her face was ruddy too, more close in hue to his own. And she was a good bit younger than Martha, not yet ten if he was any judge.

'You a girl or a boy?' she asked, and there was something strange about her speech that Errol couldn't quite put his finger on.

'A boy,' he said. 'My name's Errol.'

'Only you're wearing women's clothes.'

'It's a disguise. I was being chased. Have you been watching me long?'

'Since you got here.' The girl pushed her way out of the bush, looking up at the sky with a quick nervous glance. 'You fell out of nothing. Where'd you come from?'

And that was when he realized what was so odd about her. She wasn't speaking Llanwennog, nor even Saesneg.

Her words were perfect Draigiaith.

Benfro felt like he was being squeezed down a long narrow tunnel. He couldn't breathe, couldn't see. There was nothing but pressure and the images in his head. Had he escaped, or was this what it felt like to have your head split in two by a blade of light? He would have expected some pain, but then he had felt nothing when Melyn had severed his hand. He only hoped that the wound he had dealt the inquisitor was a mortal one; he could die happy if he knew he had avenged his mother.

But if he was dead, then why was he so desperate to breathe? His lungs burned for air, and yet whatever it was that gripped him held him so tight he could not move at all. He could do nothing but think, not even struggle.

And then he was free. Sensations burst in on him as if he had plunged his head under the waterfall at Corwen's clearing: bright light blinded him as he opened his eyes to stare straight at the sun; the wind battered his ears, filling them with a roaring sound, tugged at his wings, his legs and arms; the sun whipped away from him, and he realized he was falling head over tail through nothing. Blue sky dotted with white clouds rushed past him. And then he saw trees, rocky outcrops, distant mountains, trees again. Too close.

Instinctively he opened his wings, but he was upside down again, staring at the sun. He tried twisting in the air, but he had nothing to push against. He was falling too fast, tumbling, tumbling.

A second rotation, and this time Benfro managed to slow his spin, to spread his wings wide enough to catch the air. Then pain smashed into his right side. There was such a noise of cracking that he thought he must surely have broken all his bones, but it was just the upper branches of a huge old tree snapping in a series of dry explosions. Trying not to damage himself any more than necessary, Benfro thrust himself away from the tree. His wing tip hurt like he had slammed it against a wall, and his side burned where shattered branches scraped down it, pulling at his scales and finding all the unprotected bits of skin. He was too close to the ground now and still going too fast.

At the last moment he reared his head up, swinging around the fulcrum that was the solid knot of muscle in the middle of his back. He thrust his feet down towards the ground, trying not to tense them against the inevitable shock. He had jumped from enough trees in his young life; he knew how to do this surely.

The ground hit him like a landslide. His legs folded underneath him, and he pitched forward. He tried to tuck his head down, fold his wings tight and roll.

It didn't work.

Benfro's face slammed into the grassy earth, knocking all the sense out of him. His belly colliding with the ground squeezed all the air out of his lungs. He slid forward several paces, his head clattering up and down over hummocks and buried rocks, until he finally came to a complete halt, his nose just inches away from a large boulder.

Dazed, winded, bruised, all he could hear was a roaring in his ears as the impact of his crash slowly ebbed. Then, from somewhere nearby, he heard what sounded distinctly like a slow handclap, the sort of sarcastic applause Ynys Môn had always produced whenever Benfro did something particularly stupid.

'An especially fine landing, I must say. I especially like how you used your chin as a brake. Bravo.'

Benfro struggled slowly upright, levering himself erect with his one good arm. His wings were still spread, and he brought them into his flanks gingerly, feeling for any serious damage and finding only aches and bruises. Finally he looked to see who had spoken.

She sat in the shade of a nearby tree, a large deer sprawled on the ground in front of her, its innards in a heap where she had been grallocking it. She stood up slowly and walked towards him, stretching her wings out as she moved in a manner that Benfro found impossible not to stare at.

She was the most beautiful dragon he had ever seen.

14

Little is known of the effects of pregnancy on the manipulation of the Grym, or of the workings of the Grym on the foetus during its gestation. Few women have become adepts, and fewer still fallen pregnant to allow subjects for study. This is not, as many in the exclusively male ranks of the Order of the High Ffrydd say, because women are inherently unmagical; some of the most skilful and powerful mages of history were women, after all. It is more a tendency in male-dominated societies to view women as both the fairer and weaker sex, reducing them to the position of servant or chattel within the family structure. None of the great orders look for women at their choosings, so no women are chosen, and this is taken to mean no women have any talent beyond that of bearing children.

A perhaps surprising exception is in the royal House of Balwen itself, where sons and daughters of the monarch both receive training in the many forms of magic. And yet down the years there have been surprisingly few royal daughters, and even fewer queens. All have lost their magical abilities during pregnancy, some regaining them slowly afterwards, some swiftly and some not at all. Their offspring have all been powerfully magical, but then carrying the blood of Balwen in their veins, how could they be anything else?

Barrod Sheepshead,
A History of the House of Balwen

'Here. Let me give you a hand.'

Benfro became aware that he was lying sprawled on the ground, his face in the soft forest loam. Not in the throne room at Tynhelyg, not confronting Inquisitor Melyn and a dozen warrior priests intent on killing him. Not ducking out of the reach of that flaming blade of concentrated Grym. Not . . .

'By the moon! What happened to you?' The dragon came closer still, reaching out and taking Benfro's arm at the same time as he remembered the injury. Strange that he hadn't until now, but it was painless. At least in comparison to the aches and bruises covering his body, the raging hammers in his head. He stared at the stump where his hand had been, then up at the dragon, and found himself unable to speak.

'I've never seen a wound like it. What manner of blade is so hot it sears where it cuts?'

Benfro gently tugged his arm away from the dragon's grip and struggled upright. Close up he could see his initial appraisal of her was wrong. She wasn't quite the most beautiful dragon he had ever seen; that honour went to the mother tree in her guise of Ammorgwm the Fair. But then the mother tree had only worn the image of a dragon. This one was real.

'Who . . . Who are you?' His voice was hoarse, cracking as he spoke.

'Could say the same to you.' The dragon squatted back on her haunches, her tail twitching at the tip. She was perhaps the same size as Benfro but seemed somehow older, yet she was still by far the youngest female dragon he had ever seen. Centuries younger than any of the villagers, although he supposed she could be the same age as Frecknock.

'I'm . . . I'm Benfro.'

'Just Benfro?' Amusement twisted the dragon's face into a toothy smile. 'Not Benfro the Bold? Not Benfro of the Missing Hand, whose exploits are legend throughout Gwlad? Not Bright Benfro, Master of the Skies? Not—'

'Sir Benfro. If you insist. An old friend called me Benfro of the Borrowed Wings. My mother was Morgwm the Green, my father Sir Trefaldwyn of the Great Span.'

'Was?' The smile disappeared, the young dragon all serious again. 'You mean they're . . .'

'Dead. Yes. My mother lost her head to the same blade that took my hand.' Whether it was tiredness or the sudden return of that fateful, terrible image, Benfro didn't know, but as he got to his feet, his sight darkened and he felt the world tilting.

And then strong arms supported him. 'Here. You need to take it slowly. You're in shock.'

'Sorry. Just a bit woozy.' Benfro leaned perhaps a bit more into the embrace than he had intended, finding himself wrapped in the young dragon's arms in a manner that felt alarmingly intimate. She was warm, he couldn't help noticing, and smelled of the forest. Crushed pine needles, loam, running water, a melange of flowers and herbs and something else that really didn't help his head stop spinning.

'I think you'd better sit down again.' She lowered him gently to the ground and laid a hand on his forehead just above his eyes like his mother used to. A lump formed in Benfro's throat at the memory, making it hard to swallow. Staring at the young dragon was awkward, so he looked at his surroundings, tried to get an idea of where he was. More than that it was a forest clearing he couldn't say. The ground was carpeted in thick grass except for where he had gouged it with his landing. Boulders and smaller stones pocked the sward, putting him in mind of the clearing in front of Corwen's cave, but this was much smaller. And besides, he'd cleared all those stones away to make his corral. The trees here were different too, and the air felt strange.

'Where is this place?'

The young dragon took her hand from his forehead; it had been lingering there perhaps a little too long for comfort. 'What do you mean?'

'This isn't the Forest of the Ffrydd, I'm sure. I don't recognize it.'

'Forest of the . . .' The young dragon cocked her head sideways, giving him a look he couldn't quite read. 'There's no forest in the Ffrydd. It's a wasteland. Has been since Gog slew his brother there millennia ago. You remember the tales, surely?'

And there it was. The difference Benfro hadn't been able to put his talon on. Just the mention of the name was enough. Gog, hated brother of Magog. He shifted his focus, letting the Grym swim into his vision. His aura clung to him in weary colours, pulsing red around the stump where his hand had been, but of the rose cord there was no sign.

'It's gone. I can't believe it.' He swiped the air in front of his face, feeling for that connection that had looped into his forehead.

'What's gone? Benfro, are you all right?'

Benfro looked at the dragon, seeing her in all the splendour of her aura. His hearts fluttered in his chest and all of a sudden breathing was difficult.

'I . . . Who are you? You never told me your name.'

'Me? No one special. They call me Cerys, if they bother to call me anything at all.'

'They?' Benfro looked at the clearing again, this time seeing the Grym spread over it in a blaze of colour and health. And that was strange too. He'd struggled to see the power that flowed through Gwlad, always found it hard even to see his own aura, and yet now it was as easy as falling out of a tree. Or the sky.

'My family. My fold. Come, Benfro of the Borrowed Wings, whatever that's supposed to mean.' Cerys the dragon grabbed him by his good arm and pulled him to his feet. Benfro's head was much clearer now, his strength returning along with his wonder. Even so he allowed the young dragon to fling his arm over her shoulder and take some of his weight. It felt strange to be so close to another dragon, but it also felt good.

'Your Grace! You are wounded!'

Melyn leaned against the throne, casting his eye over

246

the damaged room. He was gasping for air, finding it far harder to breathe than the exertions of the fight should have made it. The effort of dispelling Benfro's magical flame had taken more out of him than expected. A half-dozen of his warrior priests had not fared so well, if he was counting the heaps of smoking black ash correctly.

'Where did they go?' He meant to shout the question, but it came out as a wheezy cough.

'Your Grace. Please.' Melyn felt a presence beside him at the same time as his knees gave way. Strong hands caught him under the arms, lifting him gently on to the throne so recently vacated by the late King Ballah. It took him some time to understand that it was the dragon, Frecknock, who had come to his aid. The remaining warrior priests were too busy looking after themselves.

'Stop fussing, damn you.' Melyn tried to push the dragon away, but his strength was gone. How had he become so weak? So old?

'You have a bad gash to your chest, sire. It needs medical attention as soon as possible. If you will allow me, I can help you?' Frecknock stood back, bending her head in that submissive pose of hers. Melyn went to wave her away, then noticed that his hand was red with wet blood. Benfro's severed hand lay on the floor not far from him, but Melyn's blade of light had cauterized that wound. Had the young dragon managed to lay a claw on him? The fight had been so swift, he couldn't remember.

He tried to wipe away the blood on a fold of his robe, but the material was slick, and if anything his hand came away redder. And weaker. He was having a hard time concentrating. So tired and thirsty. And cold. It was a lifetime since last he had felt cold. The Grym kept him warm, always.

'Your Grace, please.' Frecknock's voice buzzed at him like an irritating fly. She was nearby, but he couldn't see her. Couldn't muster the energy to raise his head or wave her away. Then another voice, gruff and angry, cut through his stupor.

'Get away from him or I will part your head from your shoulders.'

'Osgal?'

Melyn managed to look up, and saw through bleary, unfocused eyes his captain standing a few paces away. He held an unsteady blade of light aloft, the power of it sucking the life out of everyone nearby.

'Put your damned blade out, Osgal.' Melyn's command descended into a bubbling cough, and when he spat it was a mess of bright red. Not good. He slumped back in the throne and for the first time felt the pain across his chest, remembered the mad fury in Benfro's eyes. He reached for his robe again, finding the tear in the fabric, wet with his blood. The wound beneath it was not a pleasant sight. No wonder he was having a hard time concentrating; his body was fast going into shock.

'I can help stabilize him.' Out of the corner of his eye, Melyn could see Frecknock moving from foot to foot like a freshly inducted novitiate needing to be excused. She was quite pathetic really. Terrified of Captain Osgal and his blade of light and yet equally terrified that he might die and leave her unprotected.

'Let her.' Melyn coughed out the words with yet more blood. 'Not as if she could kill me any quicker.'

Osgal gave the barest of nods. 'Make sure you don't, dragon. You will not live a second longer than the inquisitor.'

Melyn would have laughed at the man's bluster, had he any breath left. He tried to sit up as the dragon approached, but she held out her hand for him to stay put.

'Please. Don't try to move. You've lost a great deal of blood. I'm going to try to stop the bleeding before we move you.'

Kneeling at the foot of the throne like a supplicant, Frecknock placed the palm of one scaly hand so lightly over Melyn's chest he could not feel it. He could feel the surge of the Grym as she began murmuring under her breath in Draigiaith though. It pulled in from much further afield than Osgal's blade, tapping into the whole city and out to the woods far beyond. It washed away the pain of his wound and lent him at least a little strength. Enough to fight back the waves of shock and nausea and take control of himself.

'I will do what I can, but this wound needs to be cleaned and stitched. It will take time to heal.'

'Osgal. Take your men, sweep the royal apartments. We'll set up camp in there until we've got the city under control. I don't imagine it'll be all that long before Prince Geraint musters his forces and marches for home.'

Osgal nodded once, then set off on his errand, two warrior priests falling in behind him. Melyn was left alone with the dragon, but he didn't feel in any danger. Quite the opposite; her presence was a reassurance now. That should have bothered him. All his life he had hated dragons, what they did and what they stood for. Now in a few short months he had become accustomed at least to this one. And he had learned so much from her, knew there was so much more to be discovered.

'How did they disappear? Where did they go?'

Frecknock had been concentrating on her chanting, but now she looked up.

'Your Grace?' As soon as she stopped whatever she had been doing with the Grym, Melyn felt the pain begin to swell again.

'The boy, Errol. Your friend Benfro. They both disappeared in front of my eyes. It's not the first time either. How did they do it? Where did they go? Ahh.' Melyn's chest felt like it had been ripped open afresh, and something sloshed about in his lungs as he tried to take the shallowest of breaths.

'You must keep still. Don't talk.' Frecknock placed her palm over his wound again. 'I cannot tell you what I know and perform this healing both. And truth is I do not know how it is possible. There is something dragons can do after many years of study, but never have I heard of a man . . .' She shook her head as if trying to dislodge the very idea from her brain. 'I will tell you all I know. I have sworn to do so. But first you must heal.'

Frecknock went back to her Draigiaith incantations and Melyn breathed easier, the pain lessening with each passing moment. Impatience gnawed at him, but he forced it down with the same iron will that had taken him through the ranks right up to the top of the Order of the High Ffrydd. He could not deny his injury any more than he could deny Frecknock had saved his life and was continuing to do so. But she knew something of the secret to

Errol's strange ability. He would not rest easy until he knew it himself.

'I ain't never seen a boy wear women's clothes before. What's your name?'

The young girl hurried into the shade of the tree, looking up all the time. Errol struggled to his feet, feeling the ground sway beneath them. He put a hand to the tree to steady himself and only then noticed how strange it looked. Its bark was smooth, for one thing, more like skin than anything he would have expected to find on a tree. The trunk was wider than it had any right to be too, and it bulged outwards from the base before tapering back in at the top. A tangle of narrow branches spread out from there, casting less shade than the massive oaks and beeches Errol remembered from home. He looked back over the scene, seeing it differently now from how it had appeared in his dream. Still the same place which Martha had passed through, but somehow alien.

'You OK?' The young girl stood just a couple of paces away from him. Errol guessed she wasn't much older than ten. Something about the way she carried herself reminded him of Martha, though their features were nothing alike. Perhaps it was her skinny arms and bare, dusty knees, her crop of unruly dark ginger hair and the blazing curiosity in her eyes.

'Someone hit me on the back of the head.' He reached back and touched the spot gently. It was sore, but his fingers came away clean, and the pounding he had felt upon first waking was beginning to recede, replaced by a powerful thirst.

'Who'd do a thing like that?' The girl seemed genuinely shocked at the thought. Then a cheeky grin spread across her face. 'Was it the woman you nicked the clothes from?'

'No, it was . . .' Errol stopped as a shadow rushed across the ground, something large moving through the air overhead. Without thinking, he started to walk out from under the canopy to get a better look, but the girl grabbed him by the arm, pulling him back close to the tree trunk.

'Are you mad?' She whispered the question, which made it seem all the more urgent.

'I wanted to—'

'Shh. They'll hear us.' The girl put her other hand over Errol's mouth, pressing close to him and into the tree trunk. She smelled strange. He couldn't put words to it, but there was something about her that seemed wrong. He held still, trying to puzzle it out for long minutes until finally she let go of his arm and stepped away.

'Think they're gone now. We should be safe.'

'Who's gone? What are we safe from?'

The girl looked at him as if he were an imbecile. 'Dragons, silly. Who else did you think it would be?'

'Dragons . . . Oh.' Errol felt a flush of heat in his cheeks. Of course there were dragons here; he'd seen them in his dream. Although the more he looked at his surroundings, the less it looked like his dream. There were trees, true, and a clearing not far off, but nothing was quite right.

'Where is this place?' he asked, which got him another strange look.

'You don't know 'bout dragons, don't know where you are. Who are you? Where'd you come from?'

'I'm sorry. You asked once before.' Errol held out his hand. 'I'm Errol. Errol Ramsbottom. I grew up in a little village on the edge of the great Ffrydd forest, but most recently I was in Tynhelyg, in Llanwennog.'

The girl looked at his hand, then up at his face, with that same quizzical expression. She paused a while before answering as if considering whether he was serious or not.

'Never heard of any of those places. You sure you didn't make them up? And what kind of a name's Ramsbottom? Sounds rude to me.'

'Well, I can't much help you there. It's the name I was born with.' Errol dropped his unshaken hand awkwardly to his side, took a step away from the tree trunk and peered up into the sky. 'You really think they're gone? The dragons?'

'Sure. They never hang around long.' As if to prove the point, the girl ran out to the path, then slowed as she walked along it to the clearing. Errol hurried to catch up with her. He wasn't really sure what else he could do.

'I come here sometimes, when the other villagers shout at me.'

'Shout at you? Why do they shout at you?' Errol asked, although he fancied he had something of an idea.

'Cos I'm in the way. Cos they feel bad about my ma and da. Who knows?' The girl climbed the grassy mound that swelled out of the centre of the clearing like a great green pimple. It was capped with a straggle of boulders that were far larger than Errol had first assumed, and rose higher than the trees, giving him a good look at the sky and the surrounding land as it undulated away into the distance. More of the oddly shaped trees spread away in all directions, with just occasional rocky outcrops jutting out of them. They formed a very open forest, difficult to traverse if you didn't want to be seen from above. And over in the far distance, hazy with the shimmering heat of the air, a stone ridge rose in a slow, steady climb to a flat point before dropping precipitously back into the trees. Tiny dots wheeled around it.

'That's the Twmp. That's where the dragons live. Something must've upset them. Don't normally come this way unless they're upset. Not often you see them all swarming like that neither.'

'Any idea what's upset them?' Errol looked at the whirling dots again, seeing them for what they really were. No bird could be that big.

'Not a clue, but I guess I'd better let the others know. You can come if you want. Sure old Ben'll want to meet you.' The girl jumped down from her rock and started off down the mound in the direction she had just climbed. Errol followed as quickly as he could manage, although after the climb his head was hurting badly again. And his thirst was worse than ever.

'Hold up a minute,' he shouted. The girl stopped, turned, walked swiftly back to him.

'You all right? Only you don't look it.'

'Just a bit woozy, that's all. Is there any water around here? I'm that thirsty. Don't think I've had a drink in days.'

The girl gave him that quizzical look again. 'You really ain't from these parts, are you, Errol. Don't suppose you've got a tap knife and all either.'

Errol's look must have confirmed his bafflement. The girl dug in the folds of her rough tunic, coming out with a leather sheath from which she produced a wicked-looking blade.

'Here. I'll show you.' She shrugged her shoulders at his uselessness. 'It's like having a little kid.'

She walked over to the nearest tree, then proceeded to tap the bark with the hilt of the knife, occasionally pressing her ear to it as she did so. Errol watched as she finally flipped the knife round and sank the blade into the tree.

'There you go. Should see us back to the village.' She stepped aside and he could see water dripping from the hollow hilt of the knife. He cupped his hands, letting the surprisingly cool liquid pool in them before giving it a good sniff. It didn't smell suspicious, and he was too thirsty to really care. He lifted his hands to his mouth and drank as deeply as he could.

The water was slightly sweet, cooling his head and soothing his throat as it went down. Errol drank until his stomach started to feel bloated with it, but still the steady stream came from the hilt of the girl's knife.

'You finished?' she asked as he finally stepped back, wiping his hands on his filthy travelling cloak and nodding. His head was already clearer, the pain receding. He felt more energized than he had in days, possibly months. He watched as the girl pulled the knife from the tree. Far from the water escaping in a cascade, it oozed a little, then dried completely as she smoothed her fingers over the cut, mouthing words Errol couldn't quite make out as she did so. When she stepped away, he couldn't see any sign of a hole at all.

'The Bondaris tree puts its roots down deep, where the water is. She shares with us, as long as we ask nicely. And say thank you.' The girl's voice was serious all of a sudden, and Errol understood that this was something very important to her.

'Well, she has my thanks indeed. I don't think I could have kept going much longer.'

That seemed to satisfy the girl. She cleaned the blade of her knife on her tunic before sheathing it and putting it away. Then she started off down the track. Errol fell in beside her.

'You have my thanks too,' he said, better able to match her pace now. 'That's not something I would have known to do.'

'We learn it when we're little. But not everyone gets a Bondaris knife. Not till they're older. I've only got one cos my ma and da passed.'

'I'm very sorry,' Errol said.

'Wasn't your fault.'

'No. But all the same.' He stopped walking for a moment as he realized something. 'Here you are, saving my life, and I don't even know your name.'

The girl turned, but carried on walking backwards. 'It's Nellore. Now hurry up, or we'll be walking through the worst of the sun.'

All she could remember was the pain. It came in waves, but the troughs were like nothing she had felt before, the peaks enough to make her scream. Beulah was aware of people all around her, a busyness that would have been mortifying had she been able to concentrate, think about anything at all. Only the solid presence of Clun at her side, his firm hand clutching hers, kept her sane.

Minutes turned to hours turned to days, or so it felt. Clun had carried her to their bedchamber high in the central tower of Tochers Castle, laid her out on the bed like a corpse and there she had stayed. The midwife and a couple of senior Rams had appeared soon afterwards, tried to shoo away the Duke of Abervenn without realizing what a bad mistake that was. Beulah would have laughed had not another massive contraction starred her vision and convulsed her spine. By the Wolf, how could something as natural as childbirth hurt so much?

It was Archimandrite Cassters himself who had finally given her some bitter-tasting drink that gave her a little relief. It hadn't taken the pain away so much as make her stop caring. Beulah floated above the scene, watching with a mixture of horror and fascination as the whole messy process took its lengthy time.

When the child arrived, finally, in a mess of blood and shit that made her feel like an infant herself, Beulah had been snapped back into herself by the shock. She was soaked with sweat, her hair hanging limply over her eyes so that at first she couldn't see what was going on. Clun, bless him, had wiped her brow with a soft cloth, cleaning her up as best he could as she felt the agony slowly ebb away. It was replaced with a bone-deep weariness and a horrible sense of anticlimax she couldn't understand.

And then something wailed like an infant. A fat woman Beulah scarcely recognized waddled into her view, holding a bundle of rags in her arms.

'A daughter, Your Majesty. Praise be the Shepherd. She's small but strong.'

'Like her mother, then.' Clun stood, taking the bundle

from the old woman, who did something more of a bow than a curtsy and backed away. Beulah was still aware of her presence, not far off, and that of several others. Her vision seemed to peter out after about five feet though, the room fading into darkness so that all she could see were her bedcovers, Clun and this tiny thing that he carried.

'Our daughter, my lady,' Clun said. He bent low to the bed, presenting the bundle, and only then did Beulah see it for what it was. A tiny red-faced infant stared out at her with black, emotionless eyes. It was like a person but so small. How could anything that small exist? How could it survive? It had been wiped down, but its cheeks were still crusty with birthing fluids. Without thinking, she reached out and rubbed at the mess, trying to clean it off, annoyed that someone hadn't already done so. Stimulated, the child fixed those bottomless black eyes on her, reached out with tiny arms.

'Here, take her.' Clun lowered the bundle and Beulah had no option but to accept it. The infant still waved its arms about, fists the size of angry bees flailing at imaginary enemies. There would be plenty of real ones to contend with, Beulah had no doubt.

'How do you feel, Your Majesty?' Archimandrite Cassters appeared in Beulah's limited vision, bending towards the bed with a stiff, arthritic back. The man must have been pushing eighty; it seemed absurd that he should be the one to supervise the birth.

'Weak. Weary. Thirsty.' Beulah only realized just how parched she was as she tried to speak, her words croaky in a throat made hoarse by her earlier screams of pain and curses against mankind. 'How long has it been?'

'Long, ma'am. Let us leave it at that for now. Your mother was the same with you and Lleyn both. It is something of a family trait.' Cassters waved his hand, and a page appeared bearing a small wooden bowl.

'Drink this. It will help.'

Beulah let the archimandrite tilt the bowl to her lips, took a sip of warm, sweet liquid. It soothed her throat and cleared her head a little. Enough to crook her newborn into one arm and take up the bowl with the other and then drink deeper.

'Will I take her?' Clun asked from the other side of the bed. Beulah nodded, watching the tiny face stare at her as he took their child away. It reached out with those impossibly small arms, as if trying to grab hold of her and not let go. She should have felt something for this being she had nurtured inside her almost nine months, but instead she was just relieved to have it taken away.

'We'll need to find a wet nurse,' she said as soon as she had finished the rest of the drink. The sweetness had been there to disguise the bitter herbs, she had realized after the first couple of sips. She didn't care. They would relax her, let her sleep while the maids cleaned her up, sorted out the ruined bedding. What she wouldn't have given to have been back home in Candlehall, where there was endless hot water and deep, deep baths.

'It has been done already, ma'am.' Cassters bent low again, and Beulah feared he might topple over on to her.

'Is there something else?' She knew there was, but the old Ram seemed to be having a hard time deciding how to say whatever was on his mind.

'Please do not take this the wrong way, my queen. You

have been through an ordeal I cannot begin to imagine; you are tired and perhaps not completely in your own mind. I would strongly suggest you consider raising the infant yourself.' Cassters paused a moment before adding, 'Feeding your child yourself.'

Beulah almost laughed, except that she didn't have the energy, and the herbs were beginning to make her drowsy. She was sure that she would feel something for her child when she had recovered from the trauma of the birth, but right now all she wanted was to be rid of the thing, have her skill at magic return, get back to how it had all been before.

'I will think about it, Cassters,' she said, patting him gently on the back of his liver-spotted hand. 'But now I would rest.'

15

Where accident or misadventure have rendered a limb absent or so damaged as to require amputation, then a spell of regrowing may be attempted. Success depends as much upon the patient as the healer, since the limb must be visualized within the patient's own aura to give the flesh a form around which it can grow. A dragon skilled in the subtle arts will have no difficulty creating and maintaining such a visualization, and equally will be able to speed the regrowth of the missing limb.

Accidents will all too often befall the young, however. In such a case a spell of binding may be used and the healer's own aura adopted for the task. It will be necessary to keep the patient sedated and restrained, at least in the early stages of regrowth. Once the new limb has set enough into the old flesh, the patient can be allowed to wake, but a limb regrown this way will take many months to reach full size, longer still to regain full strength.

Healer Trefnog, *The Apothecarium*

A dull throbbing pain began in the stump of his arm after a couple of hours' walking. Benfro tried to ignore it, focusing instead on the strange trees, the glimpses of exotic animals, the different scents and sounds of this forest which convinced him more than anything that he was not in the Ffrydd any more. The trees were too big for one thing, their trunks swollen like the bellies of long-dead deer, ripe to burst at any moment. Wider than his outstretched wingspan, they looked like enormous mushrooms except for the tiny branches that spiked out from their tops, clad in far too few leaves as if winter were already approaching. And yet no dead litter covered the forest floor, just dry, dusty earth and wiry brown shrubs.

He didn't know what they were called, but talking was difficult, admitting his lack of knowledge even more so. Cerys was a good companion, supporting him without complaint, at times talking, at other times falling silent. She had said it wasn't far, but without any frame of reference Benfro had no idea what that meant. Was it an afternoon's walk? A day's? A week's? With each new step he grew wearier, the pain seeping into him and draining his energy. His vision darkened, and he thought the sun must be setting, somewhere far beyond the green canopy.

'Whoa! Steady there, Benfro.' Cerys tightened her grip on his good arm as he stumbled, then regained his balance. The rush brought him awake again, lightening the view as he realized he'd almost fallen asleep walking. It put him in mind of the endless march through the forest after Melyn had killed his mother, the stupor that had allowed Magog to lure him in. The thought sent a shudder through him.

'Can we rest a moment? I've no energy left.'

'Well we could . . .' Cerys let her words trail off as Benfro started to sink to his knees. The ground here was hard-packed dirt and stone, uncomfortable, but he didn't really care.

'Or you could walk another dozen paces to Myfanwy's house. I'm sure she'll have something to perk you up. And get that hand a-healing.'

Benfro looked up and saw they weren't alone. The hard earth beneath his feet was actually a road, straight and wide, and either side of it were not the bulbous trees he was expecting, at least not immediately. There were houses, after a fashion. Quite unlike the solid constructions that the villagers at home had lived in, crafted from stone and carefully worked seasoned timbers, these were more flowing in their construction, and at first he couldn't work out what they were made out of. They were tall too, stretching up higher even than the old stone hall that had stood at the centre of his village. The hall that Inquisitor Melyn had set aflame.

'Who's that you've got with you, Cerys?'

Benfro started at the voice, at first not seeing where it came from. And then he saw it all as if a veil had been pulled from in front of his eyes. These houses were trees. Dead ones, he guessed, by their lack of branches and leaves. The trunks were darker grey, split carefully to form doors, windows. By the look of things, they had several storeys; his neck ached as he looked up to see roofs of bark shingles. Walking stooped for so long had tied his muscles in knots, and he winced as they tried to unravel themselves.

'I found him out by Bagger's Hill, Myfanwy. Says his name's Benfro. Sorry. Sir Benfro of the Borrowed Wings.' Cerys ducked away under Benfro's arm, leaving him standing on his own for the first time in hours. He swayed dangerously, convinced he was going to tumble to the road, and then another dragon was in front of him.

'He's fair fit to pass out. What've you done to him, girl?'

Benfro tried to focus, but the world was dragging him down. He felt a hand on his face, the grip firm but not unkind as it lifted his head and turned it. It took a moment for his eyes to focus, but then . . .

'Corwen?'

'Corwen? Who's Corwen?' The dragon in front of him coughed, then spat something slippery on to the ground. As Benfro studied the face he realized his mistake. This was an old dragon, most certainly. Only the passage of many years, thousands perhaps, could leave a face so wrinkled and wizened. But it was also the face of a female dragon.

'I'm sorry. I thought you were—'

'Where're you from, lad? That accent's not local.' The elderly dragon turned Benfro's head this way and that, peering at him closely with eyes that seemed too clouded to be able to see anything. She let go of his head, which drooped under its own sudden weight, then took up his arm. 'My, you have been in the wars, haven't you. How did this happen?'

Benfro gathered the last of his strength, sure he was going to faint at any moment. The pain in his arm was spreading past his elbow and up into his shoulder now, swamping what little energy he had for thinking.

'It was Melyn. He cut me with his blade of light. I had to escape. Didn't know where to go. I . . .'

The memory of it rushed up at him as he spoke. Or maybe it was the ground. Benfro thought he might have heard the old dragon mutter something, but the words were lost in the blackness.

The village was like many he had seen before and at the same time like none. Errol tried not to let his mouth hang open as he walked down the track that led from the thinning trees to the first few buildings, past enclosures with low stone walls. Goats ambled up to greet him, but they were much larger than the animals he remembered from Pwllpeiran and the few hardy beasts that lived in and around Emmass Fawr. A couple of stringy-looking dogs eyed him suspiciously from their resting place in the shade of a large tree, but they did nothing more. Everything was normal, except for the heat.

The sun, high overhead, beat down with an intensity he had never before experienced. It didn't help that his head still hurt from whatever it was Captain Osgal had used to knock him senseless. The pain was focused around a lump at the top of his neck, but it was very similar to the terrible wine hangover that was the most abiding memory of the end of his childhood. The ache pulsed in time with his heartbeat, and the glare reflecting off the dry dusty track made him squint. The drink from the sap of the tree had helped, but its effects had worn off after the first hour of walking. Now he just wanted to find somewhere cool to lie down and sleep for a week.

'Is this where you live?' Errol asked of the young girl walking beside him. Nellore said nothing but pointed further up the track. The houses either side here were single storey, windows no more sophisticated than openings in the walls. Rope curtains hung over the doorways, and

Errol thought he might have seen one or two twitch as they walked past, but he had seen no people yet.

Further up the track, where Nellore had pointed, the houses were larger, with narrow alleys between them. Some had awnings around them, over raised porches, and this was where Errol caught his first sight of another person. At first he thought the man was dead, lying in a rocking chair with his head back and his mouth wide open. But as they approached, he let out a great grunt of a snore, snapped his mouth shut and looked straight at them. For a moment his face showed only puzzlement, then it deepened into a scowl.

'Who's that with you, Nellore? You should know better than to go speaking to strangers.' The man made a great show of hauling himself out of the rocking chair and hitching up his canvas trousers. Then he clumped down off the porch and stepped into the track, eyeing Errol up and down suspiciously. A couple of other people appeared from silent doorways, and suddenly there was a crowd.

'I'm sorry,' Errol said. 'I don't mean any harm. I'm just looking for a friend of mine.'

'A friend, eh?' The man from the rocking chair looked like he had heard of the concept of friendship and wanted nothing to do with it. 'What's his name? What's your name, for that matter?'

'His name's Errol,' Nellore answered before Errol could speak, and he was surprised by the bitterness in her tone. At her age he wouldn't have dared speak to an elder like that.

'He?' The old man peered more closely, the suspicious

frown deepening on his brow as he did so. 'Looks like a woman to me.'

'I had to dress like this. Some . . . people were chasing me. Wanted to kill me.'

'Sounds like trouble, if'n you ask me.' The old man addressed his comment to Nellore as if Errol no longer existed for him. 'Don't want no trouble round here.'

'Well you just go back to your rocking chair and your pipe then, Ben Sorrenson. The lad looks half dead and I don't suppose he's seen a square meal in days.'

Errol looked up to see who had spoken and saw a middle-aged woman at the front of the crowd. She had a careworn look about her, but the smile on her face was genuine and welcoming.

'He's trouble. I can see it plain as the day.' The old man turned away, headed back to his porch muttering all the way. 'Don't want to upset the gods. Don't need that kind of bad luck here.'

'Pay no heed to Ben, lad. He's always grumbling about the gods. But we make 'em sacrifice when we can, and they leaves us alone. Come on. Let's see if we can't get you something to eat, eh?'

Errol was about to ask what gods the woman was referring to. As far as he was aware, there was just the one, the Shepherd. Something stopped him though, possibly the thought of food. His head hurt but not as much as the knot of emptiness that was his stomach.

'I'll go have a look through my da's old things, see if we can't get you some better clothes. He was about your size.' Nellore hurried off in the direction of one of the larger buildings, leaving Errol alone with the crowd.

'So, Errol. Where you from then?' The middle-aged woman took him by the arm, steering him to the opposite side of the track from the old man and his rocking chair. Too weary to resist, Errol let himself be led towards a low stone house, single storey, between larger buildings. It had no porch, just a set of wooden steps climbing to an open door.

'Where did I come from?' The question gave him pause. Not that he didn't know; he'd come from King Ballah's throne room in Tynhelyg. But that would mean nothing to these people, and for the most part they were already viewing him with suspicion. He settled for a compromise answer. 'North of here. A long way away. You'll probably never have heard of it.'

The woman gave him a knowing smile, nudged him gently in the ribs. 'Don't want anyone coming after you to know where you've gone, eh?'

'I . . . Ah, no. Not really.'

'Well, no mind. We don't get many through here anyway. Not exactly on the way to anywhere special. Just us and the gods out here.'

Again that reference to the gods. It put Errol on edge. He wanted to ask more but knew his ignorance of something so important would make him seem even more suspicious. Best to puzzle it out for himself, or maybe ask Nellore if the right moment presented itself.

He followed the woman up the steps and into a large room that took up the whole of the front of the building. It was cool inside, a welcome relief from the sweltering heat of the afternoon. Of even greater interest to Errol though was the smell of cooking emanating from a tiny stove on the far side of the room. A mixture of unfamiliar spices and rich meaty notes, it immediately set his stomach to growling.

'Dearie me, when was the last time you ate, Errol?'

'I'm not really sure. A while ago.'

'Well sit yourself down at the table and I'll bring you a bowl of stew. There's a loaf on the side there too. Cut yourself a slab.'

Errol looked to where she'd indicated, seeing a board, a knife and a loaf of darkest brown bread. He could have just torn chunks off it and shoved them in his mouth, such was his hunger, but he resisted the urge, slicing off a piece as the woman busied herself at the stove. By the time he'd turned back to the table, she had placed a wooden bowl of something brown and lumpy in front of the one chair.

'Sit, Errol. Eat. Before you fall down.'

'I'm sorry. Thank you for your kindness. This looks delicious. But I don't even know your name.'

The woman stared at him as if he were mad, then shook her head. 'Of course you don't. Silly me. I'm Murta. Pleased to meet you. Now sit! Eat!'

The meal was perhaps the finest he had ever tasted. To be fair, it could have been thin gruel and stale bread and he would have thought it was a feast, but even with hunger dulling his senses, the food was unlike any Errol had eaten before. There was a hot spiciness to the gravy, and the meat had a tender texture that suggested it had been hung for a good while before being cooked long and slow. Remembering how the drink from the tree had left him bloated, he forced himself to eat slowly, savouring each mouthful. And all the while Murta watched him but said nothing. In many ways she reminded Errol of his mother. She had that same no-nonsense air about her, a pragmatism borne of experience. He wondered how Hennas was, how her new life with Godric Defaid was working out, and a wave of homesickness swept over him.

'Oh my, Errol. You look fit to collapse.'

The feeling passed as quickly as it had come. 'Just a bit woozy,' he said. 'I got hit on the back of the head.'

Without asking, Murta walked around behind him and began inspecting the wound. 'You've a nasty lump. I don't doubt your brain's all a bit mixed up in there. Best thing you can do is get some rest.'

'I really need to find my friend,' Errol protested, even though he knew it was a waste of time. Murta was right. He needed to rest, and everything would be clearer in the morning.

'Nonsense. You'll sleep here, and I'll go help Nellore look out some more suitable clothes for you. The gods know she needs to sort out that house of hers.'

Errol stood up slowly, aware that his balance wasn't as good as it should be. He shoved his hands deep into the pockets of his travelling cloak, hoping to find the money Lord Gremmil had given him what seemed like a lifetime ago. He felt the small leather purse, then beneath it a rough bundle of cloth. The strange glass orb he'd taken from Loghtan's wagon. There was a similar bundle in his other pocket, and he was halfway to feeling what was wrapped inside it before he remembered. The two jewels, one white from Benfro's mother, one red and evil from Magog. Hastily he shoved them back, pulling the purse out instead.

'You'll at least let me give you something for your

trouble,' he said, fishing around for a coin. It was Llan-wennog money, but it was also pure silver. There were also a few pieces of gold.

'There's no need, Errol. But it's mighty fine of you to offer. There's plenty wouldn't even say thank you.' Murta nodded her head in the direction of the door, and incidentally the house across the street where old man Sorrenson was again dozing in his rocking chair.

'Well, if there's anything I can do. Cleaning up, carrying logs.'

'Best you can do now is get some rest. Come.' Murta pushed through a rope-curtained doorway at the back of the room and Errol followed. A narrow corridor led to the back of the house and a view of a sun-baked yard. Either side of it, more doors opened on to smaller rooms. The one nearest the back was sparsely furnished, just a wooden storage chest, a simple chair and a low bed with a bare mattress on it.

'My boy slept in there when he was still with us. He's with the gods now, bless him. You can have his bed for the now. The outhouse is in the yard and there's water in the well. Sleep as long as you need.'

'Thank you,' Errol said as he finished a slow turn, taking in the whole room. But Murta had already left.

Three days into his recuperation, and Melyn was beginning to regret having killed King Ballah. It had to be done, of course. There was no way peace could ever exist between the two nations, and no way they could become one while the house of Ballah still existed. But the old king's living apartments, far from being the luxurious and ostentatious waste of money he had expected were actually surprisingly small and sparse. They suggested a man who shared Melyn's asceticism and distaste of opulence, a man with whom in other circumstances it might have been pleasant to have spent some time.

Ballah's bedchamber was perhaps no bigger than Melyn's own back at Emmass Fawr, its walls hung with tapestries which depicted ancient hunting scenes and kept out the worst of the chill. A single window looked out over the formal gardens, not at their best as the summer slid gently into autumn. Most tellingly, the bed was close to but not situated upon a major nexus in the Grym. That lay beyond the bedchamber, in a small reception room where the king had no doubt conducted his important and private business. The apartments also contained a bathroom, which Melyn might have considered an unnecessary luxury were it not for the need to keep himself scrupulously clean while he healed. There was also a large library, and he longed to spend time there. An all-too-brief perusal of its shelves had revealed an eclectic mix of literature and many treatises on the forms of magic that made his natural curiosity burn bright.

But he had so far been confined to the king's bed, venturing out to the reception room only to receive reports from Osgal as the captain set about the task of securing the city. They didn't really have enough men for the task, even if every warrior priest was more than capable of taking on ten regular soldiers without even having to conjure a blade of light. It wasn't so much about fighting as running a city bigger even than Candlehall. The people were frightened and confused, the merchants clamouring to know who was in charge now. It was only a matter of time before they formed an unruly mob that would be time-consuming and wasteful to deal with. For once he wished Seneschal Padraig were on hand. A few dozen Candles would soon have the place running smoothly. Maybe he should have brought some with him, across the great forest and through the mountains of the Rim. Melyn almost laughed at the thought, but the pain stopped him.

He needed to contact Clun; that was the most pressing matter. But the wound sapped his strength and concentration both, making it all but impossible to travel the aethereal even with the help of Brynceri's ring. He had taken it off anyway, unable to muster the strength to control it properly. Time would sort things out, time and Frecknock's medical knowledge. She had cleaned and stitched his wound, found ingredients and prepared a sweet-smelling poultice which had taken away the inflammation around the edges of the cut, but she could not speed up the healing process any more than that.

'Your Grace. You're looking much better this morning. May I inspect the wound?'

As if summoned by his thoughts, Frecknock stood at the door to the bedchamber, her head bowed in that manner of hers. Self-deprecating, as if she truly thought herself worthless. Melyn suspected it was unconscious now. She shrank in on herself, made herself as small as possible whenever she was in the company of men. He tried to remember the dragon they had taken from the village all those months ago. Had she been larger then? Certainly in his mind it seemed so, although that could just have been because he was not used to seeing her around. Or it could have been that she truly had grown smaller, that all the dragons of Gwlad had shrunk over the centuries of their persecution. The thought sent an involuntary shudder through him. If dragons had dwindled in fear of men, then what had changed to lead to the existence of Caradoc and Morwenna the Subtle? How had Benfro grown from a scrawny kitling into the massive savage creature that had attacked him?

'Do what you must.' Melyn lay back as Frecknock approached. Her large hands and long, taloned fingers delicately peeled back his sleeping robe to expose the white linen bandages underneath. He was unaccustomed to the softness of the bedding, perhaps the one thing that made him think less of King Ballah. There might be something to be said for sleeping in comfort, but too much led to softness, woolly thinking and the lack of focus that had ultimately been the king's undoing.

'At least everything is clean today. I think the wound has sealed itself now.'

Melyn sat up to allow Frecknock to unravel the bandages. For the past three days they had been soiled with a mixture of blood and pus, but today they had only a light crust of the healing poultice on the innermost winding. There was no smell of infection either, which had to be a good thing. The dragon took up a basin of warm water and began cleaning the gash across his chest and the smaller one below that had almost opened up his belly. Benfro had come very close to killing him indeed; Melyn could see the irony in it being another dragon who repaired the damage.

'Why do you help me?' he asked as Frecknock gently applied a fresh poultice.

'I swore a blood oath, Your Grace.' The dragon took up a roll of clean bandages, working more swiftly and with greater dexterity than any battle-hardened field surgeon Melyn had ever seen.

'There's more to it than that though, isn't there?' Melyn pulled his robes back around himself as the dragon backed away, picking up the basin of dirtied water and dumping the used bandages into it, snatching up the stone mortar in which she had mixed the poultice. She was uncomfortable with the question.

'I . . . I never understood before, but it is our way.'

'Your way?'

'Morgwm tried to explain it to me, as part of my learning. She would never turn away anyone, be they human or dragon, friend or foe. If she could help them then she would. I thought it was just her, but it's not. It's part of being a dragon.'

'Even if it means saving the life of someone who's sworn to kill you?'

'Even so.' Frecknock dropped her head low, but it was a different kind of nod to the one she used to indicate her subservience. This was more resignation, as if she was admitting she had no control over her behaviour. Her utter spinelessness angered Melyn, although he couldn't for the life of him understand why he cared.

'No wonder your kind are close to extinction. Here, help me up. I'll see Osgal and the others in the reception room.'

'Are you sure, sire? After yesterday? Your cut—'

'I will not brief my senior officers from my bed.'

'As you command, Your Grace.' Frecknock placed the

bowl and mortar on a table under the window, then helped Melyn out of bed and into his day robes. It galled him that he needed her help, but at least she was not a warrior priest. Even Osgal, whom he had tutored since he first arrived at Emmass Fawr as a terrified young novitiate, should not be allowed to see his inquisitor so frail. Not ever, but especially not when the morale of his troop was so precariously balanced between the euphoria of their triumph and despair at being in the heart of enemy territory with little hope of any relief soon.

King Ballah's reception room was scarcely any more opulent than the bedchamber, though perhaps a little larger. It had two windows looking out on the gardens, and doors to the library and a long corridor leading to the throne room. More importantly, it had a large desk with a chair centred directly over a strong nexus in the Grym. Not as strong as the throne itself, but enough that Melyn could tap into the energy without too much effort. It was a good place to conduct the business of the city from, the thousand and one tiny details that demanded his attention and yet didn't require the ostentation of the throne room to add gravitas. It helped that the chair was comfortable too, though too much comfort could be a bad thing. Melyn set the Grym to speed his healing, knowing that he would pay for it in exhaustion later. Only once he was settled and ready did he bark the command, 'Enter!'

Osgal had obviously been waiting out in the corridor, and for some time if the look on the captain's face was anything to go by. His face was normally florid, but now the burns dealt him by Benfro's magical flame weeped slightly, taking their time healing. He should perhaps have used some of Frecknock's poultice on them, but Melyn reckoned Osgal would rather suffer. His disapproval of the dragon was written clearly in the scowl he directed at her as he clasped a hand across his chest in salute.

'Your Grace.'

'Situation report, Captain,' Melyn said. The formality irked him.

'We have dealt with all the organized resistance in the city, sir. There is unrest among the general population, but I think that's more about not knowing who's in charge. I get the feeling there wasn't a lot of love for the House of Ballah among the common people.'

'What about the merchants? I presume there's a delegation of them wanting to speak to me.'

Osgal managed a flicker of a smile at that. 'They are predictable, sir. And there are many Twin Kingdoms sympathizers. Or at least free trade sympathizers. I don't think we need worry too much about them for now.'

'And what of Prince Geraint? What of Tordu?'

'I have sent scouts south, sir. But we can't spare many men. We never planned to take the city or kill the king. Our task was to draw the armies back north.'

Melyn felt a twinge of pain in his chest as he shifted in the seat. He tried to keep it from his face, but Frecknock must have noticed as she tensed, began to step forward, then remembered herself.

'I am well aware of that, Captain. If necessary we will withdraw from the city and disappear into the northlands. In the meantime we must do all we can to secure Tynhelyg for a siege. Speak to the merchants. Assure them their interests will be well served under Queen Beulah. I will see if I can't track down Geraint and his armies.'

The captain nodded his understanding, turned and headed for the door. Melyn stopped him just before he left: 'Oh, and Osgal?'

'Sir?'

'Make sure the people have enough food, at least for now. Don't give them any more excuse to rebel than they already have.'

'I expect he'll live. He's young and strong. Going to take a while to grow that hand back though. How did you find him?'

'He just fell out of the sky. There I was minding my own business . . .'

'When did you ever mind your own business, Cerys? You said you found him over Bagger's Hill way. What were you doing there?'

Benfro heard the voices as if he were underwater, the words booming and fading in waves. He couldn't see anything but then realized that was because his eyes were closed. He tried to open them, but nothing seemed to work.

'I think he's waking up, Myfanwy. Look.'

Benfro sensed more than saw the movement around him, then he felt a hand on his forehead again, talons clicking against his scales. He was as weak as a newly hatched kitling, helpless to do anything about it as his eyelid was forced delicately open and he found himself staring at the blurred image of a dragon's head.

'Wha—'

'Shhh. You're not done healing yet.' The face moved

away from his vision, but his eye stayed open. Without moving his head, Benfro couldn't see much, but he could tell he was inside a room, the ceiling overhead hung with drying herbs. As he thought this, so their aromas began to present themselves to him: fragrant rosemary and thyme, the bitterness of wormwood root and the sharp tang of cedar bark. Other smells added to the mix, putting him in mind of the smoke in the cave where the circus master, Loghtan, had captured him. That had rendered him senseless, robbed him of what little skill in the subtle arts he had. Now he felt much the same and struggled against the shackles in his mind.

'Calm yourself, Benfro. You need all your strength to mend that hand. Best you don't move at all. Let Myfanwy's healings work their magic.' More movement, and Benfro felt the presence of another dragon slide alongside him. A smaller hand rested on his shoulder, and then a wing extended, wrapping him tight as his mother had done when he was still small and the night terrors came.

'I'll stay with him. Make sure he doesn't do himself any harm.'

'Tsk. Young things. You might want to hold your breath a moment then.'

Benfro was about to ask why, but a soft scent of smoke tickled his nose, causing him to sneeze then breathe in deeply. He should have been panicked, but instead he felt safe and warm, wrapped in his mother's embrace as he drifted off into a deep, deep sleep.

16

The aethereal trance is the most complicated of magics to perform. You must be at the same time completely aware of yourself and at once distant to all distraction. Few have even a hint of the talent, and those who do show some aptitude must study for years, sometimes decades, before they can master it enough for it to be of any practical use.

So what is the aethereal, and how might it be used? Many scholarly texts have been written about the first of those questions, and no doubt many more are yet to come. For practical purposes they are worthless. More successful might be an attempt to understand the Shepherd and his reasoning. As to the second question, well, the principal benefit of the aethereal is that it exists largely out of time and distance. An adept might leave his mundane self in Candlehall and travel to Emmass Fawr with just a thought. Messages can be relayed from one adept to another in this manner, and this is the most common use of the skill. Its one major limitation is that an adept must have been in both places in the mundane, have studied them and know every last physical detail of them, before he can be confident of safely travelling between the two.

There are those who profess to be able to wander

the aethereal at will, to use it as a means to scout out enemy terrain or infiltrate heavily guarded places. It is true that anyone achieving the trance may stray from the paths they know, but the lure of this plane, much like the lure of the Grym, is such that they will likely never find their way back.

Father Castlemilk, An Introduction to the Order of the High Ffrydd

'It was never meant for a man to sit in, was it?'

Prince Dafydd stood in the middle of the Neuadd and stared up at the vast bulk of the Obsidian Throne. Beside him, Usel the medic was fidgeting with his brown robes, obviously uncomfortable in the great open space. Dafydd could only sympathize; the place was so awash with the Grym it was hard to concentrate. And it all focused on that one huge chair.

'Take away the later additions and its design is remarkably similar to the chairs that dragons use. You can go around and see, sire. There's no proper back to it, just a space for a tail.'

'Dragons sit in chairs?' Apart from occasional visits to the circus as a boy, and their brief encounter with the dragon on the island in the Caldy archipelago, Dafydd had never really considered the creatures. At best he would have thought them wild, like large carrion birds or the mountain lions that stole sheep from the upland flocks. But that didn't square with the magnificent wings and courtly manners of Merriel, daughter of Earith.

'Most prefer benches. They're easier to get on and off.

Some designs are more elaborate than others, but this is most definitely a dragon's chair.'

Dafydd paced slowly around the dais on which the throne sat. Once you started looking it was easy to see what was original and what were later additions. 'But it's so big. Surely no dragon was ever this size.'

'Not in this realm, true. And not for very many centuries. But once dragons ruled supreme. And I've a feeling they are going to be back soon.'

'Ah, the old gods return. I've read my *Mad Goronwy*, Usel. I didn't have you pegged as one of those Guardians of the Throne fanatics.'

Usel managed to look shocked. 'I have nothing to do with them.' Then he smiled. 'Well, maybe not nothing. I am part of an order that predates the so-called Guardians of the Throne by centuries, but we both have similar goals. Only where they seek to hasten the end by killing anyone who doesn't agree with them, we just try to make sure there is a throne still here when the true king returns.'

'By which you mean a bloody big dragon, I take it.'

'Well. The throne would suggest as much.'

Dafydd walked to the front of the throne and stared up again, following the line of its tall back, those twin spires of purest black, as they rose towards the vaulted ceiling high overhead. The Neuadd was so large it felt like it had its own climate. For men to have built it, thousands of years ago, was inconceivable. That it might have been built by dragons, however vast they might have been, wasn't much easier to accept.

'Any news of the princess?' He pushed away these troubling thoughts with more pressing concerns.

'Word has been sent to Abervenn, sire. I would expect her to be here soon.'

'And what of Beulah? I don't doubt she's heard of our little adventure by now. I'd expect an army to be marching towards us at speed.'

Usel's brow furrowed for a moment, and Dafydd felt something in the Grym he couldn't quite put his finger on. The silence in the hall was all the more noticeable for the size of the place. There should have been echoes, the dull noise of the city beyond as it prepared itself for the inevitable siege. And yet here mundane sounds could not penetrate, only the silent roar of a thousand thousand worried thoughts.

'My apologies, sire. My usual contacts are not as reliable at the moment as they should be.' For the first time since he had met the man, Dafydd saw something akin to worry on Usel's face.

'So you don't know.'

'I know she was at Tochers and she gave birth to a daughter. Beyond that, I'm drawing a blank.'

'Perhaps we should speak to Seneschal Padraig. I'm sure he has spies everywhere. Fetch him for me, would you, Usel. But not here. I find this place a little overwhelming.'

'I'll have him meet you in the palace reception rooms. Best to conduct business a good distance from all this.' Usel nodded his head, which was as much of a bow as could be expected of the man, then departed, walking silently across the polished marble floor. Dafydd watched him go and not for the first time wondered just whose side the medic was on. He took one last look at the ridiculously large throne, glad he had decided it wasn't his to sit on, then followed the medic out of the great hall.

'You're awake. Good. Time to get up and make yourself useful then.'

Benfro rolled over from where he had been sleeping, a soft nest of thin branches and dried heather that had moulded itself comfortably to his shape. His mind was clear after what felt like weeks of confusion and dream. He remembered everything. The fight with Melyn, the rush to escape, landing in a clearing and the young dragon, Cerys, who had helped him. Brought him to . . .

'Myfanwy?' The elderly dragon had her back to him, her massive wings limp at her sides. Benfro struggled up into a sitting position, noticing as he did that the stump where his hand had been no longer hurt. He held it up and was amazed to see a tiny hand budding out from the wound. Instinctively he flexed his fingers and the tiny hand moved.

'The less you play with it, the quicker it will grow.' The old dragon hadn't turned to face him, but Benfro felt the heat of embarrassment in his face anyway.

'I'm sorry. I don't know how to thank you enough.'

'It's nothing.' The old dragon turned finally and Benfro got another look at that face. Free of his delirium, he could see that she didn't look much like Corwen at all. Just very, very old. The scales had all fallen from her face and neck, scarred leathery skin showing where they should have been and making her look a bit like some half-plucked chicken. One of her eyes was glazed white, but the other pierced him with a stare that saw through everything. 'I'm forever patching up wounds. You wouldn't believe how much this lot bicker and fight. Yours was just cleaner than any I've seen in a while.'

'Well I'm grateful anyway. For everything. You must let me know how I can repay you.'

Myfanwy cocked her ancient head to one side at Benfro's words. 'You're not from around here, are you.' It wasn't a question.

'I don't really know where here is,' Benfro said. 'I had to get away, didn't know where to go, so I just kind of felt out along the lines and jumped.'

'You travelled the Llinellau Grym? I'm impressed. Perhaps there's more to you than I thought, Benfro of the Borrowed Wings. Tell me, what was so terrible that you risked losing yourself completely? What did you do up at the castle that was so bad they took your hand?'

'The castle? What castle?'

'Come, Benfro. No need to be shy. None of us here have any great fondness for those stuck-up idiots and their doddering old fool of a master.' Myfanwy frowned. 'Been a while since I heard of any new hatchlings up there, mind you. Most of them wouldn't know how it's done any more. Too swept up in their studies.'

'I'm very sorry, but I've really no idea what you're talking about.'

'No?' Myfanwy left the question hanging for a moment. 'Oh well. It's no matter. You're here. Now clear out of my house so I can get some rest without having to listen to your endless snoring.'

Benfro scrambled to his feet. 'Is there anything I can do to help? I know herbs. Could fetch you fresh ones.'

'But do you know where to find them in this forest, eh?' Myfanwy cocked her head to one side again, another curiously bird-like gesture. 'No. But thank you for the offer. It's more than the last ingrate I patched up ever made. Go. Make yourself useful to the fold. Just don't get yourself injured again too soon.'

It wasn't until he was outside blinking at the bright sunlight that Benfro realized he didn't really know what a fold was, let alone how he could be useful to one. That was perhaps the smallest of the things he didn't know though. He had no idea where he was, for one thing, which was a far more pressing problem. As was how he was going to even start finding Errol. Or Gog.

'You're up. Thought you were going to sleep for ever.'

Benfro recognized the voice and was surprised at just how pleased he felt to hear it. Cerys circled overhead, her outstretched wings showing intricate patterns and whorls that it seemed somehow inappropriate to stare at. She wheeled, one wing tip almost touching the ground, then landed with perfect precision just a few paces away from him.

'How's the hand?' she asked as she folded her wings and sauntered up. Benfro took a while to gather his wits, closing his mouth at the same time as he held his arm up for inspection.

Cerys grinned at him. 'She's a good healer, Myfanwy. Rubbish bedside manner, mind you. Come on. Let's go meet the others. They've been asking all about you for days now.'

'Others?' Benfro asked. 'Days?' Cerys paid him no heed, unfurled her wings again and leaped into the air in one swift movement that was as graceful as anything he'd ever seen.

'Keep up now, Benfro of the Borrowed Wings. Wouldn't want you getting lost again.'

Benfro watched her climb steadily into the sky, uncertain what he should do. His last memory of flying was at the circus, whirling round and round the tent just above the ground. In the air he was fine, but he'd never quite mastered the art of getting there, and though he'd mastered landing after a fashion, that was under the influence of Loghtan's drugs. Even clear-headed he was fairly sure he'd end up on his belly in the dirt again. And yet Cerys had made it look so simple, so elegant.

He unfurled his wings, feeling their weight. The muscles in his back were stiff, and it felt good to stretch them. He tried a few experimental sweeps, judging the lift of each one. Could he really just leap into the air and head off like Cerys had done? Always before it had been a matter of running as fast as he could, hoping that he could get enough height before he ran out of open space, but was that really necessary?

'What you still doing down there?'

Benfro looked up to see Cerys wheeling in a thermal, and all he wanted was to be up there with her. One step, two steps and his wings came down together with enough force to lift him from the ground. Enough height that he could get another wingbeat in before he came crashing back down again. Was it really that easy? Perhaps he had learned something from his time at the circus after all.

'Why do you fly so awkwardly?' Cerys asked as he joined the thermal she was riding, gaining its lift for himself.

'Awkwardly? I thought I was good at it. Especially given that I wasn't born with these wings.'

Cerys banked, the wind ruffling the tufts of her ears as she stared at him. Her expression was inscrutable.

'You're a strange creature, Benfro of the Borrowed Wings. I can never tell when you're joking and when you're being serious. Come. Follow me.' And she set off away from the lines of tree houses either side of the wide road. Surprised, it took Benfro a while to get his wits together, longer to catch her. Cerys was swift in the air, as if it were her natural element.

'Do the others not live here?' he asked.

'Live in the woods?' The laugh in Cerys' voice only just hid the sneer. 'Dragons don't live in the woods. Well, apart from mad ones like Myfanwy. We are creatures of the air. We live in the high places.'

She sped off, and Benfro had to work hard to keep up with her. Even so it was wonderful to be flying again, to feel the wind whipping at his face, to sense the currents with the tips of his wings. The forest spread beneath him, mile upon endless mile of green interspersed with clearings, tracks and the occasional lake. Up ahead, a ridge of rock reared up out of the trees like some fossilized leviathan, rising at one end to a sheer cliff many hundreds of feet above the canopy, birds wheeling around the peak. But as they came closer, so the scale changed. Not many hundreds of feet, but many thousands. Not birds, but dragons. Caves pocked the upper face of the cliff, and on the top a flat area sloped gently away back to the forest far beyond.

'Keep close, Benfro of the Borrowed Wings,' Cerys said. 'Not all of my family are as friendly as I am.'

As if hearing her words, a half-dozen dragons split off from the main group and headed towards them at impossible speed. Benfro moved closer to Cerys but not so close that their wings might touch. They were high enough that a fall would be fatal. As the lead dragons neared, he had a horrible sense of foreboding. As if he'd met them before somewhere but he couldn't tell where. They weren't the dragons who had attacked him in his dreamwalking when he had dropped Ynys Môn's jewels, that was for sure. But he knew them from somewhere.

Two of them shot past so quickly he felt the turbulence in the air. They banked swiftly, coming in above and behind in a perfect attacking manoeuvre. Cerys ignored them, so Benfro felt that was perhaps the best thing to do.

'So this is the stray you found, Cerys. He's younger than I expected. Little more than a kitling, I'd say.'

Benfro bit his tongue to avoid answering. The dragon who'd spoken was the largest in the group and fully twice his size. His wings were massive, thick at the front edge and battered as if he'd spent his life fighting. Or crashing into trees.

'I told you he wasn't old, Fflint. And he fought off a terrible beast with claws of flame. Lost his hand escaping here. Myfanwy says he used the lines.'

'Ran away from the castle 'cause he didn't like his lessons, more like. Well, we've lost enough of the fold lately. Not going to turn away any who can pull their weight.' The big dragon wheeled lazily around until he was heading in the same direction, sinking slowly until he was between Benfro and Cerys, forcing them apart. 'Come on then. Let's see what you're made of.'

289

The dragons who had been circling in the air above the cliff top had all landed now and were standing around on the area of flat ground behind the edge. The rest of their escort landed swiftly, then Fflint spiralled down, coming to rest with a grace and precision that belied his size.

'I . . . I'm not very good at landing,' Benfro said as he and Cerys sank slowly towards the ground. There were more dragons waiting, watching, than he had ever seen. Dozens of them filling up the space he would have liked to have used to crash in. But he couldn't. Not here, not now. He'd taken off from a standstill. Surely he could manage a landing?

Cerys just laughed, which wasn't very helpful of her. She folded her wings, swooped down like a hawk towards the crowd, then snapped them open at the last minute. Some of the smaller dragons scattered as she landed, clearing a bit of space for Benfro. Being a little helpful. It still left the difficult bit to him alone. And with everyone watching.

In the end he very nearly got it right. Swooping first left and then right, Benfro clutched his regrowing hand to his chest to avoid damaging it. He had no doubt he looked like a duck trying to land on an icy pond in a high wind, but he timed everything just about right, bringing his wings down in a final, heavy beat as his feet approached the ground. It was covered in short wiry grass, which was just as well. It cushioned his fall as, at the last possible moment, he tripped one foot over the other. Pain lanced up his damaged arm as he fell heavily on it, and the last thing he heard was the braying laughter of the collected fold, the mocking tones of Fflint.

'Oh, well played. Very well played. I think I'm going to like having you around.'

'What's it like then, up the mountain?'

The third day of Errol's stay in the village, and he still hadn't discovered what it was called. After his fine meal at Murta's, an afternoon's sleep had turned into almost twenty hours, and even now he still felt weary. He longed to get started on his search for Martha, certain that this strange land was where he would find her, but Errol had to admit he needed time to recover and build up his strength.

'Up what mountain?'

'C'mon, Errol. I saw you fall out of nowhere, remember. That's mountain magic. Everybody knows that.' Nellore sat beside him on the steps outside the house where she lived. Her house, Errol supposed, although it seemed strange for one so young to live on her own. He still wore his old travelling cloak, but all his other clothes had come from the chest in Murta's son's room and another in this house. It seemed a lot of the villagers had died young.

'What happened to your ma and da?'

'You trying to change the subject?' Nellore asked.

'Maybe. A bit. Not sure I want to talk about where I came from. Least not until I've worked out where I am.'

'Fair enough. Ma died when I was little. Don't remember her much any more. Da was sacrifice last year. He's with the gods now.'

Something about the matter-of-fact way Nellore spoke the words lessened their immediate impact. It took Errol a moment to process them and realize that he didn't understand what they meant. He opened his mouth to ask, but both of them were distracted as a scream shattered the morning quiet. It went on far longer than any scream should, fading into a gurgling moan.

'What in Gwlad . . . ?' Errol stood up, scanning the track in the direction of the noise, but Nellore was already up and running. He hurried after her, catching up only as she rounded the end of a two-storey stone house and darted down the passageway between it and the next building. Past the two of them, he could see a small scrubby orchard, a ladder propped up against one of the trees.

'Hammie! Hammie! Oh no,' Nellore shouted as she ran towards the ladder. As Errol followed he could see what had happened all too easily. Hammie he assumed to be the man with the ladder, who had obviously been picking fruit from the trees. They weren't all that tall, but the topmost branches were far enough from the ground that falling from one could only end badly. A heavy branch lay alongside the prone man, still laden with bulbous pink fruits. A white smear of wood showed where the branch had snapped and, looking up, Errol could see a corresponding tear near the top of the tree.

'He's not breathing. Errol, help!' Nellore was kneeling beside the man now, her head to his chest as she listened for a heartbeat. His legs were twisted badly underneath him, but at least Hammie's neck didn't seem broken. Not from where Errol was, at least.

'Let me get close,' he said as he knelt alongside Nellore. All the medicine and herb lore his mother had taught him slotted into place as he set about checking the man over.

He was breathing, barely, and his pulse fluttered weakly. A quick look at his eyes showed he was out cold, no response to fingers prising open the lids at all.

'OK. Let's have a closer look at the damage, shall we?' Errol sat back on his haunches and tried to find the half-trance that would let him see the aethereal. He wished Benfro were here; the dragon was far more adept at healing than he ever would be. The simple fact that Errol could walk was testament to that. But that was wishful thinking. Benfro was gone, either still back in Tynhelyg and dead at Melyn's hand, or fled to who knew where. Errol concentrated, scrunching his eyes up for a moment. Then he relaxed and opened himself up to the Grym.

The man lay beside him, a riot of violent oranges and reds swirling about his lower body and legs. His head was a dark blue, cold and dying. Errol looked closer and saw the patterns of the fractures, the spread of shock as it pushed its fingers through vital organs. Slowly, methodically, shutting them down. He was going to die. Unless . . .

Errol looked for the lines of the Grym, seeing them everywhere. He reached out for the nearest, pulling the force into him as he would have done back at Emmass Fawr to keep warm. But instead of letting the heat flow through his own body, he directed it into the injured man, paying most attention to the areas where shock was threatening to overwhelm him.

It was a long, hard struggle, maintaining his concentration against a multitude of distractions. Errol was dimly aware of more people arriving at the scene, of Nellore leaving his side. A tiny part of him thanked her for understanding what he was doing and making sure he had the space to do it. Most of him was locked into the task of saving the injured man's life.

Slowly, agonizingly, the shock retreated under the assault of the Grym, something akin to health returning to the man's organs. Errol shifted his focus to the injuries. There was nothing he could do about the major fractures, but he could see numerous sites of internal bleeding, tiny little cuts and tears that would nonetheless prove fatal if not dealt with. At first he was unsure how the Grym could help, but just concentrating it on the individual points seemed to do the trick. One by one the wounds healed, the blood staunched. There was still the small matter of badly broken legs, but that was something he could deal with in the mundane.

'I think he's going to be OK,' Errol said as he let the trance slip and looked down once more at the prone form of the man. He was younger than Errol had first thought, probably not much older than he was himself. His face was slack in unconsciousness, straggly brown hair almost covering his eyes. He wore a rough tunic not unlike the one Nellore had, or the one Errol had found waiting for him on the chair by his bed in Murta's house when he'd woken. Most of the villagers wore very similar cloth. Not quite a uniform, but lacking the individuality of even the poorest inhabitants of Pwllpeiran where he'd grown up.

'What . . . What did you do? I thought he was dead.'

Errol tried to get up, but his legs didn't want to comply. A wave of weariness swept over him, the blood rushing from his head as if he were a bottle and someone had pulled out the stopper. He barely had the energy to turn away from the prone man as he fell forward, the last thing he saw as the blackness claimed him the sight of twenty or more villagers staring at him, each face a picture of disbelief.

Melyn slumped into his chair – King Ballah's chair – and focused again on the Grym. Its warmth seeped through him, washing away the worst of the pain, but it could do nothing for the weariness that pulled at his senses. A stack of reports lay in front of him, but he had no appetite for reading. He preferred to sit, letting the Grym work its slow healing on him. The bed in the other room was more comfortable, but he had never placed much faith in comfort. And it was all but impossible to maintain the respect of your men from a sickbed.

'Your Grace. You should not be doing so much. The wound will take longer to heal.'

'Do you think I don't know that?' Melyn turned too swiftly to glare at the dragon and immediately regretted it.

'I will help you back to your bed,' she said, taking a step towards him. He held up a hand to stop her and she obeyed like a well-trained dog.

'No. I won't be going back to bed just now. There is too much to do. You can help me though. You and this book of yours.' Melyn put a hand on top of the Llyfr Draconius, feeling the surging magics within.

'The book?' Frecknock tried to sound nonchalant, as if it were no great thing, but Melyn could see the hunger in her eyes.

'Yes, the book. And this ring. These are things of great magical power. They help to focus the Grym and to anchor me in the aethereal. I need all the help I can get for what I must do.' Melyn picked up the box containing Brynceri's ring and opened it. The gem set in the slim silver band was dark and lifeless, but he could sense the power coiled in it, waiting. He recalled the thrill he had felt on first wearing it, how it had aided him and his small army as they took Tynhelyg and cut off the head of the House of Ballah. With it he had reached out across Gwlad with but a thought, pulled Clun's aethereal self from him as if it were no more than a coat. It had been intoxicating to wield such power, but it had come at a cost. He would not fall into that trap so easily again. 'I would use Ballah's throne too, but I don't think I can handle it at the moment.'

'You are going to contact Master Clun?' Frecknock asked.

'That much I should be able to manage, and it approaches the time when he should be waiting for me.' Melyn breathed heavily through the pain in his chest. At least the blood wasn't bubbling in his lungs, although how long that would last he couldn't be sure. 'But first I must see if I can find Prince Geraint and his army, and that will take far more effort. Far more skill. And your help.'

Melyn found it hard to read expressions on the dragon's face. It was such an alien thing, all scales and unexpected angles. But her eyes showed her surprise at his request, and they showed something else too. There was a pride there, a happiness that she was valued, of use. A well-trained dog indeed, she would follow her master wherever he bade her go.

She stepped up beside him, taking his hand as he requested. Hers was warmer to the touch than he expected – that always took him by surprise. He felt the energy in her, stronger even than the Grym he tapped from the lines crossing beneath his chair. Melyn settled himself as best he could, shutting out the pain and discomfort, letting his mind slip into the trance state. It took longer than normal, but he pushed back his anger and frustration. No one could be expected to sustain injuries like his and hope to enter the aethereal easily.

When he did find the trance, it was not as he expected. At Emmass Fawr his small rooms or Brynceri's chapel always appeared much as they did in the mundane. The Neuadd was if anything even more magnificent when seen with the mind's eye. In contrast, Ballah's reception room, bedchamber and other apartments disappeared into a grey mist as if they had never been there. The grey continued in all directions, uniform and unchanging. There was only the throne, as far away from him as it would be were he still sitting at Ballah's desk. Melyn started towards it, but a hand on his arm stopped him.

'Your Grace, this is not what it seems.'

Melyn looked around and then up at the face of Frecknock. She was bigger here in the aethereal. Bigger even than she had appeared when she had helped him contact Clun across the maelstrom of unravelling magics that was the forest of the Ffrydd. Her dull grey and black scales had gone, replaced by striking hues of iridescent purple. Even her eyes were flecked with gold, rather than the blank, lifeless black he was used to. But it was her wings that were most noticeable: folded by her sides, they towered over her head in the same way that Benfro's had. This, Melyn realized, was how Frecknock saw herself now. Not the pathetic, downtrodden thing that inhabited the mundane world. Here she had power and purpose. Here she was growing as her fear eased and her self-confidence grew. Despite himself he couldn't help thinking he preferred her that way.

'It would appear that King Ballah has left behind many enchantments, sire. Traps for the unwary. I've no doubt that were you not so sorely injured you would have seen them immediately.'

Melyn concentrated, remembering the layout of the room he was sitting in. Slowly, the grey fog began to roll away, revealing the structure of the palace, the dull life-glows of the people moving around in it and the more focused and certain self-images of the animals.

'The throne is there to attract attention,' Frecknock said. 'It sits on a disturbance of the Grym the likes of which I have only ever seen once before. To go there unprepared would be to lose oneself completely.'

'A cunning trap for any who would try to use the king's power for themselves. Truly, Ballah was a skilled mage.' Melyn composed himself before allowing his aethereal double to rise from the chair. 'But tell me, where else have you seen such a disturbance?'

'In the great hall of the Neuadd, sire. I couldn't help noticing it when I was presented to Her Majesty. When the assassin came for her, I used the subtle arts to stop him from escaping. The Grym flows so strongly through the throne that I very nearly killed him in the process when all I had intended was to confuse his mind.'

Melyn looked back in the direction of Ballah's throne, but the walls of the palace had reasserted themselves and he could no longer see it. He could feel it though, any adept worthy of the name would have been able to feel it. And Frecknock was right, it had the flavour of the Obsidian Throne about it. But that was a mystery for another time. Now he had other more pressing things to attend to.

'Can you sense the Duke of Abervenn?' he asked. Frecknock stretched her slender neck, raising her head high and sniffing at the air like a dog. Her scales glistened in the strange light of the aethereal.

'He is at Tochers, sire. Would you like me to contact him?'

'He is with the queen?'

'Yes. And another. She has given birth.'

A child, an heir. Melyn almost slipped out of his aethereal trance at the news, catching himself at the last minute. 'Can you take me to them?'

'Of course, sire. Now?'

Melyn considered it. He would like to see them, and there was much to discuss. But the whereabouts of Prince Geraint was more pressing.

'No. We will contact them later. Reconnaissance first. Help me find the Llanwennog army.'

Frecknock nodded and held out her hand again. Melyn took it, feeling the warmth and the silky texture of those tiny scales that covered her palms. There was a moment's sensation of incredible speed, the room blurring from his aethereal vision, and then they were somewhere else altogether.

17

A dragon's true place is in the air. Yes, she is master of the ground, the mundane and aethereal planes, the Grym and the subtle arts. All these are hers to command, but it is on the wing that she will show her true mettle. Should you wish to know the true measure of a dragon, then study her in flight. Some will seek to batter the air into submission, to conquer it by main force with no thought as to how it might react to the onslaught. Such a beast will be the same in other walks of life and would make an unsuitable companion for all but the most foolhardy.

Likewise a timid dragon in the air will be a timid dragon on the ground. Too scared to climb above the greatest mountains, to battle with storms or swoop through the narrowest of passes, too scared to press the case in an argument or defend those unable to defend themselves.

And as for those who are clumsy and graceless in the air, well they are the worst. For they betray all that it means to be a dragon.

Maddau the Wise, *An Etiquette*

'Don't think I've seen anything like it. Even a hatchling knows better than to trip over its own feet landing.'

Benfro sat uncomfortably towards the back of the largest group of dragons he had ever seen, listening as Fflint and his young friends laughed and joked about the new arrival as if he weren't within earshot. His arm throbbed in time to his hearts, the tiny regrowing hand bruised and painful where he'd banged it on the ground in his pathetic attempt at landing. Darkness had fallen, the sky overhead pinpricked with a familiar constellation of stars. Or at least he thought they were familiar. Some seemed to be in the wrong place though. Not for the first time he wished Ynys Môn were with him. The old dragon had known the secrets of the night sky like no other. Where was he? What had become of his jewels? Benfro wished he had the strength to find out, but in truth he barely had enough to eat.

'They call him Benfro of the Borrowed Wings. I can see why. I suspect he's never flown more than a few yards before.'

This from one of the other young dragons in Fflint's gang. Torquil or Tormod, he couldn't be sure which. Benfro hadn't been here long, but it was enough to start understanding the dynamics of the group. Fflint was clearly the biggest and strongest, and the others looked up to him. At least the young ones did. Even Cerys was there at the front, close to the fire they had lit to roast whole deer carcasses on. There were other dragons, older and perhaps wiser, who didn't hang on his every word though. They took their meat off into the darkness, retreating to their own families perhaps, or just wanting to be alone.

'Don't mind them. They're just posturing. Fflint's been

throwing his weight around ever since his father disappeared.'

Benfro looked up to see an old dragon standing nearby. He'd been so wrapped up in his thoughts, his misery if he was being truthful, that the great creature had managed to get right alongside unnoticed.

'I've had worse,' he said, remembering the countless times Frecknock had mocked him to his face, and that fateful spell she had cast on him.

'I don't doubt it. You are young, Benfro of the Borrowed Wings, but you have seen more than your years would suggest.' The old dragon sat down beside him, curling his tail around his feet and letting out a long sigh of relief that reminded Benfro so much of Sir Frynwy that he almost laughed.

'I am Sir Gwair,' the old dragon said once he had finally settled himself. 'Although any family I might have had have long since gone. "Sir" is not so much of an honorific when you have no kin.'

'Is this not your family then?' Benfro spread his arms wide to encompass the gathering, then winced in pain.

'This lot? No. Well, there may be some distant cousins, I suppose. Go back far enough and we're all related. All descendants of the Old One. But none of these dragons are my family.' Sir Gwair laughed mirthlessly. 'And they are all the family I have.'

'What happened?' Benfro wasn't sure whether he should ask but didn't really know what else to say.

'Oh, they got old, they died. It happens even to us. Well, most of us.'

'Most of us?'

'The Old One's still alive, and he was ancient when I was a kitling. Nobody knows how old he is. How long he's lived up in the castle. But nobody remembers a time when he wasn't there, either. You'd know that, of course.'

'I would?'

'It's all right, Benfro. You're among friends here. We've all run away from something. Well, apart from the likes of Fflint and his friends. Most of the young uns were hatched here on the Twmp.'

Benfro opened his mouth to ask a question, then found there were too many to decide which one should come first. Confused, he shut it again.

'Has anyone shown you a place to kip? It can get chill out here after dark.'

'Umm . . . no.' Benfro looked at the remains of the deer haunch he'd been given to eat. He'd assumed he would be heading back to Myfanwy's house at some point, but now he thought about it the old healer had been pleased to see the back of him.

'Come on then. I'll show you the caves. You'll have quite a few to choose from. That many of us have gone recently.'

'Gone? You mean died?' Benfro scrabbled to his feet as the old dragon stood.

'Died?' Sir Gwair voiced the question as if it had never occurred to him before. Then shook his head. 'Oh no. I don't think so. They just left and didn't come back. It happens.'

He led Benfro along a path towards the cliff. It dropped down to a narrow ledge that switched back and forth down the rock face, past a dozen or more cave openings.

Some were occupied, the dull glow of candles or fires flickering from them, but most were empty.

'Any of these, really.' Sir Gwair pointed to the last four caves on the track before it petered out into nothingness. 'Not sure if they left anything behind, but they've all been empty a year or more.'

'Where did they go?' Benfro hesitated at the first cave mouth, unsure whether to go in or not.

'No idea. Back to the castle, maybe? Or south in search of other dragons. Who knows. This lot leaving didn't surprise me much, but Caradoc? That was unusual.'

'Caradoc?'

'Fflint's father. Imagine Fflint, only twice the size and half as bright. He was a good hunter, mind. A good fighter. Had some knowledge of the subtle arts too, just not the gumption to use it. No idea why he decided to up and go, unless it was to try and find . . .' Sir Gwair tailed off, shaking his head. 'No point worrying about it anyway. They're gone. You're here. You look ready to drop, so I suggest you get yourself comfortable. Make yourself at home. Tomorrow we can see how good you are at hunting.'

The wet nurse they found was called Blodwyn and she was perhaps two years younger than Beulah. Plain to the point of being anonymous and certainly not very bright, she was nevertheless the only one suitable who could be found anywhere near Tochers. Unlike the queen, she was both buxom and full of the joys of motherhood. She took swiftly to young Princess Ellyn and the child herself seemed happy enough to suckle on whatever teat was presented to her. True to her word, Beulah attempted to feed her own child, but she felt no strong maternal ties, and was happy to hand over the infant as quickly as possible. The whole business left her feeling slightly nauseous.

'She's wet again. Does that really happen all the time?' Beulah handed the child over to a waiting maid, pulling her blouse closed and wiping her hand. Everything smelled of milk, or semi-digested milk, or worse.

The maid said nothing, perhaps terrified or perhaps intelligent enough to realize that the question wasn't meant to be answered. She carried the child across the room to a waiting table, laying her down and changing her nappy with practised swiftness. Cleaned and dressed, Ellyn was handed over to the wet nurse to continue feeding. At least she hadn't wailed this time; there seemed to be a lot of wailing.

'Where is my husband?' Beulah asked. This time the maid responded.

'His Grace the Duke of Abervenn left early, ma'am. He was hoping to oversee the army's preparations for the march to Candlehall.'

'Let us hope it is ready soon, then.' Beulah felt suffocated at Tochers, couldn't wait to get back in the saddle and head for home. She still ached from childbirth, her muscles stretched in ways they were surely never designed to stretch, but the thought of once more riding a horse, feeling the wind in her hair without the swelling of her belly to slow her down, filled her with hope.

'You plan to ride with them, Your Majesty?' The disbelief in the maid's voice would once have annoyed Beulah enough to have the woman dismissed. Now she found it was simply tedious.

'I am Queen of the Twin Kingdoms. Our enemy has captured my capital, my home. I can hardly leave its relief to someone else.'

The maid stood silent for a moment, perhaps a little longer than was polite. Beulah tried to remember her name, Alicia or Astilbe or something like that. She was youngest daughter of one of the minor noble houses from the lower end of the Hendry, more sensible than most of the Candlehall girls sent to work in the queen's service. Her skill at changing young Ellyn showed as much; most of the others would have fainted at the sight of a soiled nappy.

'I will see about organizing a wagon train, ma'am,' she said eventually.

'A wagon train? Why would I need that?'

'Travelling with a child is more complicated than travelling alone. And if that child is heir to the throne then it is doubly so. The young princess will need guards as well as maids. Blodwyn too.'

The wet nurse looked up at her name, a happy smile on her face. Beulah didn't think she had ever seen anything other than an idiot grin there.

'Ma'am?' she asked.

'She will have to come with us, of course. And I assume there will be times when you will want to leave Ellyn with her. While you inspect the troops or ride out ahead? They will need to be protected, both of them.'

Beulah studied the maid again, reappraising her in the light of her words. If only her skill at manipulating the Grym and the aethereal had returned, she would have been able to skim the young woman's mind, made a better assessment of her angle. Everyone wanted something, after all. But the magic remained locked away deep inside her. It would return in time, Archimandrite Cassters had assured her. How long a time, he could not say.

'See that it is done then. Now I would be alone.'

The maid nodded her understanding, gathered up the wet nurse – still plugged into Ellyn – and together they left the room. Beulah waited until the door had closed before heading over to the fire. An autumnal chill had descended on Tochers since the day she had watched the dragons fly overhead, on their way to lay waste to Tordu's army. What had become of them? Where would they turn up next? Beulah stared at the flames, wrapping her arms around herself to fend off the cold as her frustration built. She needed to be doing things; this sitting around and waiting didn't suit her temperament at all. Maybe that was why she found it so hard to bond with her child. It represented – no, *she* represented stability, settling down, the domestic bliss Beulah's own mother had never known.

'Damn it. Where's Melyn when I need him most?' Beulah struck the heavy oak beam above the fireplace with her fist, the brief flash of pain a welcome reminder that she was alive. With it came a flicker of the aethereal sight in the flames, fleeting but enough to give her hope it would soon return fully. She strained to bring it back, trying every trick the inquisitor had taught her, but nothing worked. Frustrated, she pulled the bell cord that would summon her maid. So much for being alone. There was nothing she could do by herself these days, it seemed.

'Ma'am?' The maid appeared almost instantly, no doubt waiting in the next room. Alicia Glas-Uchel, that was her name. She remembered it now. From the Hendry bog-lands, a dozen leagues south of Castell Glas itself. They'd picked her up on their grand tour, not long after the incident with Duke Glas and the dragon.

'Send a messenger out to the city wall. I have urgent need of His Grace, the Duke of Abervenn.'

The cave was surprisingly spacious but pitch black. Benfro stood just inside the mouth for a while waiting for his eyes to adjust, then remembered what he'd learned in Magog's retreat at the summit of Mount Arnahi. He'd not tried to use the subtle arts for fear of giving the dead dragon mage the chance to attack him through the rose cord that linked them, but as far as he could tell the cord was gone, Magog's influence with it.

At a thought, the lines came to his vision. They were few and thin in this rocky, lifeless cave, but they were there. Somewhere overhead a fire blazed. It was simply a matter of reaching out for it, bringing a piece of it to him, trapping it in a fold of his aura.

The light that rose from his outstretched hand seemed bright after the near-total darkness. It banished the shadows to the corners, revealing a much larger cave than Benfro had expected. A hearth lay in the middle of the space, stacked with dry wood ready to light. More lay off to one side, but he felt no need for a fire. It was warm here, unlike the cold of the Rim mountains and the chill wind that had blown through the plains as he travelled with the circus. Wherever this place was, it must be far south of Tynhelyg.

Beyond the fire, to the back of the cave, the stone had been worked to form a private alcove. Benfro approached with trepidation – this was another dragon's home and he felt uncomfortable intruding – but there was nothing save a heap of dried heather and grass for a bed. It was close enough to get heat from the fire, but far enough away that the bedding was unlikely to catch alight. Well planned, much like the rest of the cave. He spent a while exploring, found an ancient carved desk and bench seat at the back, a locked chest he had no intention of looking inside. Here and there were little things that spoke of the dragon who had lived here, and Benfro couldn't help but wonder what had caused him to leave. Had he meant to go? Flown off without even saying goodbye? Or had something happened to him out there in the endless forest? Maybe he'd had an accident, fallen badly and broken a wing. Had he died alone, slowly starving? It seemed unlikely. So what had happened?

Benfro stifled a yawn. It hadn't been a long day, and he'd not exactly exerted himself much, but the food in his belly weighed heavy and his arm was a constant ache that only sleep could dull. Tomorrow he would find fresh bedding, maybe inspect the other caves to see if they had less of their former occupants in them. He'd start trying to find out where he was too. Maybe ask around if anyone knew anything about Gog. The old dragon, Sir Gwair, would likely tell him. If he didn't drift off into some reminiscence.

He sat in the alcove, still floating the tiny ball of flame above his hand. It was a small thing now, not nearly as bright as he'd at first thought. But it was a cheer in the dark, silent cave, and Benfro found he didn't want to lie in total darkness. Standing again, he crossed to the hearth, removed most of the logs, then rolled the tiny flame into the midst of what was left. The dry timber caught quickly, a merry little fire dancing on the stone. It would go out in an hour or so, but by then he'd be fast asleep.

'Think he's waking up. Someone get Murta.'

Errol swam back into consciousness as if he were waking from a deep, deep sleep. His arms felt heavy; his whole body felt heavy for that matter. Lying on his back, the effort of just lifting his chest up and down to breathe was all he could manage. Opening his eyes was beyond him.

'Here. Drink this. It should help.' A familiar voice nearby, and then he felt something being pressed to his lips. Until that point he hadn't noticed how thirsty he was, but as the thin trickle of liquid entered his mouth it reminded him he'd not drunk anything in a lifetime. It unstuck his tongue from his soft palate, slipped into the tiny dry cracks in his throat, blocked his airway.

'Careful you don't choke there, Errol.' The water was taken away and strong hands helped him upright as he coughed and spluttered. The movement broke whatever spell it was that had clouded his mind, and Errol woke fully up.

He was lying on a straw pallet in someone's house; he had no idea whose. It was darker but not as cool as Murta's, and there was a smell he couldn't quite place. Nor was he sure he wanted to.

'Where am I?' he asked when he'd finally cleared his throat enough to speak. The coughing seemed to bring back some of his strength, though he was still weak.

'Hammie's house.' Nellore appeared at his side, holding

a shallow bowl filled with water which she held out for him. 'You did something to him, then you passed out.'

Errol took the bowl, drank more carefully this time. A little more of his strength seeped back with the water, memories returning with it.

'Hammie? The man who fell out of the tree? Is he . . . ?'

'Shenander's fixing up his bones now. He's going to be OK, I reckon. Not that the others are happy about it.'

In his slightly woozy state Errol couldn't quite understand what the young girl was talking about.

'Who's Shenander?' he asked eventually. It seemed the easiest piece of the puzzle to get sorted first.

'Shenander's the medicine man. He patches us up if we need it. And he decides who gets to meet the gods.'

'The gods. Right.' Errol took another sip, then noticed the slightly stale taste to the water, as if it had been sitting around too long. He passed the bowl back to Nellore, wiped his face with the back of his hand. 'Why aren't they happy your friend's going to be OK?'

'Not the gods, silly. They don't care either way, I 'spect. It's the others in the village, old Ben and his chums. They all think Hammie should've gone to the gods. Reckon it's time again even if it ain't more'n a few months since Jenny went. Him falling out of the tree was a sign, they say.'

Errol shook his head. Nothing the girl said made any sense to him, but he was getting used to that now. There was still the matter of her friend though, and his broken legs. He stood up unsteadily, one hand to the wall to stop himself from swaying too much. Then, once the room had settled down a bit, he walked across to the door and stepped through the tangled rope curtain.

Beyond was another, larger room, filled with sickly-sweet cloying smoke. Light fought through shutters over two windows to the front, dimly illuminating a table in the middle of the room on which the injured man had been laid out. He was unconscious but still breathing, and his legs had been straightened out and fitted with crude splints. Errol took a step forward to inspect the handiwork, then noticed the figure sitting in the corner. Man or woman, he couldn't tell. All he could see was a pair of eyes staring out whitely from a face painted dark. Long black straggly hair matted and threaded with beads, feathers, twigs. The figure was dressed in what looked like torn strips and rags, and held a long wooden stick carved with strange looping sigils. It had to be the medicine man Nellore had mentioned.

'Are you Shenander?' Errol asked. The figure said nothing but stood up and crossed the room to where he stood. He moved with an oddly birdlike gait, head bobbing back and forth with each exaggerated step. He stopped too close for comfort, and Errol had to resist the urge to take a step back.

'You healed him from the inside. This is old magic.' The medicine man's voice was thin and grating. 'Who taught you such things?'

'I . . . My mother was a herbwoman. She taught me.' It was a lie, but Errol could hardly admit that he'd not known what he was doing.

'This is more than herbs.' The medicine man shook his head, then broke out into a gap-toothed grin. 'But it matters not. Hammie lives, and this is a good thing. The gods are pleased. Shenander is pleased.'

As if hearing his name spoken, the injured man groaned. The medicine man turned back to the table, took up a small bowl and tipped it to the injured man's mouth. He swallowed reflexively, muttered something inaudible, then fell back into unconsciousness.

'There will be many days of pain before the bones knit properly. This will help make it bearable.'

Errol looked at the splints, the careful stitches where the broken bones had been pushed back into place. The medicine man obviously knew what he was doing, assuming of course it was he who had set the bones and splinted the legs. It would be a job to keep infection away, given the heat and the general lack of cleanliness of the place, but at least the bandages looked fresh. He sniffed, coughed on the smoke. It hid any smell of decay but did little else to help.

'We'll have to take turns looking after him.' Nellore appeared from the room at the back. She took up another bowl, this one with a rag in it, and wiped the unconscious man's forehead. Errol wasn't sure what good that would do him, but it was a nice gesture.

'This is good. You will stay with him now.' Shenander raised his carved stick, waving it in tight circles as if that was an important part of the healing process. 'I will go to the forest, fetch the herbs he will need to aid his recovery. And I will speak to the gods, ask for their intervention.'

Without another word, he stalked out of the house, letting a brief flash of sunlight and a waft of fresh air in as he pushed through the doorway.

*

He woke to almost total darkness, only the dull red glow of spent coals on the hearth. Benfro lay on his side, unsure of what had woken him. And then his nose told him. That unmistakable scent wafted in over the dry wood smoke at the same time as he saw the darkness flow in the shape of a dragon.

'Cerys?' Benfro rolled over in his nest of heather and grass, sitting up and sniffing the air as he waited for his eyes to adjust to the darkness. Without thinking, he reached out along the nearest line, plucking flame from the coals and holding it in a ball of his aura. The action seemed totally natural, as if it were something he had done all his life. He had thought it was something most dragons learned early on in their lives, but the look of wonder on the face of the dragon standing in the door-way suggested otherwise.

'You can conjure a flame?' Cerys rushed across the cave towards him, her wings rustling in the still air as if she had flown here and only just begun to fold them. Perhaps she had. She crouched down, raising first one hand then the other to the tiny shining ball of light, not daring to touch it but obviously wanting to. Her face was a picture of kitlingish delight, making her seem much younger than Benfro had at first thought her. 'Does it not burn?'

'It would, if I let it touch me. The first time Ma— my master showed me how, I burned the palm of my hand badly.'

'Master?' Cerys rocked back on to her tail, recoiling from the word as if it had spat at her. 'Dragons have no masters.'

'But how can we learn, if not from our masters?'

Cerys cocked her head to one side, much like the old healer Myfanwy had done. 'We learn from our friends, our family. We are dragons. We just know.'

'He was a dragon, of sorts, my master. Both of them, if I'm being honest.' Benfro considered Magog and Corwen, two dragons as different as could be. Other than that they were both dead, of course.

'Both? How can you serve two masters? How can you even serve one?'

'Badly, as it turned out. One I would not learn from until it was too late, the other only wanted to use me so that he could live again. There is much to be said for your attitude.'

'Where are you from, Benfro of the Borrowed Wings?' Cerys settled, leaning against the entrance to the small sleeping alcove. Benfro couldn't help but notice her scent. Not unpleasant, but strange and heady and confusing. Part of him understood that the question was not meant literally, but the greater part of him leaped at the opportunity to explain.

'I was hatched at the Confluence, in a village close to the edge of the great Ffrydd forest, not eighteen summers ago. My mother was Morgwm the Green, a healer much like your Myfanwy, though she was also skilled in the subtle arts. We were different from your fold, if that's what you call your group. None of us could fly, for one thing. And the other villagers were old. Older even than Sir Gwair. Sir Frynwy was the head of the village, and he was over a thousand years old. I was the only young dragon there. Well, apart from Frecknock, I suppose.'

'Frecknock? That is a female dragon's name, is it not?'

'Yes. She came to the village as a hatchling. Long before my time. They took her in, tried to teach her their ways, but she wanted more.'

'Sounds very sensible to me. Old dragons are so staid and stuffy. Never telling you what you want to know. It's always "You're not old enough, Cerys," or "You'll find out when you've seen a few more summers, Cerys." I've seen thirty summers and more. How many must I wait before they admit I'm old enough?'

Benfro almost laughed, and the effort of not doing so made him lose concentration on his light. He could feel the heat threatening to sear his palm and let the flame die. They were plunged into darkness, even the coals in the fire now blackened and dead.

'Sorry. I can only keep it going for so long,' he said.

'Don't be. I prefer the dark.' Cerys shuffled closer so that she was leaning against him, sitting on the edge of Benfro's nest of heather and grass. Her wings brushing against his seemed to tremble and her scent was stronger still, filling his head and making it difficult to think.

'Were you hatched here? Up on the Twmp?' he asked. At his words, Cerys stilled, though she leaned close to him.

'In a cave not far from here. My mother died in a fight not long afterwards. My father ... We don't speak of him.'

'I'm sorry.' Benfro fell silent, unsure what to say. Then a question forced its way out of his mouth before he could stop it. 'In a fight?'

'That's what I'm told. I was too young to know anything about it. Myfanwy took me under her wing. Raised me. She tries to teach me herb lore and healing, but I can't tell one plant from another. And collecting them all, drying them, labelling them. It's so tedious.'

This time Benfro couldn't stop himself from laughing.

'What's so funny?' Cerys hit him on the chest, not hard, but it brought her closer still.

'My mother taught me herbs, showed me how to prepare them and store them, use them for healing or taking away pain. I hated every minute of it, but I'd give my hand –' he held up his damaged arm in the darkness, flexing the tiny talons '– my other hand just to see her again.'

'How did she die?' Cerys leaned her head on Benfro's shoulder, her wings trembling again. All he could see was the bright blade of fire, swinging in its terrible arc through the air.

'The same way I lost my hand. Only they took her head.'

'I'm so sorry—'

'I was there, Cerys. I watched it happen, and there was nothing I could do about it. She knew they would kill me if they found me. She died to give me time to escape. I swore then that I would kill them, all of them.'

'And you will, Benfro. I am sure of it.' Cerys leaned closer still, one hand resting on his chest now, one wing loosely draped across his nest of heather and grass. He remembered his fever dreams while Myfanwy was healing him. A wing wrapped around him, the warmth and security of another dragon lying close. Not his mother, nor the ancient healer, but Cerys herself, nursing him back to health.

18

In times of crisis the king must take to the road. Or so it would seem from the actions of the many kings at Candlehall. When famine hits the peasantry hard, when the threat from Llanwennog is great or the popularity of the nobility is low, then the Royal Tour will set out around the Twin Kingdoms.

Sometimes these are short affairs, taking in only the major cities of the Hafod. Diseverin IV went only as far as Tochers before scurrying back to the comfort of the Neuadd and his palaces. But other kings have worked tirelessly to unite their people, sometimes to the point of neglecting their duties back home. Had King Divitie XIX not been two years away from the Obsidian Throne, Prince Lonk would never have been allowed to embark on his mad quest, and the Twin Kingdoms would have been spared the terror that was the Brumal Wars.

Barrod Sheepshead,
A History of the House of Balwen

The feast took Errol by surprise. Days had passed since Hammie's fall, and the injured man was responding well to the rather haphazard treatment he was getting from Shenander. Errol couldn't quite fathom the medicine man. He clearly had a deep knowledge of the human body and could patch things up well if people hurt themselves. He knew something of herbs, too; more than Errol did of what was available in the region. His poultices kept the wounds from becoming infected, and the smoke he insisted on filling Hammie's front room with at least kept the flies away. And well-meaning visitors too. Errol knew from experience and his mother's many tales that it was quite often over-anxious relatives bothering the patient that hindered their recovery, so maybe Shenander's smoke was just a simple way of keeping folk away.

They took it in turns to watch over the injured man, even though most of the time he was kept in a drug-induced stupor. This, too, made a lot of sense. His wounds needed to heal, the bones begin to knit together again, before he could be allowed to move around. Errol could see that Hammie was both young and fit, so it was very likely he'd have been a bad patient had he been awake.

Murta was delighted to have someone to mother and kept Errol well fed, but she was evasive when he asked her questions about the village or the gods. After a while he stopped questioning her, happy just to gather his strength and let his own wounds heal. He would move on soon enough, once Hammie was well on the way to recovery.

Nellore was never far from his side these days, but she treated him differently, almost reverentially. She treated Shenander the same way, and Errol could only suppose she thought of him as similar to the old man, another healer. He tried to question her about the village, the gods, even her friend Hammie, but her answers made little sense, and if he pressed her for more, she would soon grow tired of it, run off on some pretend errand or other. The rest of the villagers left him alone beyond giving a polite nod if they saw him passing. Even the curmudgeonly old Ben Sorrenson, who seemed to be the closest the place had to a leader, stopped scowling at him from his favoured spot in the rocking chair on his porch. Errol wasn't welcomed in with open arms, but he was tolerated.

Which was why the feast took him by surprise.

'Ain't been a proper feast in a long time,' Nellore said as she gave Errol the news. 'Not been much to celebrate. But Hammie's going to survive, and the fruit harvest's been good.'

'When's it going to be? Where?'

'Tonight, Ben said. In the big hall.'

Errol peered through the smoky air at the doorway. It was late evening, what little light that made it through the shutters and the rope curtain fading almost to black in contrast to the candles lit around the room. That was something he'd noticed about this village. Dawn rose fast, and night fell equally so. There was no lingering dusk here.

'Who's going to look after Hammie?' They had set up a more comfortable bed for the injured man now, close to the back wall of the room. He'd been semi-lucid earlier, rambling as the drugs that dulled his pain also addled his mind. Now he slept, but Errol knew it wouldn't be wise to leave him unattended for too long.

'It's my turn, ain't it?' Nellore said.

'Yes, but don't you want to go to the feast?' Errol didn't really know what to expect of it. He'd never been to any feasts back home in Pwllpeiran until his mother's wedding, and that hadn't exactly gone well.

'Course I do. But they won't let me drink the wine, so what's the point?'

Errol wanted to say that drinking wine was much over-rated, but Murta pushed through the doorway then, interrupting him.

'They've started already. You probably want to get over there.' She carried a basket filled with food. 'I'll keep an eye on Hammie. Keep Nellore company too.'

'You sure?' Errol asked.

'Sure I'm sure.' Murta laughed, shooing him out of the cottage. 'Ain't often old Ben changes his mind, but he's taken a liking to you. Best not get back on the wrong side of him, eh?'

'My lady. Are you unwell?'

Beulah turned to see Clun standing in the doorway. He wore his cloak still, and mud clung to his boots. She envied him his freedom to come and go, even though she knew that was unfair. He must have come through the nursery or met Blodwyn on the way, as he cradled Ellyn in one arm, the tiny child staring up into his face with that rapt attention only very small children and hungry dogs can muster. She reached up to his golden blonde hair with her minuscule hands, and the smile on his face was almost enough to break through her dark mood.

'Just frustrated, my love. Each day's delay entrenches Dafydd's hold on Candlehall. We need to march swiftly, set siege before the winter takes hold.'

'We will leave just as soon as we can. But I think we should leave Candlehall well alone.'

'You think what?' Beulah turned away from the fire to

fully face her husband. He had grown in stature in the year since their wedding, and in confidence too. Still it was unprecedented for him to question her this way.

'Winter is fast approaching. Let Dafydd feed our people through the sparse months, run his supplies low. We can use the time to march on Abervenn. Root out the treason where it first flowered.'

'Abervenn?' Beulah turned back to the flames as if an answer might lie there. Clun walked swiftly over to her side.

'The city stands as a mockery to your power, my lady,' he said. 'And worse, while it is in enemy hands no siege of Candlehall can hope to succeed. If our intelligence is to be believed, then Iolwen did not accompany her husband, so she is likely still there too, her child with her. Take back Abervenn and there is every chance we can capture them both.'

Beulah allowed herself a moment's idle fancy, watching as her hated sister was thrown from the tallest tower of the old castle. The image swirled in the flames, reaching out to her for mercy.

'But Abervenn is well fortified. We could spend as long besieging it as Candlehall. And we don't have enough men for two sieges.'

'Well fortified, true. But it is undermanned. All the Abervenn men loyal to the crown are here with us. Those who sided with Anwyn and took Llanwennog gold to betray us have gone to Candlehall. That is where they will expect us to strike.'

Beulah shook her head slowly, the image of her sister's death fading away. 'It can still be defended easily. And it can be resupplied from the sea.'

'There is a way in. A small force could have the main gates open before any guard realized what was happening.'

'But Iolwen will flee as soon as she sees us coming.'

'Not if the harbour is blockaded.'

Beulah looked sideways at Clun, seeing the ghost of a smile on his lips. He had been planning this for some time, she realized. No doubt while she was incapacitated by childbirth. 'You have a plan already, my love.'

'I do. I have sent word to Lord Beylin. He controls more ships than anyone. Coast-hugging barges mostly, but they're enough to make the journey. He has men to spare, Glas too.'

'Glas? Is he not dead? I thought the dragon did for him.'

'It would seem it takes more than a goring from a dragon to kill Duke Glas. He will likely never walk again, but he will recover enough. And he is very grateful to you for allowing your personal physician to tend to him.'

The fire was getting too warm now. Beulah crossed the room, sat herself down and held out her hands to be given her child. Clun made sure Ellyn was well wrapped before handing her over, but the infant was fast asleep, frowning a little but doing nothing more as Beulah nestled the bundle into her lap. She could see from the way Clun looked at his daughter that he was as smitten with her as he had been with his queen. A shame then that she could find no stirring of anything maternal in her at all. Was that what being sent away to Emmass Fawr at such a young age had done to her? Burned out her motherly instincts? Or would she have bonded more easily with a son? So many questions and no one she could turn to for answers.

'How is it you know of Glas, anyway? And Beylin?'

'It was all part of Melyn's plan, my lady. We stationed adepts at Beylinstown and Castell Glas on our grand tour. None of them is as skilled at the aethereal as the inquisitor. Or you, for that matter. But I've been practising, going into the trance at the agreed time every day. I can find places I've been to, contact people who know me.'

'You can speak to Melyn?' Beulah almost leaped to her feet, all but forgetting that Ellyn lay in her arms. At the last moment some deep-buried instinct kicked in, stopping her.

'Alas, I have no idea where he is. Well, I have not visited the place where he is. Otherwise I would have contacted him the moment Ellyn was born.'

'How long has it been. Since last he made contact?'

'Too long. Not since just before . . .' Clun nodded towards Ellyn. Without realizing it, she had cradled the infant closer to her head, rocking her gently back and forth.

'I remember now,' she said. 'When the dragons flew over. Before they flew over. He just appeared, but you weren't expecting him. You weren't even in the trance.'

'No. He was different then, too. Much more powerful than I remember him being. He almost pulled me in. That's when I started trying harder to contact the others. Just in case something had happened.'

'Something?' Ellyn let out a little cry, and Beulah realized she had been squeezing the child close to her. She relaxed her grip a little, hoping the cry wouldn't develop into a full-blown wail.

'My lady, I am not skilled in the ways of the Grym. I do not have your years of experience, let alone Melyn's decades. But when he contacted me last, it didn't feel exactly like him.' Clun paced back and forth in front of the fire as if trying to find words for concepts his mind could scarcely process. Beulah remembered her early days under Melyn's tutelage and could only have sympathy for him.

'It felt like him, but with a larger shadow. Does that make sense? As if there were someone – no, something – else there with him.'

'The dragon?'

'Frecknock?' Clun stopped his pacing, looked up from the floor and considered a moment. 'No. I know her well enough. It was something else.'

'It helped us though, whatever it was. How else could Melyn have found you here, taken control of you the way he did?'

'That's true. And whatever it was helping him helped me too. I've found the trance far easier to achieve ever since, and I can reach out to the other adepts in an instant. No need to travel the aethereal as if it were the same as the mundane.'

'And that's how you've been in contact with Beylin and Glas.' Beulah nodded, even though she didn't truly understand. She couldn't help but feel a shudder of jealousy too, that her beloved had made this discovery on his own. She should have been at his side. They should have been exploring the higher realms together. And yet this creature, this child asleep in her arms, had denied her that chance.

'Here, take her.' She stood up and handed the baby to her husband, no longer wanting anything to do with her.

Clun took her with gentle arms and smoothed her thin hair with one massive finger. He bent down and kissed her on the forehead, utterly absorbed.

'Summon the maid,' she said. 'It's time I went and inspected my troops. If we're to march on Abervenn we'll need to get going soon.'

Wind tugged at his ear tufts, rippled at his wing tips and yet made no sound at all. Benfro soared through the air, high above the undulating forest. He felt strong, the muscles in his back firm. Flexing his hands he could almost rip the sky apart as he hurtled towards the distant mountains. And then it hit him. His hands.

Holding them up to his face was as easy as plucking a flower from a bush. He studied them as if he had never seen them before, the palms leathery, the backs coated with the tiniest of scales that glistened in the sun. Both of them the same size, they reflected a rainbow of colours. With a thought, razor-sharp claws extended, ready to slice open anything that crossed him. He was all powerful, all seeing. He was whole.

He was dreamwalking.

The understanding dawned on him as swiftly as a shiver down his spine to the tip of his tail. There was an instant when he might have fallen out of the sky, might have woken, might have lost himself completely, but he held tight to the vision of his hands and soon he was in full control.

Knowing it was a dream didn't lessen the wonder. Benfro soared over the trees far faster than he could have flown awake, and yet he could see clearly through the sparse leaves of the canopy to the spindly branches and fat, tuberous trunks. Deer darted through the undergrowth, spooked by the thought of something overhead. Or were they just the dreams of deer? The dreams of trees? There was so much he didn't know about dreamwalking. Sir Frynwy had been going to teach him, Meirionydd too, and as he thought of them Benfro let out a low keening wail at their loss. His friends, his family.

There was little time to mourn them as the forest changed, first to huge oaks and beech, then tall conifers and finally petered out altogether. He could sense that the air had turned colder, or maybe it was the sight of snow in the high mountains, now much closer than they had been just seconds before. Far ahead, Benfro's keen eyes scanned for a horizon he might recognize, but the narrow, jutting spire of rock was like nothing he had ever seen before.

And then he saw that it wasn't rock, or at least not natural. This was a tower, built by someone. Or something. And there was a terrible familiarity about it.

Closer still and he began to recognize details. He had been here before, somehow flown here with Ynys Môn's jewels. Three dragons had attacked him and he had dropped his precious hoard. They had fallen inside the wall that he could now see surrounding a building so large it made Inquisitor Melyn's monastery at Emmass Fawr seem tiny. Benfro scanned the skies as he approached, looking for any sign of impending attack. He could see nothing, not even a bird. Only the tower reaching ever upwards from the sprawling mass of buildings.

He flew over the wall as low as he dared, tail barely missing the topmost parapet. Even so it was several hundred feet to the ground. He tried to remember the previous occasion he had been here. If he had been here at all. How did the dreamwalk work? He was not physically here, surely. He was back in the cave asleep. With—

Benfro almost crashed into the ground, almost woke up. Cerys had come to him in the night. She had climbed into his nest of heather and dry grass, put her wing around him like she had done when he was still sick, like his mother had done when he was still a kitling. He had fallen asleep with her warmth all around him, her intoxicating scent.

He shook his head to get rid of the image, furled his wings and came in for a perfect landing. The ground between the wall and the vast buildings it surrounded was laid to grass mostly, perfectly flat and cropped short. Hard paths criss-crossed the area, and wide, square lakes of still black water, but there were no trees. Benfro looked around, tried to get his bearings. Somewhere near where he now stood Ynys Môn's jewels had fallen to the ground. He could see them in his mind's eye, tumbling down.

But that had been months ago. They surely wouldn't be here any more. One or other of the dragons would have found them, collected them up. Taken them where, though? Almost unbidden, his eyes looked up, following the climb of the buildings, their roofs topped with dark grey slate. Behind them the tower pierced the clouds, so tall that he could scarcely make out its top. And he knew with dreadful certainty exactly where he would find his old friend.

Benfro leaped into the air, beat down with his wings until he was aloft. In the dream it was all so easy. No need to run and jump like some fledgling bird. No fear of broken bones or, worse, injured pride. Soon he was higher than the buildings, climbing strongly and swiftly. Still it took long minutes to cross the endless miles of dark roofs, the thousand thousand sightless window eyes. He was certain somebody was watching him, but scanning the skies revealed nothing. Wherever this place was, he was alone in it.

Climbing the tower in a spiral around its outer wall was hard work even in his dreaming state. It was almost as if some invisible force were pushing him away, but Benfro pressed on regardless. He had survived the thin air of Magog's retreat at the top of Mount Arnahi. Surely this tower could not be as high as the tallest mountain on the Rim? And anyway he was not here. Not really. He was back in the cave asleep. Or was he here after all? Was this real or some parallel plane?

Higher and higher he climbed, flying against what felt like a storm. The closer he came to the top, the harder the going. And then the pressure against him was gone, as if someone had closed a window. His last powerful wingbeat shot him up beyond the top of the tower so that he had to swoop around and dive back down. A wide balcony circled the entire structure, two large glass-paned doors opposite each other giving access to a room inside. Benfro had always been curious, and this was the most intriguing puzzle of them all. He was certain this was the lair of some great dragon mage. Perhaps it was Gog's own retreat.

Movement behind the glass panes caught his eye, and Benfro circled to land. There was a feeling to the place he couldn't quite describe. Peering through the nearest door, he saw a room filled with huge tables, strange metal equipment, piles of wooden chests, things he had no names for. Hanging from a rafter off to one side, where it would be out of the draught from the door if it were open, a heavy cage appeared to be made of gold. Too small for a dragon, he couldn't see if anything was inside it, as the bars had been woven through with strips of cloth and blankets to form a den for whatever animal had been trapped inside. Or maybe not trapped; a long knotted rope draped down from the cage to the floor. Nearby, a huge fireplace glowed with the embers of a dying fire, and sitting in front of it was a tiny figure.

'By the moon! It cannot be!'

Benfro whirled, almost toppling off the ledge. Above him, far too close for comfort, a huge dragon hung in the air as if suspended on an invisible rope. Darkest black, with just the faintest shimmer of colour to his scales like oil spread across the surface of a winter pool, he sparked a memory deep in Benfro's mind. This was one of the creatures who had attacked him before, when he had dropped Ynys Môn's jewels in his dreams. Could the others be far away?

The dragon seemed not to need to flap his wings to stay aloft, drew them together far too soon to land on the balcony and yet still glided gently to the stone. Benfro felt a great wave of anger and hatred boiling off the beast, for beast was surely what he was. No great dragon mage but a warrior, battle-scarred and mad with rage. Benfro backed away, feeling first his tail slip over the edge, then his heels. He could go no further without fleeing, and there was no way he could hope to outrun such a powerful creature.

'How dare you sully this place with your presence?' The enormous dragon advanced ever closer, reaching out to him with powerful talons. The fear swamping Benfro was worse by far than anything Melyn and his warrior priests had ever produced in him. It froze him almost completely, just blind instinct making him flinch back as those claws whipped out and raked across his chest.

And then he was falling over the edge, tumbling out of control, a howl of rage and frustration ringing in his ears.

'Beulah and Clun, they are still in Tochers?'

Melyn sat in Ballah's chair at the king's old desk, letting the Grym soothe away the pain that still flared across his chest with every intake of breath. He was suppressing the cough that wanted to shake loose the liquid pooling in his lungs, but there was only so long he could manage that for. Then the agony would overcome him once more. He cursed dragons of all kinds, Benfro in particular.

'They are, Your Grace. I believe they are making preparations for the army to march out soon.'

Well, maybe not all dragons. Curled up beside the shuttered windows, Frecknock was a dark shadow in the gloom, only her large round eyes reflecting the waxy yellow candlelight.

'I must speak with them. You will help me make contact.'

Frecknock raised her head to his eye level but remained lying down. 'Sire, is that wise? You are not strong—'

'You will do as I command, Frecknock.' Melyn felt the anger surging up in him and bit down hard on the cough that it wanted to bring with it.

'Of course, sire.' The dragon rose in a lithe, fluid motion, crossed the room to where he sat, held out her hand. 'If you would join me in the aethereal.'

Melyn swallowed against the bubbling in his throat and lungs, settled his mind as best he could and slipped into the trance. It brought a moment's relief to be apart from his physical body, but he knew that Frecknock spoke the truth. He was not healing because he was not resting. Just a pity he had to be injured so deep inside enemy territory and with so much to do.

'Take my hand, sire. It will be quicker this way.' Frecknock's aethereal appearance was so much more magnificent than her drab, worldly self. Her voice had more self-confidence about it too, speaking directly to his mind. Melyn's mental defences were instinctive, and yet he knew that she would never try to take advantage of his weakened state. He reached out, feeling the warmth in her scaly palm, the strength she lent him so that he might be able to make the trip. And then with a blink, they were there.

Melyn knew Tochers from old. It was a miserable town, centred around a miserable castle with miserable, cold, dark rooms. Built to defend the pass from possible Llan-wennog invasion, it was designed to be impregnable rather than comfortable. Not the best place for the heir to the Obsidian Throne to be born.

The room to which Frecknock had somehow instantly transported him was one of the more pleasant ones in the castle. It had two windows where most had barely an arrow slit, and a fire roared away merrily in a vast fire-place. The queen lay in a large four-poster bed, propped up on pillows and cradling in her arms the tiniest baby Melyn had ever seen. There was a healthy glow to both mother and child though, which gave him heart. The queen's skill at magic was still hampered by her recent pregnancy, but it remained intact if she could be so easily recognized. The child, too, appeared fully formed, as children sometimes did, especially those of royal blood. Clun sat in a chair beside a large fireplace, but an image of him stood up, seeming to split into two people the instant Melyn turned to face him.

'Your Grace. You look unwell.' Clun's aethereal self was indistinguishable from his mundane, save for the liminal glow around him. He was far more at ease in this place than most long-practised adepts, and not for the first time Melyn wondered how a country boy from the back end of nowhere could be so strong in the Grym. And yet he'd been a country boy from the back end of nowhere himself. All those years ago.

'A little problem with the dragon Benfro. I'll live.' Melyn nodded towards Beulah, who was staring up at her husband now, still not seeing him. 'You are a father, I see. Congratulations.'

'A girl, yes. We have named her Ellyn, after her grandmother. She came earlier than we expected, but she is healthy enough.'

Melyn winced at the choice of name and the unbidden memories it raised like ghosts. He forced them away, concentrating on the present. 'The queen? How fares Beulah?'

Clun appeared to consider his words. 'It wasn't an easy birth, sire. And the queen has not yet come to terms with the change in her situation, I fear.'

'You fear? Speak your mind, boy. This is the heir to the Obsidian Throne we're discussing.'

'I'm sorry, Your Grace. I don't know how to . . . The queen . . . my lady has not taken to the child the way I would have expected a mother to. In truth she has scarcely moved from her bedchamber since she was born.'

'It will pass. Her mother was the same with both Lleyn and Beulah, though less so with Iolwen. It would be best perhaps if she returned to Candlehall. I take it our armies are marching through the passes as we speak?'

Melyn could see the anxiety as a darkening of Clun's aura, and the pause before answering was enough to tell him all was not well.

'Do I need to remind you we will soon be confronted by Prince Geraint's army?'

'It's not that, sir. General Otheng should be through the Wrthol pass by now, and a smaller army is making its way to Tynewydd from here. Tordu's army was routed by a pair of dragons, so it's unlikely they will meet much resistance.'

'Then what's the problem, boy?' Melyn's chest flared with pain, threatening to drag him back to his body.

'It's Candlehall, sir. It's been taken by an army of Abervenn men, led by Prince Dafydd and Princess Iolwen.'

Melyn struggled to stay in the room in Tochers, that same grey mist he had encountered in Ballah's private apartments swirling around him. The pain in his chest was even more severe now; he could feel each breath as a wheeze, the liquid filling his lungs and threatening to drown him in his own blood. And then a hand touched his shoulder, softly anchoring him, lending him the strength he needed to finish.

'Damn that boy. I should have known. What are your plans?'

'We will march as soon as the queen is able. The plan is to secure Abervenn first; it will have fewer men defending it. Duke Beylin and Duke Glas are sending reinforcements. Together we will take back Candlehall.'

Melyn coughed, and the pain came back double. Even Frecknock's strength was not enough, and he could sense himself losing control. Damn it, he had wanted to search the aethereal for Prince Geraint again. Their last foray had shown only that the army was leaving Wrthol. It could be halfway to Tynhelyg by now.

'Beulah knows the secret ways into the Neuadd. Use that knowledge, Clun. And keep the queen safe.'

'Always, Your Grace.' Clun bowed his head, clapped his arm across his chest in salute, but Melyn was already moving, hurtling backwards as if on a rope pulled behind a galloping horse. He could hear a voice muttering in Draigiaith, the words strangely soothing to his ears as he tensed for the inevitable bone-crushing impact as his aetheral self met his physical body in the worst possible way.

And then there was only blackness.

19

Wise Earith was the greatest of healers, or so the fables say. Where Balwen gained the Shepherd's wisdom and skill, Grendel and Malco his strength and cunning, Earith gained his ability to heal. Such was her skill, and such her generosity, that people came from far and wide with their ailments, seeking her cures. By and large she was happy to help, for the true healer does not distinguish between friend or foe, only those who are in need and those who are not.

And yet Wise Earith was not without a limit to her patience. A man who injures himself once is unfortunate; he who repeats the same mistake twice a fool. And so in her healing she would sometimes leave a reminder of the cause of the injury. For some this was as simple as a scar left where she had the skill to heal a wound without a trace. A man who would insist on picking fights she might leave weak in the shoulders, another gored by a boar after too much time spent hunting might find he had grown a fine sward of bristle where the wound had healed. These and other reminders were her gift not so much to the patient as to their family. For the careless man harms not only himself by his recklessness, but all those for whom he is responsible.

Archimandrite Zwartble, *Healing through the Ages*

Benfro woke with a start, sitting bolt upright. His hand went to his chest, felt the scales there, expecting them to be scored deep where those claws had ripped at them. Had he felt pain as the black dragon swung at him? It was all falling away as the dream faded, but he could feel the faintest of scratch marks and his hearts were thundering away as if he had run a mile.

'Where do you go, when you sleep?'

He looked up, seeing the light of dawn painting the sky outside the cave mouth in shades of pink and orange. Half blocking the view, Cerys stood with her back to him. Her wings were not folded neatly but hung limply from her back, as if she had only just crawled out of her nest. His nest. Or was it the nest of the dragon who had left this cave one day and never come back?

'I don't go anywhere, do I?' Benfro felt at the scratch across his scales, unsure whether it had been there before. He'd been in plenty of situations where he could have damaged himself and not noticed, after all. Drugged into compliance at the circus, for one.

'Not your body, no. But you were gone. You went somewhere and I couldn't sense you any more.' Cerys turned, pulling her wings in tight around her as she walked back across the cave to where he sat. 'If it hadn't been for your hearts beating I might have thought you'd died.'

'What do you know of dreamwalking?' Benfro stretched as he had done every morning of his life on waking, and for the first time felt awkward and self-conscious about it. He was used to the close proximity of dragons, up to a point. His mother had never been far from him until the day she died, and the villagers had always been happy enough to ruffle his ears, but this was very different. He hardly knew Cerys and had no experience whatsoever of dragons his own age.

'Dreamwalking? Isn't that, like, really advanced subtle arts?' Cerys dropped down on the heather and grass beside him as if that was the most natural thing in the world to do. 'I've heard Sir Gwair talk about it. Apparently the Old One can do it, and some of his cronies. But it's really hard.'

'Oh. Right.' Benfro studied his hands, trying to see whether the new one had grown at all. He was both uncomfortable and excited, and just didn't know how to deal with Cerys. 'Who's the Old One? Sir Gwair was talking about him last night too.'

'You're joking, right? How can you not know about the Old One?'

'I . . .' Benfro started to speak, then remembered his dream. His dreamwalk, if that truly was what he had done. 'I don't even know where this place is. Where's the Ffrydd from here?'

'The Ffrydd? Why do you want to know about that place?'

'Because it's where I'm from. Or you could tell me how to get to Tynhelyg in Llanwennog. That's where I last saw my friend. I'd really like to find him. Make sure he's safe.'

'I really don't know . . . Oh no. Someone's coming. I'm not here, OK?' Cerys shuffled herself to the back of the alcove, tucking herself behind the rock so she couldn't be seen from the cave mouth. Benfro frowned, looked at her with a quizzical expression and was about to ask her what she was playing at when another voice distracted him.

'Hey! Benfro of the Borrowed Wings. You in there?'

He looked towards the cave mouth, seeing the silhouette of a dragon standing there. For a moment he thought it was Sir Gwair, but the shape was wrong. Then he tasted the scent on the air.

'Fflint?' Benfro stood, glancing sideways at Cerys, who seemed to be trying to push herself into the rock of the alcove. He left her to whatever games she was playing and headed to the entrance.

'Thought you might have picked this place. Einar was a loner too.'

'Einar?'

'The dragon who lived here. He flew off hunting a year or so ago. Never came back. Figured he'd just got bored of our company, but a lot of the fold have gone missing recently.' Fflint rolled his shoulders, flexing his powerful neck as if it ached. He peered into the darkness of the cave, sniffed but didn't enter. 'You seen Cerys about?'

Something about the way the dragon spoke put Benfro on edge. It was obviously meant to sound like a casual remark, but there was far more to the question. Benfro wasn't used to subterfuge, but neither was he stupid. This was the reason for Fflint's visit, whatever else he might say. And Cerys hadn't wanted to be found. Well, one dragon had mocked him when he had landed badly the previous evening, and it wasn't the one hiding in the back of the cave.

'Not since last night, at the feast.' He hoped the lie didn't show on his face. Fflint was twice his size and had an air about him Benfro didn't trust. If ever there was a dragon who put him in mind of men and their unpredictable ways, then Fflint was it.

'She's been showing a lot of interest in you. Helped old Myfanwy nurse you back to health when you arrived. Just thought you ought to know she's younger than she looks. Headstrong. Gets funny notions sometimes. Oh, and she's spoken for.'

This last was said as an afterthought, but Benfro understood then. Not so much like men as like Frecknock, at least before she had been taken by Melyn. Fflint was jealous. Of him. If it hadn't been for the simmering sense of violence that hugged the larger dragon like a crimson aura, Benfro might have laughed.

'If I see her, I'll let her know you're looking for her.'

'No need. I'll see her before you do, I'm sure. Just remember what I said, right?' Fflint slapped Benfro on the shoulder perhaps slightly harder than was strictly necessary, then turned and leaped from the narrow path leading down the cliff face from the top of the Twmp. A snap of his enormous wings and he was speeding off into the distance.

Benfro stood and watched him go, until Fflint was no more than a dot in the distance. Only then did he sense movement behind him and breathe in a heady scent that must surely have been all over the cave.

'Thank you, Benfro.' Cerys put a hand on his shoulder, leaned against him but kept back from the cave mouth just in case.

'What's that all about? Are you and Fflint . . . ?'

Cerys gave a snort of laughter. 'He wishes. Throws his weight around like he's in charge, but I ain't spoken for by anyone. Not till I say so.'

'I don't understand how it could be any other way. I mean, you don't belong to anyone. Dragons can't be owned.'

'You really mean that, don't you?' Cerys gave Benfro a hug, nuzzled his neck, then pulled away, casting a suspicious eye over him. 'Just a shame Fflint thinks otherwise. His dad was the same. Worse even. I thought when he went things would get better, but Fflint's just as bad as he ever was.'

Benfro stretched, feeling the constraints of the cave. He needed to fly, needed to feel the wind in his face, but there were so many questions about this fold, this motley collection of dragons, that he wanted to ask as well. If he could just get them all sorted out in his head first.

'Why did they leave, the other dragons? Did Fflint chase them off? His father?'

Cerys shook her head, walking out of the cave as she spoke. 'So many questions, Benfro of the Borrowed Wings. Dragons don't need reasons for what they do. We come, we go. And now –' she unfurled her wings and teetered on the edge '– we hunt.'

The big hall was, as its name suggested, the largest structure in the village. It struck Errol as he approached it that all the buildings seemed very old. Well built a long time ago, but patched up over the years with less and less skill. Mostly they were constructed of square-cut stone fitted together so accurately there was no need for mortar. Some were rendered, their once-colourful plaster faded with time and the relentless sun, cracked and missing in places. A few of the buildings had wooden frames in their windows, and there was the occasional solid door. He couldn't remember having seen any glass though. Then again, it was so hot and dry, perhaps they just didn't need it.

Shenander, the medicine man, stood in the street outside the big hall. His bare spindly legs, wild hair and cloak of tattered rags made him appear even more birdlike than before, but he smiled when he saw Errol approaching.

'You came. Good.' His blackened face crinkled as he spoke, white eyes glistening in the last of the setting sun. 'Tonight we celebrate Hammie's recovery. The gods smiled upon us when they sent you our way, Errol.'

'He's not fully recovered yet. He'll probably never be able to walk far even when he is.'

'Nonsense. He'll be as good as new. Come. Enter our grand hall and accept our thanks.' Shenander took him by the arm and led him to the front door. Inside, torches blazed in sconces on the walls, and a huge table was laden with food. At first Errol thought the whole village must have turned up to greet him; there were more people than he could remember seeing any time before. But as he passed through the crowd, shaking hands with some he recognized, nodding politely at others, he noticed that they were all men. Murta and Nellore were away looking after Hammie, but Errol was sure they weren't the only women in the place. He'd seen others out and about, spoken to some of them. None appeared to have been invited to the feast.

'Welcome, Errol! Eat! Drink!' The question died on his lips as the suspicious old man, Ben, pushed his way through the crowd. He wore what must once have been a very expensive robe, dark blue velvet now faded, seams lined with gold, and a collar of sable. A heavy chain of office hung around his neck, the gilding worn at the links to reveal cheaper bronze underneath. Errol couldn't help but remember Alderman Clusster and his hapless daughter Maggs. He wondered how they were, what they were doing. Trell was probably ensconced in a seminary at Candlehall now, learning how to be a good little bookkeeper. The thought almost made him laugh.

'It's been an age since last we saw a stranger on the road. Hammie will be very grateful you came along.' The old man reached round to the table, bringing two heavy goblets back with him and handing one to Errol. 'Let us drink to his health and thank the gods.'

Errol sniffed the dark red liquid in his goblet. It was wine, of that much he was sure. It didn't smell as good as the drink Melyn had plied him with, but it was similar enough to bring back unhappy memories. Still, the others were all raising their tankards and jugs. It would be rude not to join in.

'The gods!' He took a sip, let the slightly sour liquid wash down his throat. He was thirsty after a few hours in Hammie's smoke-filled front room, and the wine helped. It wasn't too bad really, once you'd got past that initial bitterness. Errol took another, deeper drink as Shenander came through the crowd towards him. The medicine man didn't need to push past people; they seemed to sense his presence and move out of the way even when their backs were turned to him.

'It is truly an auspicious time. I have seen the gods massing in the western skies.'

'You have?' Errol frowned and looked at his goblet. He had not drunk much more than a mouthful but the wine was already making his head fuzzy.

'Indeed I have. When I travelled to the deep woods to fetch herbs for Hammie's wounds. It is no coincidence he fell from that tree when he did, though it seems these days the gods call to them only our best.'

'I don't understa—'

'How could you? You are not from these parts. You do not know the gods as we do. Perhaps you even sought to flee them.' The medicine man leaned in close, or at least it felt that way to Errol. He was hot, the air difficult to breathe as the massed bodies of the other villagers pressed in around him.

'You should know that the gods see everything. There can be no escaping from them.'

'I . . .' Errol tried to speak, but his throat was tight. The goblet grew impossibly heavy in his hand, slipping from fingers that had lost the ability to grip. He watched it tumble to the floor in slow motion, the dark red wine arcing out in a splash that disappeared into the black rags of Shenander's cloak.

'They wanted to take our youngest and strongest. But you, Errol, you came along at just the right moment.'

The medicine man's bird head was all he could see now, the rest of the room disappearing into the edges of a black tunnel. As his legs buckled under him, Errol felt not the floor rushing up to greet him, but strong hands gripping under his arms. His last thought as unconsciousness claimed him, how stupid he was not to have seen what was coming.

'Wake, Melyn son of Arrall. Wake.'

Melyn had not been aware he was sleeping. Before the

voice there had been nothing, as if he had never existed. Or had he been dreaming of his childhood, long forgotten in a lifetime of service to the Order of the High Ffrydd? All the mother and father he would ever need. Fleeting images tumbled through his mind as he struggled into consciousness: a castle in snow-capped mountains, the concerned look on the face of a woman he didn't recognize, a pair of dragons flying high in a cloudless sky.

'Wake!'

With a lurch Melyn sat up, then clutched at his chest in agony. The slashes that Benfro had cut across him throbbed and stung, and his lungs were weak, still choked with blood. It took too long for him to remember where he was – in King Ballah's bed, deep in the royal palace at Tynhelyg. He cast back for a waking memory, seeing Clun in his aethereal form, Beulah and her newborn daughter. How much better if she had borne a son. But how had he come to be here, sleeping?

'You were grievously injured, my faithful servant.'

Only then did Melyn realize that he was in the presence of the Shepherd. How he could have not noticed before was beyond him. That perfect bliss drove away the pain, made breathing as light and easy as it was unnecessary. The troubles and aches of the campaign melted away as he basked in the love of his god. But lying in his bed was no way to meet his maker. Melyn struggled with the heavy blankets, desperate to kneel.

'Rest easy.' There was no one in the room with him, and yet Melyn felt a firm hand push him back into the bed. Where it touched his chest, it burned like ice, spreading through him and freezing him solid. Only his mind worked, utterly at the mercy of the Shepherd. As it should always be.

'Forgive me. I have failed in your service. I had the boy Errol and the dragon Benfro in my grasp and they both escaped me.' The cold filled him, so deep he could not even shiver. It was a reflection of the Shepherd's disappointment in him, he knew, a tiny fraction of the icy torment that awaited him should he fail once too often.

'They are creatures of the Wolf, my old friend. They have his wiliness and cunning. But fear not. They will not escape you again.'

Pressure on his chest constricted Melyn's breathing even further. For a moment he wondered if he had angered his god one time too many, if this was the end and the icy pits of the Wolf's lair awaited. But then the wounds on his chest began to stretch and knit, the flesh turning stiff and hard as his deep gashes were healed. An energy flooded through him he had never felt before, the power of God made real.

'I cannot have my most faithful servant languishing in a soft bed while his body heals.' The Shepherd's voice was like warm water, chasing away the chill that had held him fast, leaving his fingers and toes tingling with pins and needles. 'Your servant did what she could, but her skills are limited.'

'Frecknock?' Melyn was surprised to hear his god mention the creature in such a casual manner. Was she not a servant of the Wolf, after all?

'She swore a blood oath to protect you, did she not? That is more powerful even than her allegiance to my ancient foe. You know as well as I, Melyn son of Arall, how few true allies you have in this world. But she is one. You need not fear she will betray you. Others you consider far closer will prove themselves less worthy first.'

'My lord.' Melyn bent his head in submission even though he had no altar, no focus for his prayers. He could feel the skin of his chest hardening, changing under the Shepherd's healing touch.

'You worry about Prince Geraint's army. You fear that they will overrun the city, take back this prize you have won.'

'I killed his father. He will not rest until one of us is dead. I would not, had someone killed my queen.'

'Ah, Melyn. Your loyalty is not in question. It never has been. You serve me well, and I will not see you fail now. It is true that the Wolf seems to have the upper hand here, but overconfidence has ever been his undoing. He sees all dragons as his creatures, their magic as his tool. But Frecknock has turned her back on him. Use her. Keep her close and she will serve you well.'

'But how can I fight him? He commands a hundred thousand men, ten thousand of them adepts. Tynhelyg is ill suited to a siege.'

'Then do not try to defend it. Take your warrior priests out to the Lantern Plains on the fifth day from this one. Set them atop Bailey's Hill and keep the dragon close by. She will hide you on the sixth dawn and by noon your victory will be complete.'

'Hide us? I don't understand.'

'Of course you don't. You are skilled in the ways of magic, Melyn. More skilled perhaps than any man on Gwlad. But do not presume to know the ways of your god.'

Melyn felt each word as a stab in his brain, an echo of the torment promised him should he fall short of the expectations of the Shepherd.

'I live only to serve, my lord.' He bent low to the bed-covers, feeling the strange stiffness in his chest restricting his movements. The pain was gone though, and his breath no longer bubbled. He felt strong, refreshed as if he had slept a week. But at the same moment as he realized he was healed, so Melyn was bereft at the departure of his god, for the Shepherd's presence had disappeared as swiftly and suddenly as it had come. He sat in his bed for long minutes, savouring the bittersweet memory of the encounter, until a gentle knock at the door reminded him of himself.

'What is it?'

The door opened a foot, revealing the hesitant face of Frecknock.

'Your Grace, I heard voices. I only wanted to be sure you were all right.'

'I am well, Frecknock. Much better than I could hope, given the circumstances.' Melyn pulled aside the blankets and swung his legs out of bed. He felt stronger than he had in days. Weeks, if he was being honest, although his chest was tight under the bandages.

'Sire, how is it that—?'

'The Shepherd moves in mysterious ways, Frecknock. Did he not bring you to me in the first place?'

'But your wound. It's—'

'Much better, thank you.' Melyn shrugged off his sleeping robes. 'I don't think I need these bandages any more.'

'Of course. Here. Let me help you.' Frecknock stepped

closer, her large hands and long fingers swiftly untying the bandages. Melyn's arms were strong as he raised them to let her work, but they felt stiff and with less mobility than he remembered. The tightness in his chest restricted his movements in a way that wasn't painful but was nevertheless awkward.

'Your Grace, I don't understand. How is this possible?'

Melyn looked up to see that Frecknock had taken a couple of steps back, the bandages held loosely in one hand. She was staring not at his face but at his bare chest, and he finally looked down to see the scarring the Shepherd's healing had left behind, for surely his god would not heal him and leave no trace of the failure his injury represented.

Only there was no scar, no livid pink tissue mapping the shiny route of Benfro's razor claws. Instead the front of Melyn's chest was covered in a plate of fine golden scales.

'Your Highness. I am glad to see you've settled in.'

Dafydd looked up from his desk to see Seneschal Padraig standing in the doorway. It wasn't his desk really; in truth he had no idea who it belonged to. Queen Beulah, he supposed, since these were the royal apartments deep in the heart of the old palace. The room was comfortably large, airy with high ceilings and tall windows opening on to a balcony that overlooked the Winter Gardens. A fire burned in the hearth, but there wasn't much need for it. Candlehall was far warmer than Tynhelyg, even as the autumn began to fade. The dying afternoon light reflected off dark red velvet drapes hung around a bed big enough for an army, and through the set of double doors beside it there was a bathroom with seemingly endless piped hot water. He was washed, well fed and had even managed to find some clothes that fitted. After months of travel it was nice to have a bit of luxury, although he could imagine the scowl on his grandfather's face if he had seen the opulence of the place.

'I would be happier if my wife were here with me.' Dafydd stood, went to greet the old man. Padraig was in his habitual black robes, slightly better tailored than those worn by the many predicants of the Candle who thronged the palace complex about whatever business they had. His hair was almost all gone, just the memory of it clinging whitely to his shiny liver-spotted scalp. Sallow skin and sunken eyes spoke of a man no longer able to make the most of his food. The haughty expression and sharp cheekbones suggested the seneschal had never been one too caught up in the pleasures of the flesh anyway.

'We will all be happy when Princess Iolwen is with us. She has left Abervenn and is coming upriver by barge, if that is why you wished to speak with me. That infernal Ram Usel said you wished an audience.' Padraig winced in distaste as he named the medic.

'Among other things. Mostly I need to know what your plans are for the city. Have you had any word from Beulah?'

'If you mean does she know her capital has fallen, then yes. I have not spoken to the queen myself since the day she left here on her grand tour, many months ago, but I have ways of communicating with the major cities of the

Twin Kingdoms. I can reach Talarddeg, even Tynhelyg if absolutely necessary.'

Dafydd could see the offer for what it was, but nevertheless he was tempted. And yet he didn't want to be any more beholden to the seneschal than he already was. 'Not for now. Perhaps when Princess Iolwen is safe here I will contact King Ballah myself.'

Something passed across Padraig's eyes at the mention of the king, but Dafydd couldn't tell what. The prince was more skilled in magic than many, but the seneschal had spent a much longer lifetime in its study. His mind was as closed as the deepest dungeons beneath the palace at Tynhelyg. Dafydd could not even tell whether the old man was being evasive or simply always had rigid control of his thoughts, although after a moment's silence he simply nodded his head slightly.

'As you wish, sire.'

'And the city? Are you preparing for a siege?'

'We are gathering all the supplies we can, sending those who have other places to go back out to the country. This city has not been attacked in many centuries though. Not since the Brumal Wars. Strange that it always falls prey to its own, never a foreign invader.' Padraig allowed himself a small smile before continuing. 'We can survive for months if the walls remain unbreached, the gates hold. But Beulah is queen, a child of the House of Balwen. There is no telling what she might know, what secrets could let her in behind our backs.'

'Would you just throw open the gates? Let them come in like you did for us?'

'No, sire. That would not serve the people well.'

'How so? I thought you wanted only to avoid unnecessary bloodshed.'

'Quite so. And you have not harmed a single person since arriving here. More, you rejected the offer of the Obsidian Throne, and I am truly grateful for that.' Padraig lowered his head to stress his sincerity, then looked up again, his pale eyes suddenly bright. 'But Queen Beulah is a very different person. She will not be kind to the city that turned its back on her.'

'She would sack her own capital?'

'Worse. I have no doubt of it. Make no mistake, Prince Dafydd. I have picked a side in this war and I will defend it to the utmost of my ability. But you must never forget what is at stake here should we fail. Candlehall and all inside its walls will burn.'

20

It is likely there has been a settlement on the site of Candlehall for millennia. Its position above the River Abheinn surrounded by the fertile plains of the Hafod make it a natural place to build. The Neuadd itself predates much of the current city and possibly even the older parts of the palace complex and the King's Chapel. It is an easily defensible spot, which perhaps explains why it has so seldom been attacked. In fact, despite or because of its sturdy walls, both the ancient Wall of Kings and the more recently constructed New Wall, Candlehall has only been besieged twice in written history.

The first siege lasted only twenty-four hours before King Diseverin IV, aided by Inquisitor Porfor and a troop of warrior priests of the then-fledgling Order of the High Ffrydd, routed the attacking army of Duke Lledrod of Dina. The second siege marked the end of the Brumal Wars and lasted just two weeks. There can be few people in the Twin Kingdoms who have not heard of King Divitie IX's massacre of the army of his unfortunate brother Prince Torwen on the plains beneath the King's Gate.

What few appreciate though is that in its entire history, spanning millennia, Candlehall has never been attacked by the army of a foreign, invading nation. It

has always been Twin Kingdoms men and more specifically Hafod men who have risen in arms, ultimately
unsuccessfully, against their own capital and king.

Father Soay, *An Architectural*
Tour of the Twin Kingdoms

'You fly well for a kitling. Though you seem to favour
your right wing a little. A shame about the landing, though.
That needs more practice, I think.'

Sun on his back and the wind ruffling the hairy tufts at
the end of his ears, Benfro was too happy in himself to be
annoyed at being called a kitling. In truth, he wasn't exactly
a fully grown adult, even if he had reached his majority
and carried the honorific title of head of his family. He
was still young, possibly the youngest dragon in this fold,
and the dragon alongside whom he flew was older than
the hills.

'Ah, I see it now. A couple of small bones that were
broken and not set correctly. How can one so young have
seen so many mishaps?'

Benfro didn't reply. He'd spotted a deer through the
tree canopy and was trying to work out the best way to
catch it. He had regained almost all of his strength since
he'd been healed by Myfanwy and arrived in such inele-
gant fashion at the fold's gathering place atop the Twmp.
There was just the small matter of his regrowing hand to
slow him down. That and his continued inability to land
without falling on his face.

'Deer. There. See them?' He didn't wait for an answer,
but folded back his wings and plummeted towards the

ground. Behind him he could sense the surprise of his flying companion. Sir Gwair wasn't the leader of the dragons, but he was the oldest and probably the wisest after Myfanwy the healer. Benfro had spent a long time trying to work out who was the leader but had lately come to the conclusion there wasn't one. Certainly they were very different to the staid old villagers with whom he had grown up.

The trees here were more of the strange things he had seen turned into houses when first he'd arrived. Tall, impossibly thick trunks were topped with tiny little branches and smatterings of leaves. With a twist of his tail, Benfro slid through the slimmest of gaps, still high enough off the ground not to worry. Something of his approach must have registered with the deer though. He'd only seen one, but a herd of them scattered in all directions. He focused on a large buck with particularly impressive antlers, angled his descent to intersect with where he knew it was going to run. Closer and closer, faster and faster, the wind pulled tears from his eyes, blurring his vision so that it was hard to judge the distance. He had to rely on memory, experience, convince himself that he could do this even with his eyes closed. And then he let out a laugh of joy. Of course he could do it with his eyes closed. He could see the life in everything around him, use the lines to judge distance far more accurately than with mere sight. They came to him easily now; there was something about this place or maybe the lack of Magog's influence. In the same instant he thought of them, they were there.

They were everywhere.

The stag was a bright point of light, moving back and forth as it tried to escape him, but the trees were even brighter still, crawling with life, glowing with it in themselves. The Grym pulsed through them in slow waves, almost hypnotic, and around them auras glowed in colours he had no names for. Momentarily distracted, Benfro almost crashed into the ground, swinging his wings down hard and pulling his head back to avoid a nasty collision. Instinctively he raised his legs, talons extended, and without realizing he was doing it, brought them together around the stag's neck. It died in an instant, the pulse of its life winking out like a candle extinguished. And with that death he felt a surge of energy fill him. Without a thought he released the body just in time to execute a perfect landing.

'Bravo, Benfro. As fine a kill as ever I saw.'

The voice woke him from some kind of trance. Benfro looked up, the Grym seeping away from his vision as he did so. Sir Gwair spiralled down from a larger gap in the canopy, landing heavily. The old dragon waddled up to inspect the dead stag.

'These trees. What are they called?' Benfro had almost forgotten the deer. He was fascinated by the thick trunks, the pulsing life within them. He walked up to the nearest one and reached out with his hand, felt the smooth surface of its bark, and as he did so a tiny jolt of energy shot from his hand into it. He recoiled, letting out a yelp more of surprise than pain. Sir Gwair must have seen, as he chuckled under his breath before answering.

'These are the earliest trees. The Bondaris. Legend has it they are the sons and daughters of the mother tree herself.' Sir Gwair stood beside Benfro now, and he too reached out to touch the smooth bark. As he did so, Benfro saw the tree glow as it took the gift of the Grym from the old dragon.

'I've met the mother tree,' Benfro said. 'She found me when I was almost dead, took me in, fed me. And all she wanted in return was a story.'

Sir Gwair patted the tree once more before speaking again, and when he did it was in a low voice.

'You are so young, Benfro. You have so much to learn. But one thing I will tell you now. Do not mention the mother tree to the rest of the fold. Certainly not to Fflint and his like. They don't hold much with such things. Kitlings' tales, superstition and nonsense. That's what they think.'

'But she's real. How can they not know that?'

'They choose not to. Same as they chose not to live in the castle with the Old One. Those of them that weren't hatched out here in the wilds, that is.'

Benfro was about to ask more. He knew so little about these dragons, knew so little about any of his kind when he thought about it. But before he could say anything a great bellowing roar filled the air above their heads. Looking up, he saw Fflint and his cronies wheeling not far above the treetops.

'Oh no. Not so soon, surely.' Sir Gwair gazed up too.

'What is it?' Benfro bent down to pick up the deer and begin the task of gutting and preparing it, but the old dragon reached out a bony hand, stopping him.

'Leave it, Benfro. You should see this, if only to understand something of what we have become.' Sir Gwair took a couple of steps towards the nearby clearing where he had landed, opening his wings and taking to the air with practised ease. Two sweeps of his gnarled and ancient wings and he was above the canopy, away.

Benfro looked at the tree towering above him, then at the dead stag. His talons had pierced its neck, killing it instantly, but it still needed to be grallocked or the meat would spoil, no matter what Sir Gwair might have said. Working as swiftly as he could, he stripped the carcass of its entrails, not easy given the lack of dexterity in his regrowing hand.

'What's keeping you, slowcoach?'

Benfro looked up from his task to see Cerys walking towards him. His hearts still leaped at the sight of her, but he was embarrassed too. She visited his cave occasionally, but not every night. Mostly she seemed to spend her time with Myfanwy, away from the Twmp, where Fflint was unlikely to bother her.

'Didn't want to leave this to go foul. Ynys Môn would never forgive me.'

'Ynys Môn?'

'An old dragon. A friend. He taught me to hunt.'

'Taught you well too. But there's finer fare than deer to be had. Leave that for the forest animals. We won't lack for food tonight.'

Like Sir Gwair before her, she turned, strode towards the clearing and took to the sky without a backward glance. Soon she was above the canopy. She turned slowly in the air, calling down. 'Won't wait for you for ever, Benfro of the Borrowed Wings. Come on or you'll miss all the fun.'

Benfro looked at the half-eviscerated carcass, then to the wheeling dragon overhead. He hated to waste good meat, hated even more to have killed such a magnificent animal only to let it lie. Perhaps the forest creatures would benefit, but it was a shame all the same. The urgency of his new family piqued his curiosity though, and that had always been his weakness.

Setting the stag against the base of the nearest tree, he ran towards the clearing, snapped open his wings and leaped into the air.

A low droning noise battered against his hearing like a fly at a grimy pane of glass. Errol tried to shake his head to get rid of whatever it was, but he couldn't move. Something held him flat on a hard surface that tilted slightly in the direction of his feet. He cracked open his eyes, wincing as the bright sunlight cut through him like a knife in the brain.

'All praise to the gods, who suffer us to live beneath them.'

Errol squinted sideways, seeing a group of villagers huddled close by. They were swaying slowly from side to side, singing a low dirge that sounded like the dying cries of distant oxen. Nearer still, the medicine man stood with his arms wide, carved stick in one hand and a blazing torch in the other. His head was tilted back and he shouted at the sky, 'Come, gods of the air. Take this sacrifice as token of thanks for the safety you have ensured us.'

Errol tried to wriggle, but he was tied down firmly, feet and hands and head. He could shift just enough to see that he was splayed out on some kind of angled rock altar.

Up above him the sky was clearest blue, the sun hanging low, which meant it must be morning.

'Grant us another year of your boon, so we may serve you as is your will.'

He remembered then, the feast and the goblet of wine. It must have been drugged, and he really should have known better than to trust these people. Now it looked like they were going to burn him alive. But maybe not; he was tied to a stone slab.

'Remember us well, Errol, when you are one with the gods. This is the highest honour we have bestowed upon you.'

Errol hadn't seen Shenander walk up close beside him, so the medicine man's voice in his ear made him start. The strap holding his head in place gave a little, but only enough for him to stun himself slightly as he slumped back on the sacrificial altar.

'Light the fires! Summon the gods!' Shenander shouted now, and as Errol tried to see what was happening, he could hear the sound of flames eating at dried wood. The sour smell of smoke filled his nose, and then thick black rolls of the stuff billowed up.

'The gods have been summoned. It is not for us to gaze upon their fearful majesty. We must leave this sacred place. Return to our homes and give worship in solitude.'

The murmuring chant of the villagers changed slightly in pitch, then slowly started to fade as they left. Errol thought about shouting out, begging them to stop, but it seemed unlikely they would reconsider after having gone to so much trouble. He still couldn't understand the method of his sacrifice. From the crackling of the flames and the direction of the wind, the fire that was giving off so much black smoke was too far away to burn him. More likely he would die of thirst or heatstroke out in the mid-day sun. He tried to move his head again, and the strap gave a little more. He strained as hard as he could, squeezing his eyes tight with the effort, and suddenly it gave way. His neck almost snapped, his chin jarring into his chest, and for a moment all he could do was lie, panting, as he recovered. When he finally opened his eyes, Errol understood.

He was on the top of a hill in the centre of a clearing, surrounded by ancient trees of the same kind he'd seen on his first day in this place. The area immediately in front of him had been cleared, but everywhere else was a jumble of large rocks. Time and weather had smoothed the faces of most of them, but the one to which he had been tied seemed to have been carved for a purpose. It was also angled so that he could see out across the sparse forest in the direction of the great rocky ridge and its summit. Even now he could see the tiny dots of dragons wheeling around it. Not the dozen or so he had expected, but hundreds.

The gods.

Errol looked at the ropes holding his arms and legs in place. They were thick, sturdy and very well knotted. There was no way he was going to escape from their hold easily. Over to his side, the fire burned strongly. It was wood, but there was some other material in there too, which accounted for the thick black smoke climbing high into the morning sky. A signal that could be seen for hundreds of miles.

He should have been panicking. Soon enough the dragons would come, and Errol had no illusions that these were creatures like Benfro, or even the long-dead Corwen and Sir Radnor. The pieces of the puzzle had been there all along; he'd just been too preoccupied, too stupid to see them. These people worshipped the dragons as gods, made human sacrifice to them. Nellore's father had been taken. Others had gone before. It didn't take a genius to work out where.

He forced himself to relax. There was a way out of this predicament. One he'd used before. This land was powerful with the Grym; all he needed to do was tap into the lines and use one to take him—

'Hold still, Errol. This ain't easy to cut.'

Errol opened his eyes to see Nellore standing by his left hand, sawing away at the rope with a fearsome-looking knife. In moments it had cut all the way through and she darted round to the other side.

'What are you doing here? It's not safe.'

'Safer 'n staying in the village.' Nellore was on to his feet now. 'They told me you'd left. Murta told me. I thought she was my friend.'

Errol sat up, rubbing the life back into his wrists and ankles before attempting to jump down from the rock. Away in the distance, he couldn't see anything circling the big hill any more, which didn't bode well.

'I think we should get away from here as quickly as possible,' he said.

Nellore looked up as if only just then realizing her predicament. 'They're going to be pissed off when they get here and there's no sacrifice.'

Errol slid off the rock, crouching while he got his sense of balance back. He was still looking for the lines, but the sight wouldn't come to him. Tied to the rock, alone, he had been calm. Now he was free and there was Nellore to worry about as well, he could hardly think straight.

'Which way is the village?'

Nellore pointed in the direction opposite to the Twmp. Now that he looked, Errol could see a track of sorts winding its way through the sparse trees. There seemed to be more ground cover the other way.

'You'd better hurry up before someone notices you've gone,' he said.

'I ain't goin' back there.' Nellore's voice was heavy with disbelief.

'Why not? They're your family, aren't they?'

'My family? Ma died havin' my little brother. He din't survive neither. And then they all said my da was chosen to be with the gods. They brought him here. Tied him up same as you. Only he wanted to go. He believed them when they said he'd become a god himself.'

Errol glanced nervously at the sky before turning back to the young girl. 'They believe what? That the dragons take you away and you become one too?'

'That's what they say. Only I saw what happened to my da, and he din't turn into no god. More like dragon dung after they ate him.'

'You saw that? Your own father? They brought you here to watch?'

'They din't know I was watching. Nobody's s'posed to watch. I hid over there, in the rocks.' Nellore pointed to the jumble of rocks that crowned the hill beyond the altar stone. As she did so, a distant screech pierced the air. Not the sort of noise you might expect a god to make.

'Is there room there for two?'

Beulah looked at the empty bedchamber, the unlit fire no more than a pile of ashes. She would be glad to see the back of this room, glad to see the back of the ancient castle and its damp stone walls. The fact that she had given birth here only made Tochers worse for her. Far better her child had been born in Candlehall, the seat of her power.

'The wagons have been loaded, ma'am. We're ready to leave when you are.' Her maid Alicia was dressed for the road already, a heavy travelling cloak over clothes chosen for warmth rather than fashion. Beulah was almost jealous of the girl's faded soft leather boots.

'Good. I've spent long enough in this place as it is. Fetch my . . . Ellyn. We will leave together from the grand hall.'

The maid nodded and hurried off. Beulah went to the narrow window, peering out at the courtyard below. Clun was down there sorting out the last few details. Most of the army had already left, but it would take all day for the entire camp to move off. He'd likely be saddling his own horse too, since no one else dared go near the great beast.

The scream cut through Beulah's musing like a knife. There was something animal about it, wounded. Before she knew what she was doing, she had crossed the room and yanked open the heavy wooden door. A short corridor led to the stairs, and on one side of it a door opened on to reception rooms that had been pressed into service as a nursery. It lay ajar, and as Beulah rushed to it she thought she saw movement on the stairs, but she was too distracted by the scene in the nursery to pay much heed.

Blodwyn, the wet nurse, sat sprawled in a chair, staring up at the ceiling as if drunk. Her dress might have been white when she put it on that morning, but now it was soaked in red, blood from the wound that gaped in her neck from ear to ear. Beulah tried to conjure a blade of fire, tuning her senses to the Grym in the hope of detecting the intruder, but the curse of her condition still smothered her. Swearing loudly, she bent and pulled out the slim dagger she had taken to carrying in her boot. Her sword was still in the bedchamber, hung useless across the back of a chair along with her riding cloak.

A groan had her whip round, crouching and ready to fend off any attack, but it was only Alicia, slumped in the corner. Her neck was intact, but she was as pale as the wet nurse's dress wasn't, a sheen of sweat on her forehead and matting her hair.

'Majesty . . . Ellyn . . . taken . . .' She reached up an arm to point at the cradle set up between the single narrow window and the fireplace, and that was when Beulah saw the blood on her maid's hand, soaking into her sensible travelling clothes.

In two steps, Beulah was at the cradle, but she already knew what she would find there. The sheets had been cast aside and the cot lay empty. The anger came to her then, boiling up like the frustration of the past nine months all condensed into that one moment. And with a snap, the magic came back. The Grym shimmered into view, weak in the room but there. Those lines connected everything, including her husband.

'Clun! To me!' Beulah may have used rather too much urgency in her calling, it wasn't something she had ever tried before. Across the room, Alicia gasped and shuddered as if she had been slapped. Hurrying back to the injured maid, Beulah crouched down, appraising her wounds as quickly as she could. Too much blood for them not to be serious. She put a hand on the woman's damp forehead, channelled some of the Grym into her.

'How many of them? Did you see faces?'

'Just one. He was tall. Thin. All dressed in black. I couldn't see his . . . Your Majesty . . . so sorry.'

'Hush. You did what you could.' Beulah sent more of the Grym into the young woman, riding in with it to see something of her thoughts. It was all a jumble, fading fast, but Alicia had spoken true. There was a man, tall and thin, his face obscured by a hooded cloak. He was leaning over the cradle, back turned to Blodwyn's twitching corpse. And then he was right in front of her, chin stubbled with grey, stinking of stale garlic and unwashed body. A bright flash of pain in her gut and a single scream before a filthy hand clamped over her mouth, pushed her to the floor.

'My lady?'

Beulah snapped back into her own head and spun round with her knife in her hand to see Clun standing over her, eyes wide in surprise.

'Alicia? Is she . . . ?' His eyes lingered on the maid for a moment, then he turned slowly on his heel, taking in the rest of the room.

'Ellyn!' He was at the cradle side in an instant, snatched

up the bedding as if his daughter could be still hiding within the folds. Beulah felt the air turn chill around her as the Grym surged away from every living thing in the room, sucked into the bright shining blade of light that appeared in his hand. With a scream of rage that was more terrible than anything Beulah had ever heard, Clun drove his other hand through the base of the cradle, not so much shattering the wood as exploding it into a thousand tiny fragments. And then he was running out of the door, shouting the name of his kidnapped daughter.

'That isn't a sight I ever wished to see.'

Inquisitor Melyn and Captain Osgal sat on their horses and gazed out across the southern plain. To the north and west of them the city of Tynhelyg was a sprawl of buildings clustered around the sluggish River Ystwyth. A brown haze hung over it, the smoke of countless fires, not all of them venting out of chimneys. Beyond it, and at their backs, the great forest marched off towards the Caldy mountains, and thence to Talarddeg and the Sea of Tegid. It was a breathtaking view even as the setting sun leached it of colour, but it wasn't what was upsetting Captain Osgal.

'The Shepherd said they would be here. Do you doubt his word, Osgal?'

The captain's horse stood motionless, but the man atop it moved in his saddle as if he had piles. Osgal's burns had still not healed properly, and Melyn could tell they pained him beneath his robes. It made him even more surly than usual, which must have been popular with the warrior priests under his command.

'Never, Your Grace. But Prince Geraint's army numbers ten thousand. A thousand of them are adepts, some few even as skilled as us. We are hopelessly outnumbered.'

'Hopelessly? An interesting choice of word, Captain.' Melyn looked south across the plain and had to admit that Osgal had a point. The lights of a thousand cooking fires dotted the darkening ground, night come early to the land. His scouts had seen the approaching army first as a dark swirl of dust and carrion birds whirling in the afternoon air, and that was when Melyn had marched the bulk of his warrior priests out of the city and up to the summit of the hill. From there the noise had reached them slowly, a low clanking and rumbling that shook the earth even though it was still leagues distant. And finally they had seen the army itself, Prince Geraint's scouts riding out ahead and the main bulk moving at a punishing speed. Riders had reached the gates of the city at dusk, then turned and raced back to report that their capital was taken. Melyn knew the distance from Wrthol to Tynhelyg, knew how long it would take a man to walk at a reasonable pace. And he knew too how many days had passed since he had removed King Ballah's head from his shoulders. Even if Geraint had known that very instant his father was slain, the two sets of numbers didn't add up.

'This army has force-marched for more than ten days. Its supplies will be strung out in a line all the way back to the pass. We are rested and we have the better ground. I have no doubt that we could deal them a dreadful blow if we were to attack now. However, none of these things matters because the Shepherd has other plans.'

'Forgive me, sir. I have absolute faith in him. I just wish I knew what those plans were.'

'All in good time.' Melyn turned his horse, riding slowly back to the camp just below the ridge of the hill. 'Tell the men to bed down. Get some sleep. No fires tonight and no tapping the Grym for warmth either. Our lord's plan will be revealed with the dawn.'

Osgal saluted, then spurred his horse on, passing the message to the troops. Some were old hands, battle-hardened and able to catch sleep wherever and whenever the opportunity arose. Most of his warrior priests would lie awake all night though. Taking on an army so much bigger than your own would worry even the most serene mind. And yet Melyn was calm. As he scratched absent-mindedly at the hard scales underneath his robes he knew that the Shepherd would bring him victory.

'You know what you have to do?' The inquisitor spoke to the growing darkness. Frecknock unfolded from the gloom, her dull dark scales the perfect camouflage. She had a leather bag slung over one shoulder, and in it the book that contained so much power. The stolen wisdom of God.

'Yes, Your Grace. I will need to find a suitable spot, but this hill is powerful with the Grym. The working should not be too hard to do.'

'Then set to it. I feel the moment is upon us.'

He sensed the working as Frecknock cast it. An invisible veil shimmered the stars for the briefest of moments, like someone passing the thinnest of silks over the whole of the hill. Melyn knew that his army was hidden. Prince Geraint himself could ride right through the middle of their camp and not see a single warrior priest. His scouts would cross this hill, find it empty, report back that all the invading forces were in Tynhelyg. The army would wait until dawn to mount an attack on those walls, confident it was not fit to withstand a siege. They would take time to rest, regain their strength, eat and maybe try to sleep. Perhaps he should try and do the same.

'Ho, Jarius. Well met.'

Captain Pelod stood guard at the main doors to the royal apartments, looking slightly nervous that his friend and prince was wandering about alone. No doubt there were other members of the troop stationed all about. Llanwennog men, not the newly recruited Abervenn Irregulars. Their darker skin marked them out as different, an easy target for anyone still sympathetic to Beulah.

'I wish I had your confidence, sir. Can't quite throw the feeling that this is some kind of elaborate trap.'

'You're not the only one. I'm just better at hiding it.'

'Well, I'll be a great deal happier when the princess is here. I think the people of Candlehall will take to their own rather better than us.'

Captain Pelod had fallen in beside Dafydd, and they walked up towards the cloisters that separated the Neuadd from the surrounding palace complex together. The sun was high in a pale blue sky, but its lack of warming heat warned of winter's approach.

'Any news from home?' Dafydd asked.

'Alas no. We have sent birds, but none has returned so far. I'm no adept, sire. None of us is. King Ballah sent all his best men to the front with your father and Tordu.'

'I know. I'd try and contact them myself, but it's so far.' Perhaps when Iolwen is here, I'll be able to get my head straight. Maybe even use that throne to help. 'I'd like to know what Beulah's up to, and for once that damned medic Usel's no help.'

They had reached the stone arch that opened on to the cloisters. Stepping into deep shade, Dafydd was distracted, thinking about how he could contact his grandfather and apprise the old king of how far he had come. He hoped his father's army would destroy Beulah's troops before they could reach Wrthol, then push them back through the pass and sweep on down to relieve the inevitable siege of Candlehall. If they could survive the winter, then there was every chance they might succeed in crushing Beulah between two armies. If they could survive the winter.

'There can be only one true king. All pretenders must die!'

The shout cut through Dafydd's musings just an instant too late. He hadn't sensed their presence, but now there were half a dozen men surrounding him and Captain Pelod. Black-clad, they merged with the shadows even more perfectly than their clothing, seeming to flit from point to point without moving through the space in between. Dafydd couldn't even be sure there were six; it could just have been one moving with impossible speed.

'Behind me, Dafydd!' Captain Pelod shouted the command at the same time as he conjured his puissant sword. 'To me, men!'

Dafydd brought his own blade to life, all idle thought gone from his mind as he tried to assess the nature of the threat. They were hemmed in by the cloister on one side, but the courtyard was only a few paces away. Out in the sunlight their attackers would lose their advantage. It was just a matter of getting there.

'No man of the north will sit upon the throne!' A dark figure lunged at Dafydd, but the assassin held no obvious weapon. Momentarily confused, the prince was almost skewered by the stiletto that appeared at the last moment in his hand. Lurching back, he felt the blade tear the front of his tunic, and instinctively swept around with his own weapon. It caught only air, then sparked off the stone of a pillar. A few paces away, Captain Pelod was fending off an attack from at least two black-clad warriors.

'In case it missed your notice, I've not even tried to take the throne.' Dafydd leaped forward and caught one of the men full on with his blade. The clothes folded in on themselves, tumbling to the floor empty. Only the faint smell of singed cloth showed that he had struck true at all.

'Dafydd. Behind you.' Captain Pelod dispatched the other attacker with a swift upward swing of his blade, turning in the same instant and lunging past the prince, who was still staring in disbelief at the pile of rags at his feet. He turned just in time to see his old friend slam into a figure far more solid than the other two. They both hit the stone wall, but it was the captain who let out a grunt of surprise. And then his knees buckled and he was falling to the ground.

'All false kings will die.' The black-clad figure held the same stiletto in his hand, only now it was red with blood, a single drop glistening on the tip.

Dafydd let out a low roar of anger, springing forward with his puissant sword held high. In the back of his mind he was aware of the approaching guards, but at that moment all his attention was on the assassin. He could barely see the man's face, shrouded in black, but those eyes locked on to his own. Dafydd glanced briefly to the left and saw his attacker's eyes go the same way. Then as the man feinted right, he let his blade extinguish, conjuring it into life immediately in his other hand, and brought it up swiftly into the space where he knew it would connect.

It felt like his whole arm had been set on fire. Dafydd had learned from the best of his grandfather's palace guard and knew the dangers of conjuring the puissant sword. The consequences of losing control of that much concentrated Grym were too terrible to contemplate, and yet for a moment he thought his end had come. It was almost as if the assassin were forcing the fire back up through the sword and into him, but that wasn't possible, surely? He fell back on his training, instinctively raising his mental defences and concentrating his attention on his blade. The flow could only be outwards, the heat pushed away from him. Anything else was messing with his mind.

As his mental barriers hardened, Dafydd saw the scene for what it really was. There was just one attacker, but he had managed to take them both by surprise. His skill was in misdirection, turning his enemy against himself. Well, two could play at that game.

'Who are you?' He threw out the question with a mental suggestion that he was truly curious, and at the same time took a step back. His old friend, Jarius, was lying very still at his feet, but Dafydd knew he couldn't afford the luxury of concern. Not now, in the heat of the battle.

'Who I am is unimportant, usurper.' The assassin ducked

and weaved, but Dafydd could see through his subterfuge. The man was a poor sword fighter, too reliant on his magic. His body gave away his intentions all too clearly. One step, two, and then Dafydd swung his blade once more. It blazed in the shade of the cloister as it passed neatly through the man's neck. His head fell one way, his body the other, coming to rest against the cold stone.

'Jarius!' Now there was time. Dafydd bent low to his old friend, feeling for any sign of life in him. Blood soaked the front of his robes, seeping into the flagstones where he had fallen as if the very fabric of the Neuadd was drinking his essence.

'Jarius!' Captain Pelod's body was heavy, unmoving, his head lolling back and forth as Dafydd shook him. And then he sensed other life around him as the rest of the palace guard came running, surrounding him.

'Your Highness. Please. We must move. There may be others.' Dafydd looked up into the concerned face of one of his sergeants and for that fleeting moment couldn't even remember his name.

'We have to help him,' he said and clutched his friend close, knowing deep down that it was already way too late for that.

Many things can corrupt an adept's skill at manipulating the Grym, but none is so potent as carrying another life within oneself. It is perhaps for this very reason that few women practise the magical arts, and those who do seldom raise children. The ability to conjure begins to fade at conception and will generally have vanished altogether by the end of the first trimester. For someone attuned to the Grym, this can be disorientating or even fatal when coupled with the more traditional ailments of childbearing.

Most adepts will regain some of their skill once the child is born, although the rate at which this skill returns can vary, as can its depth. For most women it is a slow climb to something like their former level, as if they had started again and had to relearn everything anew. Some never see or feel the Grym again, and this can weigh as heavily on the mind as the birth sickness that plagues many. And there are some few women who regain their magic in an instant, usually as a result of some great trauma or shock. This is the most dangerous way to regain the skill, for it often comes back far stronger than before. And at a time when the adept is mentally and physically least able to cope.

Inquisitor Melyn, *A Short Treatise on the Aethereal*

Benfro knew what he was going to see before he caught up with the hunting party. The smell was faint, but it was etched into his memory like no other. There were men nearby.

The dragons making up the party were circling above a rocky outcrop in the trees. A thin plume of smoke rose straight up, undisturbed until it was battered aside by the wash of wings. As he neared, Benfro could see past the trees to a wide clearing. It looked almost like an amphitheatre, with a flat slab of rock in the middle, angled slightly and carved with strange shapes. The smoke came from a series of small fires that burned around the stone, but there was no sign of whoever had lit them. He watched as Fflint, ever the first, landed in the clearing and strode up to the stone slab, sniffed at it, then kicked out at the nearest fire.

'Where is the sacrifice?' Sparks flew about the clearing, embers scattering as Fflint's tail lashed out at another fire. One by one the other dragons landed, some inspecting the slab, others wandering about the circle as if anything the size of a man could hide there. It was plain to Benfro that there were no people there, and it was plain too that there was no way he would be able to land in such a small space with so many obstacles in his way. Not without colliding with someone. He set his wings into a tight turn and wheeled overhead, hoping no one would call him down. It wasn't long before Fflint took off, climbing up to him.

'Can you see where they went?'

'See where who went?' Benfro asked.

'The sacrifice and whoever set it free. I got two fresh

scents before everyone else landed and stank the place out. Good call keeping up here. Or did you just not fancy your chances landing without ending up flat on your face?'

Benfro ignored the jibe. He was getting used to them now, as inevitable perhaps as his continued inability to master graceful landing unless he wasn't trying. 'What is this sacrifice? I don't know what we're meant to be looking for.'

'Men, Benfro of the Borrowed Wings. You know of men, I take it?'

Benfro hugged his damaged hand to his chest. It was growing slowly, still half the size it should have been, but at least it was there. 'I've come across them from time to time,' he said.

'Then you'll know they're not to be trusted. Simple-minded they might be, but they'll try and cheat you as soon as your back's turned.'

Simple-minded? Cheat? Benfro opened his mouth to speak, then closed it again. Finding out about where he was had been painfully slow, his questions rebuffed, joked away or just ignored until he had more or less given up asking. Within the fold and inside his own cave in the Twmp, he had found a certain peace and security. Enough that he had decided his best course of action was to heal, regain his strength and then renew his search for Gog, and maybe Errol too. He'd hardly thought about Errol at all recently, but this talk of men and the scent of them reminded him. No, that scent had reminded him. Different, yes. Mixed with too many other things, but Errol had been here.

'Well I'm not putting up with it. They summoned us, and here we are. Time to show them what that really means.'

Before Benfro could say anything to that, Fflint peeled out of his slow circling and shot over the clearing, shouting to the few dragons who were still wandering about on the ground. The rest of the group had already taken to the sky once more and soon a mob of a dozen or more were in formation and heading out over the trees. Only Sir Gwair held back, and Cerys.

'Where are they all going?' Benfro asked as he joined the two of them.

'To the village.' Sir Gwair sighed as he spoke, the wind whipping the rest of his words away.

'A village? Of men?' Benfro watched Fflint's group move further ahead.

'What did you think? Deer?' Cerys flew so close she clipped the end of Benfro's wing with her own, sending a shock through him at the touch.

'What are they going to do to them?'

'The villagers make us a sacrifice every year. This one's early, but who can understand men, eh? Still, they've lit the fire and left us nothing, almost as if to mock us. Fflint's going to teach them a lesson.'

It wasn't hard to guess what that lesson would be. They were still following the larger group, Benfro noticed. Part of him wanted to speed up, to join them and mete out the revenge he'd been longing to take on all men since his mother's horrible execution. But another part of him knew the picture was not so simple any more. He had met good people, and he had met dragons far, far worse than

Inquisitor Melyn. It was the warrior priests he wanted revenge on, their leader in particular. The thought of killing anyone else just reminded him of the chaos of the King's Fair, the circus, the smell of fear and burning flesh. It sickened him.

'Is there anything we can do?' he asked. 'To stop them?'

Sir Gwair let out a short bark of mirthless laughter. 'Who? Us? Look at us, Benfro. I'm too old, Cerys is too young, and you. Well, you're only half Fflint's size for one thing, and your hand isn't fully regrown yet. No, the best we can do is keep out of the way.'

The trees were thinning now, and Benfro could see rough fields marked out on the ground by low stone walls. Much smaller than those he had seen in Llanwennog and his dreamwalking to Candlehall, but they were a sign that the people here were organized. Was this village much like the one Errol had grown up in? he wondered. It seemed he was too late to find out.

Fflint and his cronies had arrived not that long before, but they had wasted no time in setting about the village. The people here lived in old stone houses, faded by the sun and neglect. The roofs were mostly flat, made from some material Benfro didn't recognize, and had openings, stairs leading up from the darkness below. Some had poles and lines, washing hanging to dry in the dusty breeze. It must have been very peaceful before Fflint and his dragons set to work.

They were ripping chunks from the roofs, flinging them into the narrow lane that ran between the houses before sweeping on to the next building. As Benfro drew nearer he could hear the screams, high-pitched like the noise a deer made when you didn't kill it cleanly. Closer still and he could see the people running in all directions, panicked and terrified. He watched in horror as one of the dragons, Tormod or perhaps Torquil, they were so alike, swooped down low and grabbed a man by the shoulders. The man's scream of pain as talons pierced his chest was cut short when the dragon bit his head off, gulping it down as he flung the limp body away.

Benfro spotted a wide area of grass at the centre of the village, wheeled on a wing tip to lose height and executed a perfect landing. The other dragons were too possessed by their killing frenzy to notice. Most still attacked from the air, but some had landed as well and were forcing their way into the houses, shattering doors too small for their bulk. Screams cut short painted all too clearly a picture of what happened to any people they found inside.

'You can't stop them, Benfro, not when they're like this.' Cerys had landed beside him, and he felt her hand on his shoulder, holding him back even before he realized he'd been heading for the nearest building.

'These men. What have they done to deserve this?'

'They called us here. They lit the fire to say the sacrifice was ready. You saw the same as the rest of us. There was nothing there.'

'And for that Fflint's going to kill them all? Who'll give him his precious sacrifice if he does that? Who will provide you with beef and lamb if there's no one left to tend the herd?'

Cerys shook her head. 'He's not like his father. Caradoc would have knocked down a house or two, maybe killed some of their animals. He'd have reminded them that they live here with our permission. Fflint doesn't understand.'

Benfro pulled away from Cerys' restraint, strode across the green to the nearest house. The roof was half off, the door pulled out of its frame. He pushed his head through the opening, seeing the destruction that had been visited on the place. At least no one had been in here, he saw. There were no bodies, and the place didn't reek of blood and shit and fear as strongly as outside. A different scent lingered here. Older but horribly familiar.

He pushed his way into the room, using his good hand to lift the debris of the fallen roof away, sniffing the air to try and pinpoint what he sought. Behind him he could sense Cerys standing at the doorway, watching his every move. Well let her. Some things were more important.

And then he found it. A wooden chest lay smashed open in the far corner, clothes spilling out of it where a roof truss had crashed into its lid. Benfro pulled truss and lid aside impatiently, hooking the garments out with his talons and flinging them aside until he found what he was sure was in there, what he hoped was not.

He wasn't well versed in the different garments people wore, but Benfro had spent enough time with the circus to know that women dressed in the main differently to men. What he held now in his half-grown hand was a woman's dress, and he had seen it before. Ripped and bloodstained, it showed all too clearly the ill treatment it had received. The faint smell of smoke still clung to it like the mud around its hem, bringing the image of the burning circus, the panic and terror as warrior priests appeared out of nowhere to hack the people down. Like the dragons wreaking mad havoc on this village for no good reason at all.

'What is it?' Cerys had overcome her reluctance to enter the building and now stood beside him, staring at the dress.

'My friend was here. He was wearing this.' Benfro handed her the dress, hurried out before she could say anything. Into the melee and hoping against hope that Errol hadn't fallen victim to it.

'Tear it down. I want every single room checked.'

Prince Dafydd stood to one side as a team of Abervenn men hammered at an old oak door in a unexceptional corridor deep in the oldest part of the palace complex. They were supervised by his own palace guards, some of whom were even helping, but so far the door had resisted all attempts to open it.

'Your Highness, perhaps I may be of assistance?'

Dafydd turned away from the noise of axes bouncing off wood like it was stone to see the medic Usel walking up the corridor as if he owned the place. Since the death of Captain Pelod, everyone else in their party travelled with company, never fewer than six to a group, but Usel always came and went as he pleased. There had been no more attacks on him or his men, no sightings of any more Guardians of the Throne. Still Dafydd wanted every room in the entire palace checked. Most had been, but this one door seemed reluctant to reveal its secrets.

'If you have a key, then by all means.' He held out an arm, pointing towards the team still hard at work.

Usel merely smiled. 'There is no key for this door, sire.

At least not one that would be of any use to you. Also your men could chop at it all day and all they would achieve is broken axes.'

'How am I supposed to open it then?'

'You cannot. Nor can any of your men hope to, unless they have something in their parentage they've done well to hide. Princess Iolwen on the other hand would be able to open it with just a touch.'

The mention of her name reminded Dafydd both that his wife should be arriving soon and that he would have the dreadful task of breaking the news to her about the attack. She had been as fond of Jarius as he was; they had all grown up together.

'What's behind this door then? What's so important it has to be protected by so powerful a spell?'

'Nothing short of the secret that has kept the House of Balwen in power for millennia. This door opens on to a passage that leads down under the Neuadd, and there the greatest treasures of the Twin Kingdoms are stored.' Usel had the faintest of smirks on his face, as if his enigmatic reply were somehow amusing him. Dafydd suppressed the urge to hit him; the man could be so infuriatingly smug at times, but he was also more helpful than not. Usually, at least. There was the small matter of the arrival of the princess too.

'I had hoped to have secured the palace before the princess arrives.'

'The palace is secure, sire, I am certain of that, and Seneschal Padraig has been as keen as any to rid the ranks of his order of these heretics. You can rest assured none of them will trouble you in Candlehall again. We can continue to vet the staff, or you can waste your time here. It's your choice.'

'Waste my time?' Dafydd bridled at the man's impertinence.

'There are but five people alive who can open this door, and none of them is close by.'

'Five?'

'Queen Beulah and her newborn, Princess Iolwen and your son Prince Iolo all carry the royal blood of the House of Balwen in their veins. That is the oldest magic and the only one that can open this door.'

'I can count, Usel. That is only four people.'

'Of course. There is one other who has the bloodline. Another son of both royal houses, as it happens. My order has been keeping an eye on him since he was born, but he seems to have disappeared completely.'

'And he has a name, this cousin of mine?'

'Oh, you've met him, sire. Young Errol Ramsbottom. He's Lleyn's son. And your Uncle Balch's too.'

The village was ablaze now. Smoke swirled through the narrow gaps between the buildings, and white flakes of wood ash floated down like snow. The stench of burning flesh filled Benfro's senses, blotting out anything else. Everywhere was destruction on a scale he couldn't quite comprehend. Ever since Melyn had crashed into his life, killed his mother and chased him halfway across Gwlad, Benfro had dreamed of taking his revenge on men. That revenge had always seen him cutting through a swathe of warrior priests, mowing them down like so much chaff until he came face to face with the hated inquisitor. Only when he saw the light fade from Melyn's frightened, startled eyes could Benfro feel his mother was at peace.

This wasn't how he imagined revenge would be. It was carnage, pure and simple. These men had no blades of fire, they couldn't use fear as a weapon. They were as powerless as a newly hatched kitling. Tiny and frail, all too easy to kill. But they weren't like the deer in the forest, the salmon in the river. These were intelligent, thinking beings. They built houses, raised animals for food and tended fields for crops. They had hopes and desires not so different from those of dragons, when all was said and done. They weren't his enemy.

And Errol had been among them. Might be among them still.

'Fflint!' The shout escaped from him before Benfro could stop it. The big dragon was busy tearing the front from one of the last houses still standing, head down, shoulders hunched in concentration. If he heard Benfro above the noise then he gave no sign. He looked more like an animal than the terrified people trying to flee the massacre. His sidekicks chased them down, pulling arms from sockets, biting off heads or just tearing weak flesh apart with razor-sharp talons.

'Fflint!' This time Benfro meant it, advancing on the big dragon, no longer really thinking, just acting on instinct. Still he was ignored. The building Fflint was trying to tear down seemed more substantially constructed than the others. There was stone in its walls and the door was heavy dark oak studded with iron nails. Its refusal to give way easily was obviously causing the big dragon considerable frustration; his face was contorted in rage, nostrils flared, chest heaving at the exertion. Close up, Benfro could see the blood smeared all over his chest scales, the char marks on his wings and the mad glint in his eye.

'Stop this!' Benfro reached out, and at the last minute Fflint registered his presence. The blow came from nowhere. One moment the dragon was tearing at stone, the next he had sent Benfro sprawling. It was like being hit by a falling tree, and as he struggled for breath, trying to get back to his feet, Benfro saw Fflint first go back to his wall, then stop, turn and glare at him.

'If it isn't Benfro of the Borrowed Wings. Here, let me do something about that.'

For all his size, Fflint was faster than a hawk. Before Benfro could move, the big dragon was on him, claws extended. Benfro raised his arms to protect his face, but Fflint wasn't interested in that. He ducked round, grabbed a wing, the same one Benfro had damaged in his fall from Mount Arnahi. Bright pain flashed through him as Fflint sank his talons deep into the muscle, then tore at it, wrenching with all his might.

'Who did you borrow your wings from, Benfro? Perhaps we should give them back, eh?'

Benfro rolled. He had no option. Resist and Fflint would have torn his wing from its socket. Barely able to focus through the pain, he somehow managed to angle his wing so it slid from Fflint's talons, but he knew this was only the start of the fight. He also knew he didn't know how to fight. He'd attacked Melyn in a rage, and see how well that had gone.

'Leave him be, Fflint! He's no threat to you.'

Benfro risked a glance to the side, seeing Cerys and Sir Gwair approaching in a hurry. Cerys still clung to the dress that Errol had worn as a disguise, which probably wasn't wise of her. Neither was approaching Fflint, not with bloodlust surging through him.

'What's this? Little lovebirds?' Fflint spun on one foot, his tail lashing out. Cerys was obviously used to his moods, but she still caught a nasty blow to her side as she tried to get out of the way. The sight of her sprawling on the dusty ground enraged Benfro, who rounded on Fflint. The larger dragon was too quick for him still, and before he even knew what was happening, Benfro felt a hand around his throat, squeezing hard.

'I told you to stay away from her, but you wouldn't listen. Thought you'd borrow her too, as well as your wings?'

Benfro struggled against the choking hold, raked the talons of his one good hand down Fflint's arm as he tried to break free. This only enraged the dragon more. Fflint first tightened his grip, then flung Benfro at the stone wall of the house as if he weighed nothing. He felt something crack in his undamaged wing as what little wind he had left was driven out of him. He could hardly breathe, such was the pain, and then Fflint's tail swept round and caught him under the chin. Benfro's head snapped back with the blow, clattering off the stone wall. His vision dimmed. His legs seemed to have lost all their strength. He heard a scream that sounded like it was a long way off, deep in a mountain cave, and then it felt like the house had collapsed on top of him. His back stretched horribly, muscles tearing and bones threatening to break.

'Can you see, little Benfro?' He was dragged to his feet,

pulled off them by the impossibly strong Fflint. Benfro could hardly focus, but he saw the shape of the larger dragon's face swim in front of him. Then colours exploded in his head, his sight gone on one side as Fflint poked a needle-pointed talon into his eyeball. He screwed the other eye tight shut, fearing he would lose both even as he started to pass out with shock.

'Pathetic. Hardly worth the effort.' The words were close, echoing in his head. It was all too quick, too violent. He couldn't understand what was happening. Benfro didn't think he could have hurt any more, but new pain lanced up his half-sized regrowing hand. Somewhere in the fog of agony and bewilderment he saw something that looked like a dragon's arm being bent and twisted a way it was never meant to go. There was a horrible cracking sound and bone gave way, thick red blood oozing out of split skin and ripped-off scales. His arm. His scales. His blood. He was going to die here, not at the hands of a man but a fellow dragon. How could this be happening? He had not avenged his mother's death yet. Had not thrown off Magog's malign influence. He hadn't found Gog, or Errol, or done any of the things he was supposed to do. How could it end here? Like this?

'You have skills he cannot comprehend, Benfro. Use them.'

The voice was his mother's, but it was also Corwen's. Hearing them, he could almost believe he had reached the end. Was this what it meant to die? To be reunited with those you loved? Maybe it wasn't so bad after all.

'Fight him. Use that dread curse of yours and burn off his face.'

This time the voice was unmistakable. The words were inside him and the thought of them brought Benfro renewed fear. He was weak, near death. There was no way he could fight Fflint and Magog both. And yet as he thought of the dead mage, so the world of the Grym opened up to him. One eye tight shut, the other gone, he could still see the village, the dragons all around him watching and waiting for Fflint to make the killing blow. He could see the Llinellau stretching everywhere. He could escape this madness if he could just get a moment to clear his head.

But Fflint wouldn't let up. He was throwing Benfro around like a doll now. Smashing his head against the stone wall of the one building that had denied him entry. Benfro could see the terrified people huddling inside. Errol wasn't among them, but that didn't mean they deserved to die any more than he did. What right did this arrogant creature, no better than a beast, have to kill just for fun? Just because he felt entitled or aggrieved? Just because anger was all he knew? He might call himself a dragon, might wear a dragon's form, but Fflint son of Caradoc was no more a dragon than Melyn. He deserved nothing less than the inquisitor.

Benfro opened his one remaining eye just as Fflint grabbed him once more by the throat. Sucking in what breath he could, he tried to reach for Fflint's arm, but his regrowing hand was too small to grasp it, closing weakly around the big dragon's wrist.

'Oh, so you are still alive. Well that just makes this all the—'

Fflint didn't finish his words. With the last of his dying

strength, Benfro breathed out pure flame. It leaped from his mouth and nostrils like a living thing, enveloping Fflint in seconds. Where it touched him, his scales turned black, cracked and fell off. He screamed as his face blistered, his eyes turning white, then bursting. Released, Benfro slumped to the ground, fell back against the wall Fflint had been battering him against, watched as the larger dragon stumbled, fell, burned. His screams were terrible, the mewlings of a terrified kitling magnified a thousand-fold. He beat at his head and chest and wings, trying to extinguish the fire that clung to him like cloth, flowed over him like water, devoured him more thoroughly than time.

Benfro could only watch with a mixture of horror and terrible delight as Fflint crumpled in on himself. His screams grew weaker, turning to bubbling sobs and then finally disappearing altogether. And still the fire devoured him, rendering him down to fine ash like the Fflam Gwir, the reckoning flame. How many jewels would they retrieve from the ashes? Benfro wondered. Not many. Maybe none at all.

He couldn't move, could hardly breathe. Something was loose inside him, hot pain jabbing him with every breath. The sight in his one remaining eye was fading now. Either that or night had come early. The remains of Fflint were shrinking away to nothing now, the magical flame that had devoured him guttering. For a moment Benfro thought that it might all be over, but then he saw the other dragons.

They had watched the whole spectacle, of course. He understood now: this was how they lived. Not noble dragons, but feral beasts. No better than animals. Caradoc had been their pack leader, but he had gone. Fflint had taken over, big and fast and stupid. Now he was gone too, and they didn't like the manner of his passing.

'What did he do?' Benfro heard the words as if his head were underwater, but he recognized the horror in them, the fear.

'By the moon, Fflint?' This was Cerys, and the concern in her voice was a sharp blade through his hearts. Benfro let his head slump back, blinking away the blood clouding his eye. The movement sent shocks of pain through him, but sharpened his vision at the same time. The entire hunting party were staring at him now, inching closer as their collective fear was overcome by anger at what he had done. He could see it in their auras, read them as clearly as the books in Magog's mountain-top retreat. Their intentions were as plain as they were simple. He would not leave this village alive.

Tormod was the first to make a move, or perhaps it was Torquil. The two of them had always been Fflint's closest allies, hanging on his every word but lacking even his rudimentary intelligence. Whichever one it was, he came at Benfro fast, screaming in rage or more likely to overcome his fear. He wasn't much smaller than Fflint, certainly strong enough to break Benfro in half. No time to think, certainly no strength to run, barely enough to breathe, Benfro did the only thing he could think of.

He reached out for the lines and jumped.

Beulah followed the trail easily enough by the carnage Clun left in his wake. She wouldn't have been able to keep up with him anyway, but it had taken time to stabilize Alicia, staunch the bleeding and find someone to tend her until the medics came. Only then had she summoned a couple of warrior priests and headed off after the Duke of Abervenn, aware all the time of the images she had seen in the young maid's mind, the words she had heard the kidnapper utter as he slid his long knife into her guts.

'The Shepherd returns. There will be no more usurpers on the Obsidian Throne.'

Beulah quickened her pace across the courtyard and out of the castle keep. At least dressed for the road she could walk without having to worry about endless layers getting in the way.

'Why were there no guards on the stairway to the royal apartment?' she demanded as Captain Celtin rushed up to greet her.

'Your Majesty, there were three warrior priests, but they swear on their lives you came down, dismissed them and climbed into your carriage.'

'On their lives?' Beulah raised an eyebrow, but in truth she had no stomach for punishment. They would need warrior priests in the campaign against Abervenn, so executing three of them just because they had fallen for some magic trick would be self-defeating. The laugh that escaped from her when she realized how much she had changed in a year was mirthless, and it must have been taken as an order by the captain.

'I shall see to their execution at once, ma'am.' He clasped a hand to his chest in salute and was about to turn away when she interrupted him.

'You shall do no such thing, Celtin. They must be punished, true. Perhaps some time marching with the foot soldiers will focus their minds on their training. But their deaths serve no one but our enemies. Enemies who can fool a trained warrior priest into thinking he has seen something that never happened. Not one of them, either, but three. Who has that kind of skill?'

'I might have believed King Ballah himself could do such a working, or Inquisitor Melyn, of course. But neither of them are here.'

'Are you forgetting our more recent run-in with an adept masquerading as a Candle?'

'Father Tolley? The Guardians of the Throne?' Celtin's face paled at the memory.

'Tolley is long dead, but we'd be fools to believe there weren't many more like him.'

Beulah set off towards the main town square, following both the physical signs of her husband's progress and the more delicate clues left by the disturbance in the Grym. She wasn't entirely sure how Clun was tracking the kidnapper, but he wasn't being very subtle about it. Carts were overturned, their contents strewn about the muddy streets. People huddled in doorways, nursing bruises and worse. The corner of one building had caved in, slashed by a blade of light if Beulah's hurried appraisal of the damage was anything to go by. In the square a group of traders had formed themselves into a huddle, arguing among themselves. She heard snippets of their angry talk, demanding who was going to compensate them for their losses, as if all of them hadn't been enriched by the presence of the army outside the city walls. As she approached, the most opulently dressed of them turned swiftly, his face a picture of righteous indignation.

'This is an outrage! We demand . . .' And then he saw who it was he addressed. His jaw dropped, eyes widening in surprise. He closed his mouth with an audible clacking of teeth, then swept into an ostentatious bow.

'Your Majesty, I am your most humble servant.'

'I very much doubt that, given your earlier comments.' Beulah scanned the edges of his thoughts, looking for signs of treason, of any complicity in the kidnap. There were none, just the weasel thinking of a man unable to admit his own fault in any situation. A typical merchant.

'My husband came through this way recently. Which way did he go?' Beulah didn't really need to ask the question, but somewhere in the gathered crowd she could feel a different kind of unhappiness, a dissatisfaction with far more than their recent upset. Out of practice after her pregnancy, and without the Obsidian Throne to bolster her power, she had to concentrate harder to pinpoint the thought and the person thinking it.

'A man ran through here not ten minutes ago, screaming a girl's name and wielding a sword the likes of which I have never seen before. He asked questions of us that made no sense, turned over our trestles, scattered our goods. Surely that was not His Grace the Duke of Abervenn?'

'A sword like this?' Beulah felt the Grym surge through her as she conjured her own blade. The merchant's eyes widened again and he swallowed hard.

'Very much like that, Your Majesty. Only his was red.'

'My daughter, Princess Ellyn, has been kidnapped. The

man who did it came this way. Do any of you know anything about it?'

And there it was, the uncontrolled thought Beulah had hoped to provoke. She focused on it, scanning the crowd in search of whoever might be thinking it. Eyes met hers and darted down, heads bowed. Except for one.

He stood in the middle of the crowd. Dressed all in black, he might have been taken for a predicant of the Order of the Candle were it not for the mud on his cloak and the smile on his face. He was thin, long lank hair hanging past his shoulders, and he gazed at the queen the way a cat might stare at a mouse.

'Your borrowed magics don't scare me, false queen.' He spoke directly to her mind, lips not moving out of that predator smile as he walked towards her. The crowd seemed oblivious to his presence and yet at the same time cleared a path for him. Somewhere in the back of her mind Beulah could still hear the self-appointed leader of the traders express his horror and concern, his words no more sincere than anything else about him. She blanked them out, hardening her mind to the smiling man.

'I have earned my magics, little man. My throne too.' She pushed out a wave of fear with her words and was pleased to see the smile flicker. He took a step back and she almost fell for the ruse. But Melyn had taught her better.

The attack, when it came, was not physical. Beulah had used fear, as was the way of the warrior priests. She expected this man to do the same, but instead what enveloped her was an overwhelming sense of pleasure. For an instant she was caught up like a giddy teenager wrapped in the arms of her one true love, overwhelmed by a passion so intense it made her shudder. It was so different to what she had been expecting, it caught her off guard, but only for a couple of seconds. Shrugging off the enchantment, she stepped up to the man, holding her blade of light aloft. His smile didn't fade, but she could see the panic in his eyes, feel the thrill of it in his thoughts.

'Is that how you bed the girls? I think you'll find me not so easy.' Beulah levelled the point of her blade at his throat, only then realizing that he hadn't backed away, hadn't made any attempt to flee. She pushed at his thoughts again, testing his barriers. Skilled he might have been, but he wasn't in the same league as Father Tolley. There was only a natural aptitude for magic and an all-too-familiar fanaticism. The plan was simple to see, poorly hidden in the tumble of images he threw at her with his mind. He was no more than a distraction, placed here to keep her and the warrior priests occupied while the rest of the plotters escaped with her daughter. They didn't need long, twenty minutes perhaps. Half an hour would be better. Then the trail would be cold and the child would be theirs.

'You cannot defeat us,' the man said, leaning in to the blade so that the skin of his neck sizzled. He still fixed Beulah with his stare, the smile on his lips making him look increasingly deranged. She tensed, holding her arm straight. It would be simple enough to let him kill himself. One less of them to worry about. She might even have his head off with just a flick of the wrist.

'No. You don't get away so easily.' Beulah let her blade shorten, ducked as the man sprang at her, and with a side-swipe took his leg off at the knee.

At the cut, the magic he had been casting over the square vanished, and all of a sudden Beulah was standing in a clear space surrounded by startled merchants and traders. Captain Celtin stood nearby, his blade of light conjured, looking from side to side as if searching for something. Then he saw her.

'Your Majesty! You disappeared. We . . . I . . .' Celtin's words faded away as he saw the injured man bleeding out on the cobbles.

'Do you still want to punish the men who were guarding my stairs?' Beulah grinned as she let her blade of light extinguish. It felt wonderful to be able to manipulate the Grym once more. She kicked the semi-conscious man. 'This one is skilled at tricking the mind, making you see things that aren't there. Chain him in the castle dungeons. I would like to find out what makes him tick. But first I must find my husband and child.'

'There is no need for that.'

Beulah whirled to see a figure advancing through the crowd. Merchants shrank back from him as he approached her, and she could see why. His cloak was ripped, his face and hands covered in blood. Even his hair was matted as if someone had been smacking him about the head with a bludgeon. But Beulah could see that Clun was unharmed. The blood was not his, but the child held in the crook of his arm was.

'Ellyn!' Beulah rushed to greet them, scooping the child into her arms. Her daughter looked up at her quite unperturbed, the only sign that anything was amiss a thumbprint smudge of red on her cheek.

'I found her in a house two streets down. They were

getting ready to leave. Didn't take too kindly to my stopping them.' Clun wiped at his face, smearing the blood rather than cleaning it away. 'They won't be troubling us any more.'

22

Look back at the history of misfortunes befalling the House of Balwen and the Guardians of the Throne will always be there. Their name is a useful shorthand for the idiocy of inbreeding, the venality of men born to power and raised away from the harsh realities of the kingdom they would rule, the failure to adequately prepare the child to become the man. Wherever fault truly lies with a generation or two of the royal family, the Guardians get the blame. And still there is no smoke without fire, as the saying goes. Shadowy factions have always fought in the background, jostling for control of the power that has ruled over the Twin Kingdoms since Balwen first built the Neuadd atop Candlehall Hill millennia ago.

Every generation believes it lives in the end times, and ours is no exception. Where most wait patiently for the rapture, or carry on with their lives as best they can in ignorance, there are ever some who would hasten the end, embrace it. Perhaps they truly are creatures of the Wolf, sowing discord as is his bidding. Or maybe they simply prefer chaos over order, war over peace. Whatever their reasons, they have found inspiration in the inane doggerel of a mad woman who died more than five hundred years

ago, and they have studied just enough history to
steal for themselves the mantle once worn by those
who would influence weak kings.

Barrod Sheepshead, *The Guardians of the*
Throne – A Noble Folly

The screams started well before dawn. Melyn woke from
strange dreams of flying through dark skies, driven ever
onward by something he couldn't understand. All around
him the camp was coming to life, the Grym ebbing and
flowing as several hundred warrior priests prepared themselves for battle.

'No one is to leave this camp without my explicit order
and no one is to use any magic,' Melyn said as Osgal
approached out of the darkness. The captain nodded and
set off to relay the instructions. Melyn stretched, feeling
the strength in the tightness across his chest, then went
off in search of Frecknock.

He found her on the crest of the hill, staring out at the
massive encampment below. The evening before it had
been a well-ordered collection of tents, with fires dotted
between them at regular intervals. Now it was like some
madman's imagination of the Wolf's lair. Fires raged
through canvas, unchecked as the men who might have
put them out ran screaming. In the darkness it was hard to
see what was causing the panic, but just occasionally
Melyn spotted something vast swoop down out of the air,
grabbing men, horses, tents or whole wagons and throwing them around like so many toys in the midst of a child's
tantrum.

'A dragon? Is it Caradoc?'

Frecknock turned to greet him, her great dark eyes heavy. 'It is he. And he has found friends. I see at least ten, maybe more.'

Melyn moved closer, taking up a spot beside her. 'Where have they come from?'

'I do not know, Your Grace. I sensed . . . something approaching. But I had no idea. I'm grateful for the spell of concealment, and the Llfyr Draconius. Without them I fear we would be suffering the same fate as Prince Geraint's army.'

'This was the Shepherd's plan all along. To use these creatures of the Wolf against each other.' Melyn gazed out across the plain, watching as the sun first tinged the eastern horizon with pink, then spread light across a scene of the most terrible carnage. The camp had been well organized, Geraint's army disciplined enough to take time over lining up the tents, corralling the horses, building basic fortifications even though their home was only a few short miles away. These professional soldiers would have made short work of Beulah's peasant army, but they were no match for a dozen dragons. More. He watched as three of them swooped on the panicked camp, huge wings blasting campfires in all directions, setting tents alight along with their hapless occupants. One vast creature grabbed a horse, carrying the screaming, terrified animal high into the air before releasing it to fall crashing back down on top of a troop of soldiers. Squinting, Melyn saw a line of archers hurl a swarm of arrows after one dragon, but the shafts simply bounced off its scaly hide. It turned, dived, taloned feet outstretched as it swept through the ranks, scattering the bowmen. Few got up after it had passed.

And so it went on as the sun rimmed the far horizon and began its climb into the morning sky. Melyn counted perhaps twenty dragons, though they swept and dived and spun and spiralled so swiftly it was difficult to be sure. They seemed never to tire, and they put him in mind of foxes among chickens. For them it was not enough to kill what was needed to survive; these creatures were in a frenzy and would not stop until everything was dead, ripped apart, half devoured.

One beast, larger even than Caradoc, landed in the middle of the camp where the biggest tents had been pitched. This was where Prince Geraint would be, his generals with him. Melyn almost pitied them; there was little they could hope to do against such an enemy. Even his warrior priests would have been hard pressed, though with a few like Clun he would have been able to drive them off.

'Why do they not use the Grym against these beasts?' Melyn asked. It was perhaps too distant to see whether individual soldiers were conjuring their puissant swords, as the Llanwennogs called them, but he had felt nothing in the Grym himself to suggest multiple adepts were tapping it.

'A few have managed, Your Grace. But the plain below is as weak in the Grym as this hill is strong. Some great disaster befell this place aeons ago. I have no idea what, but its effects persist. Much like the magics that flourished in the forest of the Ffrydd, only here the opposite is true.'

Melyn relaxed, letting the lines come into his vision.

Unbidden, he found himself in the aethereal, only this time the Grym was painted clearly over the scene as well. He could hear the noises of the battle, feel the damp of dewy grass seeping through his robes. Turning his head, he saw Frecknock both as her normal physical self and the larger, more striking dragon she perceived herself to be. The aethereal and the mundane together.

'How is this happening?' Melyn held his hand in front of his face, momentarily distracted from the slaughter going on below.

'Your Grace, this is how it should be. The Grym and the aethereal, as you call it, are but two faces of the same thing. This is central to our subtle arts. Come, let me show you something.' Frecknock stood, her aethereal self separating from the dragon sitting on the grass hilltop. Melyn rose too, feeling the weight of the world slip from him. Together they descended the hill, covering the space between them and the battle in a heartbeat.

'Will the dragons not see us like this?' Melyn asked.

'I do not think so. Caradoc, maybe. If he is looking. But the others have nothing of the subtle arts about them. They are not magical creatures. I don't understand how this can be, but to my senses they appear as base animals.'

They stood at the edge of the enemy camp now, watching in silence as the chaos unfolded. Men ran this way and that, grabbing for swords, bows, anything that might be used to fight. But the dragons swept in too swiftly to be targeted, grabbed a man or a tent or whatever came to claw, threw it about or heaved it into the air before dropping it. Nearby, one great beast had landed and was simply lashing out at anything that came near. It caught one soldier with its tail, taking his legs out from underneath him. Before he could move, much less stand, the dragon opened its mouth wide and half swallowed him before biting him clean in two. One half fell wetly to the trampled ground, the other continued its way down the beast's gullet.

'These are worse than base animals, Frecknock.' Melyn had seen his fair share of carnage. He knew the battlefield was friend only to carrion birds and the corpse collectors who would pick the dead for anything of value. He knew too that these men were his enemy, the godless Llanwennogs who had sent spies and assassins to kill Queen Beulah. There was a joy to be had in witnessing their destruction, but a small part of him, long hidden, almost wept.

And then he saw it, in the heart of the camp. One tent still stood, surrounded by the cream of Llanwennog soldiery. Prince Geraint's standard flew from a lance planted in the churned earth just a few paces from the tent's entrance. As he watched, Melyn saw the prince himself march out of the tent, place a helmet over his head and conjure into being a blade of white fire. He felt the surge in the Grym as the prince sucked life out of a place already lacking.

It happened in an instant. No brave fight, no cunning strategy. One moment Geraint was there, the next a flash of green and gold scales glittering in the low morning sunlight as something the size of a house smashed past, and then there was nothing. No tent, no lance, no standard, no soldiers. Just a helmet spinning in the flat-skimmed mud. A helmet with a head still inside.

*

404

The first thing he noticed was the noise. Like nothing he had ever heard before, it was as if the wind were whistling through distant trees, but rising and falling with a regular tempo. It was a peaceful sound, gentle after the screaming mayhem of the village, the bone-crunching violence of his fight with Fflint. Benfro couldn't see anything, had no idea where he was. He tried opening his eyes, then remembered the terrible noise of talon piercing eyeball, the hot fluid running down his cheek. Was he blind now?

Something warm and wet slapped against his face, then retreated. Benfro tasted saltwater and choked as it ran up his nose. The movement brought agonizing stabs of pain to his chest and a bubbling wheeziness to his breathing that suggested all was not well. He tried to move, but his wings were tangled around him like broken branches and he couldn't even feel his arms.

Another wash of saltwater in his face, stronger this time. He felt it surge along his body and realized he was half buried. It took all his strength to raise his head, but at least the retreating water washed out his eye so he could see. What he saw didn't make much sense.

He was lying on a beach of fine black sand, staring out over an expanse of water that faded off into a haze so distant he couldn't see the other shore. Perhaps their wasn't another shore at all. Waves lapped gently a few feet from him, most falling back before they reached his face. Every so often a larger one would break, rush up to his body and slap his legs, his belly and tail before running back like a frightened kitling. These waves were getting more frequent, bolder. Another rushed up his side, splashing his nose even though he was holding his head as high as his failing strength would let him. Benfro didn't understand how this could be happening, but he knew he had to move or drown.

But even the strain of holding his head up was too much. He let it drop back down to the sand in despair. At least he could see each wave approaching now, and stop the worst of it from going up his nose.

Something squawked just out of his line of sight, a strange sound he didn't recognize. Then the sand crunched under shuffling feet as whatever it was approached. Benfro first saw webbed orange feet and a squat black body, a round smear of white on the front of the creature as it waddled into view. It had tiny wings, more like flippers, and its head merged into its body without any obvious sign of neck. Close up, he could see it was a bird, simply by the tiny tight-knit feathers covering its body, but it was unlike any bird he had ever seen. It shuffled even closer, bending slightly as it fixed him with a quizzical stare from its black, beady eyes. It made that noise again, a cross between a gurgle and a cough, and a smell of rotting fish filled the air.

Powerless to move, Benfro could only watch as the creature looked first at him, then out at the water, then back at him again, then out at the water again. After a dozen or so repetitions, it leaned in close, pecked him lightly on the snout as if checking to see he really existed and wasn't some strange hallucination. Then it turned, gurgle-coughing to itself as it waddled away again. He heard the noise of its feet in the sand and that curious call like an argument with itself fading away gently to be replaced by the wash of the waves on the beach, the swish of the wind in unseen trees. Perhaps it had gone to get help, though Benfro doubted it. More likely it had gone to find its friends and tell them of the feast it had just found.

A larger wave rocked him, taking some of his weight and shifting his body a fraction. Benfro felt bones grinding together in ways they were never meant to, but he also felt his trapped arm free up. Pins and needles were the least of his troubles as he waited for another wave to help him. Everything hurt, and the pain in his chest made it all but impossible to breathe deeply. The short, rapid breaths he could take were unsatisfying, leaving him tired beyond belief and light-headed. Still he had to try. He wasn't going to die here.

When the wave came, the agony of freeing his arm completely almost knocked him cold. He used the pain and the momentum to roll over as best he could, trying to get his legs to work enough to at least push him further up the beach and away from the water. It sort of worked, but he was left so exhausted all he could do was stare at his new view, panting like a deer chased to the edge of death.

Benfro had grown up in the forest of the Ffrydd. He thought he knew all about trees, but the ones he was staring at now with his one good eye were like nothing he had ever seen before. They were in many ways the complete opposite of the great Bondaris trees, their trunks thin and whippy, with no branches at the top, just long spiky leaves in great profusion. They swayed from side to side in a breeze he could not feel, the motion strangely hypnotic, lulling him into a stupor. It was easier this way, he thought, to drift off peacefully, lapped by the warm water at his back. Moving was too painful, breathing was too difficult.

Perhaps if he rested a little his strength would return, at least enough to think straight.

'Dragon?'

The voice was part of his delirium, Benfro was sure. Same as the tiny weight on his head, the upside-down face peering so close that he couldn't focus on it. Just an image of red-tufted ears and black button eyes.

'Benfro?'

He swallowed, tried to speak, found he couldn't. He had no strength left to chase off this cruel hallucination. Why couldn't he be left alone to die in peace?

'Malkin fetch help.'

The weight was gone and with it all feeling. Benfro drifted away, warm as if he were nestling in his mother's arms. The soft swish of waves breaking on the sand behind him grew quieter and quieter. His eye closed of its own accord, and he welcomed the darkness. Everything hurt and he was so very tired. All he wanted to do was sleep.

How much time passed, he couldn't have said. Benfro had been listening to the slow breaking of the waves for so long that it took a while for him to realize the noise he was hearing was different. Where the sound of the water was soft, now something crunched rhythmically through the sand, heavier by far than the strange bird-like creature from earlier. It came closer and closer, then stopped. Benfro couldn't have moved if he had wanted to, but he was happy enough just to lie and wait for the end.

'By the moon! What's happened to him?'

As he heard the words, so Benfro felt the presence of someone close by. Soft hands touched his cheek, his ears, moved to his neck and shoulders. He should have felt fearful, unable to stop whoever had come from doing to him whatever they wished, but he was too weak. Too weak even to open his one remaining eye.

'These are bites. And see here, talons have done this. He's been attacked by a dragon. But what manner of creature would do this to one of its own? And why dump him here?'

There was something soothing about the voice. It reminded Benfro of his mother. He struggled to open his eye, roll over. He wanted to see her, tell her he was sorry, though he wasn't quite sure what he was sorry for. Or where he was, for that matter.

'Shhh. Calm yourself. Don't try to move.' He felt a hand on his forehead, gently restraining him. The touch was warm, comforting. An energy seemed to flow from it, easing the pain that racked his whole body. Benfro managed to open his eye, just a slit, and saw another dragon's face close to his. She was immeasurably old and yet more beautiful than he would have thought possible.

'Wh . . . Who?' His voice was barely audible above the quiet wash of the waves, the rustling of the wind in those high leaves.

'I am Earith. And you are very badly injured. Do not try to move or you will only make things worse.'

'Don't think I can. Can't feel my legs.'

'That is the least of your worries. Now rest.' With these words Benfro felt a surge of something he couldn't explain. It washed away his pain, cooled the fever he had not realized he was running, filled him with a perfect, blissful warmth. His eyelid drooped closed, but he didn't mind the darkness. For the first time in ages he felt safe as he drifted away.

The dungeons of Tochers Castle were perhaps the most dismal Beulah had seen this side of Beylinstown, hewn deep into the rock where the Grym could scarcely reach. She felt the chill in the air as she followed Clun and Captain Celtin down the narrow steps, her newly reawakened sense of magic ebbing away with each footfall. The only light came from small torches set at too-distant intervals along a wall slick with seeping dampness and green algae. Silence hemmed them in, dulling even the click of boot on flagstone, killing any thought of conversation as they passed door after open door until, finally, they reached the end.

The two warrior priests on guard came to attention as the interrogation party stopped. 'Your Majesty. Your Grace. Sir.'

'Is he still alive?' Beulah asked.

'He's still moaning, so I guess so, ma'am.'

'Open up then. I want a word with him before we leave this shitty little place.'

The warrior priests nodded, unlocked the door and stood aside so they could enter the cell. It was larger than Beulah had been expecting, hacked out of the rock with rough blows that left a jagged finish to the walls and low ceiling. A torch hung near the door, casting scant light over the room, and on the other side, lying on a pile of damp straw, the young adept lay shivering. Every so often he let out a low moan, but he didn't seem to notice them come in. The stump of his amputated leg was wrapped in a bandage, already red from his blood. The stench of the place suggested he'd soiled himself at some point, although it might just have been that this was where all the sewage in the castle ended up.

'He is awake, my lady.' Clun strode across the cell and gave the man a prod with his boot. He groaned, rolling over on to his back before opening his eyes and staring straight at Beulah.

'You came. I knew you would. Couldn't keep away, eh?'

Beulah felt the whisperings of the man's mind as he tried to cast a glamour over her, but it was a weak effort. He had lost too much blood and the wound was already turning septic, poisons flowing through sluggish veins to his brain.

'Spare us the cheap parlour tricks. Who put you up to this mad scheme? What did you hope to achieve by kidnapping my daughter?'

'A diversion, perhaps? A delay? The Shepherd is near, can you not feel him?'

Beulah skimmed the man's thoughts as he spoke. The pain was dragging down his defences, the infection weakening him yet further. She could read him far more easily in this state than when they had first met. Then he had been cocky and sure of himself. Here he was struggling, but that certainty was still rock solid. He knew his god was coming, knew that his place in the gathering fields was assured, his life of eternal bliss and happiness. But there was more to his belief than blind faith. There was knowledge there that Beulah could not quite glean.

'Can you? Can you truly say the Shepherd speaks to you?'

411

'Speaks, and more. He comes to me in my dreams. Comes in his true form. Not the god you worship, no god of men.'

Beulah saw an image unfurl in darkness. Eyes burning red like disturbed coals. Black upon black, writhing snakes and scaly skin as something uncoiled itself in the young man's mind. With an involuntary step back, she withdrew from his mind, bringing down her own mental barriers hard before she had even registered the primal fear that had made her react so. Something mad had possessed his soul long ago. They would get nothing of value from him.

'We're done here.' Beulah turned her back on the man as he slumped back down on to his bed of fetid straw. Clun looked up at her, the question in his eyes going unasked as he nodded once, then walked out.

'The torch. He'll not need that.' Beulah pointed, and Captain Celtin plucked it from its sconce on the wall. The corridor felt crowded with five of them standing by the door, but she waited until the first of the guards had made sure it was locked tight.

'Come. We're leaving. All of us.' She headed back up the corridor, sensing the warrior priests fall in behind her, Clun bringing up the rear. If the Shepherd truly was coming for his fanatic disciple, then he could find him lying in the darkness with his sliding, scuttling thoughts.

The memories came later, hidden under layers of pain and interspersed with long periods of blissful unconsciousness. Benfro remembered waking to find himself surrounded by men. It was dark, and all he could see were faces shadowed by flaming torches. He should have been terrified, but he could still sense the presence of Earith and that calmed him. Even her healing powers could not completely ease his pain as the men lifted him, straightened his wings and tail, and he blacked out again.

When he woke, it was to a rhythmic motion that he eventually realized was a horse-drawn cart, much like those that had transported him and the other circus attractions through Llanwennog. Only this was flat and open; no walls to keep him from escaping, no chain around his leg. Neither were necessary; he was as helpless as a newly hatched kitling. Whatever fate they bore him toward, he had no choice but to accept it.

The journey seemed to take for ever and yet no time at all. Benfro passed in and out of consciousness as the levels of pain in his back, his wings, his arms increased or decreased. When he was awake he first saw dark forest, the undersides of the tall trees painted flickering orange by the fiery torches the men carried. Then he was being pulled through open grassland as the dawn began to tinge the sky pink. And finally he was wheeled past buildings fashioned from stone the colour of straw, lining either side of a road so wide even Fflint could have stretched his wings without fear of hitting them, so smooth it was as if he were floating down a river on a windless day.

'Bring him inside,' he heard Earith say. Then the pain as many hands lifted him off the cart swept him back into oblivion. Benfro didn't know how he knew, but a long time passed between that moment and the point at which he woke again. Perhaps it was because the pain was gone, replaced by a terrible stiffness that gave him a new understanding of how Sir Frynwy must have felt all the time. It may have been because the loose, bubbly noises of his breathing were gone, the sharp jabbing pain in his lungs no more now than a wince. Or it might just have been because he felt rested, even if he was still more tired than he could ever recall having been.

'You're awake now. Good. How do you feel?'

Benfro opened his eyes, confused for a moment that he could see only through one. Then he remembered Fflint's talon and the horrible feeling as his eyeball had popped. He groaned at the memory of the pain.

'My eye.' Without thinking, he lifted his hand to his face, then stopped. It was his hand, the one that Melyn had cut off with his blade of fire back in the throne room at Tynhelyg. It wasn't the half-grown thing that Myfanwy had coaxed into being. This was his hand. Full size. He twisted it around, popped out his claws then withdrew them again. Flexed his talons. They felt strong, but there was something not quite right.

'My hand.'

Holding up the other one he saw what it was. Where this one was chipped and scarred, scales missing, skin tight and leathery, the other was shiny and new. As if it belonged to a dragon who had never climbed a cliff or fallen out of a tree, never spent days sorting, drying and preparing herbs, never done anything in fact.

'It will grow battered like the other in time. Of that I have no doubt.'

Benfro looked up, only then properly seeing the dragon who had spoken. She sat on a low stone bench on the other side of a surprisingly large and airy room. Behind her a wide door opened on to a courtyard bathed in sunlight. Benfro could hear the trickle of water, and as he noticed it, so other sounds began to filter in. Birdsong, wind, the chatter of voices too light to be dragons. A shiver of fear ran through him as he realized he was hearing men and women talking in perfect, unaccented Draigiaith, but before he could do anything a bundle of blurred red fur appeared at a window and dashed across the room. Leaping up on to his arm and from there to his shoulder.

'Benfro awake! Benfro better!'

'Malkin?' Benfro held up his hands again as the squirrel scampered over his head, peering upside down at him from a sitting position between his ears.

'Where Benfro's eye?' The look on Malkin's face was hard to read, inverted as it was. There was no mistaking the concern in his voice though.

'Calm yourself, Malkin. Our guest is still healing.' The ancient dragon stood up from the bench, walked slowly across the room towards him. Benfro tried to raise himself.

'Don't try to get up. You need rest, and lots of it.' She crouched down beside the raised pallet that formed his bed and for the first time Benfro noticed his nest was made of fabrics much like those that people wore. Purest white, they were soft and supportive and gave off a scent of lavender whenever he moved.

'You are Benfro, if young Malkin is to be believed.' The ancient dragon smiled and held out a slender arm. The squirrel leaped from Benfro's head on to it, scampering up to her shoulder.

'I am Benfro, and if I remember rightly, you are Earith. Thank you for healing me.'

'You're not done healing yet, Benfro. Though you are not as close to death's door as when our mutual friend summoned me to your aid.'

Benfro blinked. He was still very tired, very weak. Everything appeared sideways on, even though he knew it was just because he was lying down. He reached out a hand, missing the point he had aimed for. Everything was flat, as if there was no difference between near and far. No focus.

'My eye.' It was part question, part remembering the fight with Fflint.

'There are some things it is beyond even my skill to heal.' Earith sighed, her ancient frame seeming to deflate. 'Your eye was too damaged, and growing something like that back is . . . Well, I've never heard of any dragon who even tried.'

Benfro moved his hand back to his face, knocking himself lightly on the end of the nose as he misjudged the distance. He felt his scales, the tough leathery skin, his fangs, and then recoiled from the tenderness and swelling around his eye socket.

'Best you try not to touch it,' Earith said. 'I've healed the flesh, driven off any infection. If your looks bother you, I know a man who can make you a glass eye to match the other so no one will know.'

Benfro slumped into his bedding, staring lopsidedly at the ornately plastered ceiling high overhead. Given everything, the loss of one eye was perhaps not something he should moan about. And he could still see his aura, the lines of the Grym, the aethereal, all without any impediment. They hovered on the edge of his vision now, as if

416

the missing eye were somehow compensating. As he noticed them, so he noticed too the power radiating from Earith and more specifically the creature sitting on her shoulder.

'My friend.' Benfro looked up at the squirrel. 'How did you find me, Malkin? How did you even know where to look?'

'Swimming bird come, say big scaly whale on beach. Malkin not listen, but swimming bird not leave Malkin alone.'

'Swimming bird?' Benfro asked, then remembered the curious black and white creature and how it had peered at him before wandering off.

'Swimming bird not clever like Malkin. But swimming bird insist Malkin come see big scaly whale. So Malkin go. Follow swimming bird. Find not whale, but friend Benfro lying there.'

It was probably the most Benfro had ever heard the little creature say in one breath, but it didn't really answer the question.

'You have met Malkin before, Benfro? You know who he is? What he is?'

'He is my friend. But he is also part of the mother tree. I must have been looking for her.' Benfro's hearts started to beat harder, thump-thumping out of rhythm as he remembered Fflint picking him up and throwing him against a wall, piercing his eye, tearing his wing half off. 'When I jumped. I had to escape. Couldn't think straight. Had to get away.'

'Calm yourself, Benfro. There will be plenty of time for answers later. Now you need to rest. Heal properly.' Earith reached out, placed one old, leathery hand on his fore-head. At her touch, his breathing calmed, his hearts fell into their proper rhythm and slowed. He felt a surge of energy flow into him, but instead of invigorating him, it dragged him down. Like the stupor after a good meal. He began to slip once more into unconsciousness, but before he surrendered himself to it, he saw the cost whatever subtle arts she practised had exacted on Earith. His last sight before his eye closed was of the ancient dragon stumbling away, reaching for the bench across the room. The last he heard were her weak words: 'Stay with him please, Malkin. I must rest awhile myself.'

23

All power flows from the Grym, and all power flows to the Grym. The adept seeks to divert that flow and use it to his own ends. Most such workings are impermanent; a blade of fire lasts only as long as its conjuror can control it; a light will falter if the adept falls asleep. And yet there are some workings that will remain tied to a place or an object long after they have been forgotten by the mage who created them. Some can even persist after their creator's death, and the most potent of these are curses. For the Grym is fluid, but it can be set like a mousetrap, balanced perfectly until the wrong hands fall upon it. Then the pent-up energy of months, years, centuries will be released in moments.

Father Andro, *Magic and the Mind*

The dragons left shortly after Melyn and Frecknock returned from their aethereal tour of the battlefield. Whether their bloodlust was finally sated or there simply wasn't anything left to kill, the inquisitor couldn't be sure. His eyesight had improved noticeably since the Shepherd had healed him last, but even so he couldn't see anything moving on the plain. Only the swiftly dwindling winged shapes, fading into the pale blue sky as they headed east towards the Rim mountains and the Ffrydd.

'You can release the enchantment now,' Melyn commanded as he climbed on to his patiently waiting horse. Frecknock nodded once, and the air shimmered for a moment.

'It is done.' The dragon pulled the leather bag over her head and offered it up to the inquisitor. 'The book, Your Grace.'

Melyn stared at her, trying to reconcile the creature of the aethereal with the dragon that abased herself so in his presence. It annoyed him perhaps more that she sold herself short than that she was trying to hide things from him. Or at least from men in general.

'Keep it safe for me, and stay close.' He turned in his saddle, finding Osgal just behind him. The look on the captain's face was sour, his eyes darting away from Frecknock and back to the inquisitor. It might have been disapproval; the Shepherd knew Osgal had no reason to suffer dragons, given his recent injuries. Of course it might just have been his normal surly self.

'Fall in. We'll sweep the camp, finish what they began.' Melyn didn't say who "they" were. 'Use your judgement regarding prisoners, but be aware many of these men are not professional soldiers. We will need someone to tend the fields and work the gold mines in the north.'

Osgal nodded, barked a few orders. They moved swiftly off the hilltop and down on to the plain, covering the distance to the remains of the camp without anyone speaking. Frecknock kept pace with the fast trot of the horses, but as they came closer, Melyn could see she wanted to be elsewhere. He couldn't blame her; he could smell it too. A miasma of blood and shit, mixed in with burned flesh and canvas and the sharp scent of disturbed ground. Smoke drifted across the scene on the lightest of winds, ghost-like. At the edge of the encampment he reined in his horse, raising a hand for the army to halt.

'Split into groups of a dozen men. Spread out and cover the camp in grids. I don't want any surprises.' Osgal dismounted, the rest of the warrior priests falling in behind him. It took moments for them to form their groups and then start picking their way through the debris. A few conjured weak blades of light, but most drew their swords, delivering swift mercy to those too wounded to survive. Those still able to stand surrendered without a fight, and even with his hatred for all things Llanwennog still burning bright, Melyn could not bring himself to blame them.

He remained mounted as the warrior priests moved towards the centre of the camp, where Geraint's tent had stood. Vision sharper than it had been for years, Melyn saw one of his men stoop and pick up the helmet, shout something to his comrades nearby.

'Come, follow me.' He kicked his horse forward, Frecknock falling in behind him, and they picked a route through the destruction.

'Fancy armour, sir,' the warrior priest holding the helmet said as the inquisitor approached. 'Reckon this might be one of the generals. Maybe Prince Geraint himself.'

'It is Prince Geraint. I saw him die.' Melyn noticed the question flicker across the warrior priest's face, but the man did not ask it. 'Have you found any more of him?'

'No, sir. Just this. It was here in the middle of . . .'

The ground where Prince Geraint's tent had stood

looked like someone had taken a giant carpenter's plane and shaved off the top six inches of soil. It was clean, damp earth, fine clay smoothed almost perfectly flat. Just a line of tiny parallel grooves to mark where the vast dragon's belly had scraped the ground. It hadn't landed so much as skidded through the camp, taking tent, prince and anything else in the way with it as it clawed back into the sky. The head had left a dent in the soil as it landed, and there just beside it lay a gold chain and amulet.

'Don't touch it!' The shout came from Frecknock, but Melyn might just as easily have said it himself had he not been momentarily distracted as he dismounted. He could see the glamours woven around the chain as plain as the smoke spiralling from the nearest fire. It was too late, though. The warrior priest had bent forward, scooped up the chain in his bare hand.

His scream echoed across the devastated encampment as if the dragons had wheeled round and were even now returning for a second attack. Frecknock took a couple of steps forward, but Melyn put his hand out, placing it on her chest to stop her. The man was already dead; he just didn't know it yet.

'Nobody touch him.' Melyn's command was obeyed instantly by the warrior priests who had rushed to their comrade's aid. The man himself was oblivious to anything but pain, his hand gripping the amulet so tightly that blood seeped through his fingers. The skin on his face turned red, then started to blister as he staggered around, his screams growing weaker and weaker. Smoke rose from his robes, and his lurching strides brought him in the direction of the inquisitor. Closer and closer until he sank to his knees at Melyn's feet. His eyes were white orbs, vision boiled away by the heat coursing through him. Not a pleasant way to die at all. With his last strength, the man raised his hand up to the inquisitor, the amulet clearly visible through the bubbling mess of flesh and bone and pus.

'Bloody fool. Did you learn nothing in all your years at Emmass Fawr?' With a thought, Melyn conjured a short blade of fire and pushed the point of it deep into the dying man's brain.

Warmed by the southern sea and the waters of the Bay of Kerdigen, Abervenn's climate was markedly better than that of Tochers. The oak and elm were still in full leaf, the first tinges of yellow only now creeping into the edges of the canopy. Beulah sat on her mare alongside Clun's massive stallion and peered at the walls of the city they had not so long ago left.

'They have no idea we are here?' she asked. A half-dozen paces ahead of them the warrior priest who had been scouting the land ahead tried to hide his nervousness. Not at being in the presence of this queen; he was an old soldier, Siarl was his name, and Beulah had known him since her earliest days at Emmass Fawr. Nor was he cowed by the Duke of Abervenn, a man a third his age who had until very recently been no more than a novitiate in the order, even if that novitiate had single-handedly driven off a dragon that had killed several fully trained warrior priests. No, the thing giving Siarl palpitations was the great Gomoran stallion. No creature that wild should be so utterly, contemptibly still.

'The city gates are wide, Your Majesty. Not much traffic, but a few merchants are coming and going.'

'Did you go into the city itself?' Clun asked the question this time, although Beulah had been thinking it.

'No, Your Grace. I thought it best to raise as little suspicion as possible. If your plan is to take them by surprise, then the fewer strangers the guards see the better.'

'Very well. Return to your troop. Get something to eat and some rest. We will attack one hour after dusk.'

'Your Grace, the gates will be closed by then.'

'I am well aware of that. They would be closed before we could reach them if we just marched up there in the daylight too. Leave it to me to ensure they remain open.'

'As Your Grace commands.' The scout slapped his chest with a fist in salute, bowed briefly to the queen and then hurried off.

'You have a plan, my love?' Beulah nudged her horse a little closer to Clun's, even though it meant she had to crane her neck yet higher to speak to him. Her filly was less flighty in the presence of the huge stallion than usual, which probably meant she was coming on heat. Time to swap horses then, unless she wanted this one crushed to death.

'Lord Beylin's fleet will arrive on the dawn tide. The smaller craft are hugging the coast, but he's sent some larger ships out to sea to cut off any attempt at escape that way. I will take a small troop of warrior priests to the Eastgate at dusk. It will be closed and locked, of course, but there are ways around that.'

Beulah looked out from under the trees, judging the

hour by the tone of the light. Nightfall was not far away. Two hours, perhaps.

'Is the Eastgate not a bit small? Our men will be trapped in the courtyard beyond.'

'We won't need more than a hundred warrior priests. Maybe a hundred and fifty. Abervenn must be almost deserted. All the able-bodied men not already in our army will have left for Candlehall.'

'How can you be sure?' Beulah looked towards the distant towers, all she could see of the city from their hiding place on the edge of the woods. No flag flew, but that was normal when the duke was away.

'It's very unlikely there will be any adepts in the city to intercept me, so I will scout in the aethereal and make sure our men are not seen.'

'I will accompany you. It is best to have someone watch your back.'

Clun turned in his saddle, looking down at her from his high seat. 'My lady, is it—'

'I would advise you not to finish that sentence, my love. I am your queen, remember.'

'Always, my lady.' Clun bowed deep. 'We must prepare then. And perhaps attend to our daughter first.'

Beulah sighed, wondering where her anger had gone. Worn away by her tiredness perhaps. Of all the calamities to befall her following the kidnapping of the infant Ellyn, the loss of Blodwyn had been the hardest. No other wet nurse could be found before the army had marched out, which tied the queen into someone else's timetable of feeding and sleeping. Her daughter might have been tiny, but she was insatiable. No doubt Melyn would have had something amusing to say about that. Too bad the old man was hundreds of leagues away.

At least a week passed before Benfro could stand, possibly more as he had no idea how long he slept. It might just have been a few hours at a time, or it might have been days. Always when he woke, Malkin was there, and sometimes Earith as well. At first he managed only a few minutes before the panic engulfed him and the ancient dragon would send him back into the darkness and the peace. But with each passing day, so he built up his strength both physically and mentally. He made it out to the courtyard with just a little more difficulty than walking back from Mount Arnahi to Corwen's cave, and spent a pleasant afternoon being warmed by a sun much hotter than he was used to. It helped with the stiffness in his joints, the aches in his wings and the sudden, unexpected panic attacks when he remembered how swiftly and brutally Fflint had almost killed him. How much more swiftly and brutally he had killed Fflint.

'You never said what this place is called – where it is.' Benfro spoke in an attempt to fend off the inevitable return of those traumatic memories. He sat on a low stone bench, the perfect size for a dragon, facing the fountain and ornamental pond that were the main feature of the courtyard. The constantly bubbling water helped cool the air, as did the well-tended plants growing in raised beds all around him. The courtyard was the centrepiece of a large building, quite clearly built to dragon scale, but everywhere there were touches that reminded him of men. Lower benches, doorways through which a kitling would struggle to go, pathways too narrow to negotiate without brushing his still-tender wings against the walls on either side.

'This is my home,' Earith said. 'It stands at the centre of the city of Pallestre in the land they call Eirawen.'

'Eirawen?' Benfro recognized the name, racked his memory until he remembered where he had seen it before. The maps in Magog's repository underneath his ruined palace at Cenobus. 'Beyond the great southern sea? Past the Caldy archipelago?'

'You know something of the geography of Gwlad?' Earith raised a greying eyebrow. 'Tell me, Benfro. Where do you call home? Where were you hatched and raised?'

'I never knew the name of the village. It was just the village. It was at the bottom end of the great forest of the Ffrydd. My mother wove a spell around it so that men couldn't find the place. They always ended up at our cottage instead. Until Frecknock ruined it all, that is. It was her who invited Melyn and his warrior priests in. They killed everyone, my mother first but then the rest of them. Sir Frynwy, Meirionydd, Ynys Môn, all of them. It all happened because of her. Just because she wanted a stupid mate.' Benfro couldn't have said why he chose to give so much detail in his answer or even that particular detail. Perhaps it was the way Eirawen looked at him, patiently giving him the time to speak without interruption. Perhaps it was the frustration of days spent barely able to move, only his thoughts able to wander. Whatever the reason for his outburst, he only stopped because he needed to breathe, his lungs still weak from the injuries Fflint had dealt him.

Earith watched him for a while, perhaps considering her response or maybe giving him time to talk on if he wanted. Finally satisfied he was spent for now, she spoke.

'If you came from the great forest, then you are not of this world, Benfro. Not a son of Gog. So tell me this, when you have recovered enough. How came you to be here? How did you end up on a beach not half a day's walk from here?'

'Not a son of Gog?' Benfro's hearts had started to beat harder at the name. 'Do you mean this really is Gog's world? The story is true?'

'Ah, Benfro. So many stories are true. Yes, this is Gog's world, as you call it. This is the place he made when he could no longer bear to breathe the same air as his brother. But come, tell me how you got here first, then I will try to answer the questions I can see writ large across your face.'

Benfro didn't really know where to start, but slowly he pieced together the story of growing up in the village, learning to hunt with Ynys Môn, to heal with his mother, to read and write with Sir Frynwy and Meirionydd. He told of Frecknock and her hatred of him, and as he did so he began to understand a small fraction of what she must have felt. He spoke of Melyn and the warrior priests, and of fleeing the carnage they had visited upon the villagers and his mother. As the day passed slowly into evening he told of his meeting with Magog, his double-edged gift of wings and the rose cord that linked the two of them. Earith listened, never questioning, always giving Benfro time to gather his thoughts or catch his breath. At some point, on a silent command, a pair of men brought in great platters of food, jugs of ice-cold water sweetened with some fruit Benfro couldn't identify, pieces of finest crystallized ginger, dusted with sugar.

'This was Ystrad Fflur's favourite treat.' Benfro held up a chunk of ginger in the sunlight, then took a shallow sniff of the delicate aroma. He hadn't eaten much, wasn't sure his stomach could take anything too rich or sweet, but the smell brought happy memories and a smile to his lips.

'He would tell me stories of his travels, and if I listened long enough I'd get a treat. His jar never seemed to empty. I know how that works now, but then it was magic. I remember when he died. I cast the Fflam Gwir at his reckoning.'

'You know of the subtle arts?' For the first time since he had met her, Benfro heard an element of surprise in Eirawen's voice.

'A little. Magog taught me some things, Corwen too,' Benfro said. 'Others I sort of just did.'

Earith studied him for a moment before speaking again, and Benfro felt the weight of her gaze as if she were looking into his mind. If she found anything there she didn't like, he couldn't tell.

'You walked the Llinellau to the beach where we found you, didn't you?'

Benfro nodded. The memories of that time were still jumbled, some missing entirely.

'How could you know where you were going? You've never been here, never seen this place. There is nothing of you here to focus on. It shouldn't be possible.'

'But I did it before. When I fled from Melyn. I saw something in the Grym. It looked like a window on to a

429

different sky. I don't know. It was away from danger, so I guess I just jumped.'

'Oh, Benfro. You make it sound so easy, but travelling the Llinellau is the hardest of all the subtle arts. There are many dragons who study all their lives and never manage it. Never manage even to reach out and bring things to them like your friend Ystrad Fflur with his crystallized ginger. Very few of Gog's sons and daughters have the skill or the aptitude.'

'But Gog was one of the greatest mages ever to have lived.'

'Greatest? That depends on how you measure greatness. If killing thousands of innocents makes you great, then I suppose he is. If destroying the world just to get back at your brother makes you great, then, yes, he's the greatest. Both of them are. The last I heard of Gog, he'd driven most of his children away. The only company he keeps is his own, and half the time he hates himself as well. Most of his kind have left, turned their backs on the old ways. Gone feral.' Earith nodded at Benfro's wings, but he knew what she meant. Fflint had been no better than a wild beast, worse in many ways. Wild beasts killed for food or to protect their mates and young; Fflint had killed because he enjoyed inflicting pain.

'They were hunting people. Killing them. I tried to stop them. Stop him. He turned on me.'

'Has it got so bad? I've not travelled north in centuries. There was never much for me there anyway, nothing at all now.'

'You've seen him though? Gog?'

'Once I would have counted him a friend. His brother

430

too. But they . . . Well, you know the story as well as any, Benfro.'

'I have to go back. I have to find Gog, speak to him. I need him to show me to the place where he and Magog were hatched.'

Earith's laugh wasn't mean, but it was there. She tried to suppress the smile on her face too. Benfro had seen it before though – on his mother, Meirionydd, Sir Frynwy even, when he suggested doing something that was impossible but well intentioned.

'The Old One doesn't welcome visitors, Benfro. And how will you get there? It's thousands of miles. I've done what I can to heal your wings, but you won't be flying anywhere for a month at least.'

'I'll use the Llinellau if I have to.' Benfro wasn't sure he could. The only time it had worked before, he'd been in mortal danger. Short of asking Earith to try and kill him, he couldn't see himself facing anything like that here.

'Malkin show the way. Malkin know all the ways.'

Benfro had almost forgotten the squirrel, sitting on his shoulder as if asleep. Now it leaped down to the neatly raked gravel between him and Earith, hopping from foot to foot in that manner it had. Excited at the prospect of adventure.

'Of course. I should have seen it earlier.' Earith laughed again, only this time it was genuine mirth.

'Seen what?' Benfro asked.

'That you have the tree's protection. Malkin is her avatar. It's no accident you ended up where you did, Benfro. You leaped to safety, and the Llinellau brought you to your friend.'

'The mother tree?' Benfro looked from Malkin to Earith and back. The squirrel had clasped his tiny hands together now and was dancing around with obvious joy.

'Yes, Benfro. The mother tree. I think we will have to pay her a visit, just as soon as you are well enough to make the journey.'

The upper docks sat within the walls of Candlehall, protected from outside attack by the massive stone arch of the River Gate. The huge portcullis was raised still, and several barges were pulling in to the jetty of the upper dock as Dafydd and Usel arrived; more were queued up just downriver and waiting. In moments the first three were roped tight, stevedores lining up to begin unloading their precious cargo. None of the burly men knew their princess was on board; as far as they were concerned the boats brought only much-needed food to help the city through the inevitable siege.

'You told no one? As we agreed?' Dafydd asked the medic as they approached the middle barge.

'Not even Padraig. I thought it best we enter Candlehall the way we left Talarddeg. The princess can appear to her people once we have her safe in the palace.'

'And this lot?' Dafydd indicated his guard, already attracting more attention than was perhaps helpful.

'I would suggest you order Captain Venner to have them oversee the unloading. Make sure all the provisions are safely stowed in the public storehouses, not in some rich merchant's basement.'

'Very wise.' Dafydd turned and relayed the order, cutting off the inevitable argument before it could get started.

'You have your orders, Captain Venner. I don't expect them to be questioned.'

Venner closed his mouth with an audible click, nodded his understanding and set to ordering his men to their duties. Dafydd turned back to Usel, who once more had that annoying smirk on his face. 'Well, I had to promote someone eventually. Just a pity poor old Jarius isn't easily replaced.'

'He was a good man. Now if you'll take my hand, sire, I think it's time for us to disappear.'

There was so much going on at the docks that it probably wasn't necessary. Still, Dafydd did as he was told, and together they walked up the gangplank and on to the barge. Iolwen stood near the stern, where a rough cabin formed the captain's quarters. She had her child suspended in a sling around her shoulders and was staring up at the buildings, her head tilting back as she followed the slate roofs ever higher to the palace and the Neuadd in the middle of it. Lady Anwyn stood beside her, scowling at anything and everything. They were both dressed more like men than noble ladies.

'Your Highness. It is good to see you arrived safely.' Usel dropped his spell a few paces away from the pair of them, bowing deeply. Iolwen looked momentarily startled, then saw Dafydd and her face lit up. In that instant he forgot all about Jarius, all about the Guardians of the Throne and the fact that they were in enemy territory, facing a siege that might never be relieved. Iolwen was not fooled.

'What is it?' she asked as they embraced somewhat awkwardly, the sleeping child between them. Dafydd told her, unsurprised when tears glistened in the corners of her eyes. More surprising was the sharp intake of breath from Lady Anwyn, though she too would have known Captain Pelod well enough.

'We must move swiftly,' Anwyn said, just the slightest of cracks in her voice. 'Beulah and her consort Clun are on their way to Abervenn. The city cannot hope to hold out. Most of our men are either fighting for her side or up here in Candlehall.'

'Abervenn? Why go there? I would have thought she'd have force-marched her army straight back here,' Daffyd asked.

'I expect she intends to raze it to the ground. Beulah never did take well to being challenged.' Anwyn swept her cloak around her as if it were a barrier against the world. 'Come, let us get up to the palace. There is much to do.'

She took two steps towards the gangplank and disappeared. Dafydd turned back to Iolwen. 'Is she all right?'

'She left her mother behind. She's already lost her father and brother to this war. And she and Jarius . . .'

'I didn't know.' Dafydd took his wife's hands in his, feeling their warmth. He thanked all the gods of men that she was safe here with him.

'We should probably go, sire. The less time we spend out in the open here the better.' Usel came forward, holding out his hand, and Dafydd took it once more. He thought he could feel a change in the texture of the air, though it might have been his imagination. Otherwise everything was the same, but they walked unhindered and unnoticed off the boat, past Captain Venner and the palace guard supervising the unloading, up the narrow back alleys and in through the poorly guarded servant gate into the palace complex. Only when the medic started to pull them in the direction of the great reception hall and the queen's chambers did Dafydd stop.

'Not yet, Usel. There is still that room, remember?'

The medic paused a moment before nodding. If he was annoyed at the detour he didn't show it, and they were soon standing outside the door. Looking at its black oak surface and heavy iron fixings, anyone could be forgiven for doubting a team of men had been attacking it with axes just a few days earlier. There wasn't a scratch on the surface, though a few chips in the stone arch surrounding it looked crisp and clean.

'What is this?' Iolwen asked. She still carried Prince Iolo in his sling around her shoulders.

'This, Your Highness, is your birthright. Something only a very few people outside the family of Balwen have ever seen.' Usel produced a heavy iron key from his robes and held it out.

'I thought you said there was no key,' Dafydd said.

'Perhaps you would like to try it, sire?' Usel had been offering the key to Iolwen, but now he presented it to Dafydd. The prince took it, feeling a weight in it that was greater than the volume of iron from which it was made. How many generations of kings had held this key before him? He studied the door more closely; it had an iron ring set in one side to pull it closed, but there was no sign of a keyhole.

'How am I supposed to use this?'

'Your Highness, if you would place your hand on the door.' Usel addressed the princess. She looked confused but nevertheless did as she was told. It occurred to Dafydd that he was being monstrously selfish, dragging her up here after her long journey. They should have gone straight to the royal apartments he had commandeered for their use, settled his infant son in and given them both time to rest before doing anything else. But all such thoughts evaporated the instant Iolwen's fingers touched the smooth dark wood. Something shivered in the air, and a keyhole appeared alongside the iron ring.

'The oldest of magics, as I said before.' Usel's voice was steady, but his eyes were wide with excitement like a little boy at a feast.

'Where did you get the key from?' Dafydd asked.

'Seneschal Padraig had it for safekeeping. It never leaves the castle, even when the monarch is away.'

Dafydd noted that Usel hadn't actually answered the question, but he was getting used to that. He slid the key into the newly appeared keyhole and turned it. The lock was stiff, as if rarely used. Or resisting the attempts of a usurper, perhaps.

'Would you turn it, my love?'

Iolwen clasped the key lightly, turned it with no more effort than if it were a spoon in a tureen of soup. The lock *clacked* and the door swung open to reveal the top of a spiral staircase leading down into darkness.

24

The lost cities of Eirawen are a thing of wonder to behold. What cataclysm overtook them, and what happened to the people who built them, can only be speculated upon. Histories tell of violent earthquakes and eruptions driving the people from their paradise north to the lands that would become the Twin Kingdoms. But in truth the remains of the cities in that vast southern land are too well preserved to have suffered such a fate. Overgrown by forests, they are nevertheless largely intact, the great halls still standing, spires competing with the trees in a race towards the withering sun. It is as if the people simply decided one day to leave their marvels of stonemasonry and architecture behind and walk off into oblivion.

From the travel journals of Usel of the Ram

The screams stayed with him for days.

They made it to the rocks just before the first dragon came swooping down on the clearing. Errol had never seen a creature so big before; it was twice Benfro's size at least and it thundered around the clearing in search of the sacrifice promised by the smoking fire. Nellore whispered 'Fflint' before covering her eyes, shrinking further back into the gap in the rocks. Errol suspected that Fflint was the dragon who had killed her father. He didn't have to watch the beast for long to realize that he was short tempered. The lack of any sacrifice seemed to enrage him, the arrival of more dragons merely stoking his anger to new heights. They all took off shortly afterwards, flying in the direction of the village. And then the screaming started.

Errol had assumed the village would be some distance from the altar, but the sounds carried as clearly as if it were just the other side of the hill. He was about to clamber out of their hiding place in the rocks when yet more dragons flew over, sending him and Nellore deeper into the warren of cracks and crevices, far from sight but at the same time unable to see what was going on. Instead they were left with their imaginations fuelled by the noises of extreme violence. Morning passed into afternoon with yet more sounds of mayhem, though at least the screaming had stopped. The two of them said nothing all day, just sat and waited for the dragons to leave, shivering despite the warm air and the harsh sun baking the rocks all around them.

It was late afternoon turning towards evening and the sudden onset of dusk when they heard the swish of wings high overhead. Peering up through a gap in the boulders, Errol watched dragon after dragon fly back towards the distant Twmp. He hadn't counted them in, and nor could he be sure that he'd seen every one that passed, but the giant, Fflint, did not seem to be among them. Only when a full hour had passed since the last dragon struggled slowly behind the others, nursing a wounded wing by the look of things; only when the darkness had fallen completely, did he finally speak.

'I think they're all gone now. We should move. While we can.'

Nellore sniffed. She had curled herself up into a ball beside Errol, and he suspected she had been crying to herself. There was scarcely enough light to see anything, but he thought he saw her nod her head in agreement.

'They've never done that before,' she said. Errol thought better than to point out the obvious fact. If they had done that before, at least in living memory, then there would have been no villagers to drug him and tie him to the altar.

'That big one, Fflint. It was like he was mad or something.'

'They were like that before, with my da. Fighting with each other. Kicking and biting like wild animals.' Nellore's voice was very small, and she looked younger than Errol could remember seeing her.

'Let's go, OK? There's nothing to be gained from hanging around here.'

They stepped quietly into the clearing. Errol strained his ears to hear anything above the quiet rustle of the wind in the leaves of the nearby trees. The fire that had brought the dragons in was nothing more than a few dull embers in the darkness beside the altar stone. A brighter glow rose in the direction of the village, orange and flickering.

'I need to see. If anyone's still . . .' Nellore didn't finish, just set off in the direction of the glow. Errol followed, and they were soon at the outskirts of the village. It had always seemed a little ramshackle, but now it was just ruins, picked out in orange by the flames of a thousand fires and lent a more hellish hue by a gibbous blood moon rising over the scene like an omen. Most of the single-storey buildings had been flattened, rubble strewn across the street. Flames danced on wooden beams, floorboards and furniture, and everywhere was wispy smoke in the moonlight, the occasional crash as something structural gave way.

Murta's house was less damaged than most, just a section of the front wall missing where something heavy had smashed into it. Errol stepped through, searching for any sign of life. He found none, but in the back room where he had slept the chest had been smashed open and clothes were spilled all over the floor. He looked around in panic, then relaxed a little as he saw his travelling cloak still hung over the back of the chair. He checked its pockets, finding the two jewels where he had left them, his purse and the strange orb too.

Back outside, he found Nellore standing at the remains of Hammie's house. The injured man might still have been inside, but if so he was quite clearly dead. The building looked as if a great weight had been dropped on it from above, the roof caved in and walls pulled down around it. Behind, in the orchard, all the fruit trees had been crushed like so much firewood. Thick trunks snapped like twigs, roots pulled up, foliage stamped into the ground as if its existence were an affront to nature.

'Errol. Look.'

Errol turned to see where Nellore had gone. Across the street and along a ways the village hall still mostly stood. Unlike the other buildings, its door was solid wood. It lay in the road where it had been ripped from its hinges. Smoke still wafted out from the darkness beyond, bringing a smell of burned hair, cooking meat. But it was what lay in front of the hall that had caught the girl's attention.

A pile of ash, purest white despite the dark orange glow of the moon, lay a few paces from the hall. The light breeze that was keeping the worst of the smell away also whisked the ash into the air, carrying it off like a thief. Nellore squatted close, poking around in the pile with her finger.

'There's something in here.' She brushed ash aside, reached in and pulled something out. 'Oh.'

'What is it?' Errol hurried over as Nellore rose slowly to her feet. She turned to face him, held out her hand and opened it up to reveal a tiny, clear crystal.

'It's . . . I think it's Fflint. The dragon. I can sort of sense him.'

Errol looked at the minuscule jewel, then at the pile of ash. The wind had taken most of it away now, almost as if it was dissolving in the air. There were no other jewels to be seen, but surely a dragon should have many. And bigger than this one. Even Magog's final, unreckoned jewel, wrapped in heavy cloth in his pocket, was many times bigger.

'If it is Fflint, then he is dead. And more, someone has burned his body, reckoned his jewels. Well, his jewel.' Errol looked at the empty street, the broken buildings and smelt the undeniable stench of death in the air. He couldn't begin to guess what had happened, but he knew also that there was nothing left here for either of them. Nellore still held the jewel out in her palm, poking at it with one finger. Her tongue protruded from the side of her mouth in an expression of utter absorption.

'You should be very careful with that,' he said. 'If you must keep it, then wrap it up well. You'll lose your mind to it otherwise.'

Nellore ignored him, so he reached out and snatched the gem, dropping it into a fold in his cloak. For the briefest of instants he felt something of the dragon who had laid waste to the village, battered away at the buildings, ripped people apart. He felt Fflint's rage, and then another dragon facing him, battered and bruised, but recognisably Benfro. Then a roar of flame enveloped the dragon.

'Hey! That's mine! I found it.' Nellore made a grab for the jewel, but Errol backed away swiftly. Folded up in the fabric of his cloak, the magic dulled away to nothing.

'I'll give it to you, I promise. But first we need to get as far away from here as possible. They'll be back. I'm sure of it.'

'Where . . . Where are we going to go?' Nellore's eyes were wide, glistening in the moonlight. It was a very good question.

'I came here looking for my friend. Martha. I'm sure she met some dragons not far from here, but they didn't kill her. They took her somewhere though.'

'Da always said there were people in the north. Wise people. Up in the mountains. Don't know anywhere else. I've always lived here.'

Errol looked up at the moon and the stars speckling the night sky. They were mostly familiar, at least enough to get a rough sense of direction. The Twmp and Fflint's dragons lay off to the west, the road he'd come in on to the east. North was forest, undulating hills and nothing much to the hazy horizon, if he recalled the daylight view.

'OK then. We go north. But see if you can find a bag or something, and salvage any food. I've a feeling it's going to be a long walk.'

The walls of Abervenn were old, perhaps even older than all but the central parts of Candlehall, the Neuadd and the Wall of Kings. In the aethereal it had a solidity about it that only a structure steeped in generations of lives could achieve. The newer houses seemed thin and ghostly in comparison.

Beulah had never really considered the aethereal much before. Melyn had taught her how to access it and how to control her movements through it, but she had always thought of it as merely a means of communication over distance. Denied access to her magic for the long months of her pregnancy, she now found she was savouring her abilities more, enjoying them for themselves as much as for the advantages they gave her over her enemies. Only here, confronted with the walls of Abervenn, she found even her power thwarted.

'How can we hope to get through?' She floated up to the oh-so-solid stone, placed an aethereal hand upon the surface. It was warm to the touch, like skin, and rough like the callused hands of the ancient masons who had built it, repaired it, altered it down the centuries.

'We could simply float over the top, but that might attract unwanted attention.'

'Attention? I thought you said there would be no adepts here.' Beulah faced Clun, drinking in his brilliant aura. He glowed like the sun, gold tinged with crimson around the edges, and if anyone was going to draw attention it was him.

'Father Tolley was an adept of great skill, as was the man sent to delay us in the market square back at Tochers. These so-called Guardians of the Throne seem to have skills more normally associated with the senior warrior priests and quaisters of the Order of the High Ffrydd. I cannot be sure there are none here. It's likely that there are, given that Abervenn seems to be the centre of the revolt against the House of Balwen.'

Clun's aura darkened, the crimson threatening to over-whelm the gold as his anger rose. Abervenn had been given to him – it was his responsibility – and he felt that deeply, personally. Once again Beulah wondered how it could be that someone raised a common merchant's son could be more noble of spirit than any of the fawning courtiers who had plagued her life at the palace.

'I don't think we need fear the Guardians,' she said. 'We have met them twice and bested them both times.'

'But we still do not want to alert them to our presence needlessly. There is another way in, my lady.'

Beulah followed, gliding just above the ground as Clun led her towards the spot where the Eastgate stood. The sluggish water of the Gwy entered the city through an iron grille close by. Its bars were spaced wide enough that a thin man might slip between them, but Beulah knew the river was ducted through deep tunnels all the way to the centre of the city. Even a strong swimmer with powerful lungs would drown before they saw daylight again.

'We cannot pass through the water channel. It's too dangerous.'

'But we can go through the Eastgate itself. See.' Clun gestured to where the road met the wall. The indistinct aethereal forms of two guards stood, one either side of the track, and between them, where the solid oak gates should have been closed at this time of the evening, a hazy, ill-formed veil only slightly distorted the view beyond.

'How is this possible?' Beulah asked.

'These walls are a thousand years old. More. They are part of the land now, solid and immutable in this plane as well as the mundane. But the gates were rotten and failing. Carpenters were replacing them when we came here just a month ago. They used green oak from trees not fifty years old. With time they will harden in the aethereal as they harden in life, but for now they are ill-formed things. Easy to penetrate.'

Clun walked forward to the shimmering veil, placed his hand on it and pushed through. 'See? There is no resistance whatsoever.'

Beulah floated forward, conscious of the guards either side of them but excited nonetheless at this new understanding of something she thought she had known most of her life. Touching the space where the gates stood felt like brushing the surface of a warm bath.

'Come, my lady. Take my hand. We shall enter my city together.'

Beulah reached out with her aethereal form, took Clun's outstretched hand in her own. Together they moved forward, him walking, her floating a few inches off the ground. The veil that was the gateway parted as lightly as a silk sheet, and then they were inside.

'We must move swiftly, my lady. I will cover the ground if you will be my eyes.' Clun increased his pace to a run, dragging Beulah along beside him as he crossed the small square behind the River Gate. Beulah didn't know Aber-venn well, but her husband seemed to have the lie of the place imprinted in his memory. His skill at navigating the aethereal was not so much surprising as unbelievable in one who had only learned of its existence a year earlier, and yet she had no time to dwell on the mystery as they moved with increasing speed through the city. It was all Beulah could manage to scan the streets for signs of people. They sped past the Kingsgate, adequately guarded for a city in peacetime, but hardly enough men to give a troop of warrior priests any worry. The Westgate was even less well defended, though its stout construction and towers meant a handful of well-provisioned guards could keep an army out indefinitely. There were few soldiers on duty at the barracks, which left only the castle itself to worry about. Clun avoided it, and they were soon back at the Eastgate.

'It is as I thought. The city has few soldiers left to guard it. Most must have gone to Candlehall.'

'Then we should strike at once. Break down this gate and rush the guards at the other two.' Beulah began to relax, feeling her aethereal self pulled back towards her body, but Clun stood motionless, midway between the flickering half-images of the two guards.

'I see no need to rush, my lady, when we can just ask these two to open the sally port.' He reached out and touched one guard in the area where the man's head should be. A moment's pause in which Beulah felt something like spiders crawling over her skin, and then Clun crossed to the other guard. She shuddered at that same strange sensation, but it lasted mere moments.

'We should return to the camp now, my lady.' Clun took her hand once more, and with a step they were there. Beulah sank back into her body, waking from the trance with a groan. She felt more weary than at any time since giving birth, a deep tiredness in her bones. Travelling the aethereal had left her this way when she had first learned the skill, many years before, but it was an age since she had felt that way.

'Take ten of your men. Go quickly to the Eastgate. You'll find it open and the guards asleep. Secure it but do not enter. We will be along soon.' Beulah struggled upright as she heard Clun outside the tent, giving orders like he was born to it. She staggered to the entrance, looking out upon a dark scene of rushing bodies as the small army of warrior priests readied themselves for battle. The motion dizzied her, weakening her knees, and she had to grip the tent fabric tight to keep upright. When had she become so pathetic? She'd not felt this way since she was a little girl.

'My lady, please. You must not overexert yourself.'

Strong hands took hold of her, and for a moment Beulah's anger flared at the thought that someone could dare to be so familiar. And then she remembered. How had she forgotten? Her mind was as sluggish as her body, drained by their short reconnaissance.

'Clun, my love. I must lead the assault. This city has defied me once too often. I must see that it pays the penalty for its actions.'

'We cannot both go, my lady. It is too dangerous. One must stay behind to look after Ellyn. The future of the House of Balwen depends on it.'

'I am more than capable of looking after myself.'

Beulah said the words even though she didn't feel as if they were true. She was weak still, far weaker than she liked to admit.

'I have seen you fight, my lady. You are the equal of any warrior priest, better by far than most. But you are still not up to your full strength.' Clun steered her towards the camp bed and Beulah cursed him silently for doing so. The last of her resolve crumbled as he lowered her.

'You made this my responsibility when you made me duke. The people of this city have defied you, but they have defied me too. They kidnapped my daughter. Abervenn will not forget my wrath. What little of it survives.'

Close by, Ellyn lay in a tiny cot, sleeping silently. Beulah looked at her face, so much of her father's features already showing. Soon the infant would wake and need feeding again, and heroic, loyal, formidable though he was, that was one task Clun could not perform.

'Go then, my love.' Beulah kissed her husband with more urgency and passion than she had intended. It was too long, but not long enough, and finally she pulled away from his embrace.

'Spare no one. This night Abervenn will burn.'

'If I may?' Usel stepped forward, conjuring a tiny ball of light that hovered just over his outstretched palm. The glow illuminated steps worn down in the middle by the passage of many feet over even more years.

'Have you been down here before?' Iolwen asked before Dafydd could himself.

'Never, Your Highness. I have heard stories, and it should be perfectly safe; there are few others who can

448

open that door and only one key. But I will go ahead, just to be sure.'

The medic set off slowly down the steps, holding up his light more for Iolwen and Dafydd than himself. The staircase was wide and the ceiling above them higher than necessary, but it still took a long time to descend deep into the rocky heart of the hill on which Candlehall had been built. Dafydd didn't notice the glow at first, as it was outshone by Usel's light, but slowly he came to see a dull red tinge to the stone walls. The air grew warmer too, and young Iolo stirred in his mother's arms, not waking but troubled by the dreams of infants. Then they rounded the final turn in the steps and stopped.

It was a huge cavern. Whether it was a natural cave deep beneath the Neuadd or had been hewn out by main force, Dafydd couldn't have said. It didn't really matter; that it existed was enough. The ceiling rose from the edge where they stood, arcing up towards a point a hundred spans or more up. A central pillar climbed to that apex, and Dafydd didn't need telling to know that the Obsidian Throne sat directly above it.

'What is this place?' Iolwen walked slowly forward to the nearest of a series of stone walls that radiated out from the centre, rising twice the height of a tall man. Small alcoves had been cut into each wall, hundreds upon thousands, and they all glowed with a dull red light that whispered terrible mad things in the silence.

'The treasure of the House of Balwen. The jewels of every dragon ever slain in King Balwen's name. More besides.' Usel walked slowly towards the centre of the cavern, passing close to the nearest wall with its dully vibrant load. 'I never thought I would see this. Hoped it wasn't true.'

'There are so many. And they're all so lost, so frightened.' Iolwen reached up to one of the alcoves, fingers hovering over the small pile of jewels that lay inside.

'I would suggest you don't, Your Highness.' Usel was suddenly at her side, one hand wrapped around her wrist and pulling it away. Dafydd could have sworn he'd been twenty paces away, more even, and yet he had covered the distance in the blink of an eye.

'Are they dangerous?' Iolwen asked.

'Not so much dangerous as lonely. This is not how a dragon should live after its mortal existence is done. This is not how its jewels should be left, either. This whole place is deeply unnatural. I had heard rumours, but the truth of it is much more terrible.'

'How so?' Dafydd stepped further into the cavern, feeling the swirl and ebb of the Grym all around him. 'Men have collected dragons' jewels for centuries. They are highly prized.'

'And do you know why that is, Prince Dafydd?'

'They are a short cut to the Grym. They help an adept focus its power to his own use.'

'That is how they have been used, it's true. But if you knew just what it meant to treat a dragon's jewels so, you would weep for these countless tortured souls.'

'Tortured? How? Surely they are dead.'

Usel went very still, as if he were struggling to control his temper. Dafydd was reminded of one of his old tutors. Tolt Moorit had been his name, a good teacher but not prepared to suffer fools. Tolt had known better than to strike a prince of the royal house, and had adopted this very same motionless pose whenever Dafydd did something particularly stupid.

'Do they sound dead, Prince Dafydd?' the medic asked eventually. Then he cocked his head as if hearing something unusual himself. 'Come. Follow me. And touch nothing.'

He headed off at such a pace they wouldn't have had the chance to touch anything even had they wanted to. The walls, which had looked like they formed simple spokes from the central pillar, were more like the walls of a maze, narrowing and branching with bewildering complexity. Without constantly glancing up at the stone roof of the cavern and the pillar, Dafydd would soon have been hopelessly lost, and even with them he wasn't sure he could easily make his way back to the exit. Usel seemed to have no such problem though, leading them swiftly past an uncountable number of alcoves, each with its collection of jewels, until the colours of the light suffusing the cavern changed. In a pace the red switched to bright white, almost blinding after so long in near-dark.

'This is what a dragon's jewels should be like.' Usel put his hands into one of the alcoves, coming out with a pile of glowing white gems. 'You can touch these, but I'd recommend you don't hold on to any for too long.'

Dafydd picked up one of the clear stones, marvelling at how pure it seemed in comparison to the red ones. Its edges were perfectly cut, though in a complex pattern he couldn't quite understand. Nevertheless it felt right, lying in the palm of his hand with a sense of satisfaction. And then the images began to fill his mind: of flying high above the trees, the wind warm against his skin, the distant line of mountains tipped with white snow that glared in the bright afternoon sun.

'These are ancient, some of the first to be collected here if I read the design of the place correctly.' Dafydd's mind lurched back to reality with such a shock he almost fell over. Looking down, he saw that Usel had taken the jewel from his hand and was placing them all back in their alcove. Such potency was astonishing; he had never felt anything like it before and even now could feel the desire to experience it again creeping up on him.

'What do you mean, the design of this place?' Iolwen asked.

'A dragon's jewels are inherently magical. They focus the Grym in ways you and I cannot begin to understand. To some extent they are the Grym. When they die, dragons are traditionally burned with the Fflam Gwir, the true flame. It returns their earthly form to the land and sets their jewels to this white, pure state. The jewels are taken to a secret place and added to a pile, so that in death they may commune with others of their family or fold. Their shared wisdom and experience is not lost with their physical forms, but carries on in Gwlad. All knowledge is there, for those who know how to access it.'

'This doesn't look much like a pile to me.' Dafydd walked up to the great stone pillar rising to the ceiling high above. It was round, polished smooth and carved with symbols he didn't recognize.

'That's because this place is an abomination. All these jewels are being kept apart from each other by lifeless stone. Bad enough that men have hunted and killed dragons for centuries – longer – but to keep them in this state of living death afterwards . . .' Usel tailed off, as if the horror he was seeing were too much for him to take. Dafydd had never seen the man so agitated.

'We should go,' Dafydd said even as he felt the tendrils of that one white jewel reaching out to his mind. 'There is nothing we can do about this here and now. When the throne is secure and Beulah dealt with, then we can turn our attention to righting this wrong.'

The city of Pallestre was not large, Benfro discovered over the days of his recuperation. He longed to go in search of the mother tree, and each morning when he woke he would have the same conversation with Earith about the journey, but as he grew stronger and ventured out of the house with her, he had to admit anything more than a short stroll was beyond him. The thought of flying left him in cold sweats, his wings were so tender.

'I don't think I'll ever get used to seeing men and dragons together like this,' he said as they paused at a corner of one of the larger squares towards the centre of the city. Awnings in a hundred different bright colours shaded market stalls where men traded food, clothing and all manner of things Benfro had no names for. A few dragons wandered through the crowd, pausing to view wares or chat with the stallholders much as the men and women did. Everything was on a scale somewhere between just a little too large for men and a little too small for dragons, but it seemed to work.

'Dragons and men have always coexisted peacefully in Eirawen. It used to be the same in the north, until Gog and Magog fought their pointless battle.' Earith led the way to one of the nearer stalls, which Benfro could smell sold ginger even before they arrived.

'M'lady Earith.' The stall keeper nodded his head by way of greeting, then did the same in Benfro's direction. 'Sir. Could I interest you in some fine ginger?'

Benfro looked at the man's wares laid out on a wide table under the awning. Wooden pails were piled high with chunks in various sizes and to one side lay a pile of what he imagined must be the root itself, before whatever magical process turned it into the delicious product he remembered so well. Behind the man a stack of large wooden barrels were covered with heavy cloth sacking and chunks of ice. Some of them had taps hammered into their fronts, reminding Benfro of the barrels of wine that had always been a feature of village feasts, even if he had never been allowed to sample their contents.

'Perhaps you'd prefer a sip of the ginger beer? Best brew in all of Gwlad.'

'Really? I'd heard that the best ginger came from Talarddeg.' Benfro wasn't quite sure why he said it, most likely because he wasn't used to conversing with people. The ginger seller gave him an odd look in return.

'Talarddeg? Sir must be a lot older than he looks. Hasn't been a living soul in that city in thousands of years. And you'd be hard pressed to grow anything up in all that ice and snow. Let alone sweet, sweet ginger root.'

'Benfro is not from these parts, Master Boggs. The Talarddeg he knows is very different from the one you may have read about, I suspect.' Earith reached into the leather satchel she had slung around her neck and pulled out a shiny silver disc, offering it to the man. 'We'll have some of your ginger beer though, I think. It's a hot day, after all, and I'm told there is none more refreshing.'

'I thank you for the offer of your coin, M'lady, but I wouldn't dream of taking it.' The ginger seller produced two large wooden buckets from under his counter as he spoke, filling first one then the other from the barrels at his back. 'You won't get finer anywhere. Trust me.'

Earith inclined her head towards him slightly by way of thanks, then reached for the first bucket, passing it to Benfro. 'Don't drink too fast,' was all she said.

Benfro sniffed the slightly bubbling surface of the liquid within, smelling the aroma, familiar but somehow sharper. He took a tentative sip, then a slightly larger gulp as the flavour exploded on his tongue. The drink was cold and refreshing, but the bubbles seemed to go up his nose and make him sneeze.

'Not too fast, I said.' Earith scolded him but with a smile on her face. 'Come. Let us sit a while.'

She led him to the edge of the square, where dragon-sized stone benches were shaded by more of the tall thin trees that Benfro had first seen on the beach. Earith set her ginger beer down beside her before speaking again.

'How strong are you feeling, Benfro?'

'How strong? Perhaps as strong as I was before Magog gifted me with my wings. Not as strong as I was when I fled Corwen's clearing. I'm sure I could walk all day if I had to, but I don't think these wings are up to much at the moment.' He opened them tentatively, stretching them only a little way, expecting the pain to jab into him at any moment as it had done every other time he had tried. It didn't come, but his joints were stiff and the muscles in his back felt the weight on them instantly.

'In my youth I would have healed you much faster, Benfro. Alas, I am old and can no longer summon the energy as once I did.'

'I have no complaints, Lady Earith. Quite the opposite. You saved my life, took me in. I am for ever in your debt.'

Earith looked at him, her head half-cocked to one side in a manner that reminded Benfro of Meirionydd and sent a pang of sorrow through his hearts at her loss.

'Your mother raised you well, Benfro. You are a credit to her. Never lose sight of what she taught you. Too many of the dragons in this world have done that, as you know.'

'Fflint.'

'He is but one example. There are few now who study the subtle arts. We have lost our connection with the Grym, with Gwlad herself. I've felt it for a long time, a slow dying as if our race is coming to an end. But you have changed things, Benfro. You are here when you shouldn't be. And you give me hope.'

Unsure what to say, Benfro took another drink. He followed Earith's gaze, trying to see what she saw in the same way he had tried to see what Ynys Môn saw in the forest when they were out hunting. He looked out across the square, impressed by just how well it had been designed to accommodate both men and dragons. He'd wandered through much of the rest of the city too, and it was all built that way. What he didn't see was many dragons. Lots of men, women and children going about their business, yes. But when they had entered the square there had only been two others of his kind at the market. Now there were none.

'How many dragons live here? In Pallestre?'

'You've noticed. That's something else about you, Benfro.' Earith sighed and the sky seemed to darken a little despite the burning sun overhead. 'When Gog and Magog broke the world, I brought my people here. Men and women as well as dragons. We left behind so much, but there wasn't enough time to do anything other than flee. Over the years we've built something of what we once had. This city is very much like a dozen that used to grace the shores of Eirawen. But we dragons are few now, whereas men increase in number with each new day, it sometimes seems.'

'It was the same in my village,' Benfro said. 'I was the first dragon hatched in a century at least.'

'We have never been as prolific as men when it comes to breeding, but I can remember a time when there were hatchings every month.' Earith shook her head slowly. 'Gog and Magog did something to us when they tore Gwlad apart. Whether they meant to or not, I don't know. But dragons have never been the same since that terrible day. And now it is all unravelling, I fear for us all.'

'Unravelling?'

'Have you not seen it? No, of course you haven't. You're too young. Too close. But some of us remember Gwlad when she was whole, before the split. Something of that is coming back. And it gives me hope, in a small way.'

'I'm sorry, Lady Earith, but I don't understand.'

Earith laughed again. 'You do not need to call me

457

'Lady', Benfro. You of all dragons. Not when you bring me hope. You see, I lost a dear friend recently. A dragon, my daughter Merriel. She flew off to visit the islands of the archipelago, off up to the north, and never came back. She is not dead, I would know it if she were. Instead it was as if she had simply disappeared. I feared she had been carried off by the likes of Fflint, somehow seduced into their way of thinking. Now I suspect I know what has happened to her.'

'She is in my world.'

'Exactly so. The walls between the two are beginning to crumble. You are over here, so she is over there. I suspect others have gone that way too, and more will find themselves in this land. If they are men and they meet the likes of Fflint, then I fear for them, truly I do.'

Benfro remembered the cave where he had slept while with Fflint's fold. The dragon who had lived there before had disappeared over a year earlier. Fflint's father, Caradoc, had gone too. Had they somehow slipped through the veil that parted Gog's world from Magog's? Were they wandering confused in a land populated by men who would hunt them down and kill them? He held up his newly grown hand. 'My world is not exactly friendly to dragons. It was a man who took this.'

'Which is why I asked you if you were feeling strong, Benfro. I fear you will need to be in the coming days, weeks and months. I have put the word out that I would speak with the mother tree, and tomorrow we will go in search of her. The time has come to put right the wrong done to her so long ago.'

25

One chip to slow it
Two chips to still
When both are joined as one the heart shall beat
once more.

The Prophecies of Mad Goronwy

'You wish to petition the queen for more favourable
trading conditions? Tell me, gentlemen, where were you
when the former Duke of Abervenn was fomenting
rebellion in the south? Were you enjoying favourable trading conditions with him?'

Melyn sat on King Ballah's throne, basking in the
power that it radiated. It hadn't taken long for the news
of Prince Geraint's death and the near-total massacre of
his army to reach the city. With no hope of rescue from
Tordu's scattered forces in the south and less chance of
any organized resistance in the north, the people of Llanwennog had bowed to the inevitable and accepted they
were now subjects of Queen Beulah. Some were more
openly cooperative than others, most notably the merchants, who sensed an opportunity to renegotiate duties
now they were no longer trading with a foreign country.
And so here he was, facing yet another delegation of
self-important pompous idiots who thought that just

because he wasn't born of the royal house he couldn't read their thoughts as clearly as if they were written in big letters above their heads.

'Your Grace, Her Majesty the queen is a wise and noble ruler, but even she must realize that this war has cost both countries dear.' An odious fellow by the name of Squiler presented the case for all of them, affecting an easy familiarity that anyone who knew Melyn would have known was a mistake. Perhaps it had worked with the palace major domo, or even someone lower down the food chain, but it was never going to work with him. By the Wolf he wished he had a few predicants of the Candle to hand this work to.

'Which is precisely why I am maintaining taxes as they are. Pray I don't decide they need raising to pay for defences against this new dragon menace.' Melyn could see a weak counter-argument forming in Squiler's mind and pushed it aside with a thought, planted firmly in the minds of all the merchants, that they needed to leave now before things got worse for them. 'Now it is time for you all to go. I have much to do.'

Squiler opened his mouth to speak, then closed it again. He bowed deeply, backed away from the throne through the midst of his fellow merchants, then turned and left, the rest of them scurrying after him.

'They will be back, Your Grace.' Beside the throne, Frecknock had been lying silent during the morning's appeals. It pleased Melyn to watch the faces of the people presenting their cases when they saw her. None had seen the dragons that had torn their army to pieces and he wasn't about to explain that the largest had been ten times

460

her size. Let the citizens imagine that he controlled the beasts, that they were his weapon to use at any time should they become too unruly.

'Alas, this is very true. I can only hope that Seneschal Padraig can send me some of his predicants soon. This bureaucracy gives me a headache at the best of times.'

'Does your wound still bother you, sire? I can look at it for you if you would like.'

Melyn stopped scratching at his chest, only then realizing that he had been doing so. 'No, Frecknock. That won't be necessary. It's healed fine. I cannot fathom why the Shepherd felt the need to remind me so of the creature that struck me in the first place, but his reasons are often mysterious to us.'

'It would be presumptuous indeed to even try to understand him. I am grateful every day only for his continued protection.'

Melyn looked for irony in the dragon's words but could find none. She might once have been a creature of the Wolf, but she was his to command now, as loyal as any warrior priest.

'What do you make of this throne?' He ran his hands over the arms of the great carved wooden chair, feeling the heat of the Grym course through them and into him.

'It is very much like the Obsidian Throne back at the Neuadd, Your Grace. Although more human in scale. I suspect it has a similar function, focusing an unnatural nexus of the Grym and allowing those with adequately trained minds to channel that force for their own subtle arts. Someone attuned to its magics but not as strong-willed as yourself would surely be driven mad by it. Or lose themselves entirely.'

Melyn stood, not because of Frecknock's words, although he could see the truth in them. The throne had a certain quality about it that made it all too easy to let the mind wander. All too easy for it to go so far it might never find its way back. And yet she was right too about the unnatural feel of it. Something powered this throne, and if it was the same as flowed in the Neuadd he had a suspicion he knew what that would be.

'When Benfro appeared here, just before he attacked me, where did he come from?'

'Behind this screen, Your Grace.' Frecknock stood and walked to the carved wooden relief that formed a backdrop to the dais on which the throne stood. 'I assumed he had come here by the same subtle art with which he escaped. Something he should not even know about, let alone be able to perform. But . . . Oh.'

Melyn went over to see what she had found. His warrior priests had checked every inch of the throne room for hidden doors, finding several allowing servants to come and go unseen and one that led to a series of hidden passageways to various royal apartments. No one had discovered anything behind the throne though. Now Frecknock stood beside an archway in the wall that he could have sworn hadn't been there a moment earlier. Stone steps climbed downwards, spiralling out of sight, and a dull red glow reflected off masonry walls, not flickering like torchlight but solid and unwavering.

'I didn't see this before, Your Grace. I'm sorry. It was hidden by the most sophisticated of subtle arts.'

'If what I suspect is down there, then they would have to be. Come, we shall see.'

Melyn set off down the steps, feeling the air thicken around him. He stopped after a while, looked back and saw Frecknock still standing at the top.

'I said come, Frecknock. This is something you should see.'

'Your Grace. It is forbidden. I—'

'Will accompany me.'

The dragon paused a moment longer, then nodded once before treading carefully down the steps. The passageway was just wide enough for her to follow as Melyn led the way. The stairs spiralled deep beneath the castle, into the rock upon which it was built, before opening out into a vast cavern. Pillars cut in the rock held up the high vaulted ceiling, and into each of these had been cut hundreds, thousands, of small alcoves. Every one was piled with glowing red jewels.

A week of walking through the strange forest, and Errol was beginning to wonder if they would ever see the mountains. It wasn't hard going; there was a fairly well-worn track that worked steadily north, deviating only to skirt around the larger hills. They crossed rushing rivers on sturdy stone bridges, well made but clearly ancient. They slept during the heat of the day in caves, under massive rocks tumbled from the hillsides or in the root bowls of the vast trees that spread away in all directions. Walking was easier at night, when the air was cooler and there was less chance of being spotted from above, although neither Errol nor Nellore had seen a dragon since the day the village had been destroyed.

The young girl was fascinated by the jewel she had found in the ashes, so Errol spent the time teaching her all he knew of dragons, their magic and the memories that crystallized in their brains. He taught her of the Grym and told her of the world he had grown up in, though whether she believed him or not he couldn't be sure. It was a good way to organize his experiences in his own mind, Errol found, to begin unpicking the mess Melyn had made of his memories. Nellore was a quick learner too, mastering the art of seeing the lines far more quickly than he had. Perhaps the jewel helped her in that respect, but it didn't seem to dominate her the way the single white stone from Benfro's mother had transformed the young dragon. Neither did it sink its magical tendrils into her like Magog's unreckoned gem. Both of them weighed heavily in Errol's pockets, nestling with the pure glass globe he had taken from Loghtan; he was sure he could hear them calling to him as he slept.

Water wasn't a problem for the first ten days. Nellore's special knife gave them all they needed from the massive-trunked Bondaris trees. As they moved towards the end of their second week of walking though, these petered out, replaced by more familiar stands of oak and beech, huge elms and hemlocks. There were enough streams and rills that they didn't go thirsty, but Errol was all too aware they had no water skins. The food they had scavenged from the ruins of the village had only lasted a couple of days, but the forest provided, and Nellore was well versed in its lore. The further north they travelled though, the less she recognized and the thinner their meals became.

'I'm hungry,' she said as they lay side by side at the base

of a massive tree in the heat of the afternoon on their fourteenth day. It wasn't the first time she had said it either.

'We need to hunt,' Errol said, though in truth he wasn't sure how. And neither had they seen much in the way of wildlife on their journey, though that might have had something to do with their lack of stealth.

'Why don't you just reach out and take what you want? From the lines?'

Errol almost laughed. He'd told Nellore about Benfro, of course, and he'd told Benfro's stories of how his extended family had provided for themselves. What he hadn't told her was the other part of the tale, of how Benfro had only managed to fetch a raw turnip when he'd tried. And Errol had never managed to bring food to himself. Didn't begin to know how.

Except that he did. He'd done it before, reached out along the lines to bring dry clothes from his home back to Corwen's clearing. Only he'd brought the whole chest instead of just the tunic and breeks he was looking for.

'I could try. But I don't know where to start. I don't even know where I am, let alone anything else.'

'Well how do you s'pose your friend did it then? Benfro?'

'OK. Let me think.' Errol shuffled himself until he was sitting upright, his back against the tree trunk. The shade made it easier to see the lines as he conjured up the vision. They were rich here, but static. The place teemed with life, most of it plant based. Only the tiny intense flickers of insects hovering under the canopy and the occasional higher bursts of birds in flight were moving at all. But the lines were all interconnected, the trees and the shrubs and the insects and the birds. And yes, he and Nellore, and the dragons over the Twmp. Everything was joined, all part of Gwlad.

Without realizing he had done it, Errol found himself reaching out into the lines. For a moment he panicked; he knew all too well what happened to people who ventured too far away from themselves. But he could still feel the tree at his back, hear Nellore's soft breathing beside him. Using that centre to focus himself, he pushed out further.

The forest went on for miles, but at the speed of thought it was but a blink to the foothills. Still there was nothing with that spark of intelligence that would suggest domesticity and food. For a moment Errol wondered if he should have gone the other way, to the Twmp, where the dragons lived. But then he'd seen what they ate and how they behaved. He didn't want anything from them. And while Fflint might not have shown much in the way of magic, there was nothing to say some of the others might not sense him, track him down.

Then he started to feel them: thoughts that were not his own. An unmistakable clatter of noise that reminded him of Emmass Fawr. Concentrating harder, he tried to single out one voice, one person. Someone hungry but anticipating they would soon be fed.

Errol had his eyes closed tight, and now he saw as if he was in a dream. Or maybe stumbling through one of the dreadful swirling fogs that occasionally spilled out of the great woods and swamped Pwllpeiran for days. Pwllpeiran! Why hadn't he thought of that? He knew Clun's house like his own, knew the store at the back where the cured meats hung, the barrels of apples were kept. For that matter, there was his own house out on the edge of the forest. His mother always kept a well-stocked larder.

The vision faded, and Errol could feel the ropey bark of the cedar tree cutting into his back. He was losing it, dropping whatever connection he had found. With a last push of effort, he tried to get it back.

And found himself looking down at a pair of hands that weren't his own. Young hands, their fingernails worn smooth and short by hard work. There was something familiar about them. Was this the boy whose mind he had ridden in his dreams? But he wasn't asleep now. So where was he?

As if answering his question, the view changed, revealing a long wide corridor. Stone walls rose into a vaulted ceiling high overhead. More like a great hall than a passageway. The hands reached up for a heavy iron ring set into a wooden door, twisted it and pushed. Inside was an empty room, a long refectory table taking up most of the middle. A line of silver serving dishes sat on a sideboard along one wall, and at the end of them a large piece of roast meat was dripping on to a carving board. Errol could see the glistening fat, the crisp burned skin. He could almost smell it. All he needed to do was—

'What're you doing in here, boy?'

Errol lunged for the roast at the same time as his view changed. The eyes he was borrowing swung round to see a large bearded man standing in the doorway. He felt the meat, hot beneath his fingers. Gripped it tight even as a terrible fear washed over him, sent him spinning back to himself.

'Hey! You did it! Wow!'

For a moment Errol couldn't work out where he was. Who he was. And then he couldn't understand why it was so dark. The sun had set, nothing but shadows under the cedar tree. Nellore was sitting at his feet, cross-legged, no longer beside him though he had no memory of her moving. He could scarcely make out her expression in the darkness and had no idea how hours could have passed in what felt like seconds.

But there was no denying the rolled joint of roast beef burning his hand.

'Malkin going home again. See mother!'

The squirrel leaped from Benfro's shoulder on to the nearest branch, scuttling up the tree and disappearing into the canopy for what felt like the hundredth time since they had left Pallestre. Alongside him, Earith walked with a steady gait that seemed slow but nevertheless ate up the distance with surprising swiftness. Benfro had long since given up trying to talk; it took all his strength just to match the older dragon's pace as she forged a path through the forest. His beating had left him weak as a kitling.

'Do we know where we're going?' he asked, pausing for a moment and resting his arm against a massive cedar. It was the first time in a while he had noticed, but the forest here was quite unlike that through which they had first walked. When had the trees changed, the air cooled?

'The mother tree is where she wants to be, Benfro. You should know that. If she grants you an audience, then we will find her soon enough.' Earith didn't pause, just swept aside the next branch and plunged on into the trees.

Benfro found himself momentarily alone, only the familiar noises of the forest for company. If he ignored the aches and pains in his body and wings he could almost persuade himself that he was back home in the Ffrydd. There were stands of giant cedar not more than a couple of hours' walk from his mother's cottage. These could easily be them. All he needed to do was turn east, listen out for the sound of the river, perhaps pick up one of the deer trails that criss-crossed the whole area. He could go home, and his mother would be waiting for him, a look on her face that was a mixture of scolding and relief. And all this nightmare would never have happened.

'Benfro come!'

Malkin reappeared from the branches of the nearest tree, upside down for a moment, then swinging acrobatically to leap on to Benfro's shoulder. With a weary sigh, he pulled his heavy wings tight around him, stooped low and pushed through.

It was like stepping from night into day.

One moment he was in deep forest, surrounded by ancient cedars reaching skywards and ranging in all directions. The next he was standing at the edge of a vast clearing, the ground dropping away in a gentle grassy slope towards its middle. And there in the centre she grew, the most enormous tree possible, her branches spread wide, each sporting a different kind of leaf, a different kind of life. Confused, Benfro turned back the way he had come. He should have known better than to expect to see the forest he had been walking through. He was several paces into the clearing, and the edge was marked with dense bramble bushes, fat with juicy blackberries and pure white flowers.

'Come, Benfro. Don't dawdle. It doesn't do to keep the mother tree waiting.'

Benfro turned again to see Earith just a few paces ahead of him. He could have sworn she was not there a moment earlier, but then he had been somewhat distracted by the sight of the tree. He nodded, stepped forward to join her, and together they walked down the slope to the great spread of branches. They were almost there when a voice rang out.

'Gog! You came back!'

Benfro stopped mid-stride as a dragon appeared from under the canopy. He was shabby, limped badly on the leg that had been shackled for so long, and his wings were never going to lift his body from the ground, but he had a grin on his face that wasn't the mad thing Benfro remembered.

'The lady said you would be here soon. She is very kind to me, you know.' Sir Tremadog waddled up to Earith and sniffed her much the way a dog sniffs a lamp post. 'You are not the lady.'

'Sir Tremadog, this is Earith the Wise.' Benfro distracted the old dragon before he did something embarrassing.

'Pleased to meet you,' Sir Tremadog said, then wandered off across the grass, stooping every now and then to collect flowers.

'What's the matter with him?' Earith asked.

'He was captured by a circus. They took his jewels out, one by one, to make him biddable.'

'Actually I meant his wings, his size. He's an old dragon but he's barely bigger than a kitling. And he could never hope to fly.'

Benfro remembered the circus arena, Sir Tremadog in his guise as Magog running around in circles, flapping his stubby wings and leaping into the air like a cockerel. 'He is big for a dragon from my world. And his wings are much the same size as most. We are small, drawn in on ourselves to avoid being noticed. Our wings were never big enough to fly, at least not until Magog gifted me with these.'

'Actually they were, Sir Benfro. But Gog played a cruel trick on his brother's kin when the two of them broke the world apart.'

Benfro and Earith both looked up to see the mother tree standing in front of them. She wore the guise of the dragon Ammorgwm, though she appeared aged from the vision of perfect beauty Benfro recalled at their first meeting.

'Lady Earith, it is good to see you again. And thank you for nursing young Benfro back to health. He has a dreadful habit of injuring himself.'

'I suspected you might have sent him my way. Young Malkin only ever visits when you are near.'

'I am always near.' The mother tree smiled, the fine glittery scales around her eyes sparkling in the sunlight as they moved. 'But you are right. I've had my eye on Benfro for a while. He holds the key to undoing the great wrong his ancestor wrought on the land.'

'He . . . I . . . What?' Benfro looked from Earith to the mother tree and back again. Sir Tremadog wandered up, a bunch of flowers in one hand. He seemed perplexed by the presence of two female dragons, holding up the flowers and waving them slowly from side to side as if unsure who he should be giving them to. After a few seconds of this he shrugged, then pushed the whole bunch into his mouth, chewing thoughtfully.

'Let us sit a while, and perhaps eat something a little more savoury.' The mother tree waved, and behind her now there was a table laden with food. Benfro's stomach growled, empty after half a day's trek through the deep forest. He tried not to appear too eager as he clambered on to one of the low benches and cast a hungry eye over the incredible selection on offer.

'To be young and have such an appetite.' Earith smiled as she took her place alongside him more slowly. The mother tree herself seemed not to walk so much as slide from where she had been standing and into her chair. Sir Tremadog, tiring of his flowers, lumbered around to the other side of the table and began helping himself, humming a little tune as he did so.

The mother tree watched him indulgently, then turned to Benfro and Earith. 'Please, eat. You have travelled far to get here, and Benfro needs to build up his strength.'

Benfro needed no second telling. He was perhaps a little less hasty in his eating than Sir Tremadog, but he had a powerful hunger nonetheless. As he worked his way through a plate heaped high with delicious-smelling vegetables, the mother tree spoke, her voice slow and measured.

'You know the story of Gog and Magog, Benfro,' she said. 'You know Sir Frynwy thought of it merely as a tale. Told to warn of the perils of too much power and pride, but a story nonetheless. And you also know that it is much more than that. You know that it is true. What you don't know is the cruel trick Gog played on his brother when the worlds were split. And you, dear Earith, don't know the extent of Magog's evil concerning his brother. Gog gave knowledge of the subtle arts to the men in his brother's world, set them on the path of destruction that has seen Benfro's kin all but wiped out. And Magog sowed the seeds in his brother's line that you see flowering today. The abandonment of study in favour of hunting and feasting. The loss of all connection with the Grym and the subtle arts. These are his gifts.'

'But Benfro is born of Magog's world and yet here he is,' Earith said. 'Surely the magic that tore Gwlad apart is unravelling now. And if what Benfro has told me, if Magog truly is dead, then it can only be a matter of time before the spell collapses completely.'

'Not while Gog still lives. Nor while Magog's jewels spread their unreckoned influence across his world. The two Gwlads will remain apart, but closer than they have ever been. Dragons, men, places long lost. All of these have begun slipping between the worlds, in both directions. I can feel myself, my other self, in a way I've not for millennia.' The mother tree shuddered as she spoke, as if some degenerative disease were eating away at her.

'Are you not the same then?' Benfro paused with a perfect roast potato poised in front of his mouth. 'Not the mother tree I met in the great forest of the Ffrydd? Nor the one who helped me escape from the warrior priests at Tynhelyg?'

'The same, but not. It is hard for me to put into words, Benfro. When Gog and Magog split the worlds, they split me too, for I am Gwlad in many ways. I am incomplete. You cannot imagine what agony that is for me.'

Benfro put the potato back down on his plate somewhat unwillingly. He had some small notion of the pain the mother tree must have endured. Had he not watched helplessly as his own body sorted through the pile of jewels in Magog's repository? Had he not suffered the cruel influence of the rose cord that connected him to the dead mage?

'You have suffered much, Benfro. There can be no denying it. But I have been in this terrible limbo for many thousands of years. And now I can finally see a way to be whole.' The mother tree – or was she really Ammorgwm? – fixed Benfro with a sad, serious look. 'But I will need your help.'

'My help?' Benfro swallowed even though there was nothing in his mouth. All eyes were on him, even Malkin and Sir Tremadog had stopped their self-absorbed feasting and now stared his way. 'What can I do? I'm just . . .'

'You are the last of Magog's line, Benfro. And you are joined to him, joined to his essence more fundamentally even than that.' The mother tree's eyes shifted ever so slightly to that point in his forehead where the rose cord had attached itself to his aura.

'But it's gone. He has no influence over me here.'

The mother tree dropped her stare, let her head droop. 'It is true he cannot reach you here in Gog's world. Not while the Old One lives at least, and not while Magog is so distracted elsewhere. You disrupted his plans when you scattered his jewels from their nest in Mount Arnahi, but the link between the two of you is still there. Even if you cannot see it.'

Benfro couldn't stop himself from reaching up to his face, as if he could touch the insubstantial loop that linked him to Magog. He could see his own aura, healthier now than it had been for days. It flowed around him constantly, pulsing with strength. He could see the lines of the Grym, almost too bright for his aethereal sight in this most magical of places, but of the rose cord he could see no sign. Of Magog's influence he could sense nothing.

'Are you sure?' he asked.

'As sure as anything.' The mother tree waved her arm, in the same instant transforming from the image of Ammorgwm into the slender white-haired creature Benfro had seen once before. The Grym shivered as she moved, as if it lay on the surface of a pond and someone was stirring the water. And then he saw it, motionless where all around was motion, the palest shade of pink in among the blinding white.

'I am sorry, Benfro, but you will never be free of Magog until his jewels are reckoned. Even then something of him will remain with you, but it will have no power over you.'

'Then I have no choice. I must find Gog, persuade him to take me to the place of his hatching. Magog's bones are there. I can breathe the Fflam Gwir. I just need . . .' And then Benfro remembered the one thing that was missing. 'The jewel. I don't have it. Not my mother's either.'

'You don't have them?' A flicker of worry spread over the mother tree's pale face, and the sun dipped behind a cloud, dropping the temperature in the clearing in an instant. 'Where are they?'

Benfro tried to think back past the beating he had taken from Fflint, past losing his hand to Melyn's blade of fire, past the rage that had cleared his mind at the circus and the long weeks he had spent with Loghtan, Tegwin and the crew. It felt like a lifetime ago that he and Errol had fled Corwen's clearing, and then Errol had gone back for the jewels. Errol had taken charge of them, wrapped in cloth and hidden at the bottom of his hastily made bag. But the last time he had seen Errol, watched the boy fade away along the lines to the moon-knew-where, there had been no cloth bag slung around his shoulders.

'I have to find Errol. I have to go back to the village. He was there.' Benfro pushed away his plate, stood up and looked around the clearing as if his friend might be hiding there. With a wave of her hand, the mother tree made the table and all the food vanish, much to the astonished indignation of Sir Tremadog. Earith stood more slowly, her great age showing in that one difficult movement.

'I can take you there, Benfro. But you must realize that your friend is most probably dead. Men have not fared well in Gog's world.'

'No. Errol yet lives, Earith, and he is not at the village where Fflint, son of Caradoc, met his end.' The creature that was the mother tree approached the two dragons, and as she did it was as if the vast tree itself approached too. The canopy of every kind of leaf loomed overhead, blotting out the sun, and the great trunk of the tree swelled and widened even as it drew closer and closer. Then there was just the tree; no strange, thin, white-haired woman, no Malkin, no Sir Tremadog, and when he looked around, no Earith either.

'Where . . . ?'

'They will be well, Sir Benfro. Do not worry for them. Time is of the essence though. I have felt something move in this land that should not be here. You must hurry or we may all fail.'

'I don't understand.' Benfro watched as a line in the trunk split open to reveal a narrow tunnel, rapidly widening. Soft green light spilled out, and he remembered his first encounter with the tree.

'Your wings are still not healed enough to carry you. This is a quicker way to Gog's castle. The last I saw him, the boy Errol was heading that way too. There is something there of great value to him.'

'I should thank Earith and Malkin.' Benfro paused at the tunnel entrance. Looked back. He could see nothing in the gloomy darkness of the canopy.

'They do not think you rude to leave so, and neither do I. Go, Benfro. Find your friend. Together you can undo this terrible wrong.'

Whether there was some compulsion in the words of the mother tree or not, Benfro couldn't tell, but in the end they were not necessary. He could not stay in Pallestre with Earith, could not linger with the mother tree no matter how much he wanted to. He was healed, apart from his eye, and he could see well enough. It was time now to restart his quest. Nodding his head in silent thanks, he stepped into the tunnel.

Thick black smoke spiralled in the air, making some streets all but impassable as Beulah rode through the remains of Abervenn and down to the seafront. She had spent the night sleeping fitfully between bouts of feeding young Ellyn, her dreams invaded by the screams of the dying as the second-largest city in her realm was put to fire and the sword. For too many years Abervenn had been a thorn in the side of the House of Balwen, a place whose citizens looked to the sea and the whole of Gwlad rather than to Candlehall and their rightful ruler. Now it was time to cleanse it and start afresh.

'This is a sad day, Your Majesty.' Captain Celtin rode alongside the queen, a guard of two dozen mounted warrior priests surrounding them and scouting ahead for any potential trouble. So far they hadn't seen a living soul. Not even a cat or dog.

'Sentimental, Captain? You're not an Abervenn man, are you?'

'No, ma'am. Emmass Fawr is my home, and the order is my family. This purge was necessary, but it still pains me to see such destruction.'

Beulah didn't reply. He had a point, after all. They should have been putting Wrthol and Tynewydd to the torch, not their own back yard. And after Abervenn, what would she have to do to Candlehall?'

'Your Majesty, it is good to see you well.'

They had reached the docks, where a large number of ships were moored, unloading an even larger number of men and equipment. Lord Beylin had been allowed to approach through the circle of warrior priests and knelt on one knee in front of the queen's horse.

'Looks like you arrived in the nick of time, Beylin. I don't suppose you've seen my husband anywhere in this mayhem?'

'His Grace the Duke of Abervenn is up at the castle.' Lord Beylin rose, looking up in the direction of the smoking, blackened towers.

'Has he found my sister yet?'

A dark frown spread across Beylin's face. 'She is nowhere to be found, ma'am. The Lady Anwyn is not here either. Only the dowager duchess, old Lady Dilyth.'

'She still lives?'

'As I understand it, yes. The duke had her taken to the barracks. He intends to interrogate her himself once he has finished searching the castle. I believe he has certain skills in that area.'

Beulah allowed herself a small smile. Lord Beylin had no skill at magic himself and was uncomfortable around those who did. No doubt Clun had been completely oblivious as he told his ally how he intended to conduct his search. The smile was short-lived though. Iolwen had escaped, of that Beulah was sure.

'Accompany me, Beylin. I will speak with Lady Dilyth myself.'

Lord Beylin bowed, then turned and shouted to a group of men at the quayside. Within moments his horse was being led through the crowd. Mounted, he fell in beside the queen and together they headed towards the Kingsgate and the barracks.

'I was delighted to hear of the safe delivery of your daughter, ma'am. You must be overjoyed.'

Beulah stared at Lord Beylin. On the face of it, the question was innocent enough, but it irritated her nonetheless. What was it that had changed in her that he felt he could be so familiar? Was it that he had brought men and ships to aid in the retaking of Candlehall? Was it that they had met once before, shared a few meals together? That she had once used his first name to address him? Or was it that the very act of giving birth made her a woman first in his eyes, queen second? She had a suspicion it was this last one, and that annoyed her more than the familiarity itself.

'How went the battle?' she asked, pleased to see Beylin stiffen as he heard the rebuke in her tone. He rallied quickly though; the man was all charm.

'Better than I could have hoped. We sustained minimal casualties, and only a handful of ships slipped through our blockade.' Beylin frowned again, as if this was a personal insult to his skills. 'Your husband is a cunning strategist, ma'am. I don't know who he studied warfare under, but the man is a genius.'

'Clun claims he learned everything he knows about warfare from playing games with the other boys in his village.' Beulah smiled at the thought of all those learned generals with their maps and strategies, pitted against someone who had spent long summers trying to capture another boy's hideout in the woods. 'I suspect he may have picked up one or two things at Emmass Fawr, though.'

Lord Beylin said nothing to this, and they soon arrived at the barracks. A commotion at the far end of the parade ground turned out to be the great Gomoran stallion Godric. The beast had been left untethered, as was Clun's usual practice. Normally it would stand stock still until its master returned, moving only to threaten anyone who came too close, but now it was prancing around in a circle, throwing its head this way and that as if battling faeries.

'Your Majesty. Perhaps it would be best if we kept our distance.' Lord Beylin reined in his own horse a good distance from the stallion, but Beulah pressed on, her filly more excited than fearful. Too late she remembered that it was probably coming into heat.

It made no difference. The stallion was far too caught up in whatever strange battle it was fighting to notice. Beulah watched it as she came closer, beginning to see a pattern to its dance. And then she remembered a cell deep underneath the castle in Beylinstown, a mad predicant by the name of Father Tolley who had managed to hide himself in plain sight. Relaxing gently into the aethereal trance, she saw the scene differently. The stallion still pranced, even more magnificent in this plane, if that were possible, but its movements made sense now, darting and kicking out at another figure. A young man Beulah didn't recognize and yet who had such a strong aethereal presence she could see his features as clearly as she saw Clun's. He was too preoccupied with the horse to notice her, concentrating on not having his head caved in by one of those massive hooves.

Dismounting from her horse, Beulah glided across in her aethereal form. At her approach, the stallion calmed, settling to just a nervous pacing back and forth. The young man, sensing his opportunity, darted to the side, bringing him right in front of Beulah's aethereal self. Only then did he seem to notice her, too late to defend himself. She reached out to his mind, unguarded in his moment of surprise, and turned it off.

'Your Majesty. Are you all right?'

The words were the first thing she heard as she returned

to her body, slumping in the saddle as the inevitable weariness hit her. Shrugging it off, Beulah dismounted, ignoring Lord Beylin's concern as she marched towards the great stallion, now standing perfectly still, its head down and breathing heavily over the prostrate form of a young man dressed all in black.

'My thanks, Godric. That's another one I owe you.' Beulah held her hand out to the beast and it dipped its head to her before scraping a hoof against the hard-packed ground and shaking in triumph.

'Secure this man. Keep him sedated.' Beulah shouted the command to the warrior priests guarding her, none of whom seemed all that keen to get too close to the horse.

Finally Captain Celtin shouldered his way through, marching up with a good impression of fearlessness even though his regular glances at the stallion gainsaid his confidence. He rolled the unconscious man over, pulling his arms behind his back.

'See he is brought with the army to Candlehall,' Beulah said. 'I will interrogate him once we have taken the city and I have my throne back. I grow tired of these so-called Guardians and their secrets.'

26

And the Shepherd went away from his people, meaning to draw the Wolf from its lair. But in his thoughts he was troubled, for the Wolf was cunning and powerful. He had no fear that he could not defeat his foe, only that the Wolf might leave behind creatures of its own foul creation to wreak havoc in its name. And so the Shepherd reached deep into his own chest and drew out his heart, the heart of all Gwlad. And he took his heart and hid it in a place no man would ever find, guarded by forces of wonder and amazement. Then, when he was sure the land was safe, protected by his heart, he set off in search of the lair of the Wolf.

The Book of the Shepherd

Melyn had only taken a few steps across the smooth floor towards the nearest alcoves and their collections of jewels before Frecknock called out to him: 'Your Grace. You must not touch them. It is not safe.'

He looked back to see the dragon standing on the bottom step of the staircase as if she didn't dare trust herself to the floor.

'Do not worry, Frecknock. I have handled many dragon jewels before.'

'But these are unreckoned. Raw. To touch them is to bind oneself to the poor beast from whom they have been taken. Why have they not been reckoned? Why are they all separated like this?'

'Why do you think men have hunted dragons all these centuries, millennia? For their jewels and the power that lies within them, of course.' Melyn walked up to the nearest alcove and took one ruby-red jewel out. It was as big as a hen's egg, but jagged on the edges. It pulsed with a life of its own, random thoughts and feelings jumbled together. True, someone with no skill or training might be entranced by the whirling images, the sensation of flying or deep ecstasy a dragon's jewel could bring, but he knew how to block those parts and concentrate on the raw Grym that flowed through it.

Frecknock finally committed herself to the floor. 'This place is the work of men?' She stepped as lightly as Melyn had ever seen across the shiny, polished marble and peered at the alcoves from a healthy distance. He could feel the fear boiling off her, but it was a different flavour to the terror-panic that she had shown around him and the warrior priests during the early days of her capture. This was a deeper fear, something in her bones. It unsettled him that she could feel this way here.

'Does it upset you, to see this?'

For a moment Frecknock didn't answer, and Melyn had the distinct impression she hadn't heard him. Then she turned away from the alcoves, making sure no part of her body, not even her tail, came within more than a wide pace of the stone pillars.

'It is the most horrific thing I have ever seen. Imagine,

if you will, coming across a hall piled high with the bones of your warrior priests. Knowing that they had all died a slow, terrible death and yet were still in some manner alive. This . . . This is a hundred times worse.'

Melyn placed the jewel back in its alcove, feeling a fleeting sense of panic as he released it. He had handled hundreds, thousands of dragon jewels in his lifetime, but something of Frecknock's fear rubbed off on him then. He dismissed it with a wave of his hand.

'This place is a focus for the Grym, nothing more. The dragons who gave up these jewels are long dead. You have nothing to fear from them.'

Frecknock had turned back to the steps and was looking up at the massive black pillar around which they wrapped. Melyn noticed for the first time the inscriptions carved in its surface, recognized something of the language and the story they told. He had seen something similar out in the northlands, he realized. That old disused chapel in Lord Gremmil's castle. The godless Llanwennogs might have taken over this place, corrupted it to the ways of the Wolf, but it had once been a shrine to the Shepherd. No, more than that. His god had once lived in this place. He was sure of it.

'King Ballah's ring. You have it with you?'

Frecknock looked startled for a moment, then went to the bag she had slung over one shoulder. It had the Llfyr Draconius in it as well as the various magical artefacts that had been found in the palace after Ballah's death. Melyn didn't like to admit it, but he felt they were safer in her keeping than entrusted to any warrior priest. The temptation in them was too great, let alone the myriad curses and enchantments weaved around each one.

'I have it here, sire.' The dragon held out the small box. 'I studied it as you asked. It is a thing of great power, but it is inert as if whatever lies within it is asleep or dead. I cannot fathom it, but I sense no more danger in it than the one you wore before.'

Melyn reached into the pocket of his robe, taking out the velvet bag in which he had placed Balwen's ring. Wearing it for any length of time left him weary, though the power it gave him was intoxicating. Without knowing quite why, he slipped it on to his left ring finger. As he did so the whispering of a thousand thousand voices, the dead dragons entombed in this giant repository, rose up like the threat of a storm. It should have been disquieting but instead was quite the opposite. He knew that all these lives were his, all their knowledge just waiting to be used.

As he reached for the second ring, presented in its tiny wooden box, Melyn noticed his hand trembling slightly. He hesitated for a moment, unsure whether he should continue. But the Shepherd had told him, even as he had healed the wounds on his chest, given him the vigour of a twenty-year-old. This ring was his to command too. And who was he to second-guess the great plan of his god? Soon the Shepherd would return to Gwlad in his true physical form. Melyn wanted nothing more than to be there to greet him.

A shudder ran through him as he took out the ring, raised it close to his eyes so he could study it more clearly. It was so very much like King Balwen's own, gifted to him by the Shepherd, passed down to Brynceri and cut from the belly of the dragon Maddau when it had finally been slain by Ruthin. Had the Shepherd favoured others as well? It made sense, perhaps. If Balwen's task was to unite the Twin Kingdoms, then maybe another had been charged with taking his word to the north. Another who had plainly failed at some point.

Clasping Ballah's ring in his right hand, Melyn felt the familiar touch of his god, and with it came a better understanding of the writings on the great central pillar. The story was familiar, but the arrangement of the writing, more like runes than letters, hinted at something else. Something hidden deep within the pillar itself.

And then he saw it. Encased in the very living rock, protected by a spell woven into the words. The source of all knowledge, the heart of the Shepherd himself.

'Your Grace—'

'Silence, Frecknock. I know what I am doing. I know why I was called to this place.'

Melyn took King Ballah's ring, slipping it on to his finger on the opposite hand to King Balwen's. At that moment the pillar shimmered in front of his eyes, the stone seeming to melt and flow as the heart of the Shepherd oozed through the rock towards him. He reached out, cupping both hands to receive it. As it neared, so the fiery red glow of it grew brighter, matched by the light of the two rings. The blaze was so intense, Melyn had to close his eyes. The heat felt as if it would sear away his skin, but there was no pain. Only the joy of being at one with God. The whole cavern hummed with a low noise like the distant murmured singing of a thousand-strong choir. Ten thousand strong.

As the heart of the Shepherd fell into his hands, he sank to his knees under the weight of it, felt the power surge through him in ever-growing waves. He understood so much, knew so much, remembered so much. The memories of his childhood came flooding back: the great castle with its endless, enormous corridors; the winding stairs to the top of the tower where the likes of him were not supposed to go; the room with its massive windows opening out on to a wide balcony so high up in the sky you could almost believe you were flying; the ancient dragon, so big he scarce seemed to fit in the room, patiently explaining the wonders of the Grym and the subtle arts. Thoughts and images tumbled through Melyn's mind as if it were not him thinking them so much as someone else picking through it all, trying to find out what made him tick. For a moment he understood what Errol must have felt like when he had his memories altered, only Melyn didn't have the luxury of wine to dull his senses.

It all coalesced into a single word, a name, a pinprick point of hatred so intense it could have shattered a mountain. Melyn forced open his eyes as the word escaped from him in a ragged shout. He saw there the truth of it all. And the lie.

'Gog!'

Lady Dilyth of Abervenn had seen better days. Beulah knew a little of her history; the girl who had fled Tynhelyg when her father's family had fallen out of favour with the young King Ballah. Distant cousins of the king, they had embraced the House of Balwen, bringing both court secrets and invaluable trading links with them, and the young Dilyth had found love in the arms of Angor, heir to the duchy of Abervenn. In another world Beulah might have admired her, might have sought her advice on matters of state. She was a strong woman in a world dominated by men, after all. And she had been a good ruler; that much was obvious from the way the people of Abervenn had rallied behind her in their act of mass treason. In another world they might have been friends.

In this world she was a woman nearing her end, and she knew it. She was dressed much more simply than a duchess might be expected to, dowager or otherwise. Her long skirts and dark blouse were the sort of thing the serving women wore, as were her heavy leather boots, speckled with mud and ash. Her old face was creased and blackened with smoke, and there was a swelling around one eye that suggested her capture hadn't been entirely without a struggle. She sat on a stout wooden chair in one of the smaller barrack rooms, no doubt an officer's quarters if the quality of the furnishings was anything to go by. She wasn't bound though; all the fight gone from her.

'Where is Princess Iolwen? Is Lady Anwyn with her?' Beulah stood back in the shadows as her husband asked the questions, probing gently with her mind to see what Lady Dilyth's thoughts betrayed. So far not much; the woman had formidable mental strength and knew how to block out an enemy.

'A very long way from here, Clun Defaid. Both of them.' Lady Dilyth still spoke with a Llanwennog accent, even after all these years. Or maybe she was laying it on thick to annoy Beulah.

'What did you hope to achieve? Inviting Iolwen back here, kidnapping my daughter?'

At this last question Dilyth's guard dropped. Just for an instant, and not long enough for Beulah to sense anything more than a brief flash of surprise. But it was enough.

'She knew nothing about that. I'm guessing she knows nothing about the Guardians of the Throne either.' Beulah came out of the darkness, pulled a chair away from the table in front of the duchess and sat down.

'Oh, I know a great deal about the Guardians, false queen. I just never held much by their prattling nonsense. The Shepherd is a myth, an invention to keep the simple people in line. He's no more coming back to claim his throne than I'm walking from this room alive.'

Beulah had to admit she was impressed. Lady Dilyth was perfectly calm, resigned to her fate. But then she was an old woman; her husband was dead, her son too. Only her daughter remained and was in all probability just as far away as she said. Her heresy was perhaps understandable, Llanwennogs were notoriously godless anyway. Her plain speaking was probably just a means to hasten her end, and the old Beulah would have happily cut off the woman's head for her words. But the old Beulah was gone. Her impetuousness with her.

'So tell me about these Guardians then. Since you're such an expert.'

Lady Dilyth peered through puffy eyes, pausing a moment before deciding to speak. 'You know of Mad Goronwy, I take it?'

'I've read one or two of her doggerel poems, yes,' Beulah conceded.

'You're the cuckoo child in a nest of thieves. At least that's what they say. You should be honoured. Not many people get a poem written about them.'

'Who say? I thought you had nothing to do with them.'

'They come and go. Usually Rams, but the occasional Candle. Never a warrior priest or quaister of the High Ffrydd though. Melyn always was good at maintaining discipline.'

'They know the truth. The Shepherd walks among us. Most are just too blind to see him.' Clun's voice was tight, and Beulah could see he was rising to the bait Lady Dilyth was laying.

'Ah yes. A true believer. You have him well trained, Your Majesty.'

'His Grace the Duke of Abervenn has felt the touch of the Shepherd. He does not have to believe any more.'

'Oh, I don't doubt Master Defaid has felt the touch of something. Candlehall is full of strange magics. But your precious Shepherd? I doubt it.'

Beside her, Beulah felt Clun tense and then relax. 'You seek to taunt me with disrespect for my title, Lady Dilyth,' he said after a while. 'But all you are doing is reminding me I wasn't born to it. It was a gift from my queen.'

'Your queen, yes. I wonder what the good people of the Twin Kingdoms would think about her if they knew half the things I know. How her sister Lleyn really died, for instance. Gallweed, wasn't it? Very hard for a young girl to come by.'

'I think there's little to be gained from continuing this interrogation, if all you're going to do is bring up old gossip about my sister.' Beulah pushed hard at Lady

Dilyth's mental barriers, feeling her begin to struggle. Something gave, and a few images, snippets of ideas started to leak out.

'Half-sister.' The old woman relaxed and Beulah almost tumbled into her memories, trampling around them like a novice. Too late she realized that this was what Lady Dilyth had planned all along.

'What do you mean, half-sister?' Clun asked.

'Did you not know? Why, it was quite the scandal back in the day. Queen Ellyn's dalliance. Oh, there's no doubting old Diseverin fathered Lleyn on her, but he was in no fit state by the time it came to your beloved. Couldn't cope with the throne, poor man. It takes some that way.'

Beulah tried to speak but found herself tongue-tied and horrified as the words came backed with solid images of the court, of her mother still young and alive, of her father still hale and hearty but passed out with drink. And there, in the background, someone else keeping a firm hand on the reins of power. Keeping the Twin Kingdoms together.

'You see it now, don't you, dear?' Lady Dilyth's voice was all around her, and Beulah cursed herself for being so fooled. 'Oh, he rallied, after a while. I've no doubt Iolwen is his; she has his nose after all. You've always taken more after your mother. Well, up to a point. You have your father's temperament, his scheming nature. His eyes too, now I come to think of it.'

'Make . . . Make her stop.' Beulah only whispered the words, but Clun was already there. With the faintest of whispering noises, a slight chilling as the Grym leached out of everything nearby, he conjured a short blade of fire and slid it swiftly into Lady Dilyth's chest, through her heart. Riding her thoughts as she died, Beulah saw one last image. The view through a partially opened door, a spy's view of a familiar bedchamber. She knew it, had visited her father there on the last day of his life. A couple were in the throes of passion there, his strong naked back scarred by some ancient injury. In those final moments Beulah saw her mother sit up, drape an arm around the neck of her lover, caress his chest as he took her again. And then, as the light began to fade and Lady Dilyth's essence was sucked back into the Grym, the man turned side on, looked briefly towards her and winked. His face young but unmistakably that of Inquisitor Melyn.

The beef lasted them three days, supplemented by the increasingly familiar plants and herbs Errol was now finding. The trees were more and more like the great forest back home, and the land began to climb, undulating ever upward into the foothills. They caught glimpses of the mountains beyond, rising grey and menacing against a darkening sky. Bad weather was on its way, winter with it.

'I'm cold. What's happened to the sun?' Nellore sat in the shelter of a rock tumbled across the path from a nearby cliff face. A chill wind had picked up since dawn and the clouds were doing their best to end the day early. Errol wondered if they could chance a fire. It was unlikely they'd attract any dragons this far from the Twmp. Unless there were other groups out there.

'I told you about the Grym, didn't I? Just tap the lines to keep yourself warm.' He'd fallen back on his novitiate training and the earlier foundation he'd learned from Sir

Radnor, but Nellore didn't have the same knack. She could see the lines, was fascinated by them and constantly pointed them out to him. And yet she found it impossible to get her head around using them.

'I'm sick of this place. Sick of walking and walking. Are we ever going to get there?'

'I don't know, Nellore. I don't even know where there is. But it's got to be better than . . .' Errol turned, looking back down the track the way they had come.

'Still cold.' Nellore rubbed at her legs. She wasn't dressed for the mountains, and neither was Errol really, though at least he had his travelling cloak.

'We'll stop here, OK? There's not much daylight left, and I'd rather find somewhere dry to camp before the rain comes.'

'Rain?' Errol wouldn't have thought it possible to put so much despair into one word, but Nellore managed it.

'There's bound to be caves in those cliffs. Let's find one we can use. I'll gather some wood and we can light a fire. I'll even see if I can get us some more food.'

That seemed to cheer the young girl up. They spent the next half-hour clambering over scree and rockfall until they found a perfect spot to camp, tucked into a narrow cave formed by a split in the cliff face. Errol even remembered to check right to the back just in case it was already occupied, then they collected all the dry wood they could find and piled it up far enough back that any firelight wouldn't be visible from afar.

Errol had seen Benfro breathe fire. He knew the warrior priests could conjure flaming blades, knew even how it was done, in theory. But it had been a long day's walk after weeks of the same, and they'd found little food. He knew that if he were to attempt to use the Grym to set the kindling aflame it would go horribly wrong. It was remarkable enough that he'd managed to reach out along the lines and take food before. He didn't think he'd be able to do that again.

He was staring at nothing, wondering how best to go about sparking a flame, when he smelt woodsmoke wafting up through the still air of the cave. Focusing, he saw that Nellore had taken a couple of the smaller twigs and some dried leaves and somehow managed to coax them into fire. He drew up his legs, crossed them over and tried to get as comfortable as the rock and hard-packed ground would allow as the young girl nurtured her flame like a newborn babe, breathing on the embers and feeding them small twigs until they caught. Soon they had a merry, if small, fire burning away.

'At least we'll be warm now. Be nice if we had something to cook on it.'

'Where did you learn to do that?' Errol didn't really want to know; he just wanted to put off the inevitable.

'Da taught me. Course we had drier wood to work with.' Nellore fed another branch to the fire, her face lit up by the flames. Outside had gone very dark with the approaching storm, and the air felt heavy as if it were being squeezed by the weight of the clouds above. Errol was glad of the shelter but worried about being stuck in the cave for any length of time without food or water. They should perhaps have collected more wood too.

'I will see if I can find us some food,' he said after too long an expectant silence. The change in Nellore's expression lightened up the cave and lent Errol much-needed energy. It was hard to be too morose in the company of such simple enthusiasm. 'I'll need you to keep a watch on me and the fire both, mind you. I don't want to get lost wandering the lines.'

Nellore nodded, moving close to where he sat. Errol settled himself back against the rock and stared at the flickering flames, waiting for the lines to come to his vision. It took a while, ignoring the rumbling in his stomach and the occasional chill gust of wind that whipped around the cave. Then, when they finally did swim into view, he wondered how he could have missed them.

For all that the cave seemed a barren place, it was filled with so much Grym the lines blurred into a continuous glowing sheet, covering everything. Nellore was a bright point in the midst of it all, but Errol knew there was no point searching in her direction. He tried to relax, stretching his senses in ways they weren't used to going. He sniffed but not with his nose, listened but not with his ears. The cave was a weave of noise and smell so pervasive it was almost impossible to pick out individual threads. Still he persevered, racking his memory for the exact image of the long corridor with its vaulted stone ceiling, its heavy iron sconces and flickering yellow torches, the huge black oak door that would open on to a room full of food.

The image solidified in his mind the more he recalled of it. Errol tried to remember what it had smelled like, what noises he had heard, the feel of the cold flagstones under his feet. But these were memories of an earlier visit to this place, a different corridor and a wide stone staircase spiralling up. He knew where that staircase led. Up to the top of the great tower and the golden cage where Martha was trapped.

A gurgling spasm ran through his gut, reminding Errol of why he was here. Not that he actually was; he was back in the cave with Nellore, and the time was surely passing swiftly there. He needed to find the dining room, hope there was food there again and hope that nobody caught him this time.

As if in a dream, the view changed from the staircase to the heavy oak door. And then before he could even worry about not actually having any hands with which to open it, he was inside. It was darker this time, but the sideboard still carried a selection of silver platters, their domed covers casting strange bulbous reflections in the half-light. There was no joint of roast meat this time, but a wooden bowl filled with ripe fruit. There was enough to feed the two of them for days, if he could just work out how to get it back to the cave.

Something tugged at him, like a distant cry of alarm. Errol felt himself losing the trance again, and stretched out with invisible hands for the bowl. He thought he could feel something, but the scene darkened, fading away into a whirl of blackness and stars as he crashed back into himself. Such was the force of his return, he jerked his head back, cracking it against the rock of the cave wall. Dazed, it took a while for him to see that the fire had burned low, longer still to notice the bowl, still full of fruit, lying in his lap.

'Well, well, well. What have we here then?'

In his stupor Errol registered that the voice speaking

was male, but he couldn't see who spoke. He was desperately tired, confused and hungry. Too late he realized what a male voice meant.

'Who?' He shook his head, hoping to clear it enough to work out what was going on. And then he saw them, three men dressed in dark cloaks sitting on the other side of the fire. One of them had Nellore held tight, a leather-gloved hand over her mouth to stop her screaming. Errol struggled to get to his feet, tipping the bowl and its precious fruit on to the cave floor.

'Let her go.' His voice was hoarse, throat cracked and dry. Nellore's eyes were wide with terror, darting from his face to a point above his right shoulder and back again. He understood the warning, but he was too exhausted to do anything about it. Too slow. As he turned to see the man standing behind him, the fist connected with his face and everything exploded into blackness.

27

The hall of kings will echo with the screams of ancients.

And a new god will sit upon the twice-spurned throne.

The Prophecies of Mad Goronwy

'The people await, Your Highness. Your people await.'

Prince Dafydd looked up from the desk in the royal apartments where he had been composing a coded letter to send back to his grandfather, but the announcement was not intended for him. Seneschal Padraig stood at the door to the reception room flanked by two Llanwennog palace guards.

'Is it time, then?' Princess Iolwen greeted the old man nervously. She had not brought much in the way of formal wear on their travels, and she had not fancied borrowing any of her sister's clothes. In the end they had found a room full of dresses that must have belonged to her mother, and then Iolwen had closeted herself away for days with an army of seamstresses, trying to decide what would be most appropriate to wear in front of the people of Candlehall and then altering and cutting. The dress she had finally emerged with was stunning, but she didn't look comfortable in it. Dafydd could only sympathize; he wasn't too keen on formal wear himself. This was the hard part of being a ruler. Living up to the expectations of the people.

'It is, ma'am. Would you like me to accompany you?' The seneschal shook gently as if he was frightened, but Dafydd knew it was not fear. He was an old man, close to his end. Perhaps another reason why he had been so ready to cede control of the city to them.

'That won't be necessary, Padraig. This isn't a coronation. I am not queen. Go and see to the preparations. It cannot be long before my sister comes back for her throne. We need to be ready and well stocked for the siege.'

Padraig nodded, the relief evident in the lines of his old face. He turned away, walking somewhat more briskly from the room than at his arrival. Dafydd almost laughed.

'Let's get it over with then.' Iolwen held out her hand to him, and Dafydd escorted his wife from the room. Guards went on ahead, and they were followed closely by yet more, even though the palace had been checked for potential assassins. Usel was never far away, though the medic often disappeared from view, flitting from shadow to shadow as he double-checked their route. After the death of Captain Pelod, no one was taking any chances with security.

Their route took them through the cloisters where Jarius had died, and Dafydd felt a pang of loss for his old friend as they passed the spot. The air seemed colder here too, as if the death were imprinted on the stones and the captain's ghost haunted the open walkway. He shook away the superstition, concentrating on the great bulk of the Neuadd, rising above them all in impossible splendour.

Those huge oak doors were open as they approached, and Dafydd could sense the thoughts of hundreds, maybe thousands of people within. He dropped back a couple of paces so that he was following Iolwen rather than leading her. This was her realm after all, not his.

Conversation buzzed around the great hall as they climbed the wide stone steps to the entrance, but it fell to hushed, expectant silence the moment the first guard crossed the threshhold. A little behind her, Dafydd watched as Iolwen was swallowed by the shadows, and a moment's panic swept over him. Then he too was inside, eyes adjusting to the scene.

It couldn't have been the entire population of Candlehall, but it felt like that many people thronged the hall. A wide aisle had been left for them, leading straight to the dais upon which the Obsidian Throne sat empty. Dafydd remembered the cavern deep below their feet and the panic rose again. What if the floor collapsed, plunging them all to their deaths? It was foolish, of course. Just the effect of being in such a crowded space, the sense of anticipation that hung heavy in the air.

Iolwen paused just over the threshold as if she too was having difficulty accepting the reality of her situation. Their plan had always been to make sure their son, Iolo, was born in the Twin Kingdoms, to cement his claim to this throne in later years. Neither of them could have anticipated that they would get this far, achieve this much.

'Leave me. I am safe among these people.' Iolwen dismissed her guards, who obeyed despite their obvious trepidation. Then she walked slowly up the aisle to the dais. Dafydd followed but kept well back. She would invite him up once she had claimed the throne. For now he would stay just close enough to help should trouble arise. Relaxing his mind and feeling out across the collected audience the way his grandfather had taught him, he sensed that trouble was unlikely, at least for now. These people were rapt, their anticipation of something wonderful almost palpable. It didn't say much for Beulah that her sister's return could be greeted with such enthusiasm.

Like the steps to the door, those that rose to the dais were low and wide. Iolwen took her time climbing them. If Dafydd hadn't known her better he'd have said she was milking the moment, but it wasn't showmanship holding her back so much as fear. She stopped in front of the great throne, stared up at it, her head tilting slowly back as she looked all the way to the top of the ornately carved back. Then, even more slowly, she turned and faced the crowd.

'I was only five years old the last time I saw this place. My mother had just died and my father thought it would help foster peace with our neighbours to the north if I was sent to live with them.' Normally Iolwen's voice was quiet, but something about the acoustics of the Neuadd and the power of the throne behind her made it sound as if she was standing right in front of Dafydd. He looked around and, judging by the expressions on the faces close by, the effect was the same for everyone present.

'Despite what you may have heard to the contrary, the people of Llanwennog are friendly, peaceful and warm-hearted. I was welcomed at King Ballah's court, treated as an equal and raised as if I were his own daughter. I won't say it was easy, but I grew to love them, and one of them won my heart.' Iolwen held out an arm towards Dafydd, beckoning him to her. He felt the heat rise in his face as all eyes turned to him, but there was no backing out now. Climbing the steps to stand beside her was more difficult than any part of their journey all the way from Tynhelyg.

'Prince Dafydd is second in line to the throne of Llanwennog, and he is also my husband. The father of my son, Prince Iolo. One day, perhaps soon – I certainly hope soon – our two nations will be one and we can stop this petty warring.'

That brought a cheer from part of the crowd, which spread around the hall to become a chant of 'Queen Iolwen! Queen Iolwen!' which went on for quite some time, until Iolwen herself raised both hands and called for quiet.

'I am not queen. My sister is queen. And I cannot take this throne from her just by sitting on it. I will not sit on it.'

Silence filled the vast expanse of the Neuadd as a thousand people held their collective breath. Dafydd wanted to ask what she was doing, but one look at Iolwen's face stilled the question in his throat. She had seen what he had seen, deep beneath their feet. And she knew the history of the Obsidian Throne, how it had driven kings mad. Her fear of it was obvious, but it wasn't that which was keeping her from climbing the steps cut in the black stone up to the uncomfortable seat. It was one thing to sit in a chair, no matter how big that chair was, quite another to rule a kingdom.

'My sister has forfeited her right to rule the Twin Kingdoms by waging unnecessary war. Let me end that war first, and then I will take this throne and all the responsibilities that go with it. Until then let no one sit upon it.'

Iolwen's words echoed across the Neuadd, falling away to nothing as the crowd took in what she had said. And then a lone voice near the back started a chant: 'Iolwen! Iolwen!' It didn't take long for everyone to join in, the volume rising to uncomfortable levels. Dafydd took his wife's hand and squeezed it tight, drinking in the adulation like the most intoxicating of fine wines. This audience wasn't exactly the whole of the Twin Kingdoms, but it was evidence nonetheless that she had solid support. Her sister was not loved anywhere near as much.

Something crashed to the ground outside with a force that rattled the massive, jumbled windows and cut the chant off like an executioner's axe. The palace guards at the doors ran outside, well trained to the last. Everyone in the great hall heard their screams. Then the huge doors were shoved aside, and in that instant Dafydd finally accepted that it was dragons who had built the Neuadd, that the scale of the place was entirely appropriate for their size. The creature blocking all the sunlight from the doorway loomed over the crowd like a giant surveying a meeting of pygmies. It opened its mouth, unintelligible sounds spilling forth in waves so loud they could have shattered glass.

And then the screaming really started.

'Your Grace, the men are getting restless. Winter approaches, and they want to know if we are staying here or moving back to Emmass Fawr.'

Three days since he had discovered the cavern

underneath King Ballah's throne room. Three days since he had held the heart of the Shepherd in his hands and understood a truth too horrible to admit. Three days since he had either eaten or slept, and Inquisitor Melyn was still in no mood for company.

'Are they not trained warrior priests, Osgal? Are they so lacking in initiative they cannot find tasks to keep themselves occupied? Are you so lacking in leadership skills you can think of nothing either?'

Captain Osgal had been standing at the foot of the dais, his head at Melyn's waist height, bowed slightly as was only proper in the presence of his inquisitor. Now he climbed the shallow steps until he was on the same level as the throne, forcing Melyn to crane his neck.

'Sir, you are not yourself. You sit here for hours on end with no one for company save this . . . this dragon.' Osgal indicated Frecknock with a dismissive sweep of his hand. She was lying curled up beside the throne, but raised her head as he spoke. Melyn reached out a hand and patted her between the ears. Sooner or later he would be angry. That was how he should have been reacting, a part of him knew. He'd been waiting three days for it to come now, but all he felt was a vague annoyance. The mindless chattering presence of all these people in this city was like a swarm of flies he couldn't bat away, buzzing around his head when all he wanted was some peace and quiet, time to take in all that he had learned and decide what he would do about it.

'Frecknock has proved her loyalty beyond doubt, Captain. She has saved my life many times, saved all of our lives in the forest. Even yours. Are you forgetting that?'

'No, sir.' Osgal choked the words out as if he would

rather eat his own shoes than admit any kind of debt to a dragon.

Melyn almost laughed at the irony, letting out something more like the bark of a kicked dog instead. The captain stood up straighter at the sound, taking it as a rebuke.

'I will tell the men to barrack themselves for the winter, sir. Start allocating some administrative work. I take it we won't be seeing any predicants of the Candle soon, with the situation at Candlehall?'

Melyn found it hard to concentrate on the captain's words, hard to concentrate on anything much at all. But the man just stood there, looming over him like some giant mindless oaf, waiting for an answer.

'What? Oh. Yes. Organize them, Osgal. And I suppose you'd better start vetting the Llanwennog administrators too. We'll need them to run things eventually, and I doubt we'll be seeing any Candles soon, as you say. Now leave me. I have much to think about.'

Osgal looked for a moment as if he was going to speak, then thought better of it. He nodded briefly, making a half-hearted salute with his fist, turned and left. It was some distance to the great double doors that opened out into the main reception hall, but the captain disappeared into the gloom long before he reached them. Melyn had ordered the windows shuttered, the only light in the whole room emanating from his two rings and the single large red stone sitting on one arm of the throne. The heart of the Shepherd.

'Is it wise to treat your men so, Your Grace? They need your leadership now, more than ever surely.'

Melyn picked up the heart stone, feeling the weight of

it in his hand. Closer to King Balwen's ring, they both glowed brighter, the ruby light spreading over Frecknock's dull grey scales and turning them so black she almost disappeared. Only the twin orbs of her eyes reflected back the power that swelled in the room.

'Did you know?' Melyn asked. 'Have you been laughing at me all this time?'

Frecknock's eyes widened in fear. 'No, Your Grace. Never. I don't even know now. Not fully. This jewel means something to you, but I don't know what.'

'This jewel.' Melyn lifted up the stone. It was as big as his closed fist, heavy like solid glass and roughly shaped. It might have looked a bit like a heart, or like a squashed ball that had been chipped away in a couple of places. 'Interesting choice of word. You think it a jewel. A dragon jewel no less.'

'Is that not what it is? I know it is huge, larger than any I could imagine, but it was down there with all the others. Almost as if they were there to protect it.' Frecknock's confusion was as plain to Melyn as her thoughts. She had no idea that he could read her so clearly now. The rings and the heart stone made everything so easy, at the same time as they softened his rage.

'You're right, of course. It is a jewel, and it has come from a dragon. One of the mightiest ever to walk these lands. It is also the distilled essence of the Shepherd. My god. His eternal presence in Gwlad, you might say.' Melyn twisted the stone this way and that, inspecting it for flaws. The more he saw of it, the more he understood. The two rings, one for King Balwen, one for some distant, ancient ancestor of Ballah, had identical crimson gemstones in them; both skilfully cut from this larger jewel, fashioned so that even an adept such as he would think them born of the deep earth rather than grown in the brain of the very beasts he had dedicated his life to eradicating. And yet they had been a bond, linking every inquisitor since Ruthin to the heart stone hidden deep beneath Tynhelyg. No wonder he had always felt drawn to the place, jealous of the race of men that lived here.

'I . . . I do not understand, sire.'

'No. I don't suppose you do. And neither do I. At least not yet. Tell me, Frecknock. How did Errol slip away from us, vanish in front of our eyes? How did Benfro leap from this very throne into nothing?'

Frecknock's eyes were transfixed by the heart stone now, like a dog taunted by a tasty morsel. Melyn could have waved it around and her gaze would have followed, her head swivelling from side to side as if she were on strings. Instead he placed it back on the arm of the throne and waited for her answer. In among the maelstrom of his own thoughts and everything the stone had unlocked in him, he knew what it would be. Easier to let her tell him though.

'It is one of the most complex of the subtle arts, Your Grace. Few master it completely. I have told you how we can reach out along the Llinellau Grym and bring things to us, food and so on? Well this is similar, but instead of bringing things to us, we go to them.'

'We? You can perform this magic yourself?'

Frecknock bowed her head. 'Only over the shortest distances. I have to be able to see my destination, know it like I know the scales on the back of my hands.'

'And yet Errol Ramsbottom managed to travel from

King Ballah's execution block a few hundred yards from here all the way to my private chapel at Emmass Fawr. Somewhere he had never seen before. How is this possible?'

'For one such as he, it should not be. Even if he knew how to step into the Llinellau, he would surely end up dissipated over the whole of Gwlad.'

'Could Benfro have taught him?'

'Benfro?' Frecknock's eyes widened and her gaze finally shifted from the heart stone to Melyn. 'Benfro is only a kitling. He hardly mastered the hiding spell before . . . He couldn't even manage to see the Llinellau when Sir Frynwy and Meirionydd were trying to teach him. But . . .' She fell silent, her eyes dropping away from his.

'But what?'

'There was his dreamwalking, sire. That puzzled even Sir Frynwy. He shouldn't have been able to do it. Our dreams are when we are at our most helpless and vulnerable. And yet Benfro walked them as if he had been born there. He didn't even know how.'

A memory stirred then: Queen Beulah noticing a dragon form flying around Candlehall in the aethereal. Melyn had encountered it himself, recognized the dragon Benfro had become. That dragon had breathed fire at him too.

'So Benfro walks the aethereal in his dreams yet lacks the skill to see the Grym. He is a kitling of just seventeen years but can fly like no other dragon. He breathes fire that burns only what he wants it to, as poor Captain Osgal found to his cost. How do you suppose he has learned to do all these things in only a year?'

'I cannot say. Even Sir Frynwy couldn't do these things, and he was over a thousand years old. And he had the Llyfr Draconius to help him.' As if she anticipated his asking for it, Frecknock pulled the heavy book out of her shoulder bag and handed it to him.

Melyn took it, feeling the weight of more than leather and parchment and ink. The knowledge contained in its pages had its own destiny, tugging at his mind and adding to the chaos of thoughts and images bubbling away just under the surface. Only the mental discipline from all his years in the Order of the High Ffrydd kept him from going completely mad. And that same mental discipline would help him bring order to it, claim it all for his own. His entire life up to this moment might have been built on a lie, but Melyn knew an opportunity when he saw one. He laid it across his lap and took up the heart stone once more, feeling the heat build within it.

'Who do you suppose wrote your precious Llyfr Draconius?' he asked of no one in particular. A face seemed to swim into view in the red-tinged darkness, the ancient dragon who lived at the top of a tall tower in a vast castle. Somewhere Melyn knew but didn't know.

'It is said to have been begun by Gog, Son of the Winter Moon, though many others have added to it down the generations. I've always believed Gog to be a myth though, like Arhelion and Rasalene, Palisander of the Spreading Span and Ammorgwm the Fair.'

With each name Frecknock spoke, so Melyn saw another dragon's face in front of him. Some old, some young, but all vast and magnificent. In his long life he had hunted and killed their kind almost to the edge of extinction, but never had he seen any as majestic as these. Nor had he understood the rage and hatred of their kind that had driven him to do so. It had just always been that way. Until now.

'They all existed, long ago. All the tales are true. It's the ones they don't tell you that are more interesting though. The acts of petty jealousy, greed and lust. I thought us men were bloodthirsty, but we are amateurs compared to your kind.'

Melyn stood again, suddenly anxious to do something. Or possibly just to dispel the ghosts of long-dead dragons. The turmoil in his mind was settling down now, his new understanding of Gwlad and his place in it beginning to make sense. And as he examined that sense, that place, so his old friend anger began to heat up.

'Here, take this.' He handed the Llyfr Draconius back to Frecknock. 'Show me how you use the lines to travel. It needn't be far, but I want to watch you.'

'Of course, Your Grace.' Frecknock nodded, putting one hand flat on the cover of the book for a moment before tucking it back into her bag. As she did so, Melyn summoned the trance state that would let him see the aethereal, bringing the lines to his vision at the same time. There was a brief instant when Frecknock appeared to him as she saw herself – a far more pleasing shape even he had to admit. And then that form was leached of its vibrant colours, becoming the same hue as the Grym itself. There was the briefest of hesitations, then the dragon dissolved in front of his eyes, reappearing a few dozen paces across the room. First as her ghostly Grym outline, then solidifying into her mundane self.

'Again,' Melyn commanded, and he watched her perform the trick once more.

'Again. And again. And again.' He studied closely as Frecknock performed like a well-trained dog. And then finally, when he was sure he knew what she was doing, he reached into the Grym, concentrating on the spot where she now stood halfway across the throne room, and stepped forward.

'Your Grace. How is this possible?' Frecknock caught him as his knees buckled. He was close to her, too close, and the smell of her was strangely intoxicating, her cradling arms strong as they wrapped around him. It brought back yet more memories, the life before he came to Emmass Fawr that his initiation into the order had all but obliterated. Still seeing the aethereal and the Grym, Melyn shook himself free of her with greater reluctance than he expected, turning back to face the throne some twenty paces away. He had crossed that distance with a thought, but it wasn't the first time he had done that.

'When Benfro escaped, did you see which way he went?' Melyn scanned the edge of Frecknock's thoughts as he asked her the question, seeing her memory of the event in a blur of motion and concern. Concern for her own safety, for his, and yes, for the young dragon as well. Even though she had despised him all his short life, still she had not wanted to see him dead. He could understand that, up to a point, but it didn't help his rising temper. All his life he had been lied to, manipulated by her kind, but it went back to that first, great betrayal.

'He was moving towards the throne, Your Grace. I think he saw something there. It all happened too quickly.'

Melyn pushed out with senses he couldn't put a name to, feeling the lines and the power of the Grym coursing through them. There was a flavour to their ebb and flow, like the smell of the cold stone corridors in the depths of the monastery, the river as it flowed past the great rock upon which the Neuadd was built, the trees in Ruthin's Grove. And there, above the throne, was a different scent. As if someone had opened a window on to another world. Tantalizingly familiar.

And then he noticed the heart stone, sitting on the arm of the throne. It glowed with a fiery light, echoing that of the two rings on his fingers. Melyn felt a familiar surge of power, and the Shepherd was within him. Only it wasn't the Shepherd at all. He tried to push it away, but it was far too late for that. It had been far too late for most of his life.

Stepping away from Frecknock, Melyn flowed into the Grym and was gone.

'Damn it, where is he?'

Beulah woke herself from the aethereal trance, coming back to her real body with a snap that had her leaping out of her chair as if she'd been stung. A quick look out the barge window showed that the sun was low in the evening sky. She had been searching for Inquisitor Melyn for hours, pushing further and further into the unknown, driven by an insatiable need to know the truth. Haunted by the dying image Lady Dilyth had planted in her mind.

A soft gurgling cry told her what had broken her trance. Young Ellyn was awake and would need feeding. She wasn't a bad child, really. Quiet most of the time, almost diffident in her requests for feeding and cleaning. Clun doted on her in a way that made Beulah almost jealous, but the queen herself couldn't feel the same stirrings of unconditional love. Not for the first time on their journey she mourned the loss of the wet nurse Blodwyn and hoped that a new one could be found soon.

'You may enter.' Beulah sensed the hovering presence of her maidservant, another from the Hendry, though not as competent as Alicia. The door opened hesitantly, and the girl shuffled in. She curtsied nervously, then went straight to the baby's cot. Beulah was about to complain that she hadn't closed the door when it pushed open further and Clun stepped through.

'No luck, my lady?'

'None. It's as if he has closed his mind off completely. And all this damned water doesn't help.'

Beulah looked through the window again, watching the grassy bank slide by. Lord Beylin's barges were much swifter running up the river than they had been creeping around the coast to Abervenn, but it had still taken them several days, held back by the bulk of the army still travelling on foot.

'I'm sure he's fine. If anything had happened to him we would have heard by now. I'm certain he isn't dead; I'd have felt that. All the warrior priests would have felt that.'

Beulah thought about reminding Clun that he was not a fully trained warrior priest, but in truth his connections to the Grym and the aethereal were so strong he would likely have been the first to feel something like that. She was distracted from commenting by the maidservant, bowing nervously and presenting the newly clean Princess Ellyn.

Beulah took the infant, wondering how long it would take for her to feel anything but mild annoyance at the child, then shrugged open her blouse and let her feed.

'We have some news at least. Birds from General Otheng. His troops have secured Tynewydd, so the Rhedeg pass is open. He is waiting for confirmation from Cachog on the situation at Wrthol, but the last he heard, Prince Geraint had turned back to Tynhelyg.'

'And that's meant to make me feel better?' Beulah shifted, trying to find a position that was comfortable and failing. 'The larger of Ballah's two armies is heading his way and Melyn has only five hundred warrior priests to defend a city?'

'He has no need to defend it. He can just retreat into the northlands, cut around behind Geraint's men and march south through either pass.'

'Do you think Melyn would turn and run like that? That's not his style and you know it. And he's changed too. Somehow he's more powerful in his magic than ever before. You felt it, didn't you? When he dragged you into the aethereal.'

Clun frowned at the memory. 'The dragon, Frecknock, has taught him something of their subtle arts. But there is more, as if something is standing behind him, pushing him ever further.'

'The Shepherd?' Beulah's skin tingled at the thought of it. She remembered the night Clun had come to her possessed by his spirit. The night Ellyn had been conceived. As if sensing her change in mood, the infant stirred at her breast, opened her eyes and let out a tiny wail. Beulah lifted her up, stared at her tiny face and those impossibly black eyes. Was she marked by the Shepherd for great things? Would she rule over a united Gwlad?

'Shall I take her, ma'am? Little un's probably full now. She never takes all that much.'

Judging by the pain in her nipples, Beulah had to disagree, but she handed her child over to the maid anyway, swiftly rebuttoning her blouse. She was getting to her feet when a sharp knock at the cabin door broke the silence. Clun was there in an instant, putting himself between it and his daughter rather than his queen, Beulah noticed.

'Enter,' she said.

Lord Beylin stepped into the room, ducking slightly to avoid hitting his head on the low lintel. He took in the whole of the cabin with a swift sweep of his head before bowing extravagantly.

'Your Majesty. We are approaching the lower docks. My scouts inform me that the River Gate is down and the upper docks sealed. Too much to hope we could have entered the city that easily.'

'They've prepared themselves for a siege this time? I'd have thought that coward Padraig would be throwing himself upon my mercy. Anything to protect his precious city from harm.'

'Is it not your city, ma'am?'

'It was, Petrus. And it will be again. And I'm not going to let the people go unpunished for their treason.'

28

Many have speculated on the original craftsmen who built the Neuadd, atop Candlehall Hill. In design, architecture and construction it is markedly different from the buildings that surround it, even the ancient walls of the city and the King's Chapel. And yet it is clearly much older even than these.

Then there is the scale of it, and that of the great Obsidian Throne within. Although many generations of the House of Balwen have sat upon it, the throne is clearly not designed for any man to occupy. In many respects it diminishes the king, making him appear small, detracting from his regal appearance.

In looking for answers, it is necessary to find comparable structures, and the closest still in common use are the great religious houses. The monastery at Emmass Fawr is of similar construction to the Neuadd, and has rooms that overwhelm the senses by their vast size in much the same way. And here is a clue as to the true purpose of the Neuadd and the Obsidian Throne – awe.

This is the Shepherd's hall. By its vastness the primitive people who laboured on its construction were reminded of just how insignificant, how unimportant they truly were. And at the same time the great throne, visible from every corner of the enormous hall, reminds the visitor that however insignificant they may be, they can always be seen. The building is thus a metaphor for the Shepherd himself.

Father Soay, *An Architectural Tour of the Twin Kingdoms*

A cold breeze rustled the dying autumn leaves in Ruthin's Grove, toying with Melyn's hair as he stood at the edge of the cliff and gazed across the forest of the Ffrydd. To the casual observer he might have appeared a statue, so still was he on the outside. Inside was another matter.

The Grym flowed through him like nothing he had ever known before. It soothed away his aches and pains, healed old injuries he had long since grown accustomed to. It nourished him and brought him information from all over Gwlad. He could sense the thoughts of the novitiates and quaisters in the monastery nearby. Picking an individual was as easy as tuning into a conversation in a crowded hall, but he was not interested in their petty, everyday lives. Everything they stood for was a lie anyway. Now he remembered. Now he knew.

Other thoughts babbled close by, the stable hands, workmen, cooks and a hundred different professions who kept the monastery working. Outside it, the village that had grown up in the shadow of the great arch muttered contentedly to itself at the approach of evening and the end of a hard day's work. Only the almshouses where the mindless failed novitiates lived were quiet. No thought there, just empty husks waiting to be fed and watered and cleaned, as if that was somehow kinder than just putting them out of their misery.

With a single step Melyn was outside the long stone building that served as the almshouses' central refectory. Anywhere else the complex would have seemed big, but against the massive hulk of the monastery the buildings looked little more than doll's houses. Inside, upwards of a hundred men would be sitting patiently in their chairs. Soon the youngest novitiates would come out from the monastery to tend them, feeding them thin gruel before taking them back to their beds. He wasn't here to see any of this, could scarcely bring himself to care. He knew so much more about the Grym now it was hard to feel sad for people who had lost their minds to it.

The door was locked as usual; most of the inmates were catatonic, but a few had been known to wander around, aimless as cattle and just as destructive. Melyn pulled on the stout rope that rang the bell, waited patiently for it to be answered. All his life he had chafed at the slowness of others, their slowness at learning, slowness at responding to his commands, slowness at understanding his skill and acknowledging his superiority. Now he knew better, understood just how unimportant time was. His anger still burned bright, but it was controlled, directed. In time he would unleash it, and the whole of Gwlad would tremble at his fury.

'Your Grace? I thought . . .' The man who opened the door was dressed in the plain brown robes of a novitiate, but he was older than the inquisitor by many years. Few who had been candled by the order remained in its service; most slunk home with heads low or moved far away to build new lives for themselves. One or two in each generation hung around, maybe hoping for a second chance, and every so often they might be given it, although they would never again set foot inside the great monastery. Tending to the mindless was considered a high honour, although Melyn couldn't begin to understand why. Wiping another man's arse was not something he would undertake.

'That I was away? That I might not survive? I would have thought you knew me better than that, Eifion.' Melyn pushed past the old man into the entrance hall of the building. The smell that confronted him was at once familiar and dreadful, the stench of soiled bodies and rot. He headed straight for the door that would take him to Eifion's office. The air would be slightly clearer there, away from the mindless.

'No, sire. Of course not. I just hadn't heard the warrior priests returning. Normally the noise echoes from miles out. Not that these old ears are up to much these days. None of us is getting any younger.' The old man shuffled along after Melyn, complaining all the while. He closed the door firmly behind them, then went straight to a low sideboard where a tray held a jug and a couple of goblets. 'Wine?'

'The army is still in Tynhelyg. I came here alone.' Melyn took the offered drink, savouring the smell of it before slaking his thirst. How Eifion managed to get hold of the good stuff was anyone's guess, and it had been a while since the inquisitor had drunk anything as fine. 'I needed to see you.'

'Me? Why?' The old man slumped into his seat behind

the untidy desk that sat by the only window in the room and took a drink from his own goblet. Melyn felt the stirrings of his old anger at the overfamiliarity and suppressed it. True, Eifion was no longer a member of the order as such, but even so he should have shown a little more deference. Then again the old man had known him longer than most.

'I have some questions. About how I came here, how I joined the order. My family before that.'

Melyn saw Eifion's eyes widen in surprise, rode that sensation into the old man's thoughts. It wasn't as if he needed to use subtlety; the man was an open book.

'Your Grace, surely the order is—'

'The only mother and father I will ever need. Yes, I know. I also know the order was founded to serve the Shepherd, to defend Gwlad from the creatures of the Wolf, to prepare for the time when he would come and take us to the safe pastures. Yes, Eifion old friend, I know the scriptures and I know they're bunk. So, tell me about my family. Tell me where I came from.'

Too late the old man tried to put up a fight. He was hopelessly outclassed, no better than a wet-behind-the-ears novitiate. Worse even, with his brain addled by age and wine. Melyn's questions brought the images, the memories, to the front of his mind. So easy to read, so easy to see. But far from the relief he craved, the release from the madness, Eifion's answers only compounded it.

'They brought you to me. The villagers. Said they'd found you walking in a daze near the edge of the Faaeren Chasm. Reckoned you were a novitiate who'd lost himself to the Grym, maybe escaped from here. But you weren't like the others, and you were too young to be a novitiate. Your mind had wandered out along the lines, but you came back. Took a while – weeks, months. I've been tending the mindless eighty years now and I've never seen one of them come back. Except you.'

As Eifion spoke, so Melyn saw the memories, faded at the edges with time. The north fields, strewn with boulders and pocked with the occasional scrappy tree, marching towards the edge of the precipice that plunged a thousand feet into the chasm. And there, on the other side, the southern flank of the Rim mountains. It was a vista he knew well, one he had seen almost every day of his adult life, and yet now it felt wrong, incomplete. As if something had taken a vast swathe of the land and ripped it away.

'And no one ever knew where I'd come from.' It wasn't a question. Melyn tightened his grip on the old man's mind, digging for any hidden secrets. The sour-sweet smell of urine suggested to him that he might have been a bit less brutal about it, but the inquisitor found he no longer cared. Eifion was a failure, had always been a failure, and the kindest thing to do would be to put him out of his misery.

'Farewell,' he said and stopped the man's heart with a thought. His ancient frame slumped in his seat, tilted forward and knocked over the goblet. Red wine spilled across the chaos of papers, dripping to the floor to mingle with the piss.

Melyn cast his mind out further, sensing nothing. Only the empty husks of the mindless remained in this place, and that suited him just fine. With a single step he was standing in the main hall, staring at them as they sat motionless in their chairs. The teaching of the order had it that the mindless were in service to the Shepherd, that they had gone to join him in his fight, but it had always been accepted that they were kept alive as a warning to novitiates not to try and run before they had learned to walk. Melyn knew it was also guilt on the part of the quaisters and senior members of the order. They had let these young men down, maybe chosen unsuitable candidates or not paid enough attention to their charges. They were a constant reminder of the need to try harder. They were an abomination.

The ball of fire he conjured was not large, but it burned with a heat as hot as any furnace. Ancient wood caught swiftly, filling the hall with thick white smoke. None of the mindless moved. Not even as the flames licked at their feet, caught their clothing and singed their hair. They would not be mourned or missed.

A memory tugged from Eifion's mind came to him as he stood in the hall, listened to the crackling flames. Again Melyn saw the view from the northern fields where he'd been found wandering and mindless as a boy. A blink and he was there, gazing out across the chasm as the first few stars pierced the deep blue evening sky. He couldn't recall being found, only slowly coming to life in the old alms-house now burning merrily a mile behind him. But this was where it had happened. This was where it had started. Melyn looked around, his mind seeing the aetheral even as his eyes saw the mundane, and layered over everything the lines of the Grym. There was something about this place, this spot, that tugged at him, called him. Focusing on a patch of sky, he could make out stars that were different somehow to those he had known all his life.

Then he saw it, silhouetted against the darkening sky, a tower taller than the highest mountain. The sight of it sent a shiver through him, not of cold or fear, but of joyous recognition. A single word formed on his lips.

'Home.'

And then the floodgates opened in Melyn's mind, the mental blocks of a lifetime dissolving with dizzying speed. His memories returned with a force that would have rendered a lesser man senseless, but he stood firm against the deluge, letting it wash over him, around him. Letting it fill him completely. He knew then what had happened to him, how he had ended up at Emmass Fawr, how he had been touched by a god and then discarded like some unwanted plaything. Well, he was a god now too, and his vengeance would be sweet indeed.

'Your Highness, take my hand.'

Prince Dafydd was still transfixed by the dragon standing in the great doorway to the Neuadd. It was twice the size of the one they had seen in the islands, its head bigger than an ox cart. It wasn't attacking, didn't need to really. The people were doing far more damage to each other trying to escape than one dragon, however large, could ever hope to achieve.

'What is it?' Dafydd heard the idiocy in his question even as he asked it.

'It's a dragon, Dafydd. A bloody big one.' Usel's normally calm demeanour had vanished, replaced with a calm urgency. 'Now I think it would be best if we left.'

'I cannot.'

Dafydd and Usel both looked to the princess, who stood tall, staring at the creature that had gatecrashed her homecoming.

'Iol—'

'It's not attacking us. Please, Usel. You have to speak to it. Find out what it wants. I will try to calm everyone down.'

Dafydd took a moment to understand what Iolwen was saying. His instinct, Usel's too, had been to hide, escape. But Iolwen was more concerned with the safety of the panicking crowd than herself. He felt both humbled and ashamed.

'Use the throne. Calm them,' she said to Dafydd, then turned to Usel. 'You speak Draigiaith. Tell me what that creature is saying.'

Her words galvanized them both into action. Dafydd reached out for the throne, feeling the power of the Grym that surged through it like nothing he had ever experienced before. It was intoxicating even from a distance; how much more so would it be to sit on the thing? He shook away the question, concentrating instead on smoothing out the waves of panic surging through the crowd. There were smaller exits on all the other sides of the Neuadd, and already people were fighting to get out. Most were heading for the north doors, so he sent out a suggestion pointing out the other exits. Groups of terrified people started to break off from the main crowd, and soon they were flowing out through all three sets of doors. Only he, Iolwen and Usel stood on the dais, their backs to the great throne, and Dafydd couldn't help but notice that none of the panicked people clambered up on to it. No one even ventured on to the first of the low, wide steps.

'Who are you, little man, to wield the subtle arts with such skill?'

Dafydd froze as the words boomed in his head. Slowly he looked up at the dragon, still standing in the main doorway and gazing down on the mayhem its presence had sparked. Beside him, Usel was shouting in that guttural, glottal language he had used with Merriel back on the island, but the dragon seemed to be ignoring the medic. Then it shifted its gaze, eyes the size of cartwheels fixing on Dafydd himself.

'This place. What is it? Who built it?' The voice in his head spoke Llanwennog, or at least that was how it seemed to Dafydd, and the compulsion behind it was enough to weaken his knees. He could no more refuse to answer than stop breathing.

'This is the Neuadd. Home to the Obsidian Throne. Seat of the kings of the Twin Kingdoms.'

'It has the smell of the Old One about it, even if it is overrun with vermin. You would do well to leave before the rest of my fold arrives. Some of them like to hunt your kind for sport.'

This time the dragon's words came with an overwhelming urge to flee. Looking around, Dafydd could see that most of the people had left the great hall, just a few walking wounded still struggling to get away. Usel had given up his shouting and was standing perfectly still, staring up at the dragon as it lumbered slowly into the Neuadd. Turning his head, Dafydd saw that Iolwen too was transfixed by the beast.

'We have to go.' He reached out and took her by the hand, his touch breaking whatever spell held her in place. Iolwen shuddered as she came back to herself and nodded her agreement.

'Usel. We must leave here. There are more coming, and they aren't as friendly as this one.'

The medic made no sign of having heard him, so Dafydd grabbed him by the arm, pulling him away. They could go round the back of the Obsidian Throne and head for the west entrance, except that Usel resisted, his eyes still fixed on the great beast.

'Can you not hear him?' he asked, his voice dreamy.

'I can, and he suggested we leave.' A wave of fear shivered through Dafydd far more potent than anything his tutors in magic had ever managed to instil. Across the almost empty hall, he saw the last of the injured scrabbling to escape, dragging themselves towards the doors. Only one or two figures lay crumpled and still. 'Come, Usel. Now.'

Dafydd pulled harder at the medic's arm, and eventually he let himself be dragged away. Almost as if Usel had been single-handedly keeping the dragon at bay, the great beast pushed further into the Neuadd as they backed towards the west doors. It reached a point midway between the main doors and the throne, reared up on its hind legs, head reaching almost to the ceiling, spread its wings and let out a deafening roar. Dafydd didn't need to pull the medic any more. All three of them were running as fast as they could as the great stained-glass windows erupted outwards in a million lethal shards.

Outside, the courtyard was chaos. People stumbled

around, covering their ears, screaming for help, running from the glass, which had flown as far as the cloisters and beyond. Dafydd's ears were still ringing from the noise so the whole scene took on a surreal edge. Part of him wanted to stop and help, but he had to get the princess to safety.

'What's the quickest way back to the royal apartments from here?' He shouted the words, but they still sounded flat and distant. Usel cocked his head to one side, shook like a dog trying to get water out of its ears, then reached out and took Dafydd's hand first, then Iolwen's.

'I'm sorry for the intrusion. I would not normally do something like this without asking first, but the circumstances . . .' His words tailed off and only then did Dafydd realize that the medic was talking directly to his mind.

'How . . . ? No, that's unimportant right now.' He mouthed the words, hearing them only in his head, but Usel and Iolwen seemed to hear him fine. 'We need to get to safety.'

'Agreed. But I'm not sure the palace complex will be any safer than the Neuadd. Not when Sir Morwyr's friends arrive.'

'Sir Morwyr? How do you know his name? Have you seen this beast before?'

'Not here, sire.' Usel pulled the two of them towards the cloisters. They cut through the milling masses, somehow always managing to be avoided even though no one gave any indication of seeing them. Usel must have been hiding them, Dafydd reasoned. He was happy enough to be led, though his heart went out to those less fortunate. Panic could be cruel, and many of the people who had come to see the princess take her rightful place on the throne would likely not last the day. Maybe not even the hour.

They ducked through the cloisters at a run, kept up their speed down long corridors that finally ended in the palace kitchens. Only then did Usel finally let go of their hands.

'Why did you bring us here?' Iolwen asked, ignoring the startled looks from assorted cooks and serving girls.

'My apologies, Your Highness. This is the quickest route to the royal apartments if you don't mind taking the servants' stairs. Given the circumstances, I think it wise to get to Prince Iolo as fast as possible.'

'Lead on, Usel. But I must speak with Seneschal Padraig, muster our forces as quickly as possible. This is no forest dragon wandering in confused. That creature flew here, and it was powerfully magical.'

'I suspect it was drawn here, though from where I don't really want to speculate right now. Come this way.' Usel led them to the far end of the kitchens, where a door opened on to a narrow plain corridor. Dafydd grinned at the flustered cooks, bowing and curtsying at the sudden appearance of royalty. He had spent much of his childhood hanging around in kitchens not so different from these. They were the warm beating heart of any palace.

'One moment, Usel.' Iolwen stopped them before they could leave, turning back to the collected kitchen staff.

'There has been a terrible accident up at the Neuadd,' she said. 'People are hurt, some grievously so. It's still dangerous so I won't ask any of you to go up there, but please boil water and make preparations for the wounded. I will talk to Seneschal Padraig as soon as I can find him. Please don't be alarmed.'

There were long moments of silence, as if none of them had ever been spoken to by a princess before. Then a grey-haired old woman pushed forward. She wore a heavy sackcloth skirt, her blouse sleeves rolled up past her elbows, and looked like she had made enough bread in her life to feed the entire Twin Kingdoms.

'It will be done, Your Highness,' she said in an accent so thick it was almost impossible to understand. Then she turned her back on them and started barking orders.

'Your sister would never have given a thought to the injured,' Usel said as he led them along the corridor and up a flight of narrow winding steps that opened on to the end of the main corridor of the royal apartments.

'My sister would most likely have engaged the dragon in combat, Usel. I've never had much talent for that kind of magic.'

They hurried along the corridor, back to the rooms they had left only hours earlier, arriving just as Seneschal Padraig appeared from the other direction.

'Your Highness. Prince Dafydd. You are safe. Praise the Shepherd.' The old man was puffing as if he had run all the way from the Neuadd, but he hadn't been at the ceremony. Did he even know what had happened up there?

'You have heard the news, Padraig? This changes everything, you realize. We must send for warrior priests straight away. We cannot fight this creature.'

Dafydd looked up in surprise at his wife's words, his own confusion matched by that of the seneschal.

'Warrior priests? Send for them?' Padraig paused a moment to catch his breath. 'But they are already here. At the gates.'

The first thing he knew was cold. Errol shivered in his sleep, reached out instinctively for the warming flow of the Grym and found . . . nothing. The shock of the discovery jolted him awake, and he jerked backwards with a snort of inhaled breath. His head hit rock, starring his vision and sending jabs of pain down his neck. He lifted a hand to feel the lump he was sure was there, and that was when he noticed the chain.

It hung from a seamless iron bracelet around his wrist, too tight to slide off no matter how hard he tried. Errol lifted his hand up to his face, the better to examine it in the poor light, only he couldn't raise it close enough.

'Don't want you escaping on us now, do we?'

Errol looked up as he heard the voice, only then starting to take in his surroundings. His thoughts were strangely sluggish, his predicament dawning slowly.

'Where—'

'No questions. No speaking unless spoken to. Them's the rules, unnerstand?'

He was in a cave, but not the cave he'd been in before. There was no fire burning merrily at his feet for one thing. This place was damp and cold, and it smelled really bad, like rotting eggs and dog mess. And there was no sign of the Grym anywhere. Try as he might, Errol couldn't see the lines. It reminded him of the deep cellars at Emmass Fawr, where he'd helped Usel the medic carry out his examination on dead Princess Lleyn.

'I said them's the rules. Unnerstand?' The words came with a sharp pain in his leg as someone kicked him. Errol shook his head to dispel the fog that was making it so hard to concentrate. He saw a face leering at him out of the semi-darkness, pale and round with a wisp of straggly hair growing out of the top of an otherwise bald pate. The man wasn't so much dressed as wrapped in swathes of heavy material, dark brown and stained down the front, frayed where it scuffed the rocky ground.

Errol opened his mouth, but wasn't able to speak before the man kicked him again.

'No speaking, right? Mister Clingle, he don't like the new grunts speaking.'

Errol nodded and his head throbbed.

'Gets up then. Work to do.' The man tugged on Errol's chain, pulling him so that he had no choice but to comply. His legs almost gave under his weight, the cave swaying alarmingly. He put out his unchained hand to steady himself, but scarcely had time to brush the rock with his fingertips before he was being dragged stumbling towards a narrow, low doorway, the darkness beyond it made deeper by the smoky torches burning either side. Sharp pain cleared his thoughts a little as he banged a shoulder into the doorframe, but his captor merely laughed and kept pulling him onwards.

The tunnel went on for ever, or at least that was how it felt. Errol still couldn't quite get his thoughts together enough to work out how he had come to be here, or indeed where here was. There was something missing too, but the pull of the chain on the bracelet around his wrist was impossible to ignore. He shivered at the cold, trying to wrap his cloak around himself with his one free hand. Something weighed it down, but before he could feel in the pockets to see what it was, he tripped on the uneven floor and tumbled head first into a large cavern.

Laughter rippled around the space, echoing in the ill-lit darkness. Many voices, but not much mirth. It was more the noise of men happy to see someone else suffering. Errol pushed himself up from the floor, noticing as he did so that the smell was much worse here. His hands came away sticky, caked in a thick dark ooze that stank so badly it made him retch. The insistent tug on the chain stopped him from investigating further, and all he could manage was to wipe one hand on his cloak.

'Take.' The man who had dragged him down the tunnel handed Errol a long-handled shovel.

'Dig.' He pointed at the ground where Errol had just lain.

'Fill.' He pointed at a wooden cart on four solid iron wheels nearby. It had a metal hoop on one end, shiny where it had been repeatedly rubbed by something. Errol watched as the man took his chain and clipped it to the hoop. 'When it's full, push it up there and empty it on to the pile. Then start again.'

Errol slowly started to take in his surroundings. The cavern was huge, disappearing into darkness high overhead. It was a little warmer in here, but the smell made breathing almost impossible and really didn't help his muddled thoughts. He stood at the edge of an enormous pile of the same sticky dark material that had covered his hands, the source of the smell. His wasn't the only cart; there were dozens of them, each with a man attached to it by a long iron chain. Some were busy shovelling, a few had stopped to stare at him. They all looked thin and weary, faces sunken around their eyes and cheekbones. Most were wrapped in layers of rags like the man who had dragged him here, though a few shivered in thin tunics and breeks.

'Get on with it then! The lot of you. Back to work!' The shout came with a kick that sent Errol sprawling into the muck again. And that was what it was, muck. He couldn't be sure what animal had made it; something that ate meat rather than the more pleasant offerings from the horses at Emmass Fawr he'd helped shovel out in his pre-initiation days at the monastery. The middens there had been huge, but the endless mountain of dung here made them look tiny by comparison.

'Ten loads, then you can eat. I'll be counting.' The man shoved Errol hard between the shoulders, leaving no doubt as to how things were going to work from here on. Still confused, his thoughts whirring in the chill, fetid atmosphere, he set about his task.

'You are aware that there's a bloody great dragon laying waste to the Neuadd right now?'

Dafydd followed Seneschal Padraig back along the corridor towards the main palace reception rooms. He had left Iolwen with Usel to go and see that Iolo was safe. He suspected Usel was going to try and persuade the princess to pack some belongings and flee the city before it was too late – if it wasn't too late already. He also suspected Usel wouldn't have much luck with that. Iolwen was not one to change her mind easily, nor to back out of a fight.

Padraig stopped at the entrance to the king's waiting chamber, a worried frown creasing his elderly face. 'I'm sorry, Your Highness. Did you say dragon?'

'Yes, dragon. And I don't mean the sort of creature we have in the circus back home. This thing flew in. It barely fits through the doors.'

As if to emphasize the point, a loud thud like a distant clap of thunder shocked the air around them. Swiftly followed by another.

'But I . . . The army . . . The queen!' Padraig flapped his hands like a man who's accidentally pissed on his fingers, then set off across the room to where a set of tall glass windows opened on to a balcony. 'The queen!'

Dafydd shook his head. The man was obviously losing it. But he was also moving at considerable speed for his age, still muttering 'The queen' under his breath. Padraig reached the windows and flung them open at the same time as something vast swooped past them. It cast a fleeting shadow over the balcony and the seneschal jumped back in surprise.

'By the Wolf! What is that?'

Dafydd caught up with him, keeping back from the open window until he was sure it was safe to step outside. The balcony was to the front of the palace, looking out over the parade ground beyond and then down the hill over the rooftops of Candlehall. Behind him, he knew, the buildings climbed to the Neuadd, but it was the view out over the city walls to the plain below that caught his breath and snatched it away.

He had assumed most of Beulah's army would have marched north through the Rhedeg pass from Tochers to

Tynewydd, not wanting to get caught in the pass by the winter snows. A small force could have laid siege to Candlehall, keeping them locked in and using up their supplies over the cold months, before mounting a more serious attack in the spring. Instead she appeared to have brought her entire army back with her and was even now preparing siege engines to pound the walls.

'How is this possible?' Dafydd whispered the question under his breath, unaware that Seneschal Padraig had joined him on the balcony.

'Lord Beylin has brought men and barges from the Hendry. Duke Glas has sent more men too. They took Abervenn just a few days ago. Sailed upriver. Your Highness, I am so sorry. I had hoped only for peace between our nations.'

Dafydd ducked as something vast swooped overhead. A gust of wind followed, threatening to knock the seneschal off his feet. He spun round and looked up, saw not one but five dragons, each as big as the creature Usel had called Sir Morwyr. They circled the Neuadd, snarling and biting at each other, play-fighting like gigantic crows. Occasionally one would swoop low over the buildings, raking slates from roofs with outstretched talons. His ears still rang from his earlier close encounter with the dragon, but as they cleared, so Dafydd could begin to make out the sound of screaming.

'In the Shepherd's name, where did they come from?' Seneschal Padraig's voice was very small as he made the sign of the crook across his chest. 'What do they want?'

Dafydd stared in horror as one great creature clawed its slow way up into the sky above the Neuadd, clearly carrying something in its huge claws. Then with a great sweep of its wings, it let go of its trophy. Arms and legs flailing in the air, some poor palace guard tumbled screaming to his death. Before the figure could hit the ground, it was caught in the air by another dragon, tossed around like a mouse being played with by a cat. Dafydd turned back to the seneschal, unable to watch any more.

'I don't know. But I think Beulah's army is perhaps the least of our problems.'

29

One city will falter
One city will burn
One city will suffer
For the old gods return

The Prophecies of Mad Goronwy

It didn't take long for the tunnel walls to turn from wood to stone, neatly carved and locked together with joints so tight they barely needed mortar. Benfro felt the ground beneath his feet change from grass to loam and then to smooth cobbles as he walked towards a distant pinpoint of light. It began as green, sunlight filtering through summer leaves, but with each step so it brightened to a harsh white. The temperature dropped too, his breath escaping from his nostrils in great steaming gouts as if there was a fire in his belly. At least he felt warm inside, filled with the mother tree's food and protected by her blessing. Still there was much in what she had told him that was troubling.

Benfro couldn't have said at what point the tunnel stopped being anything to do with the tree and changed into something entirely dragon made. It wasn't really important, although when he noticed the roof arching ever higher above him he turned once to look back at the warm grassy clearing where he had started, only to see a dark stone corridor leading into black. No going back now, he had no option but to press on.

By the time he reached the end of the tunnel, he already knew where he was going to find himself. Benfro looked out across the flat open expanse between the great outer wall and the buildings of Gog's castle. Far distant and seeming to climb into the clouds, the central tower was even more impossible in reality than it had been in his dreamwalking state. And Benfro was sure this was no dream. He was here now, in flesh and scale and wing, not a hundred paces from the spot where he had dropped Ynys Môn's jewels. How long ago had that been? It felt like years, though scant months could have passed.

Snow covered the ground where before there had been grass. It hid the paths, and the nearby ornamental ponds showed only as indentations in the ground, which was otherwise perfectly flat and white. There was little chance the jewels would still be where they had fallen, or that they had ever been there given he had been dreaming when he had lost them. Still, Benfro walked across to the spot he thought was right. It wasn't easy to judge. He was seeing the place from a new perspective – he had never landed in his dream – and yet he was sure now he was here, building the image in his head in the same way his mother had taught him to remember the herb store back home. His one eye noted the position of the outer wall in relation to the nearby buildings and the distant tower, and his blind eye layered the Grym and the aethereal on top of that vision, painting a history of what had happened here – the living creatures that had passed by and left some measure of themselves upon the fabric of the world. The Grym flowed through this place with a single-mindedness he had not encountered before, everything converging towards a single point. Benfro didn't have to look up to know where that point would be.

And then he noticed, just off to one side, a subtle bend in the lines. A junction where he would not have expected one to be, it had a familiar feeling to it but one he couldn't fathom. Like the softest hint of a smell can trigger a memory of something long forgotten. He hurried to the spot, brushed aside the snow until he reached the neatly trimmed grass beneath, then parted the sward with fingers that shook more in trepidation than cold to reveal the tiniest of pale white jewels nestling against the frozen soil. Without his strangely enhanced sight it would have been just another ice crystal, oddly shaped but not so unusual for that. And yet Benfro knew better. He plucked it from the ground with something akin to reverence, balling his hand around it in a tight fist.

'Benfro? Is that you?' Ynys Môn's voice floated into Benfro's head. It was weak, distant, as if the old dragon was a mile away, shouting into the wind.

'It's me,' he whispered and saw the great forest of the Ffrydd surround him in his memory. He had just run like a mad beast after a deer, bringing it down by hand despite the bow hanging at his back. His friend and mentor and perhaps the closest thing to a father he had ever known was standing nearby, grinning at his idiocy. Soon they would make camp for the night, settle down to food and stories.

'I can't see anything. Don't know where I am,' Ynys

Môn said, and the memory burst like an eyeball pierced by a talon. Benfro clutched the jewel so tight he could feel it dig into his palm. He scanned the ground, using all his senses old and new to find more of his old friend, but there was nothing. And then he sensed something else, something threatening.

'Well, what have we here? An intruder.'

They spiralled out of the sky like massive black snowflakes, three great dragons that Benfro recognized as the ones who had attacked him in his dream. Their true forms were larger even than their aethereal bodies, larger even than Fflint. They were older too. The biggest of them landed just a dozen paces away, dark as the night and with no discernible pattern to his scales in the flat white light of the snow. He swept the ground with a final arc of his wings, sending up a fine flurry of powder that hung in the air between them like a threat. Benfro knew him then for certain, recognized the dragon he had encountered in his dream. Reflexively his hand went up to his chest, feeling for the scratch across his scales that wasn't there.

'Do you lot never learn? You are not welcome here.' The great beast folded his wings tight, the bony joints rising high above him as he spoke. Benfro was aware of the other two coming in to land behind him, taking up positions for an attack.

'I don't know who you mean by "you lot".' Benfro lied. He knew perfectly well who they took him to be, but he also knew he could not fight them. 'I am Sir Benfro, son of Sir Trefaldwyn of the Great Span and Morgwm the Green. I have come here seeking Gog, Son of the Winter Moon.'

Something like fire flashed in the black dragon's eyes as Benfro spoke the name of Gog. He heard the other two take in simultaneous sharp breaths.

'How dare you speak his name? How dare you even set foot in his castle?' The black dragon advanced on Benfro, who stood his ground. He should have felt afraid, he knew. He'd almost died in his fight with Fflint, lost his hand to Melyn, succumbed to Tegwyn and Loghtan without even realizing he was being attacked. This huge beast could rip him apart, and the two behind him weren't much smaller. And yet all he felt was calm. Any doubt as to whether he was in the right place, whether Gog was still alive, had evaporated at those words.

'I dare by right of birth,' Benfro said. 'And in the name of Magog, Son of the Summer Moon.'

If naming Gog had enraged the black dragon, naming his brother seemed to plunge the whole castle into a deep freeze. Everything stopped. Even the wind, whistling about the crenellations and around the distant tower, fell to nothing. Silence blanketed the world like newly fallen snow. And then a low growl, so deep Benfro could feel it in his legs, rose from the black dragon. His breath steamed out of his mouth as he crouched in readiness to spring, wings half-opening, talons extended. Behind the beast Benfro watched the aethereal doubles of the other two dragons inch closer. Deep in his own stomach the flame began to grow. He would use it if he had to; he hoped that he wouldn't.

'I will kill you where you stand for uttering—'

'You will do no such thing.'

The voice slammed into Benfro. He was battered by it,

his knees buckling under an impossible weight. The black dragon clearly felt the same way, cringing like a kitling scolded. Benfro looked up to see another dragon circling as he descended. He landed with considerably less grace than the others, sending snow in all directions and shaking out his wings before walking slowly up to the group.

'Have you become so like your feral cousins you treat all visitors this way, Enedoc?' The black dragon abased himself even further as his master passed him, and Benfro finally saw what he knew he would see. The newcomer was old. As old as Earith perhaps. Maybe even older. He wasn't as large as Enedoc, but he had more presence. His aethereal form was so overwhelming Benfro had to avert his blind eye.

'You are Gog.' The words were foolish, but he said them anyway.

'And you are Sir Benfro. I've heard a lot about you.' The ancient dragon held himself erect and peered down his long nose at Benfro as if he were some curious specimen found under a rock.

'You . . . you have?'

'Indeed yes. Mostly from your friend Ynys Môn. A fascinating dragon. Such insights. I take it you found his last jewel there.' Gog nodded towards Benfro's fist. 'It would have been better if you'd not dropped them in the first place, but given the circumstances of your arrival, I think it can be forgiven.'

'Is he all right?' Benfro clenched the tiny jewel harder.

'All right? My dear Benfro, he's dead.' Gog let out a long wheezing laugh that ended in a cough. 'Dear me, this cold doesn't agree with my old lungs. Come, let us continue this conversation somewhere warmer.' He turned away, snapping open his wings. Two long strides and he was in the air. Enedoc and his companions leaped to follow. The three younger dragons wheeled away over the first building, while Gog headed straight for his high tower, leaving Benfro alone in the snow as he climbed swiftly. Only when he was halfway there did he slow, wheel in the air, then speed back, landing once more in a cascade of snow.

'Why do you not follow?' Benfro couldn't help but notice the wheeziness in the old dragon's voice, the rapid breathing.

'My wings were damaged. They need more time to heal.'

Gog came closer, cocking his head to one side as he peered more closely. 'Lost your eye too, eh? Out beyond the wall, I take it.'

Benfro nodded. Close up, he could see Gog's great age painted on his features, but he also saw the similarity to Magog. Or at least the image of a dragon in his prime Magog had chosen to project. With his blind eye, Benfro could tell that Gog was well past that. The effort of flying even a short distance had shrunk the magnificent presence, and now the old dragon's joints glowed dull yellow with arthritis, his aura clung to him like a purple miasma. There was a weakness about him at odds with the way he held himself.

'They grow worse with each passing year. Regressing to the mindless beasts our kind were back at the birth of Gwlad. They have no appreciation of the subtle arts, grow no jewels.' Gog indicated Benfro's hand.

'It was your brother's parting gift. His curse to your world.'

Gog raised a grey and bushy eyebrow. 'Indeed? And how could you know this?'

'The mother tree told me. Same as you cursed my world, gave men the magic that killed Ynys Môn. Killed my mother.'

Gog's head drooped, though whether from shame or simple tiredness, Benfro could not tell.

'It has been thousands of years. I am not the dragon I was back then. Nor could I have foreseen the ultimate result of my rash actions. I am sorry, Benfro. For all the good it does.' He shivered again, ruffling his wings against the cold. Even Benfro could feel it now, seeping into his feet. He was surprised to see that the sky was darkening, the sun setting already.

'We cannot stay here all night though, and you can't fly – I can see that much is true. We can't walk; that would take days. It seemed a good idea building this place so big when I was young. I can see I was foolish then.' Gog shook his head, held out a gnarled and twisted hand. 'Come then, we will use the Llinellau. Here, I will help you.'

Benfro hesitated, unsure whether he could bring himself to take the hand that had, in a way, caused him all his troubles. 'I know how to walk the Llinellau Grym,' he said. 'That's how I got here, after all. To your world.'

'Really? And so young? I am impressed. Then you'll have no trouble following me.' Gog withdrew his hand, turned on the spot and vanished. Benfro's good eye barely registered what had happened, but his blind eye showed him the Grym in far greater detail than he had ever been able to see it before. The route the old dragon had taken wasn't hard to see, easier still to follow. And besides, he knew where he was going. In a step he was there.

It was back-breaking work. The dung stuck to his shovel unless he heaped it so high he could scarcely lift it to the wagon. The first load seemed to take for ever, and all the while the stench of the place, the bad air and the mesmerizing pull of the chain on his wrist made thinking all but impossible. Finally when the wagon was almost overflowing, Errol stopped digging, put his shoulder to it and heaved. The iron wheels ran on metal rails that at least made moving it relatively easy once he had got it started. The rails led through a short tunnel to an even larger cavern, and here he was directed to unload the dung over a cliff edge into a bottomless black pit. At first Errol used his shovel to scoop great chunks out of the top of the wagon, but then one of the other workers silently showed him how to open the end and operate a tipping mechanism. It was a small act of kindness in a world of utter and inexplicable misery that earned the man a kicking from the overseer.

'Why . . .' Errol croaked out the word before remembering the warning about speaking. He shut his mouth again quickly, hoped no one had noticed, but the act reminded him of just how thirsty he was, how tired and hungry. Wheeling his wagon back to the start of the rails and the mountain of manure, he looked around for water but saw none. There was only the cavern, its rough stone walls broken by the entrance to the passageway leading back to the room where he had woken. Torches lit small

546

pools of light around the working area, but the space felt somehow much larger. Looking up into the darkness he thought he might have seen something moving, a different shade of black in the torchlit gloom, and then a cry behind him had him whirling in surprise.

'Incoming!'

It was the overseer, the man who had chained him to the wagon. He too had been looking up, but now he ducked and ran for the narrow opening in the rock. A couple of other men not tethered to the line of small wagons did the same. Everyone else simply cringed, some covering their heads with their hands.

'Get down, boy!' It was the man who'd shown him how to unload, tugging at the hem of Errol's cloak, a look of terror in his eyes. Unable to work out anything, let alone what was happening, Errol did as he was told, hunkering down beside his wagon at the same time as he heard a whistling sound echo through the cave. There was an explosion like the wet slap of a giant fist, followed by a wave of air even more foul than that he'd been breathing. And finally a wave of sewage rolled down the heap, far looser than the stuff he had been digging up. It splattered the side of the wagon, rushed around the iron wheels and over Errol's boots. The fresh stench made him gag, but his stomach was so empty all he could manage was a dry heave. Retching made his head spin, and with a sickening sense of inevitability he felt himself toppling forward. He put out both hands to steady himself and sank up to his forearms in warm, wet shit.

He thought he was going to die. Nothing made sense; he couldn't remember how he had come to be here, and when he tried to think what he could remember last, his head hurt even more.

'Right then, everyone. Back to work. Shit's not going to clear itself.' The overseer emerged from the safety of the tunnel, his voice muffled by rags held over his mouth and nose. Errol started to climb back to his feet, but the compulsion in the man's words was less now, his own head a little clearer. The muck covering his hands brought with it something other than heat, the tiniest sense of the Grym in this dark and lifeless place. Instinctively Errol reached out for it, drawing it into him as he had done on those cold lonely nights in the empty dormitory back at Emmass Fawr. He still couldn't see the lines, was certain there were none this deep underground, but the dung crawled with life touched by magic.

'On your feet, boy. There's work to do and you don't eat till it's done.'

Errol's sense of relief was cut short by a sharp blow to the back of the head. Before he had a chance to react, someone grabbed him by the collar and hauled him upright. As his hands sucked out of the dark liquid, so the cold and confusion came back.

'By the Old One, you stink.' Errol's shovel was pushed into his chest so hard he had no option but to take it. He clung to the wooden shaft as tightly as he clung to the feeling of the Grym. It had given him much-needed strength and it had brought back memories: his escape from Melyn's clutches, the villagers sacrificing him to the dragons they considered gods, the long trek north in search of Martha.

'Dig, damn you!' The overseer followed up his barked

command with a swift smack across the thighs from his heavy stick. The pain buckled Errol's knees, forcing him down into the rapidly cooling mess at his feet. Around him a few of the other workers laughed, the sound choking away to nothing as the overseer shouted, 'Get back to work, the lot of you. No one eats till this new fall's cleared, and if that's not done quick enough no one eats at all.' He kicked Errol again, not hard enough to knock him over but hard enough to wind him.

Errol knelt in the muck for a few moments catching his breath before hauling himself back up. He sank his shovel deep, hauling the stinking mess into his wagon. It was still mindless, muscle-tearing work, and he still had a raging thirst, but his mind was starting to clear now, things falling into place. With each swing of the shovel he let his gaze wander over the cavern and the mountainous pile they were clearing. He studied his fellow labourers too, and snatched sidelong glances at the overseer. Watch, learn, plan. If he had learned nothing else from the Order of the High Ffrydd it was that. He would bide his time but stay alert for any opportunity to escape. He had to. Who else was going to save Martha? Who else was going to save Nellore?

The afternoon was turning to evening by the time the royal barge had docked and the horses had been disembarked. Beulah's filly had taken only moments to unload, and was saddled and ready for her in just a few minutes. It was Clun's great warhorse that caused all the delays. It had grown accustomed to being around people in the months since the queen had bought it for him and even tolerated the presence of one or two grooms, but coming off the barge it had been as flighty as a mare with the wind under her tail, throwing its great head around and kicking out at anyone unlucky or stupid enough to get too close. Only Clun himself had been able to calm it, and even then only up to a point.

'I don't know what got into him, my lady,' he said by way of apology for keeping her waiting the half-hour it took to get the beast harnessed.

'Something's spooked him badly. Was there a problem on the boat?' With Clun on his back, the horse seemed to quieten a little, but it still quivered with barely controlled power, sweat shining its black flanks.

'Oh, he's not frightened; Gomoran stallions don't understand the concept of fear. No, he's excited by something. He can smell it, or . . . I don't know, taste it?'

Beulah looked once more at the placid filly, remembering that she had thought it might be coming into heat. But the stallion was showing no interest in her. Just as well, since the thought of being caught between the two of them was not appealing.

'Something's coming? A storm maybe?' She glanced up at the sky, but it was pale and clear, just a few wispy clouds high overhead, some eagles soaring in the distance.

'I don't know. Perhaps a gallop will calm him down.'

'A gallop? Is that wise?'

By way of answer, Clun squeezed his knees into the stallion's flanks, giving it some rein as it moved first into a trot, then a canter. Before she had managed even to get her own horse moving, he was away across the docks at high speed, heading for the road that followed the river's course before it branched off towards the King's Gate. A troop of warrior priests struggled to keep up.

'Perhaps we would be better proceeding at a more gentle pace, Your Majesty.' Lord Beylin led his own grey mare up, mounting with the particular care of a man who has had many riding lessons but little practice.

'I think that is very wise, Lord Beylin. It is good that His Grace the Duke of Abervenn has already fathered an heir to the throne. If he carries on like that he won't live long enough for another.'

The rocky cliffs on the south side of Candlehall reared above them as they rode out through the docks. From here it wasn't possible to see the palace complex or the Neuadd, but as they passed through the trees and out on to the plain, so the city opened up in front of them. Beulah had seen it many thousands of times before, riding out for the day or returning from months spent at Emmass Fawr. It never ceased to inspire her, only this time it filled her with deep anger too. This was her home. These were her people. At the top of that hill was her throne. And yet they had rejected her as solidly as the massive oak doors that closed the King's Gate far ahead of them.

She rode through the busy camp, nodding in silent approval at the efficiency with which her soldiers set about their tasks. Away in the distance she could hear the sound of trees being felled and hammering as the carpenters set about building siege engines. No doubt the warrior priests would try a more subtle method of breaching the walls first, but it never hurt to have a backup plan. If all else failed, there were ways a small force could enter unseen, but she would have to be among them, and she was still regaining her skill with magic. Best to keep that option in reserve for now.

Finally they arrived at the centre of the camp, where a series of command tents had been pitched, ready for battle planning to begin. Godric stood motionless at the entrance to one of the tents. Beulah dismounted a few tens of paces away, not out of fear of the animal but thinking of her page and the rest of the royal retinue. She handed over her reins, then walked slowly up to the stallion. His flanks still glistened with sweat, his muscles tense. He held his neck high, ears pointing straight up.

'What is up with you?' Beulah asked, offering the horse a hand to sniff. He bowed his head towards her, nostrils the size of her palms flaring even wider, and then tossed his head. For a moment Beulah thought she was going to be kicked, all too aware that one blow from those great feet could take her head clean off. But Godric kept all four hooves on the ground, instead throwing his head back and forth as if trying to indicate something. No doubt alerted by the noise, Clun came running from the tent at the same moment as Beulah turned to see what the horse was staring at. What it was trying to fight, she realized.

'By the Shepherd.' Clun's voice was almost a whisper and all the more frightening for that.

Beulah's eyes tracked up the great steep hill of Candle-hall, past the slate roofs of the merchants' town houses, past the palace complex and up to the huge edifice that was the Neuadd itself. The eagles she had spied earlier were circling it, swooping and diving over the city. Only they were far too large to be eagles. Far too large to be anything that should have existed.

'Dragons. How is this even possible? Where have they come from?'

It was Lord Beylin who asked the question, though Beulah was thinking it too. She fancied now that she could hear screams from behind the city walls, and she watched as one of the flying beasts swooped, raking the roofs with its claws. She knew those houses, knew exactly how big they were. This dragon was fully the size of Caradoc. Bigger, even. And as she followed its flight back up to the Neuadd, so she counted six, seven, eight more. They scrapped like crows around a buzzard, attacking each other for the sheer fun of it, then peeling off to vent their frustration on something in the city below.

'My lady, we should move. It is not safe here.' As Clun spoke, his great horse nodded its head in agreement. Beulah nodded too, but she couldn't take her eyes off the largest of the dragons, wings spread wide as it whirled high above the great hall. Then it turned, and she could have sworn it locked its eyes on only her. There was no way she could have seen from that distance, but somehow she just knew.

And then with a roar like thunder in the mountains, it pulled its wings tight to its sides and dived.

30

Legend tells of a vast city hidden in the inaccessible heights of the Rim mountains north of the great monastery of the Order of the High Ffrydd at Emmass Fawr. Nantgrafanglach, as this place is called in the ancient tongue, is said to be on a scale that makes even that vast building seem small, and at its centre rises a tower so tall it is often hidden in cloud. Despite the bitter cold, gales that blow in across the Caenant plain and snows that never clear the high peaks, this city is habitable, indeed most pleasant to live in, because it is both protected by ancient magics and heated by hot springs. The people of Nantgrafanglach are said to be tall and fair-skinned, with pale blue eyes and hair the colour of the snows that surround their great city. And as is always the way with such legends, the city is awash with gold, jewels and other riches, the tower itself is said to house the greatest library in the whole of Gwlad.

If you travel far enough into the foothills you will find old mountain men, trappers and other social misfits who may claim to have seen Nantgrafanglach from afar, to have caught a glimpse of that tall tower reflecting the setting sun. Some may even tell you they have met the city's strange inhabitants, traded with them for precious metals. And yet none can say where this magical place lies, even though they know the high mountain passes better than any save perhaps the wild goats and the lioncats. It is possible that the same magics that make the place habitable also hide it from those not welcome within its walls. It is far more likely that Nantgrafanglach does not exist at all, no more than a story made up around a hunting campfire to chase away the fear that lurks in the darkness beyond.

Father Keoldale, *Travels in the Rim Mountains*

Benfro stepped from icy snow into fire, felt the tip of his tail singe and whipped it out of the flames just in time. He found himself in the large room at the top of the tower he had seen in his dreamwalk, too close to the great fireplace for comfort. If anything the room was bigger than he had imagined it, the distance between the two vast glass-paned doors almost as wide as the clearing where his mother's cottage still stood. Clutter filled most of one end, but in front of the enormous fireplace an area had been cleared around a writing desk very much like the one in Magog's repository underneath the ruins of Cenobus. The golden cage that had hung in the rafters now sat on the floor alongside it, door wide open, and as Benfro peered into the darkness within, a figure emerged.

'Errol!' Benfro covered the distance between fireplace and cage in three large strides, then stopped as he realized the person staring up at him was not his friend. She was female for one thing, with long untidy hair hanging down over her shoulders, and she wore a dark green cloak that was torn and tattered at the edges. At his single word she looked up at him, cocking her head at a quizzical angle exactly as he had seen Earith do.

'You're not Gog,' the woman said, frowning. 'Where is he?'

Benfro looked around the room, realizing then what had been missing. 'He should be here. He left before me.'

'Ah, Benfro. You made it. Splendid.' Both Errol and Martha turned to see the ancient dragon emerge from the stone arch at the top of the spiral staircase. A young man walked by his side, dwarfed by the dragon's bulk, carrying a tray with a large silver cover over it. 'I noticed young Xando here bringing Martha her supper and thought I'd help him with the stairs. It's a long climb if your legs are short.'

The young boy blushed at the dragon's words, ducked his head deferentially and hurried towards the young woman with his tray. He was strangely familiar to Benfro, especially when his blind eye took in the boy's aura.

'You are so like Errol,' he said. 'And yet you're not him.'

'Errol?' The young woman had been looking at the approaching boy, but her head shot up at the name, eyes fixing on Benfro. 'Errol Ramsbottom?'

'You know . . .' And then Benfro's brain caught up with Gog's words. 'Martha. You're Martha. The one who Errol's been looking for. The one I saw in the cage when I was dreamwalking. I thought you were his prisoner.' He nodded in the direction of Gog, who was standing a few paces off, smiling at some inner joke.

'I was, at first. Until I convinced him that I had come to

learn.' Martha took the tray from the young boy and placed it on a nearby table. Benfro caught a whiff of something meaty and wonderful, his stomach rumbling even though it was not long since he had eaten his fill at the mother tree's table.

'And a fine student she is,' Gog said. 'Better far than any dragon apprentice I have had in recent years. They have lost their appreciation of the subtle arts, my fallen sons and daughters. Most are interested only in hunting, fighting each other and fornicating. Sometimes all at the same time.'

Benfro felt heat in the tips of his ears at the words. Unbidden, an image of Cerys sprang into his mind. He shook his head to dispel it; he wanted nothing of her after what Fflint had done to him.

'Most are so feral now they no longer grow jewels in their brains.' Gog ambled over to a large wooden bureau close to the writing desk. He pulled out a drawer and removed from it an ornate wooden box, handing it to Benfro. 'Your friend, Ynys Môn, had a fine set when he died. Long memories and great experience of the subtle arts. I am sure though that he would prefer to be whole.'

Benfro opened the box to see a small mound of perfect white jewels nestling in a blue silk lining. Memories of Ynys Môn rose strongly from them, like a scent trapped for too long and finally released. He held up the last jewel, tiny even in his growing hand, and then dropped it into the pile. The sense of peace, of relief, was palpable, and he heard a distant voice mouth the words 'Thank you, Benfro' in his head.

'He should lie with the rest of his family, his fold.'

Benfro gently closed the lid but did not put the box down. 'And to do that I must ask you an enormous favour. I must know how to find the place of your hatching. The place of your brother's hatching.'

Gog's brow furrowed. 'But why?'

'So that I can retrieve Magog's mortal remains and breathe the Fflam Gwir over them.' As he spoke the plan out loud, a horrible feeling settled over Benfro. He had long since lost his mother's leather bag, had no pockets in which to store anything. Errol had been carrying Magog's jewel. And Morgwm's. He had to find him and not just because Errol was his friend. Without the unreckoned jewel, all was lost.

'Mortal remains?' Gog's voice was almost a whisper as he stepped forward, peering at Benfro with white eyes that seemed to see him all the better for their blindness. 'Can it be? Is he truly . . . dead?'

'He has been dead more than two thousand years,' Benfro said, and as he did a bright pain flowered in his forehead. With his missing eye he saw the looping cord of red spring into being. The old dragon had been close, but now he stepped back, leaning heavily on the writing desk. Benfro sensed something about the room change, as if a great power had been extinguished somewhere or the temperature had dropped.

'How can this be? The wall between our two worlds should have dissolved as his essence flowed into the Grym.' Gog slumped on to the bench in front of the desk. 'I should have known.'

'I was always the better mage, brother mine.'

All heads turned as one towards the spot by the

fireplace where the voice had come from. Benfro didn't need to see to know who it was, though he couldn't begin to understand how he was there. He had to have travelled the Llinellau, but how was that possible?

'Melyn? Melyn son of Arall? Is that truly you?' Gog peered at the man standing by the fireplace, and for the first time Benfro noticed the way the old dragon seemed to look without focusing. His eyes were milky with cataracts; did he see the world the same way Benfro now did himself? A mixture of the mundane and the aethereal, superimposed one upon the other? Or could he see only the aethereal now? Only the auras of the people and dragons around him? And how could he possibly know Melyn?

'There is no Melyn any more. Melyn was your plaything. You discarded him when you had no further use for him. Cast him out into the Grym to die.'

'That's not true. I taught you the subtle arts, raised you above the ignorant folk you grew up with. You were my first, most promising pupil. And then you were gone.' Gog stepped towards the man standing by the fireplace. It looked like Melyn, sort of. But there was something very wrong with his aethereal form. It shimmered and switched between the hated shape of the inquisitor and that of a much smaller figure, a young boy. And behind it all Melyn's aura was completely suffused in a menacingly familiar dark crimson. Yet somehow Gog did not appear to see the peril. 'I mourned you, my young apprentice. I thought you were dead.'

'Keep away from him. He's dangerous.' Benfro put an arm out to pull back the old dragon. Had it been his good hand, maybe he could have stopped Gog, but his grip was weak still. Gog shrugged him off, turning his back on Melyn as he did so.

'Melyn is not dangerous, Benfro. He is my—'

But whatever he was, Benfro never knew. There was a surge in the Grym as the inquisitor conjured two blades of light, fiery red like the jewels atop the stone pillar in the depths of Mount Arnahi. They blurred through the air, so swiftly did he move, and then in a horrible repetition of his worst nightmare, Benfro watched as Gog's head parted from his shoulders and tumbled to the floor.

'Ah, by Gog's hairy balls! Stand firm, men. Are you warrior priests or children?'

Beulah was so transfixed by the sight of the dragon diving towards her that she scarcely heard her husband's words. Her every instinct was to turn, run, but she couldn't move. The same couldn't be said of the soldiers nearby, who were fleeing in all directions as panic hit. Among them were more than a few warrior priests; so much for them being elite fighting men and masters of magic.

'Lord Beylin, protect the queen.' Clun's command brooked no argument, and before Beulah could even react he had spurred his massive stallion forward, galloping out into the field between their camp and the city walls. She watched in horror as the dragon shifted its dive, flaring its wings wide into a swoop that would bring it into direct collision with Clun as it skimmed just above the ground. Any normal horse would have stopped, reared, unseated its rider and fled, but Godric merely increased his speed. He covered the distance with a fluid grace, flowing over the undulations like water, tail and mane spraying out in the wind. Beulah wanted to turn away, terrified of what she was going to see, what she was going to lose. But she could only stare as horse, rider and dragon came closer and closer together.

At the last possible moment Godric finally reared, but not in fright. He kicked out at the dragon's head with his enormous iron-shod hooves. Clun stood tall in his stirrups, so high that the dragon must surely pluck him from the saddle with its enormous talons. Instead it raised its head awkwardly to avoid the hooves, exposing the soft underside of its neck for an instant. Even a good distance away, Beulah felt a drain in the Grym the like of which she'd never known before, saw twin scarlet blades of fire appear in Clun's hands.

A flash of light, and the great dragon seemed to crumple in on itself, tumbling to the ground with a crash that rocked the earth under Beulah's feet. Clun and Godric disappeared in a cloud of dust and flailing wings, lashing tail, and then they were out the other side, wheeling at a slow trot, then a walk, finally coming to a halt alongside the struggling creature. Clun's blades had half-severed both wings, cut deep gouges in the beast's soft underbelly. He dismounted slowly, one blade extinguished, the other still burning bright, and approached the dragon with confident steps even though its head was almost as big as he was tall. A vast eye stared at him with angry malevolence. For a few moments it seemed as if the two of them conversed, though Beulah could hear nothing over the distance. Then the creature struggled to its feet, black blood pouring from its wounds. It tried to rear, opening its mouth wide to bite Clun in half, but it was weak and slow and arrogant. With a swift step to the side, the Duke of Abervenn ducked low and brought his blade up through the open mouth, deep into the beast's brain.

A cheer went up among the gathered warrior priests and soldiers as the dragon slumped to the ground, dead. Beulah realized she had been holding her breath and let it out in a long, slow sigh. And then a screech high above sent a shiver through her. So transfixed had she been by the fight, she had completely forgotten that more than one dragon was attacking the city. Two more great beasts wheeled overhead, descending in slow loops that allowed them to see the whole army drawn up on the plain. Beulah expected them to avoid Clun, who was even now striding away from the carcass and back towards Godric, but instead they landed lightly a few dozen paces away from him. One of them screeched again, the ululation sounding like speech as it carried on the breeze. Then Beulah heard Clun respond, his words lost in the distance but their tone showing he spoke the language of dragons.

'My lady, how is it they have not killed him? Or he them?'

Beulah turned to see Lord Beylin standing just behind her. At least he hadn't run, though he gripped his thin steel blade inexpertly.

'I do not know, Petyr. The Duke of Abervenn is full of surprises. Perhaps one day I will find out where a lad of scarce nineteen summers learned all that he knows, but for now I am just glad to have him around.'

Beylin opened his mouth to speak again, then shut it, his eyes widening. Beulah turned to see Clun extinguish his blade of fire, climb back into Godric's saddle, turn and ride slowly towards her. The two dragons flanked him, their movements strangely catlike as they matched his speed but kept a few dozen paces behind. They stopped a hundred yards from the encampment, leaving Clun to ride on alone.

'What manner of sorcery is this? Are you bewitched, my love?' Beulah approached the great black stallion without fear and it dipped its massive head to her, flaring its nostrils in recognition. Clun dismounted again, letting the reins fall slack.

'Quite the opposite, my lady.' He took her hand in his, lifted it to his lips and kissed it, the mischievous glint in his eye making him seem barely those nineteen summers.

'Then what, pray, are those two beasts doing?' Beulah nodded in the direction of the dragons. They had hunkered down on the grass and now were as motionless as statues.

'The one on the left is Sir Sgarnog, if I've got the pronunciation right. The other is his mate, Angharad the Red. The beast I killed was their leader, Sir Chwilog. I tried to speak to him, but I think he was a bit mad. These two are really quite happy to see the back of him.'

'I didn't ask who they were, I asked what they were doing.' Beulah felt a certain sense of safety so close to Clun and Godric, but she was still nervous at the closeness of the two dragons. Neither was as large as Caradoc, but between the two of them they could destroy half her army if they so chose. And there were more wheeling around the Neuadd to contend with too.

'They are awaiting my command, my lady. I have

defeated their leader in combat, so as far as they are concerned I am their leader now.'

For an endless moment there was silence, as if the whole of Gwlad held its breath. Then the air grew thick, squeezing his lungs until Benfro could scarcely breathe. A terrible wailing screech built up, so loud he thought his head must surely break. And then the great glass doors burst outwards, shattering into a million pieces that were whipped away on the wind. Massive stone benches flipped into the air as if thrown around by an invisible hand. Papers exploded out of bookcases, strange instruments flew about the room, some clattering against the walls, others disappearing out of the windows. Flame billowed from the fireplace as if some great beast had blown down the chimney. Benfro covered his face to avoid losing his other eye and just caught the movement as Melyn sprang at him. He ducked and rolled, narrowly missing the swinging arc of the inquisitor's blades.

'I will kill you all now and claim both of these worlds as my own.' Melyn's voice cracked with madness as he circled the body of Gog. Benfro backed away, risking a glance to see Martha and the young boy cowering beside the golden cage, trying desperately to avoid being sucked out of the windows by the gale that had sprung up from nowhere.

'Run!' he shouted even as he knew running was pointless. And then there was a commotion at the doorway as Enedoc appeared at the top of the stairs, closely followed by his two companions. They took only an instant to appraise the situation, then Enedoc launched himself across the room, wings wide, claws extended in attack. Melyn moved in a blur, his twin blades screaming in the wind. Enedoc reared up at the last minute, narrowly missing going the same way as his master. He spun smoothly on one leg, whipping his tail around to cut Melyn off at the knees, but the inquisitor just laughed, leaping like a man a third his age. One blade swung down as he rose, and Enedoc let out a howl of pain and rage.

'There will be no sons of Gog in my world,' Melyn shouted above the wind. 'Only their jewels will remain, and I will tap them for their power.'

Their power. Benfro saw the body of Gog lying by the now-empty fireplace. His head lay just to the side, and in it were surely the greatest jewels ever to have grown inside a dragon's brain. Benfro knew then that unreckoned they would be Melyn's – Magog's – to control. And with them the inquisitor would be truly unstoppable. He would have to do something about that, but first he had to get Errol's friend to safety.

'You have to go. Take the Llinellau. Get as far from here as possible.' Benfro spoke the words quietly but pushed them at Martha with his mind.

The young woman looked up at him, shouted back, 'I can't leave Xando. And we can't use the lines anyway. Look at them!'

Benfro did and instantly saw what she meant. The Llinellau here were all crimson, power pouring through them into Melyn. How the inquisitor was not devoured by them he couldn't begin to understand, but trying to step into them was plainly suicide.

'Get to the ledge outside,' Benfro said. Martha looked

around, saw the two dragons in the doorway at the top of the stairs, then ducked down as Enedoc flew overhead. Dark gouts of blood spattered the floor and walls, but the dragon once more took the fight to Melyn.

'Go!' Benfro shouted, then turned back to the fray. He could feel the fire building up inside him, the Fflam Gwir. The reckoning flame. He just needed to get a little closer. But Melyn stood between him and Gog's body now. Benfro might have just burned them both, but he remembered the casual ease with which the inquisitor had brushed aside his flame before. He couldn't risk that happening again.

Then Enedoc launched himself once more, and this time Melyn's blades were not swift enough. The dragon wrapped his claws around the inquisitor's body, the two of them tumbling together, knocking the writing desk over. Benfro took a deep breath and then released the flame.

Palest blue, it leaped on to Gog's body as if it were alive, enveloping him totally in an instant. Through the glow Benfro thought he saw Gog rise in his magnificent aethereal form, and then something crashed into his back, knocking the wind out of him.

'What have you done! The master!' Blows rained down on him as Benfro tried to escape from a weight pinning him to the floor. One of Enedoc's companions had seen him breathe the reckoning flame and had assumed he was attacking Gog.

'He's dead, you fool.' Benfro managed to get his weaker arm underneath him, pivot and roll. The dragon fell from him, momentarily stunned. This gave Benfro just enough time to get to his feet and run for the broken window as he saw a blade of light spear up out of the middle of Enedoc's back. Out on the ledge Martha and Xando huddled against the wall, shivering in the bitter cold. 'Grab hold of each other. Tight.' Benfro shouted above the wind. It wasn't really necessary; they were all close together anyway.

'You will not escape me, Benfro.' The voice was Melyn's, but the surge of fury that lit up the rose cord looping away from his forehead was all Magog. Benfro screamed at the pain as the long-dead dragon mage poured all his efforts into breaking him. His vision dimmed, both eyes robbed of their function. His limbs froze and it felt like a giant hand had reached into his chest and was squeezing his hearts. He could feel his strength ebbing more swiftly even than when Fflint had thrown him repeatedly against a wall.

And then the pain was gone.

'I think we should go now.'

Benfro opened his eyes, seeing the rose cord tied closed with a loop of dark green aura, strong and solid as it flowed from Martha. She had her arms around Xando, and they both stood at the edge now, teetering over a thousand-foot drop.

He didn't need to turn to see the inquisitor rushing towards him; Benfro's blind eye showed him both the man and the dragon that had overtaken him. In that last instant he saw too the twin points of crimson light where each blade of fire began, and the way the Grym bent towards Melyn, feeding him with energy that came from . . .

But there was no time to explore that. Benfro bounded to the edge of the platform, swept Martha and Xando into the tightest embrace he could manage even as he opened his wings further than they had been since his fight with Fflint.

And then he jumped.

An Apology

This book has been a long time coming.

I began writing The Ballad of Sir Benfro over ten years ago. At the time, I was working on a livestock research farm in mid Wales and beginning to learn Welsh. During one evening class (Dosbarth Nos), we were discussing the county names and Sîr Benfro came up. Sîr is the Welsh equivalent of the English 'shire' and Benfro comes from Pen meaning 'head' or 'end' and Fro, an old Welsh word for the land, so literally the Headland or the end of the land, which anyone who knows Pembrokeshire will realize is very apt.

It is also, as my better half pointed out to me at the time, the perfect name for a dragon, and thus Sir Benfro was born.

He started off as a rather ungainly fellow, and because I was working on a sheep farm it made perfect sense for his arch-foes to be sheep (at least it did in my mind at the time). I wrote a couple of short stories exploring the characters and mythology of this world I had imagined, and then decided there was enough in it for a fantasy epic.

It took the wise counsel of my good friend Stuart Mac-Bride to convince me that sheep would never be taken seriously as evil foes. I changed them to men, but kept their names. Some of you will recognise such breeds as Llanwennog, Clun Forest, Beulah Speckle-Face, Torwen and Tordu. It is no coincidence that the god of these people is called the Shepherd.

Perhaps unsurprisingly, I found it very hard to find a publisher for this sprawling tale of magic, dragons and ~~sheep~~ men. I wrote three of a planned five-novel series, then realized that even if a publisher did pick up the first one it would be several years until they needed book four. I was dabbling with crime fiction at the time too, which was something of a distraction. Eventually I self-published both my first two crime novels and the three Benfro books that were already written. I had no great hopes for huge commercial success, but liked the idea of them being out there.

That's not quite how things worked out.

The crime novels, featuring Edinburgh-based Detective Inspector Tony McLean took off spectacularly well, selling hundreds of thousands of copies. The Benfro books were very well received too, and I started getting emails from people wanting to know when the next one was coming out. Soon, I'd tell them, and then get a call from my editor asking when the next McLean book would be ready. My initial deadline of summer 2012 passed by, then summer 2013 was gone. I always meant to get the book written, but there just never seemed to be any spare time.

Then my editor at Penguin decided he too liked the Benfro series and wanted to publish it. This knocked the schedule back even further, as I had to review and edit the first three books all over again before even thinking about writing the fourth. And there was another problem. Books one, *Dreamwalker*, and two, *The Rose Cord*, came in at a reasonable one hundred-and-twenty thousand and one hundred-and-forty thousand words respectively. Book three, *The Golden Cage*, in my original self-published version, was almost two hundred-and-thirty thousand words. Too long for a paperback, and out of keeping with the flow of the earlier books. Something had to be done.

So after much soul-searching, I took the decision to cut a large section from the end of book three and use it as the opening to book four. There is a natural point in *The Golden Cage* where this works well, and the Penguin edition of the book is thus shorter than the original DevilDog version.

The beginning of this book, *The Broken World*, will therefore be strangely familiar to some of my earlier readers, and for that I apologize. I hope you don't feel short-changed; there's well over a hundred thousand words of new story in here!

I must also apologise for the long delay in picking up the story again. You have all been very patient, and I promise not to take so long with the final instalment.

Thank you all for being such wonderful readers. I hope you enjoy this latest chapter in the adventures of Benfro and Errol.

James Oswald
Fife – May 2015

Acknowledgements

I may have been the one sitting at a desk in the wee small hours dreaming of dragons and magic (and sheep), but an army of people have helped to bring those dreams to the wider world. I run the risk of upsetting people by not including them in this list, but I must thank Alex Clarke, Sophie Elletson, Hugh Davis and all the rest of the team at Michael Joseph for polishing my words into something readable, and for wrapping them up in such gorgeous covers. Thanks too to Roy McMillan and Wayne Forrester for the truly wonderful audiobook editions.

I wouldn't be where I am today without the irrepressible Juliet Mushens, agent extraordinaire, friend and now cat lady in training. Thank you seems somehow inadequate, so I'll just have to keep sending the pink fizz.

A shout out to Stuart MacBride, who probably never realised all those years ago how his advice to ditch the sheep would pay off. And thank you to my long-suffering partner Barbara McLean, who first pointed out all those years ago that Sir Benfro would be great name for a dragon.

And finally the biggest thank you of all to you readers, who not only took a chance with an unknown, self-published author, but also stuck around this far. I could probably do it without you, but it wouldn't be half as much fun.

J D OSWALD

THE BALLAD OF SIR BENFRO

Errol and Benfro's epic tale finally comes to a magnificent conclusion as the fate of the war-torn Twin Kingdoms is decided once and for all.

The Obsidian Throne

The final instalment of the Ballad of Sir Benfro

Available 22/09/2016

JAMES OSWALD

NATURAL CAUSES

AN INSPECTOR McLEAN NOVEL

A young girl's mutilated body is discovered in a sealed room. Her remains are carefully arranged, in what seems to have been a cruel and macabre ritual, which appears to have taken place over 60 years ago.

For newly appointed Edinburgh Detective Inspector Tony McLean this baffling cold case ought to be a low priority – but he is haunted by the young victim and her grisly death.

Meanwhile, the city is horrified by a series of bloody killings. Deaths for which there appears to be neither rhyme nor reason, and which leave Edinburgh's police at a loss.

McLean is convinced that these deaths are somehow connected to the terrible ceremonial killing of the girl, all those years ago. It is an irrational, almost supernatural theory.

And one which will lead McLean closer to the heart of a terrifying and ancient evil . . .

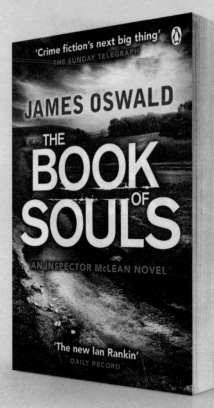

'Crime fiction's next big thing'
THE SUNDAY TELEGRAPH

JAMES OSWALD

THE
BOOK
OF
SOULS

AN INSPECTOR McLEAN NOVEL

'The new Ian Rankin'
DAILY RECORD

Every year for ten years, a young woman's body was found in Edinburgh at Christmas time: naked, throat slit, body washed clean.

The final victim, Kirsty Summers, was Detective Constable Tony McLean's fiancée. But the Christmas Killer made a mistake and McLean put an end to the brutal killing spree.

Twelve years later, and a fellow prisoner has murdered the Christmas Killer. But with the festive season comes a body; naked, washed, her throat cut.

Is this a copycat killer?

Was the wrong man behind bars all this time?

Or is there a more sinister explanation?

McLean must revisit his most disturbing case and discover what he missed before the killer strikes again . . .

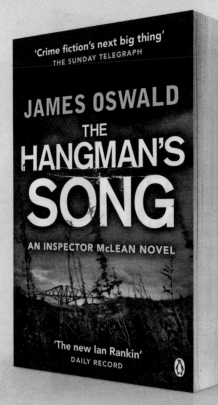

The body of a man is found hanging in an empty house.
To the Edinburgh police force this appears to be a
simple suicide case.

Days later another body is found.

The body is hanging from an identical rope and the noose
has been tied using the same knot.

Then a third body is found.

As Inspector McLean digs deeper he descends into a
world where the lines of reality are blurred and where the
most irrational answers become the only explanations.

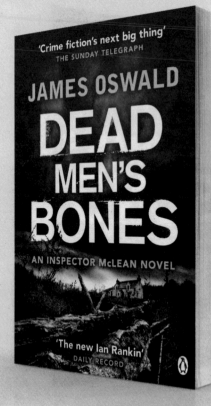

'Crime fiction's next big thing'
THE SUNDAY TELEGRAPH

JAMES OSWALD

DEAD
MEN'S
BONES

AN INSPECTOR McLEAN NOVEL

'The new Ian Rankin'
DAILY RECORD

**A family lies slaughtered in an isolated house
in North East Fife . . .**

Morag Weatherly and her two young daughters have
been shot by husband Andrew, an influential politician,
before he turned the gun on himself.

But what would cause a rich, successful man to
snap so suddenly?

For Inspector Tony McLean, this apparently simple but
high-profile case leads him into a world of power and
privilege. And the deeper he digs, the more he realises
he's being manipulated by shadowy factions.

Under pressure to wrap up the case, McLean instead
seeks to uncover layers of truth - putting the lives of
everyone he cares about at risk . . .

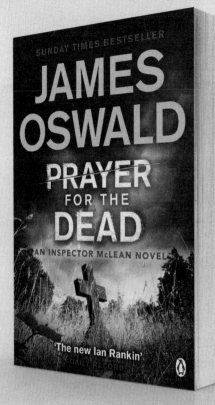

SUNDAY TIMES BESTSELLER

JAMES
OSWALD

PRAYER
FOR THE
DEAD

AN INSPECTOR McLEAN NOVEL

'The new Ian Rankin'
DAILY RECORD

**In a cave beneath the streets of Edinburgh a man is first
ritually purified – and then murdered . . .**

When the body of missing journalist Ben Stevenson is found deep
within Gilmerton Cove's network of caves, DI Tony McLean is
handed one of the darkest puzzles of his career.

Not only is there a troubling lack of forensic evidence at the scene
of this particularly gruesome killing, but there are also peculiar
elements which strain even McLean's understanding of the possible.

What is clear, however, is that he is on the trail of a killer driven by
the blackest of compulsions who will strike again unless McLean can
make sense of the apparently senseless . . .

He just wanted a decent book to read ...

Not too much to ask, is it? It was in 1935 when Allen Lane, Managing Director of Bodley Head Publishers, stood on a platform at Exeter railway station looking for something good to read on his journey back to London. His choice was limited to popular magazines and poor-quality paperbacks – the same choice faced every day by the vast majority of readers, few of whom could afford hardbacks. Lane's disappointment and subsequent anger at the range of books generally available led him to found a company – and change the world.

'We believed in the existence in this country of a vast reading public for intelligent books at a low price, and staked everything on it'
Sir Allen Lane, 1902–1970, founder of Penguin Books

The quality paperback had arrived – and not just in bookshops. Lane was adamant that his Penguins should appear in chain stores and tobacconists, and should cost no more than a packet of cigarettes.

Reading habits (and cigarette prices) have changed since 1935, but Penguin still believes in publishing the best books for everybody to enjoy. We still believe that good design costs no more than bad design, and we still believe that quality books published passionately and responsibly make the world a better place.

So wherever you see the little bird – whether it's on a piece of prize-winning literary fiction or a celebrity autobiography, political tour de force or historical masterpiece, a serial-killer thriller, reference book, world classic or a piece of pure escapism – you can bet that it represents the very best that the genre has to offer.

Whatever you like to read – trust Penguin.